WOLF TECH 2

WOLF TECH 2

ADAM WEBSTER

CONTENTS

This book is dedicated to all those who have supported me in learning to write my stories and have been along for the ride since I started posting the stories to Wattpad and encouraged me to continue my stories.

Author Note

Thanks to Jo Anne Failla, Sonya Brown, and everyone else who had given me constructive criticism to help me edit this book on Wattpad.

Native Words are used as close to correct from http://www.rockymountain-nakoda.com. Any incorrect usage, or other issues are my own.

This is a work of fiction. All resemblance to any actual place or person living or dead is either a coincident or used fictitiously.

There are a couple chapters which have quite a bit of violence in it, do keep it in perspective they are not human, so human moral values are not in effect.

Wolfdogs:
While many people enjoy having wolfdogs or other wolf hybrids as pets, as they can be very affectionate, playful, loyal, and smart, not all are suitable as pets. Their traits and behaviour, not just their looks, vary dramatically between individual animals, not always just from how much wolf is in them. Some of the negative traits include fearfulness of humans, high prey drive, high energy, territorial, destructive, extremely independent, and being escape artists. If you are considering them, make sure to check out the resources available, including Wolfdog and Wolf Sanctuaries, as the staff at those places likely can give you more details, other local resources, and any restrictions for your area.

As with any plans for bringing a new animal into your home, research needs to be done before doing so, as they are a living being, and don't understand why you have to leave them or why you abandon them to a shelter, where often they are not able to be placed with others. Committing to any sort of animal should be a life-long commitment, and never just for the status of having the animal as a possession.

Prologue

B rook was born a Werewolf. She not only had her human form, a wolf form, but also a third form which stood on its hind legs and looked like a huge wolf, and she could shift whenever she wanted. For the most part, werewolves lived separately from humans, as they had different outlooks on several key ideas, including physical contact and beliefs. It had caused many packs to not have the option to stay with the humans as technology advanced, due to needing to keep their secrets.

Brook was a trainer for her pack, as she had skills to help the youngsters—which they called pups—to gain the basic skills for fighting hand-to-hand and with basic weapons. She was frustrated on how the world seems to be leaving them behind with the lack of technology. The pack kept ruling the secrecy of werewolves was more important than a good internet connection, as there was nobody who had the skills to manage the technology, and especially nobody to know how to bring it in without the humans being involved enough they would be seeing too much.

Adam was a human who had been out taking photos in the mountains near the territory claimed by Brook's pack. Brook and Adam had a chance meeting while she was out running off some energy and frustration. This meeting led to the discovery that Brook and Adam were mates. It didn't even take him a moment to decide to accept her as his mate, as he had thought werewolves *could* exist, and had thought about *what-if* enough to know he would accept immediately if he ever was told they existed. He quickly decided, when he was promised a place within the pack and help moving, to toss his human life and move to the pack. It helped he was bored with his tech job and wanted to do something new, just lacked the means to do so.

Finding the state of the Pack's technology being stuck over two decades in the past and with his technology background, it took little work to talk the Alphas and the Elders into bringing them up to the level of the humans. It surprised Adam he was placed in charge of all the technology upgrades, even as he was learning what he needed to know before he could become a werewolf, what the werewolves called *Turning*, so he could fulfil his life-long dream of being a wolf. He was able to bring major technology changes, which would have made many companies envious, even as they maintained their secrecy.

In between training to learn the skills which he was expected to know to function in his role and rank within the pack, he trained the others on how to handle the technology they now had at the pack. He also started to bring the technology to the security side of the pack. Initially, he had been limited, but then was shown how the current ways were clearly lacking and left gaping holes in their security when an enemy breached the pack house, even to those who were reluctant to change, and the permission was given.

The security changes were done just in time to detect a surprise attack before the attackers were ready, so they were able to mount a surprise counterattack. Following the successful repulsion, they found enough issues for them to start planning a return attack.

When they were recovered, Adam and Brook did a trial run, since an informal check had them almost meeting the speed they were expected for the rank of Second, which since the Alpha had offered them the Second position, which is the second-in-command of the pack, and generally lead the pack whenever the Alpha is not available, so has to meet the same standards. They met the standard, with five minutes to spare.

This is the continuation of the story...

Chapter 1 – Promotions

Adam knocked on the open door. Both Brook and Adam were freshly washed and wearing matching outfits of a long sleeve turtleneck leotard, and a knee length skirt. Their hair was pulled back in a ponytail and still damp from their shower. Adam enjoyed the nice light feeling of a skirt, leaving his legs bare. His wolf also loved since they shared clothes, as they took on a little bit of his mate's scent too, which added to the scent of their mate they each had from their mating bond. He also enjoyed wearing matching clothes to his mate as it was just one more way for others to know they were together.

Gareth refused to comment on their clothes as they seemed to just take too much amusement about the comments, as they knew when to dress better, but for around the pack, clothes were clothes. He knew of others who did so as well and didn't say anything to them either. "Come in and close the door." He told them. He personally had no issues with what anyone wore, other than a rare time they were representing the pack to outsiders, at which point he expected them to wear something respectful. He was sure he wouldn't need to tell either of them about it.

Brook closed the door behind them, as they moved over and joined him in the sitting area. There were two piles of several binders in front of him.

"I have talked to the Elders and my Seconds. All are in favour of you officially being Acting-Seconds and starting the training. We are moving fast here, as the Seconds have asked to step down immediately due to the attacks we have had recently." He didn't need to add on their age as well. "I have been able to get them to agree to hold off till the Spring Trials at the end of April, where I expect you will easily hit the standard for Alphas and Seconds. I have asked them to advise you, but you have already started doing the duties and taking on the responsibilities. We are just adding on the authority and privileges." He didn't bother saying he had already had their pay adjusted to reflect it as well. The details were in their forms in the first binder.

Both nodded. Even Brook was a bit stressed about the offer. Being the pack's Seconds was a big responsibility, but both were willing to take on the challenge.

Gareth continued, "We will also be qualifying your fighting skills, in all three forms at the Spring Trials. These books are the training information for Seconds and include some additional details you must know; mostly about interacting with other packs. These are not to be read by anyone else, as they contain information which is restricted to Alphas and Seconds. There is also an oath you must memorise and give to the pack at the next Full Moon Howl. That gives you three weeks to do it; by then you should have reviewed all the information as well."

"But I haven't finished Turning. I can't shift to Were yet." Adam complained. His life was changing even more than he expected and he didn't feel ready for it to change even more. He already doubted if he met himself where he had not met his mate and had stayed being a tech, he'd understand how he got to this position of almost leading the pack from where his life had continued, as it seemed to never change.

"I think by the weekend you will have completed the shift; the Turning Scar is almost gone." Brook commented with a grin.

"I agree," Gareth replied in agreement, "Your scent has only a hint of human left, and if one of the humans had been here before you, I wouldn't even be able to detect it at all." He knew of the betting pool, but as long as nobody was cheated, he never took official notice to them; let those who wanted to have their fun and risk something they could do without. He knew Brook occasionally joined into them.

"But I've had only nine weeks since I was Turned! It usually takes three to four months!" Adam exclaimed. He was shocked it was happening so fast. His wolf snorted at him in amusement; he felt it was only right and proper.

The other two chuckled before Brook commented, "You took the mating changes very fast, too. I expected the turn to end about now, so have been watching the signs."

"I still think that I won't be ready at the Spring Trials this year for the Were shape tests." Adam commented, a bit frazzled on how fast his life kept changing, not letting him get his balance before needing to leap again; he kept feeling like he was going to fail and fail badly. Now, a failure would not be just him and maybe his mate, it would impact the entire pack. His wolf nuzzled him in his mind, reminding him he was not alone, and had others helping him.

"The Were is more of learning what works for you, as most of the skills are those learned in the other two shapes. I think you'll be fine. I'd be willing to bet money you'll qualify." Brook replied, teasing him at the end.

Shaking his head, Adam deferred to Brook, "If you say so, you have been right so far, Love." He refused to accept most bets against her, and never ones she offered money, as he rarely won them and those only because he knew tech more, for now. "I will do my best." He had heard most of the pack refused to do them too.

Turning back to the position and the main part for this meeting, Adam clarified, "So this is fully official, and we can announce it?"

Gareth grinned, "Yes. New IDs are in the binders showing your new status as Seconds."

They chatted for a bit more about what their position would entail, which included travel and meeting other packs in the place of the Alphas, and if the Alphas had to go himself to the meeting, they would stay and lead the pack in his place. It also meant everyone had to obey them, and they were answerable only to the Alphas alone. It was on par with Next-Alpha, which was usually the pups of the Alpha, and always had the Alpha ability, and the order of control between them and Seconds depended on skill and age. Until John and Bri returned from their training and passed the Spring Trials, they officially didn't have the title as well, so until they were confirmed as passing all the training in the spring, they would technically outrank them.

The position of Second was usually the Alpha's most trusted advisors. Gareth stopped for a moment, "Even though you have only been here under three months, Adam, I feel I have known you for centuries. Also, you have seemed to settle in and get our ways right from the start. Many in the pack also listen to what you have to say. I am thinking you are my grandfather's spirit come back to the pack. It is rare to have someone return so soon. I feel that as long as you listen to your wolf and your mate—as you have been doing—you will do well. I'm not sure you noticed, but you have much access to the pack with everyone instinctively respecting and obeying you. I know you have not broken contact with all in your previous human life, yet you have only told your immediate family, and you even asked. I trust you totally; even when I gave you the right to hand out punishments, you have mostly kept them low key and only where they were necessary." Gareth grinned, "Not that you won't make mistakes, I know I have made my fair share of them, but you will work to correct them before they get too big and apologise to anyone harmed."

Brook smiled and could see they had been trusted, with the number of rights they were given were rarely given out, with most needing the Alpha's approval. They had been given nearly unlimited access to pack funds, given authority to hand out punishments without having to check with the Alpha beforehand, and basically assigned to be a contact with the Longview pack. Usually, it was only the Seconds who had those rights. She had only realised it after the Alpha had commented about them doing the duties, the fact they had started doing them.

"Oh, and when you're at Longview, start the work to get them set up to network. Hank is the tech manager there, in addition to being Second. Send him the specs and the contact to get the hardware, and how they need to set it up." Gareth ordered.

"The Were-Net idea is a go?" Adam asked.

Gareth shook his head, "Don't have enough packs signed on, yet. Longview is a pilot to see if we can get the two networks not only secured well, but also with secure channels between them. Other packs want to see how it performs before they start spending the money on the equipment. Once it is working well, I suspect it will expand to be global quickly."

Adam nodded, "Will do. I will have them set up and have Chris as the security contact. He has already found several holes I hadn't secured and already filled them in. He is wanting to start an agreement for network penetration testing from an outside vendor. They will at random times try to break into the network and will report back to us on the attempts. Some of their people have started off as hackers, and now instead of doing it for kicks or bragging rights, do it for their job and get paid for it. The one which Chris wants to use, the US federal government and FBI use to test their network." Their bragging rights was in the reports to the company they broke into, generally with how to secure it before the next attempt, to makes it even more of a challenge. For most, the pleasure was in the doing, the fact they got paid well for doing it was the bonus.

Gareth grinned ferally, "I love that idea! Go with it."

Adam looked off in the distance, quickly linking to Chris, *I have approval for the network testing. I am putting you in charge of it, as I just got handed a couple whoppers of work: getting Longview networked and connected securely to us, and Brook and I have been promoted to Acting-Seconds—Don't tell anyone until the official announcement is made. Let me know when the agreement is ready to sign.* Getting an acknowledgement back, with a congratulation on the promotion, he nodded to the Alpha, "I am letting Chris handle it, as it was his idea. I think he'd be the best to run it, since he is the one responsible for the security of the systems."

Looking at the stack of learning he had to do, "I'm thinking I may need to get a server management team together, to deal with the servers, as soon I will be too busy to be doing it." Adam complained, "But I don't know of anyone qualified or even interested in the pack."

Brook and Gareth laughed. Gareth advised, "That is what happens to the seniors in the pack, they have to delegate more and more. I will put the word out within the pack. Ask Hank if he knows of anyone qualified, who wants to change packs."

Adam nodded, "Adding it to my list." He stated as he wrote it down in his notes.

After they discussed other more minor items and pack information they needed to know, Gareth felt his stomach complain and looking at the time, was startled it was lunchtime, "Well, it's time we headed for lunch. I'm going to announce it to the pack at dinner tomorrow if you're around. You can tell others, and I suggest you tell your pups; just have them keep it quiet."

Adam and Brook nodded, picked up their binders, took them quickly to their rooms, and pulling out the new IDs, showing 'Second' as the title, and 'All-No Restrictions' access. Adam smiled, putting the neck strap around his head and tucking it under his shirt; he didn't need it out, but should have it with him. Brook did the same.

He wrapped an arm around his Mate, and kissed her cheek, before heading out for the lunch.

The rest of their group was there, including their pups, when they reached the table. Adam pulled out his old ID and handed it to Martin, with Brook following. "Don't need this anymore," he commented, before switching to silent to just tell the table before anyone asked why, *We have been promoted to Acting-Seconds and have new IDs. The official announcement is tomorrow at dinner; keep it quiet till then. The Seconds decided they have had enough and are stepping down. Brook and I are hoping to pass all the tests to qualify for taking over when they do after the Spring Trials.* Smiling, "Our run this morning just passed the Alpha benchmark and we are now qualified for the Wolf Run section," The wolf run was considered the hardest for most, as it was a long run, and was the most key. Runs on the other two forms were less essential but still had standards to reach. With the snow they had been working on it, but the tracks were not in the condition for them to get out in them.

As they all dug into their lunch, the others at the table congratulated them, and those not there thought it was just for the run.

I guess I am going to be loaded with more duties? Erin commented, since she had mostly taken over working with those dealing with the tech in his absence during his Turn and he hadn't really taken them back, as he was loaded with other work she would not ever want.

Yes. I'll also be having Robin working some with you for a bit. Let me know what you want and don't want over the next while. He replied. *I don't want to burn you out.* Adam had hated when temporarily taking on duties 'for a short time' became a permanent addition. He did like how the pack had already bumped her pay up while she was covering, and Gareth had mentioned she would now have the new pay made permanent, if she stayed doing the duties.

I'll do that. I'll also see if there is anyone else wanting to do tech. There are a couple of pups almost of age who are interested. Aurora has mentioned she would be interested in working more with the servers. Erin advised.

If she wants to, let her handle the tasks. Let me know if there are any others, and I'll pass it onto the Alpha. Adam agreed. *I have projects which Chris and I are working on. I'll pass her the details too.* It seemed even if he hadn't known, someone was interested in stepping up for what he needed. He would totally let her do it.

*****

Once lunch was done, Adam and Brook headed out with the others who were going to take control of the now Nameless Pack, what had been the Shadowed River Pack before being declared rogue. Losing their name was the first of a list of punishments given for a pack going rogue under the Treaty. There were five packs which were in the area around the rogue pack, and all wanted to have the pack dismantled as soon as possible. Most packs were willing to accept the women and children, but only MacLaren and Longview were willing to accept non-fighter males.

The fighters who had laid down their arms and gave up without a fight, were being investigated. Adam had been able to talk Gareth into not killing them outright, from the way Duncan and Keanna were treated, they may have had not been able to leave, and when they had a chance to not fight but give up, they took it. Even his wolf had to think about what he said and had decided it was the best way; it took Adam even more work to convince his wolf to see his view, than it took to talk Gareth around. He wanted to minimize the bloodshed and to give a second chance which showed those who gave up could keep their lives. It was why many refused to stop fighting, as they knew death waited for them and wanted to go down fighting, instead of having it at a time and place of another.

Adam was in control of the pack which was on the offensive, with Brook at his side. The two of them had flipped a coin for who was in command this time, and had already agreed the other would be the next time. Working together gave both a new view but tempered with the thoughts of old. The Alpha was also using it as a way to see how they could work on their own without anyone giving them instructions, and everyone looking to them. They had already sent the vehicles on the roads, as they had to go around several mountains, and the wolves could use the alpine level passes and go straight through the parks. With the wolves not liking being cooped up in a vehicle which caused them lots of stress, the run would be better, as while they would need work to make sure to not exhaust anyone, they would be much less stressed about being cooped up in a vehicle, and werewolves had huge endurance.

Adam and Brook headed to their room to double check they had everything stowed in their packs well, including rope, a few edged weapons, and their load of restraints for both human and wolf, including wolf-muzzles to keep pesky teeth secured. before putting them on. On a human, the packs seemed to fit lower on the back and sides with a low vest built in. Although it didn't look at all comfortable, it was reasonably comfortable. They had designed the packs in a way so when they shifted, they would be as comfortable for their wolves. Brook shifted to her hybrid, and held the door for her mate, who shifted to wolf. To identify themselves at a glance, both had their IDs around their necks, with the badges tucked into the clear pouches on the shoulder strap of the pack, to keep it out of the way. It would identify them to the wolves they were attacking and show they had the seniority to negotiate if they were willing to surrender.

They were met with the half the pack's fighters, which was the force they were taking, just outside the pack house. Seeing that all the support gear was loaded, Brook shifted down to her wolf. The group was fairly noisy with chatter of barks, yips, and growls and many had issues standing still. Most were excited to have an actual fight, not the endless rounds of patrols.

Adam gave a demanding howl, *Anyone missing?* He asked when everyone had settled down. Getting no response, he started his short speech, *We fought off the Shadowed River Pack. We lost three packmates, but we took down one of the worst packs in the area.* He got a howl of celebration, but tinged with sorrow, *Today, we dismantle the rest of their pack. We are here to take out any of their fighters. Anyone who resists or attacks already has a death sentence. Use whatever force is needed to take them down, alive, if possible, but don't take risks.*

Before becoming a wolf, he didn't think he could ever do anything to cause anyone to die, and here he was; ordering the death of many people—they may be werewolves, but they were still people to him. *Any who surrender without a fight are to be treated with respect but watched. Alpha Gareth has given permission to even save the non-combatant males. Treat them well, as they may become packmates.* Pausing to let his conditions of the battle sink in for a few moments he continued, *Any questions?* With many headshakes and most unable to stay still, he turned and unerringly started to trot, *Then off to the fight we go!* He gave a low howl which was not only picked up by his attack-pack, but all the pack-mates staying behind, as a wish for all of them to return safely.

On the four-hour run, they discussed tactics, and how they wanted to start the battle. There were some fast, stealthy wolves who had taken off ahead of the main group to try to find out the number of sentries and layout of the pack. The official reported number in the pack to the Council of Alphas showed they had taken out over three quarters of the pack already. Either they were foolhardy, and they did only have a quarter of the pack left, or the reported numbers were incomplete, in which case they had no idea how many were at the pack house. For most of the last century, in this area, pack boundaries were generally fixed due to the number of humans around, since the coming of the railroad making it easier for large numbers to reach the area limited them from changing as they fought over territory. The Inter-Pack Treaty in this area had the borders mostly fixed but with parts for expansion or contraction of pack sizes but had a set distance so they would not encroach on other packs without a specific agreement between the packs. Pack numbers were how their neighbours knew if they needed to negotiate for expansion.

Reaching the edge of the official territory of the former pack, they had a ring of scouts watching out for any of the remains of the rogue pack to appear. They slowed down to a walk, as they had expected more resistance than they were seeing. Adam was seeing an ambush at every turn and at every thick spot, but there was nothing, not even any wolf tracks. Not even any scents lingered, showing they had not been there since the last snowfall, and likely it was long before then. They startled a fox and a coyote, showing there had been no wolf in the area for a very long time, as both of the smaller canines rarely were in wolf or werewolf territories.

*****

By the time they had reached the much smaller perimeter the scouts were actually covering, they had travelled more than half of the distance to the location they believed the pack house was. The pack had exercised their own right of not reporting the location of their pack house, which few packs exercised, as most had a road going to it, so were easily found these days. There were only a few scouts out, and Adam had several groups split off and surround them. They only found one Beta they had been able to see, and he seemed to be trying to get himself declared as Alpha loudly, ignoring the fact their patrols were falling silent.

Adam decided to show himself. Brook was beside him, and there were another four who were behind them. Two he had shift to Were and stand back but showed themselves. The rest stayed out of sight.

They moved in, ignoring the scouts and even the other guards, heading straight to the Beta. Adam could sense he was a Beta rank at most, and stared him down in a clear challenge as he moved forward, his tail proudly erect, stating wordlessly his authority. Getting five metres away from him, and not having the challenge answered, he decided to tell them why they were here, *We are here to dissolve the Shadowed River Pack. Under the Inter-Pack Treaty, a Triad of Pack Elders—* Although after the fact, they had discussed it with many more packs, and all had agreed with the actions and what they wanted to do. *—Has found the pack to be in contravention of three Inter-Pack Treaty Rules. One: unlawful and untruthfully declaring of a pair of wolves who wished to leave as Rogue instead of Lone, simply to prevent them from finding a new Pack. Two: Unprovoked Attack of non-combatants in another pack who was not at war with them, while trespassing on that pack's territory. Three: Unprovoked attack of a pack by stealth. Following the attack, a fourth was added: Use of wolfsbane for an offensive measure.* Adam commented in open mind-speech which all who were nearby could hear. You could use open mind-speech and any Were, or even human who had a telepathic ability, could hear you; it was as if you shouted it. When face to face, you could talk privately with those not in your pack, but unless you knew them well, you could only talk with your pack when they weren't in sight. Some wolves didn't have the ability to speak silently to those not of their pack, even if they were in front of them, but most just shrugged it off as a difference between individuals.

Brook smiled inwardly as he sounded clearly in charge, and as confident as an Alpha needed to be. She had no sense of his hesitation nor how he didn't think he was worthy, which he had confided to her he felt.

Adam let the orders sink in for a few minutes, still staring down the Beta. Wolf-Adam really wanted to show who was in control and take him down. *All who are willing to leave and be absorbed into another pack are to put down their weapons and surrender. By the Authority of Alpha Gareth and the Triad of Packs, I am granting it also to any male, not just females and pups. Any who fight will be killed as the pack has been declared Rogue. You have one hour to decide.*

He had discussed it with Brook on the run there. They decided that if they give them time to decide to give up, they might be able to get more to surrender, and make it out of there without any deaths from their pack, even though it could make it worse for them by giving the rogue pack time to get positions to attack. Backing up slowly, Adam and Brook sat on the edge of the clearing. Adam hadn't even taken his eyes off the Beta.

Two scouts walked up to them, hands up, and with their weapons secured in their spots, "We don't need an hour to decide that we would rather leave this pack behind. It's been sick for a long time. All the senior pack members were on what they called a raid." Motioning with his head, "He's the only Beta left. There are a handful Deltas, and the rest are Theta or Omega. Most of the few Deltas left are the ones who don't like the way the pack was going but were too afraid to leave."

Adam traded a look with Brook before moving to keep the Beta in his sight, *Would they be willing to surrender, if we guarantee their safe passage to another pack?*

"I am sure most would take the chance. When the Alpha took most of the fighters, we felt it may be the end of us if they failed, as males are just killed, usually." Several had already suicided when the Alpha fell; not waiting for another pack to show up, expecting to be dealt harshly as they had been taught. Others had to be put down by packmates as they went Rogue with the loss of pack bonds and attacked others around them.

Go talk to them. If you can, get inside and see how many we can get out before those that want to fight work up their courage. Randy, go with him. He told them, sending one of the two in Were form, leaving it so all there could hear his agreement, before switching to Randy alone, *Treat him well, but keep a watch out for a trap. Have one from another group be a silent and unseen shadow for your safety.* Adam got a wordless reply of agreement, as he headed off.

They stood at a standoff with the Beta, with more and more of the pack surrendering, being snuck away, and put on several old school buses they had brought, getting them out of reach once their name, what rank the pack gave them, and what rank the organising wolf thought they should be at was noted. Talking with some, it seemed the Thetas contained many wolves who should be higher ranked. They didn't ask them any details about why they had what they felt was a wrong rank; whoever did a longer interview would be doing it at MacLaren. The official pack record seemed to not record many lower than Delta was something they had found as the records were rarely, if ever, looked at if there wasn't a good need to do so.

Passing the numbers already on their way, which put the pack as larger than reported back to Gareth, he got a savage mental growl which had *him* wanting to roll on his back even at this distance, *Fifth reason for taking the pack down. I always thought their reported pack numbers were very small but had no proof to support an investigation. You can do whatever you want there with my blessing now. I'll pass it onto the Elders.*

Taking a deep breath and a body shake, Adam replied, keeping his mate linked into the discussion, *There are also twenty Omegas which we have collected already. They are in bad shape; it seems they only got the scraps of dinners, only enough to keep them alive, and then worked from sunup till after sundown. I have them separated from the others, and I want to get into the pack records to see what their charges are. I suspect many will be cleared by another pack, from the few stories I have heard.*

Gareth gave another mental growl, *If the Alpha wasn't already dead, I'd want to tear him apart, alive, for how he treated the pack. If you get the records, keep them safe. We will need them for the Triad. Have you got any Elders?*

So far, maybe one. One Omega looks like he could have been, and I haven't seen someone with such trouble moving since leaving the city. He moves like a ninety-year-old human. He is already on his way to you for a debrief. I did promise he would not be harmed. Adam hoped he had been an elder, as they would have knowledge on how the pack worked, and how long the illness at the top had lasted. For an Elder to be treated with such disrespect had him nearly frothing at the mouth over it. He had sent them in a SUV with two guards and the one younger wolf they had to lean on, to get back separately from the rest. Likely, they would be able to give much more details about how the pack went bad.

Chatting some more, he brought the Alpha up to date. The Alpha went to go brief their Elders and have them pass it onto the other packs which had asked to be informed what they learned. Twenty Omegas was a sky-high number. The fact it had not been reported was also very bad. According to their reported records, they had none. Pack numbers were reported, so other packs could know if they had enough territory to support them, or if they needed to be allowed to expand. It was also, for if they called for help, the other packs who respond knew how many they were helping. While this was minor, compared to the other issues, it was another mark against them.

*****

The Beta burst out of the pack house as a slate-grey wolf, growling up a storm. Adam had expected that, so had pulled off his pack, so he could fight easier, even if it meant he didn't have the armouring against bullets, which was a trade-off both him and Brook felt was an acceptable risk. Several from their pack were watching for any stealth attacks being attempted. He stepped forward, walking slowly towards him, *I see; your answer is 'no',* He answered mildly. His wolf really wanted to just tear his throat out, but realising what his human was wanting to do, felt a savage pleasure.

His wolf grinned in their mind, **I guess my savage side is rubbing off on you,** He laughed, giving control to the human side. It was going to be much more painful and not just physically for their opponent, unless they surrendered. He stayed close to help his human fight, as he hoped it would be a good fight.

I am now the Alpha of Shadowed River. Get off my territory before I kill you. Came the snarled response. Adam, Brook, and many of the senior Enforcers they had with them felt no need to follow his order, and actually could feel they were more powerful than this wolf pretending to be an Alpha.

Your pack has been dissolved due to your breaches of the Inter-Pack Treaty. You no longer have a pack. Adam replied, just as calmly, and stepped neatly to the side when the other wolf lunged. He chomped down on his tail-tip as it passed, getting a loud yelp.

Adam started circling the slate-grey wolf, acting very casually about it. He was a good ten centimetres taller at the shoulder, if not more. His bulk from the month of steady workouts and training showed. The other wolf was rangier and didn't have even close to the mental 'presence' Adam had, not even what he felt from some of the senior enforcers MacLaren had.

Adam kept dodging the grey wolf leaving behind sharp bites, but seemingly staying calm, which infuriated the other wolf; he had yet to land a blow. This fight appeared to be till one submitted or was dead, but Adam acted like he fought them every day or this was just a minor training bout. It showed how little training the wolf had taken.

The grey wolf snarled when his jump was missed, and he rolled in the dirt. Lunging again, Adam was not where he expected. He yelped at the sudden pain in his flank, while Adam sauntered away. The many bites were turning his pelt red.

Adam started circling, *Again: your pack has been dissolved due to the actions of the last alpha. This is your last chance to save your life.*

I'll never surrender! I'd rather die! Came the snarled response.

Adam let him take a bite, but it was his undoing, as Adam used his momentum against him, rolled him on his back, took his neck in his mouth, and letting out a chest-deep growl, as he bit down just a hair from breaking the skin. The grey wolf fought and tried to force him to release, but Adam just bit down harder, and started to taste his blood.

Again, he growled, and again the grey wolf refused to surrender, even though he could hardly breath. Adam then bit down hard, cutting off his breath and severing his artery. He knew from the amount of blood pumping into his mouth, the wolf was dead. Stepping back, he was growling savagely. He could feel the disgust and disappointment from his wolf of how easily they beat this wolf, and how they couldn't stand to be wrong and submit.

Brook stepped up beside him, leaned into Adam's flank, sent him calming and loving thoughts as they watched the grey wolf twitch out the last movements. She felt Adam's anguish over having to take a life come to the fore as his anger and battle-thoughts drained away. *You gave him more chances to respond and to give up than is required. He refused, and as he said, he'd would rather die than surrender. This happens, and we just have to live with it.* His tail drooped as she licked the blood from the one bite he had allowed, sealing it so it would heal.

Adam gave a nuzzle to his mate, *You're right. I chose this life, and everything it entailed, even this.* He let his breath out in a sigh, *I don't like it, and may have a bad dream or two, but I'm not going to dwell on it. We have work to do here.* With the support of his wolf seeming on one side and his mate on the other, he pushed the memory into a corner so he'd be able to get through the job; when they were back, he could deal with it in private.

Calling out, pushing the power they had only started to be taught to use, *Stand down. Your last Beta has been defeated in death. Any who do not fight will not be harmed.* Switching to just those in the pack in the area, as he had been taught, *Move in. Take any who attack down. Deadly force is authorized. Any who submit are not to be harmed and will be taken to the processing. If you find pack records, try to protect them, and let us know.* Adam ordered, sounding strong. He decided to give a warning, *There might be wolfsbane bullets still here. Take care; I don't want to have any deaths.*

The other Were, dropped Adam's pack on him, and buckled it on, as it was not impossible, just really hard, to do it as a wolf. Adam wagged his tail in thanks and lead their group in the still open front door to the pack house. The vest parts of the pack's harness had armour plates installed. It would protect parts of him if attacked with bullets. It did make it a little stiffer, and harder to fight in, but generally he would rather be safe than dead. He hoped it wasn't needed.

Chapter 2 – Cleaning House

Heading in the door, they were met by two wolves, in just cheap, ill-fitting clothes. Adam stopped, with Brook right at his flank, and the others arrayed behind them. He could see they were acting submissive, and the stench of fear was billowing off them, *Speak. I don't think you are to attack us; we won't attack unless you do.* Adam ordered.

"They aren't here to attack you, but we are!" Said another voice to their side. Instantly spinning with his wolf-reflexes, had a battle-axe crashing down right where Adam's neck had been less than a breath before. His wolf took control and launched themselves at the attacker. Before they could recover Wolf-Adam already had the attacker's throat ripped out. Using the attacker as a springboard, Adam bounced back to the ground as Newton's Third Law of Motion was proved true, as they were thrown back into the other two before they had realised the axe had missed, as the first choked on his own blood as he died. Wolf-Adam relinquished control as he spat out the chunk of flesh he had ripped out, disgusted at the taste. He stood almost in the same spot as he had before the three had attacked, ready for more.

My fur is all bloody now! Wolf-Adam whined, disliking the way the werewolf's blood clumped his beautiful fur. His human side just chuckled, as they looked for another attacker, but the only ones were the two others they had already taken out.

The two were just struggling from under the larger male who had attacked them. They were helped up by two of Adam's pack, in their Were form, and had their hands cuffed before they could get their whit's together.

Bring them here. Adam ordered. One of their faces was familiar. Standing in front of the other, *Take him away. Put him with the fighters we have caught.*

Shifting to human, Adam studied the other till it clicked: this was the one who's face he lifted from Duncan's mind, "You know Duncan and Keanna?" He asked generally. Getting a flicker of fear before he smoothed his face and shook his head, Adam grinned as he could smell the silent lie. *This one gets special treatment. He is the root of the cause of all this issues,* He told his pack silently, not letting them know his orders for dealing with him, *I want a death-watch on him. Duncan is to have him arrive safe and sound for his judgment. A little rough handling if it can't be avoided would be acceptable.*

They nodded, and two in Were shape moved to flank him as they escorted him to a Light Armoured Vehicle which had been parked right outside the door. Adam watched as he was hauled into the rear passenger compartment of the vehicle which looked like an eight-wheeled tank with no top gun. Adam had been surprised they even had one let alone three, but they had been acquired when the armed forces had downsized. They had two more which were tanks, but the muzzles had been welded over; they really looked intimidating, but the worst they could do was run someone over. They had been retrofitted as armoured transport vehicles, and mostly used for rescue under fire or pure mental warfare.

Even he knew the saying, 'Before the battle of the fists, is the battle of the minds.' And how just acting like you have won before you started could win your battle. Having one of their tanks coming at you? Adam had been told of skirmishes which had turned into a rout of the attackers just by having it drive towards them and point the barrel where they were hiding.

The tanks were very hard on fuel, so he had not called them in. Although they had been trucked close for if they were needed, he hadn't bothered having them off-loaded from the flatbed trailers. By the end of the night, he thought they would be able to send them home.

Turning to the nearly forgotten two, they cringed when his gaze landed on them. They submitted by showing their necks. Smelling the increase of fear from them Adam sighed, "I am not going to harm you, as long as you don't attack." Nodding at the cooling body, "He attacked with intent to kill. My wolf saw the deadly threat and took it out. He doesn't see you as a threat."

Both sighed and the scent of fear decreased, "I had been the Alpha's clerk, until I made an error and gave him the wrong report. He made me an Omega for it. I know where he kept the files and know as of yesterday, he hadn't changed the combination."

Adam smiled at his luck, "What rank were you before you were demoted?" He felt like he should have been much higher ranked.

"Beta." Came the wistful reply.

"Well, we will need to check on your case, on all the Omegas in fact, but as long as you're telling the truth, you would be restored your rank with no record of being Omega. An honest mistake like that was should not have made a case for a demotion at all, let alone being made Omega."

He looked at Adam with hope in his eyes, "The Alpha demanded perfection. If he didn't get it, he invoked the Alpha Law and made us Omegas. Also, he didn't allow anyone to leave. There was very rarely anyone who escaped. In my years, only two mated pairs escaped, everyone else was captured and tortured before being executed. Or we have word another pack killed them from the reports of them being Rogue." He shuddered, "And everyone was made to watch the executions done here. When the second pair were protected by MacLaren and not treated as Rogues, it made him go crazy. He was still having enforcers out searching for the other pair."

Brook had shifted to her Were to be better protection, pulled out the sword which fit her size from the sheath along the spine of her pack, and guarded Adam's back. Reaching into his bag, she pulled out his shorts, and handed them to him to pull on, as he still preferred not to be running around without something on but didn't want to pull his pack off more. Both were just carrying the basic, generic clothes supplied by the pack, as there was a good chance they would be not wearable after this attack.

After a quick discussion, Adam and Brook decided the files were more important for them to personally deal with. The others were working well to deal with those there, but the shock of their seniors being taken out was causing more to give up without a fight.

Adam nodded to the two, "Lets go get the files, so we can reverse the decisions."

*****

Coming out of the office with a big stack of files, they headed to the nearest door and started loading boxes of files into the van. There had seemed to be endless files. Just dumping them in boxes and reloading them was going to take all night. Luckily, they had found all the rest of those who were fighting them and freed all the females from the cells in the basement.

The buses and tanks, along with a good escort of the pack, were on their way and should be arriving at their pack house just in time to have breakfast. At dawn, it had been arranged to have Arctic Shadow Pack relieve them; they would start a full search of the building, and all the outbuildings for anything hidden. Adam was glad he didn't have to deal with it as well, as it had already been a very long day. On the way back, many were going to sleep and let the wolf-side take them home.

Adam was still concerned they had not found any of the wolfsbane. He thought it might be still hidden here, as he doubted they took it all on the attack; they expected to return.

Adam was directing everything from where he sat on the ground near the door, leaning back against Charlie, who was taking a nap.

Brook was also asleep, with her head in his lap. He had got a couple hours of shut eye while Brook handled it, and now was her turn to rest.

All packed. All the paper which was in the alpha's office and his rooms, has been packed up. We're heading out. Came the call, just as the sky started to lighten.

Good. Take as many as can go with you and leave the fastest runners. We'll keep it secure till the Arctic Shadow Pack arrives. Adam called back. There were only a few left around. Most were tired and were looking forward to getting back. They had a good run but could turn over to their wolf-half and let the exhausted human-half sleep on the way back. Many were like him, resting in pairs or trios, keeping up a guard position around the pack house.

There was nothing amiss till Adam heard the loud howl of the other pack as they came in. Brook woke with a start, sitting up, "It's just Arctic Shadow Pack coming in." Adam murmured to her, as he stood up. The pack came in from the north, where their territory had a large number of former glaciers and alpine land. The legend was the members who set up the pack had thought it was a shadow of the arctic. Another story was they had the name because the wolves they saw from that pack were all white furred.

The largest white wolf walked up to Adam and Brook and shifted to human. "Betas Adam and Brook, I presume? I'm Second Mark." He introduced himself, without any preamble.

Adam smiled and gave him a hug in greeting, "*Acting-Second* Adam, and this is my Mate, Brook."

Mark grinned, "Acting-Second? Congratulations on the promotion." He too had just recently been deemed 'trained' and took over fully as Second of their much smaller pack than MacLaren.

"Thanks. We're doing the official announcement tonight. We only got it recently and are still getting used to it." Adam replied as he led him into the Alpha's office, "This is the Alpha's office. We already have secured all the records we could find. As you know, the Alphas and Elders for five packs are wanting a whole picture here." Checking they had reasonable privacy, "We have already found out they had twenty-four Omegas, and as far as I can tell, all were demoted for minor mistakes, with several in the last year. We plan on reversing the decisions. We also found out three quarters of the Thetas were not in the official records." He paused to make sure they were alone, and to close the door, "Also, I suspect there is a stash of liquid wolfsbane hiding somewhere here. When they attacked us, they had hollowed bullets filled with it on them. If you find any, secure it to be sent to us. I'll have an armoured vehicle come pick it up with some Betas. I will give you their names when you contact me, and they will have the orders in writing, signed by us, if we don't come in person; I really don't want it to fall into a Rogue's hands." He might be new to being a werewolf, but for some reason he had memories of werewolves dying in agony from wolfsbane poisoning.

Mark went pale, "That is major issues. Glad I'm not dealing with them." Wolfsbane was a major issue, as possessing it was an immediate death sentence. A pack found to be making it, was alone a reason for dissolving the pack. At the security precautions, he nodded, expecting something similar. "SUV or LAV? I saw one heading off as we came in." Not only was wolfsbane one of the few reasons for immediate dissolution of a pack, even before the treaty by traditions which were over a millennia old, possessing it was a provocation and a valid reason for other packs to attack.

"LAV. They are much stronger, and much harder to fake. Even if they are a pig on gas." Adam answered with a grin.

Brook nodded, "Mostly we are dealing with the Wolfsbane. Adam took Duncan and Keanna under our protection, and since we have been promoted, Alpha Gareth is having us deal with most of the work. He's using it as a Second Trial."

Adam gave a wary smile, "We've already qualified on the wolf-run, and I don't even have my Were, yet!"

Mark laughed, "I heard you were only recently turned and joined us. From your scent, I couldn't tell and the way you act, you are well on your way to being a seasoned wolf soon." He blinked, "Wait, you said you *qualified* your wolf-run test? Where did you find a clear and dry track?"

Brook laughed, "We did it just after the latest snowfall. We had ten centimetres of fresh snow which had only lightly been packed. It hid most of the ice under enough traction for our paws."

Mark shook his head, "How long was the trail?"

"One-Fifty kilometres. Ran it in eighty-five minutes." Came Brook's proud reply.

Mark's eyes bugged out in shock, "Our Alpha runs that speed on the Spring Trials, on *clear ground*!" He shook his head again, "I'd hate to have to try to run away from you!"

Adam laughed, "This pack's most senior surviving member tried it. The first time, when he was running from the pack house, he got away. I worked hard so he couldn't do it again. When the pack attacked, I was able to use some trees to have him stop."

Mark laughed, wincing, "Even my wolf now doesn't want to take you on! Did you want me to keep you informed if we find anything?" Mark thought he knew the wolf who still lived, and if it was, he had the nickname of 'White Lightning' since he was faster than anyone else. If they could take him out in a paw chase, they were faster than their Alpha! From the power radiating from the two, he would not be surprised if they were soon the Alphas of their own pack. He could feel his wolf submitting to them, even though technically he was more senior to them and they were treating him as an equal. He led them to the door of the office and opened it back up.

Adam nodded and reached into a pouch on his pack, pulled out a card, "It has my contact information, I haven't had a chance to get the new ones yet so has the wrong title."

Mark nodded, and handed over one too, he had only a small pouch around his neck, "I want one of those packs! Can you shift with them on?"

"Yes, even Were. As long as your load is balanced and not too heavy, you can even fight with them on, and are designed so you can get them off or even on while wolf, although it isn't easy to get it buckled while wolf." Brook replied, "Come down to our pack after this is all done, and we'll get you fitted for one." It would be a fairly basic one, but they were one of the products they did trade or sell to a selection of other packs and were fairly expensive.

Mark nodded, "I will do that. I've never been to your pack house; I've heard some stories of how beautiful it is and want to see if they are true." Even his wolf perked up at the invite to their pack house. Other than the Alpha and a few helpers, none from his pack had visited it. He had been told the description of it didn't do it justice, and the description had him very envious.

Adam nodded, smothering a yawn with his hand, "Well, time for my pack to let yours get to work. If you need anything, let me know."

Mark nodded, "Enjoy your run."

MacLaren Wolves, gather outside the main doors with all your gear. Adam ordered the wolves who were left, *It is time we headed back. Arctic Shadow Pack is now in control.*

*****

The run back, with mostly the faster wolves, was limited only to the speed which their Hybrid wolfdogs could run, and as they didn't need to conserve their strength, took only a couple hours. Most, including Adam and Brook, had given control to their wolves, so their human-minds could sleep.

Adam's wolf nudged him awake as they arrived back at the pack house, mid morning, *All of you are dismissed. You are excused from all duties till tomorrow, noon at the earliest. Check for your next duty shift. I do recommend being on time for dinner tonight.* He knew most of them knew of his promotion, as it was hard to hide the fact when his ID was visible. Those whom he had told or mentioned it, he had asked for it to be kept quiet for the official announcement, but Brook had commented it was likely everyone would already know. Since they were on-duty the entire time, it was either three 8-hour shifts or four 6-hour shifts, depending on how they worked, the time off was normal for those on an extended duty. Those who had stayed would have already been slotted in to cover their shifts as needed, or others who were considered reserves would have slotted into the shifts needed. The inner patrols sometimes were done by the Junior Enforcers, those older pups who had passed the training and qualified as Enforcers, with a single senior Enforcer to guide them. Some may even have a longer break from other work they had done.

Jess, Joshua? Could you bring something for us to eat in our room? We're not gong to make it to lunch and need a few hours sleep. We were up all night. Adam called. His wolf gave him a tired mental nudge, as while his human-mind got a few hours rest, they were physically exhausted.

On it, Came the quick reply from Joshua, *Welcome home, Dad.*

Shifting back to human, they dumped their packs just inside their room and stretched. They took a quick shower to wash the blood and grime off their skins and reassure each other they were fine. Luckily, the one bite which Adam had taken to get control of the Beta in the fight had already closed, and although still red where his fangs had penetrated, was healing nicely. Both had bruises, but nothing which wouldn't clear up quickly. Their other injuries from the first fight, would be fully healed within a week. They didn't bother with clothes, as they were heading to bed after they ate.

Coming out, they were led by their nose to a nice small feast which Jess and Joshua were laying out for them. "When the Chefs found out who it was for, they whipped up some food fast just for you, and ordered us to make sure you didn't go away hungry." Jess commented, as she gave both a hug.

"Martin took us for training this morning, so we didn't miss two sessions in a row, and we'd better get back to it." Joshua commented, as he gave them hugs as well.

His wolf growled appreciatively at the food and passed a suggestion to his human. Adam nodded, "After dinner, we'll go for a wolf pup play time. Let any pup know who is interested."

Both Jess and Joshua grinned as they nodded. Seniors calling a wolf pup play time was rare, but was always fun, "I'll make sure there are enough adults as well." Joshua said, knowing most if not all the pups would want to be there.

Both settled in a seat and started eating like the ravenous wolves they were, as their pups helped put their hair in a simple braid to keep it out of the way while they ate before letting themselves out.

There was not much left, when they pushed back with a sigh, "That was good." Adam commented as he swayed over to the bed, nearly falling on it. Charlie had already sprawled on one side, his belly distended slightly from a large meal as well.

Brook slid onto the bed, pulled a blanket over them, and snuggled into her mate with a tired smile, as replying being too much work.
*****

Adam was awoken by Jess stroking his cheek softly, and he smiled as he stretched. He had to wince, as he was stiff, "What time is it?" he asked.

"Twenty minutes before dinner. And you need to be there." Jess replied with a grin. It had taken a full ten minutes to wake him up.

Adam looked over and smiled; Joshua was trying to wake up Brook and having no luck. Adam grinned and kissed her on the lips. Brook lifted an arm and held his head to her lips for a second kiss before opening her eyes, "Guess it's time to get up?" She commented.

Adam nodded, "Almost dinner, and we need to be there for the announcement. They held it off for us to do the take down of the pack."

Brook nodded, sliding out of the bed. She went to the closet and grabbed just some comfortable slacks and collared shirts; since they were going to be up in front of the pack, they needed to dress better, to not offend the 'conservative' members. Brook had almost given both skirts but decided against them. Also, it was to show everyone they took their promotion seriously by dressing more respectful of the formal-ness of the occasion.

Dressed, they each wrapped an arm around their pups, "You two are coming with us for the visit to my mother for her birthday," Adam told them, "You're as much our pups as Robin and Toby are."

Joshua smiled, "I thought so, just with everything going on, you forgot to tell us. We're all packed in wolf-bags."

Adam pulled him close in a side-hug, "You are excellent in your anticipation."

Entering the room, Adam smiled as it seemed many of the pack already knew and were trying to keep it down for the official announcement. There was almost a scent of anticipation from the pack. All the seats were full, and there were others standing around as well.

It usually happens this way, Brook commented, amused, *Most, if not all, found out about major promotion before it is announced. It shows we care.* It also showed how hard it was to keep a secret within a close-knit pack as they cared enough to want to talk about changes in their packmate's lives.

Adam chuckled, as they sat down, to wait for the Alpha to arrive, *It also shows we have a hard time keeping something like this a secret.* He replied, amused, giving words to her private thought.

The Alpha walked in, and didn't need to call for silence, as it very quickly went quiet, "As many of you have already found out," He commented, amused as well as a close-knit pack is something he always strived for, "Our current Seconds are wanting to retire. It seems we have finally been blessed with replacements as well. Adam and Brook," He had to stop for the long, loud howl. He ended up holding a hand up to get everyone to quiet down, "Have shown they are up to the challenge. They have qualified already on the wolf-run, as most saw them zipping around the one-fifty trail a few days ago." Their run had become the talk of the pack, as it was rare for the seniors to really run, especially when the ground wasn't totally clear, "Their official time was just over eighty-five minutes."

Again, the pack howled; it was a very good time, and needed to be calmed down before Gareth continued, "They then lead the force which dealt with the rogue pack's remaining members. Adam took down the Beta who was acting as their Alpha in a fair fight, and also the next strongest when they were ambushed by him and two others. He also uncovered more violations of the Inter-Pack Treaty rules. Those, the elders have decided, qualify as his Leadership and Fighting trials. They were also able to carry out the mission without any major injuries and no death of any of the pack." The pack howled louder, as it showed the two not only could lead, but both would work to keep everyone alive and well and not spend their lives needlessly.

Waiting for the pack to calm down before continuing, "We will have the official party and oaths given for them at the next Full Moon Howl. The current Seconds are working to pass the duties over to Adam and Brook and will be officially stepping down at the end of the Spring Trials. By then, I expect Adam and Brook to be fully qualified." Neither Adam nor Brook wanted a party for their taking on the role, but the pack wouldn't let them not have one, so they were just having it join the normal full moon party. For once, the chef hadn't complained about the added work.

Using this time, Gareth decided to inform everyone what was happening with those recovered, "Onto other news, since I have everyone here: From the Rogue Pack, we have recovered quite a few who either felt they had no option but to fight or were left behind with inadequate protection. Many are here now, as our guests." He nodded to the clump of them in the corner. Two others had already found their mates among his wolves, and others had found new friends and were mingled among the pack. Some others had formally approached him already about joining the pack and had been passed the laws and other details to read before giving their oath and formally joining, having to reassure them they had Guest Status, and it would not be revoked. "Others who gave up at the fight are being cleared before release from detention. We will be folding some of them into our pack, and others will be going on to other packs which have agreed to take them." There were several who had said they had contact with a different pack, and those packs had, in every case, extended an invite to visit, to see if the pack would be a good fit, and already had left to go there.

A howl of greeting was given. Stories about what they had to endure had been making the rounds since they arrived just after dawn.

"Those who we captured, which are those who fought, are currently sitting in our Rogue cells awaiting the compiling of the charges against them, and getting what information out of them we can. They will be dealt with, eventually." He commented with grim pleasure. They would deal with them after everything else was dealt with. Currently, while they were in a room which barely had any warmth, they had a clean, comfortable place to stay, and for the most part, they were with one or two others. They were provided food and knew they were looking into the records for confirmation of their stories before they could be released or as humanely as possible put down if they couldn't overlook their details. "We have a large amount of their pack's records which are being gone through by our elders, and their helpers. It is going to take a while."

They all had been told they wanted to give them back their lives if they could, and if not, would have a respectful send off if they were at least respectful to the guards. The couple who had not been respectful had been separated and already dealt with quietly as they had believed the lies of their Alpha and supported going after any who tried to leave. With how the pack dealt with dissenters, they were not treating any who was respectful as supporting the decisions of the leaders and were looking into other details.

"Many of those who had been declared Omegas were done in contravention of what I would consider right and were done for minor infractions. We are going through the records recovered, will be reversing the demotions, reinstating them to their former rank, and exonerating them of the charges. Many of the pack only stayed there because of the fact the Alpha didn't allow any to leave. If he couldn't capture or kill them, he would inform the other packs of them with fictions or half truths of what they were to have done, and state they were dangerous and needed to be killed on sight." Taking a breath as a growl swept the hall, "Sadly, in one instance we helped. In another, we unknowingly helped protect them. I have had that family relabeled as lone wolves and they are living on the south-west edge of our territory with my permission. They had been there for years without our knowledge and had not caused any problems. They have been invited to join the pack, but they are still hurting from the way they had been treated." He had sent out a wolf to provide them the information of their old pack no longer existing, and the leaders were dead along with a formal letter which had the signatures of the Alphas for three packs to label them as Loners, not Rogues. The letter actually had been passed to other Alphas too, and there had been a supplemental letter from several which not only reputed the Rogue status too, but also offered them sanctuary if they wished. So far, they had rebuffed the offers of Packs, but had accepted the papers as the gift they were. They would help, if they ever encountered a different pack which hadn't received their changed status.

Pressing on the pack through the bonds Gareth gave an Alpha order, "They are to be left alone, unless they approach you. I don't want them pressured at all."

Taking a breath, "The others we saved were Duncan and Keanna. I am not going into details, but they fled and had asked for sanctuary before we got their fictitious notice. By then, I had seen they were quite different than what was declared. I had them watched, but by the time they asked to join us, I had decided it had been faked, and let them join with a clean record. Since then, they have been exceedingly loyal and have caused no problems." Finding them in the pack, he gave them a nod, "I have them down as taking the Delta Qualifications at the Spring Trials, as they are not Theta in skills. They have much more skills than that. As I have always stated: I go more by abilities than by what rank your parents have. I do not like a stratified pack, where those who wish to move up can't and those unqualified for the position are given it just because they were whelped by ones who did."

The statement caused a stir, especially among their guests, who's pack had not allowed them to move more than one rank up in their life, and even then was hard enough most didn't bother. "If anyone wants to sign up for training, let them. If you can't talk to your supervisor, talk to myself, our new Acting-Seconds, Martin, or Rein and his mate Mikan," Each had waved a hand when he had given their names, "And they will be able to help you with getting you set up with some training."

Seeing he was starting to lose some, "Now: let's eat!" Gareth called out to much laughter.

The hall settled down to mostly sounds of everyone eating, as those who were not left the area. Adam and Brook smiled as there were many mental calls of congratulations, and many of thanks in bringing the group back safely.

Adam continued to love the ability to talk while eating, and not need to worry about a mouth full of food but trying to reply to many people all at the same time was giving him a headache.
*****

After dinner, Adam and Brook shifted to their wolves in their room, and padded out the door to wait for the pups near the front door. There was a large tumbling of wolf pups out the door already, followed by Alpha Maria, Jess, Joshua, and a few other adults. Adam and Brook dipped their heads and folded their ears back in respect to the Alpha.

I thought you could do with some help. It seems many of the pups want to come out and play. It is rare for open play periods. Was Maria's amused response.

Adam dangled his tongue out in amusement, *I love playing with pups, and my wolf very much enjoys it too. After this week, we need the time to relax and think about the good in life, not the bad.*

Opening up to the pups frolicking around him, seeing no more coming out, and it being fifteen minutes after he said he was leaving, *OK pups, we're going for a short run out to the training meadow, and play there.* He had decided on the meadow, as it was well within the secure perimeter, and had enough room to play. It would allow for them to enjoy themselves without needing too many adults to watch but was a place they didn't usually get to go, as it was outside of the parameter permitted for the younger pups. The older ones would have been permitted under supervision to be out there for their training.

Taking off at a slow trot, he led the puppy pack, with adults keeping watch on the outside, and Maria taking up the rear to make sure they didn't have any stragglers. They arrived quickly, as it was not far from the pack house for an adult.

Adam lay down and indulgently let the pups use him as something to climb over. His wolf was very much happy to play with the pups and enjoyed the time to relax with them. After a while, he started to use his muzzle to poke them, making many roll over. They were trying to get them more control and were gentle about it. When he stood up, he ended up with three pups sprawled across his back. Wolf-Adam enjoyed the fun and walked around a bit, trying to make sure to keep it smooth enough not to lose them, before he sped up to a trot for a bit, then flopping back down in his original spot, and shook them off, to their yelps of fun as they rolled to the ground.

All too soon, it was time to head back, and most of the pups were complaining tiredly, but a couple had already fallen asleep. Adam picked one up in his mouth, and Brook the other, as they took the puppy-pack back to the pack house. Handing over the snoozing pups to their parents, they were given a quiet thank you, and they watched over the other pups till their parents collected them. Those who were asleep were gently picked up and taken to bed by their parents, with looks of gratitude from their parents, as sometimes the pups were hard to put to bed.

One was left and was cuddled against Adam's side as he lay there, *Where's your parents, Jake?* He asked, gently.

He let out a whimper, *My mom is out patrolling for the night; she had to cover a shift for another. My dad was James,* Came the soft reply, as the young pup cuddled more into his side with a whimper.

Adam looked at his mate in surprise, wandering what to do with him as the name clicked in his mind.

Chapter 3 – Recovery

Brook came over and nuzzled Jake gently, *You can come curl up with us. I have let your mother know where you will be.* She too recognised the name as being one of the three they lost in the attack on the pack.

Adam nodded and stood up, nuzzling the pup – he looked like a yearling wolf, but was still much smaller than him; he could walk under his belly without trouble, *How old are you, Jake?*

Turn ten in the spring, Came the reply. Adam could feel the anguish in his voice over losing his father as a raw wound to the pup's spirit. It called to something within both halves of Adam. For the human, it was he had been in the place Jake was at, and he had no trusted male to talk to. For the wolf, it was more of the shared memories from his human side, and the need to protect a vulnerable pup which needed some comforting from an adult male.

Give us some time? Adam asked, *I remember how I felt when I lost my father. I can give him some comfort.* He was remembering the day they found his father's body, when he suicided. Nobody had realised he was even depressed, let alone had gone so far as to see it as the only way out. He had been in school, and the principal had come personally to tell him his aunt was picking him up, and her telling him of it. He barely remembered anything else from the next few days, but it had always stayed with him.

Brook nodded, *I need to go speak with Sam and Lea's parents. I will leave you be with him. I'll have Jess drop off some sleep shorts for him in our room.*

Adam nodded, and nuzzled the pup again, *Come, you're staying with us. I have a couple of things to talk to you about.*

When the pup stood, Adam stood and shook his fur, before leading him slowly around the pack house to his door. Heading inside, he shifted, and grabbed some shorts, offering the pair in the pup's size which Jess dropped off, "Shift, and we can curl up on the couch and chat."

The pup did so and had a hurt and vulnerable look in his eyes when he looked up at Adam. He led him over to the couch and pulled him into his arms as he started to cry, letting out the pain and loss he had been feeling, now he was with a dominant male wolf which he trusted to protect him. Adam held him close and just gave him a safe place and a caring shoulder to cry on. He knew it was sometimes all which was needed.

Silently sighing at his wolf, he commented, *I wish I had this growing up. I lacked a male role model; I barely saw any of my uncles and didn't really have a close family friend I saw very often which I felt I could lean on much.* Others had told him years later how he seemed to be very angry all the time... and realised he had blamed his father for years for abandoning him, and took a long time to realise his father had a mental illness nobody had noticed, so he hadn't gotten any help for it.

Wolf-Adam just gave a mental nuzzled to his human and shared his strength to help him. He could see this was bringing back many memories from when he was young, and how alone he felt then, and only once he had his wolf was some of it dealt with.

Eventually, he stopped crying, and Adam handed him a tissue to wipe his eyes and blow his nose. Taking another to wipe his own unshed tears, having been just a quiet shoulder to cry on, as he did his own remembering.

"Feeling a little better?" Adam asked gently, still holding him close.

"Not really," Came the honest reply.

Adam decided to share parts of his own story, "I too lost my father when I was your age. Unlike you, I didn't have a pack and lots of friends who cared about me. Nor did I have my wolf-half to keep the loneliness away; talk with your wolf, and if you ask for help, he'll help support you and give you strength to get through this."

"Does the pain ever go away?" Jake asked quietly.

Adam sighed, "Not really, sorry to say, it never does really go away. Time does put it at distance, and lets you continue on, but at times it rears its head, and you just need to have a good cry. I will make one offer: if you need someone to talk to, or even just a shoulder to cry, come find me. If I'm not available, any of my pups might know some of what you're feeling, and be able to help, as they lost their parents. Jess and Joshua lost theirs a while ago, Robin lost his, and Toby lost his father."

"I guess," Jake commented, sounding lost.

Adam just held him firmly against his chest, "I am not going to try to replace your father. Just remember, he died protecting the pack. If we had failed, they planned to harm the pack. You will eventually feel proud about that."

Jake wrapped his arms around Adam's chest and held on tight, his head on Adam's shoulder, "Nobody will tell me how he died, just he died fighting the other pack." He sobbed, with his nose tucked close the pack's Second; the scent of a dominant male helping to comfort him.

Adam settled to just holding him, "I might not be able to find anything, but I will ask around to see what I can find out. It may take some time before I can get what you want, though.

"You'd do that *for me*?" Jake asked, his voice muffled by Adam's neck. His nose was pressed into it, breathing in his dominant musky scent was helping to calm him down. His voice was wolf-growly, and Adam could sense he had called his wolf forward to help him, which was a good thing.

"I just said I would. I keep my word, and will find out for you, as much as I can. I know when mine died, I wanted to know how, too. Even though it was suicide."

Adam switched the topic, otherwise he'd start crying, and he was trying to support the pup, "So did you enjoy the play time this evening?"

"Mmmhmm," Came the sleepy reply. It seemed Jake had worn himself out, at last. Brook slipped in just as Adam sensed him fall asleep.

Get the bed ready, Love. He just dropped off to sleep. Adam asked silently, not wanting to wake the pup.

Brook nodded, and moved to open the blankets, careful to not disturb the sleeping Charlie. Although they had a dog bed for him, it lay unused, as Charlie had always preferred curling up with them on the bed. Adam crawled in, putting his back to Charlie, and Jake on the other side, as Brook got ready for bed. She slipped in on the other side of Jake.

Adam sighed and looked at the sleeping pup curled up against his chest, *He really reminds me of myself. I don't want him to grow up with no male he trusts to ask whatever he wants without any concern. I don't want to replace his father; he'd resent that, but still be there for him. Even if it is just to be a shoulder to cry on, for now.*

Brook nodded sadly, *I do hope his mother doesn't go the way most mates go, and pine away for their mate.* Giving Adam a hard look, *Only if she does, will I permit you to add him to our family. I will fight to keep her his guardian; he is probably why she is holding onto life right now. I did ask Martin to keep her to her shift runs for now, for Jake's sake, as he needs her around. I did tell him that if they had nobody, we would do the patrol instead of her. Also asked him to keep a close eye on her, as he's the one she looks to.*

Adam nodded in understanding, *It hurts when we lose a pack member and I don't want him to lose both parents, so I will not do that. Could I be a trusted Uncle to him?* He asked his mate.

Brook nodded, and softened, *That you can. It may also help his mother. Maybe we can give her your mother's contact information, for an-

other woman who has been through something similar? From what little we have talked, I'm thinking your parents were mates, even if they weren't Were.

Adam nodded, closing his eyes. Even though they slept most of the day, he was getting tired again, *We can ask her first, when we see her this weekend.*

Quickly, they both fell asleep, but their wolves prowled forward. They would protect the pup from any more pain. Bending his nose, Wolf-Adam sniffed the pup's head, taking in his scent and making sure it was imprinted in their memory, so they wouldn't forget it before relaxing their body, so it could rest and recover from the extremely busy week. He slept lightly, keeping an ear and nose out for anyone coming near them and the pup they were protecting.

*****

Friday morning came all too early. Adam stretched before curling back around the pup, pulling him close. He growled as someone moved beside him before realising it was his mate.

"You two better get moving, if you want breakfast." Brook scolded, "I know you are both awake."

Adam opened his eyes and blinked for a few times, before smiling at Jake, who was smiling back up at him. "Have a good sleep?" Adam asked.

Jake nodded, "But I'm hungry now."

Brook laughed, "Good thing it is breakfast time then. Not sure who, but someone dropped off some clothes for you to wear." Knowing Jess and Joshua, it was one of them as they enjoyed anticipating their needs and having things ready to go before they had to ask. Their wolves knew them enough and trusted them when they slept, they wouldn't wake their humans if they entered.

Jake nodded and wiggled out of Adam's hold to put the clothes on, before scampering for the door, "See you later," He called walking out.

Adam shook his head, as Brook tossed him a sleeveless robe. "Hurry up, I'm hungry, too!" She complained, "We can shower after breakfast."

Shaking his head, Adam pulled the robe on and pounced on her gently to give her a kiss, "Come on then; lets go for breakfast."

They quickly gathered their food and plopped down. Toby and Robin were sitting across from them, and smiled as they dug into their breakfast, *Saw you had Jake in with you last night.* Robin commented, *Is he OK?* He was taking his duties as a senior pup very seriously, and had been keeping an eye on Jake since he collapsed in the saferoom, when the bond to his father snapped at his death. Lea had cuddled him till he woke up, just as they released them from the saferoom. She didn't think anyone else noticed, as they had gathered around his mother who had shrieked just before passing out herself.

Adam nodded, *At first it was to just watch him while his mother was on patrol, but he reminds me of myself when I was his age, and I lost my own father. He's doing as good as can be expected, when you are just recovering from your dad's death.* He replied, looking at both pups, *I suspect you can both understand what he's going through*

Both looked down at their food, remembering losing their own fathers, before nodding.

I do hope you two can keep an eye on him. Adam asked his pups.

Both nodded seriously, *Already have been; I saw him collapse when his bond to his dad was broken. Lea and I kept him close till his mother was able to care for him, and we were let out,* Robin replied, *Been trying to keep an eye on him since.*

Turning to Brook, *Did either other of the two who died have pups?* He didn't want any other pups who were having to deal with this sort of thing to do it without knowing there were others who could help.

Brook shook her head, *No, as far as I remember, they both were single. I will check to make sure.* If they did, she would make sure both the surviving mate and the pups would have someone they trusted keeping an eye out for them. It seemed the pack didn't have as much as she thought for support of the pups who lost parents; Jess and Joshua had just been thrust to being responsible for themselves without any help, and others didn't have the support which she had thought the pack supplied. She would look into it, she silently promised herself.

So, what did you do for your shadowing afternoon yesterday while we slept? Adam asked, wanting a happier topic, and to catch up on their pups.

I got to help monitor and calibrate some sensor alarms in the control room, Toby answered, eating his second helping. *A few of the movement sensors were triggering when rabbits ran above them. I got to input the sonic signature to the system as one to ignore. Sam worked on automating some camera sweeps.*

Lea and I helped train some of the elders on how to use their laptops, with Alpha Maria keeping an eye on us. Robin commented proudly. Being able to help an Elder with something was quite an achievement, *Lea is very good at translating tech-talk into something the elders could understand, since they didn't even have typewriters when they were growing up!* He commented with a laugh. *She found a funny video on You Tube called 'First Tech Support Call in History' about switching from scrolls to books. They could relate to that!*

Adam had to laugh, as he had seen the short video, *I agree, it does help those who don't know tech to understand how hard we have to work sometimes to keep frustration under control.*

Several others decided to look it up when they had time, as they could feel Adam's amusement at the video. After the week the pack had gone through, they needed the amusement.

Adam turned back to the main discussion and made sure his pups got some praise for being so self-directed, while they were dealing with other issues. *Toby, excellent! You get to help keep us all safe from attack. Robin, excellent; it helps all of our lives be a little bit easier.* Adam commented, praising his pups. *I need to catch up on my work for this week, as I have barely had a chance to even check my email all week! Hopefully I can get it all done today.* he complained.

*Remember, we aren't doing a run tonight, but make sure you have the stuff for the weekend, as we're seeing Adam's mother, and will be running *for most of tomorrow; we're taking some of the former-Shadowed River Thetas and a few others to Longview with us.* Brook commented. Most of those going with them didn't even have a change of clothes to their name and had been given some when they came; they had been wearing clothes which were almost rags.

Suddenly, Adam remembered about what they had been getting together as a family gift, *Did you finish the picture frame?*

Both pups nodded vigorously, *We had to modify it when you two took in Jess and Joshua. We even added them to your pictures and used what you taught us to make the adjustments. It looks like they were part of the original shots.*

Adam laughed, *I meant to do that, but it's slipped my mind! I'm glad it was a family job.* He shared his happiness with the two, on how proud he was of them.

It even breaks apart into smaller parts, to fit into a Wolf-Pack easily for the run. I'll get it and bring it over this morning Robin replied, with some pleasure.

Adam nodded. He used the rest of the breakfast time, to catch up on everyone's lives, as he had three helpings of the excellent sourdough pancakes. He sent an image of him getting fat to his wolf, who snorted at him, **We're healing, and had to use reserves, as we were too exhausted yesterday. We can start recovering now, especially since we need to help protect the pack more being Seconds. I won't let us get fat and slow.**

Adam was amused at his wolf's comment, but as he had never lied, even when teasing him, he stopped worrying, and enjoyed eating whatever and how much to fill him up without worrying about getting fat.

*****

By the time breakfast was done, and they were leaving, Adam wrapped an arm around Brook's waist, "So any plans for today?"

Brook nodded, "While you are dealing with the paperwork," She replied with a shudder, "I am going to go inspect how much the pups have done with the old gear and any of the new stuff, to see if we need to order more or anything different or find them more work to do. I'm also going to check up on Erin and her crew and do an unannounced inspection of the server rooms. When you're done, I plan on giving Steve his trouncing; he's probably thought I forgot about it. He forgot about my wolf. *She* is still annoyed at his disregarding us." She gave a feral grin which promised pain to someone, and it sent shivers down *his* back, and he wasn't the one it was for.

Make sure we never get on her bad side, like Steve has. I don't want that sort of grin pointed at me! Adam told his wolf.

Wolf-Adam gave a mental shudder in reply, ***I hope so too, she could be vicious when fully aroused.*** He commented, before sending an image of her as Ralph's mate, and tearing into a Were who had harmed a pup. ***Senior She-Wolves are usually worse than a She-Bear who is protecting a cub, when angered. Try not to piss them off, as they usually need a good fight to calm down.*** He advised.

Human-Adam shared an internal shudder with his wolf and gave an agreement to the feeling. He had always felt she could be very dangerous if she chose or was pushed to her limits. He never wanted to be the cause. Both were looking forward to watching her fight, even if it would be mostly one-sided, with Steve being human.

Remembering the night before, "How did your talk go with Lea and Sam's parents?" He asked as they walked out of the dining hall.

"They had no problems with it. I let them know we were thinking they may be mates; from the discussions they had with their daughters, they had to concur. We will just have to wait till around the time they come of age for confirmation. They felt honoured we were willing to take them under our wing, even before our promotion, and with the promotion, they are nearly beside themselves in happiness." Part of it, she felt, was due to the seniority which it would bring them to. She wasn't sure, as when their pups had been low ranked, they hadn't liked the boys even being friends with their daughters, but now they were ranking higher, they were all for it. It was a feeling she was not liking to find out some supported.

Walking into their bathroom, he stripped the robe and his sleep shorts off, before getting in the shower. Brook followed him in and smiled, giving him a kiss before starting on his hair. She gasped, looking at his shoulder.

"What?" Adam asked, concerned.

"Your scar is gone!" Brook exclaimed happily, as Adam tried to look at his shoulder. "Your turning scar is gone. You have finished turning. Right when I thought it would for you." She added happily. There had been a betting pool going on in the pack, and appears she won it.

Adam let out a whoop of joy, "Then I'm going to steal you to learn how to shift to Were and get used to it, after I get to watch you deal with Steve."

Brook laughed, "Deal! You seem to be getting too much enjoyment out of the thought of seeing me trounce him."

Adam smiled, "Partly, it was me who brought up the idea of them joining us, and the first thing Steve does is disregard you. Another reason is I am always too busy with my own fight to watch you fight. That is one thing I want to see, more than Steve get his punishment. How are you looking to deal with him?"

They spent the rest of the shower figuring out some tactics and what they wanted to do. Since they didn't want a lethal fight, Brook agreed to just staffs. She had wanted to use swords, while Adam had doubted Steve had the skills to handle the weapon, and it was one which could accidentally cause serious injury or death without meaning to, was why he had talked her out of it.

Coming out, Robin was waiting for them, showing off the frame with the pictures already in it with some pleasure. Adam grinned, as it showed their entire family: Adam, Brook, Jess, Joshua, Toby, and Robin. All six had their wolves standing with them in the main picture. Each individual shot had the human head with the wolf head behind them. Adam and Brook were facing each other at the top, and the four pups were two to each side, facing in. The group shot was in the middle.

"I love it! It really shows we are not just our human side. Now, how does it split for travelling?" Adam asked.

Robin turned it over, and poked a couple releases with a screwdriver, and popped the bottom part from the main picture, then the top.

"If you take in any others, I can add another section below for them, and we can change the group photo to include them." Robin stated proudly, "That was Toby's idea, since then we'd not need to make an entire new frame. We have made two extra sections with the same wood, each which could fit up to four head shots.

He tucked pieces of foam over each piece of glass, and then between the three sections, and wrapped it all in a bubble-wrap and tucked it into a waterproof bag.

"It should fit into your pack, now." Robin commented, handing over the package to Adam.

Adam grabbed his bag from the beside the door where he dropped it, clearing it out. He noticed his shorts were already gone; Jess or Joshua already must have grabbed them. He emptied the bag out and slid it into the main one along his back. It slid in easily. Setting the bag down on the table, he went and selected all the clothes he'd need for the weekend, needing three changes.

He used them to pad the package, and packed it well, making sure it would be comfortable, and then packed a couple of his weapons, but most was staying here, as they weren't going to a fight. Nor did they need to have restraints, although he did put one set into a side pocket, just in case. They were each going to carry their own clothes, and any card or gift they were bringing, but beyond that, they didn't need much else.

Finished with the pack, Adam headed over to deal with the paperwork, and his personal e-mail which had built up, if he had time.

Robin and Brook left to do the inspection tour, as it was something which Robin could take over, even at his age. Brook knew what they needed to inspect, and would make sure Robin knew, too.

Adam groaned at the number of messages which had built up. He dealt with approving the ordering of more equipment and laptops, and for some specific hardware for Chris to do his security work, including a more powerful firewall for the warehouse area and prepare for the second network. Chris had been busy and had worked out exactly what Longview needed for their network to work with theirs, and what infrastructure they needed to get it working. He was glad he had documented the work he had put into setting up MacLaren's pack, making it available on an internal shared location, so Chris could expand from it, and used his own experience in securing it to make it even better.

Chris had also forwarded they would already need to expand the Wi-Fi link to the pack house, and also a rough cost for running a fibre link. Thinking for a minute, he ordered the Wi-Fi gear, and let everyone know about it. They'd deal with it when it arrived. They would just need to install the gear at both ends and plug it into the switch; the existing fibre run to the pack house from the cliff's cave was more than enough to service the link.

The fibre link was something he had been considering but would need to deal with permits and the humans, at least till the edge of their property. They could run it to the secondary data centre and link it in there. It would impact the forest less than trying to run it to the primary. They could easily beef up the link between the two of them to handle the traffic.

Creating and submitting the recommendation for the link took a bit of time. He had to build in a "Now" which would support one pack, "Soon" which would support the five packs, since he knew the other four were interested, too, and "Future" which was a larger cost but would then have the bandwidth to handle the entire global future network. He did show projections and the costs to change and do upgrades would affect everything much worse later, along with his recommendation to build the "Future" as it would be cheapest in the long run. The Wi-Fi would be a backup link, for if the fibre went down, they could maintain a slower connection, but not go down.

After a short snack break, since he wasn't used to spending hours sitting at a computer anymore, he forwarded the information about expanding the link to Hank, so he had all the records, and said he would answer questions when they were out there the next day. He gave basic setup details for their network and to work out their service and support agreements.

They had agreed that having each pack trained to provide their own support would be best and set up a support network of peers to share knowledge, instead of having to wait for an out-sourced support tech to arrive. It also allowed for another channel of inter-pack cooperation and discussion. It was also another source to employ their pack members and would mean they didn't need to trust anyone outside the pack with their secrets.

Adam had barely got to his personal e-mail by the time lunch came. He had several offers of outsourcing of their support, their servers, or their data, as well as offers for supplying their equipment. He politely declined each real offer, stating security and privacy concerns. Some he would have to deal with several times before they would stop, he had already found. There were also many he thought might be scams, or less truthful about what they could offer compared to what they would also be doing with their access.

Once the server connections started to come online, he knew there would start to be inquiries on available services from other companies. He'd have to discuss it with the Alphas and Chris about doing some hosting, to generate more money for the pack. He wanted IT to be a revenue stream, not just be a major item which they had to continually pay money out to deal with. The Inter-pack networks would generate some money, but he wasn't expecting a very large funding stream from it, let alone a profit, at least to start. They could use the space at the warehouse for hosting the resources for the humans, and leave their main data centres for hosting any supernaturals they came across.

He had found out those who had jobs outside of the pack paid part of their wage to the pack, to help support it. They had a stake in the restaurant in town and had a fair amount in investments, but the money had to be moved around a bit, to not have it noticed how much they had. The grants and funding for the wolfdogs was another major stream of funds, although they were using actual dogs for most of them; since they had mind-speech, they could tell the dogs what they wanted them to do and be understood.

Most of his personal e-mails were mailing lists, which he had decided to unsubscribe to many of them, as he didn't have time to deal with them. Some of the sites he used to frequent, he turned down or even off the messages he was getting. Others which no longer interested him, he completely shut down his accounts.

Adam was whittling down what personal items he was getting, and it was getting to the point it was getting manageable. He set up some auto-forwards for some e-mail, so Erin could deal with them without him, and have the contacts for them, like making orders for additional computer equipment. He fired off quick messages to the suppliers authorizing her as an approved contact and could make decisions up to a certain dollar amount without him.

Heading to lunch, he grabbed his food and rubbed his eyes, "I don't know how I could stand sitting at a desk staring at a computer screen all day. I'm glad the afternoon is going to be more physical." He commented to those around him.

Brook came up and rubbed his shoulders for a bit, "I don't know, either. We get to have fun this afternoon, though." She reminded him, *By the way, I passed on to the four pups that Lea and Sam were being moved to the two other rooms of ours. All four seemed excited. I'm thinking they are going to pair off and swap rooms. I think they are old enough we don't need to worry about them, though.*

Excellent; they need help moving? Adam asked. He agreed, if they wanted to pair off, they were old enough, and their wolves would help them.

Not yet; I think their parents want to help them. Both pups, due to their jobs, have access to the elevator, so they don't really need us. Was Brook's reply. *I did let them know that* this *was a permitted use of it.*

Martin laughed as he sat down, unaware of the silent discussion, "The long-awaited Trouncing. I can't believe it got put off by almost a week!"

Brook glared at Steve who seemed to sink in his chair, and want to disappear, commented softly, "If you will accept an apology and take it easy on me, I'm very sorry to not have followed your advice. It won't happen again." He was *not* looking forward to this. He had seen how some of the wolves trained, and he had no way to even come close to their speed. Martin had pushed him to spend time training, so he wouldn't immediately be pounded on, and had spent as much time as he could training.

Brook gave a feral grin, and her eyes looked very much her wolf, "Nice try, and maybe a little easier, but you still will get a good trouncing. You get to thank Adam for talking me out of using swords. You can't get out of it."

Steve visibly shuddered but didn't make any further comments.

Adam turned to Erin, and as he ate, he passed on what he was going to be having her deal with, before turning to Chris and doing the same.

Martin was just sitting there with a grin on his face. Discipline fights were always fun, as long as you weren't the one in the wrong.

End of lunch came all too soon for Steve. Going down to the training room, if he had a tail, it would have been tucked between his legs. Brook bounced along, and changed in their room, as Adam and Martin headed down to the training room. She bounced in, picked up a staff from the rack, stepped into a large challenge circle, and stood still in a relaxed pose, facing the change room, waiting for Steve to emerge.

Chapter 4 – The Fight

Steve came out and picked up a staff, "OK, let's get this over with!" He commented, stepping into the ring. As this wasn't a hard fight, but a punishment, Brook didn't need a referee. There were many other packmates who stood back and watched, as they waited for the punishment fight. He had been told to just ignore them, as they didn't matter for the fight.

Adam and Martin chuckled. If needed, they would step in if it went too far but doubted it would. A bit of blood was fine, maybe a broken bone, but anything more and it would be stopped. Bruises were expected.

"I bet Brook will come out without any bruises or anything worse," Adam said quietly, pulling out a twenty from a pocket he had put in it just for this.

Martin grinned, "You're on!" he replied, putting his own twenty on it. He would be surprised to lose this bet as Steve had some skills with the staff. All it would take is a single bruise and he'd win; he seemed to forget it wasn't just Brook-the-trainer, but Brook-the-Second now.

Brook shook her head at them, but knowing it was in fun, and was only for a twenty between friends, didn't say a word.

Stepping forward, she called out in a loud, clear voice for all to hear, "Steve, you are being punished for disregarding the knowledge of a senior wolf and putting your own life at risk with the disregarding of their knowledge. Defend yourself!"

Steve brought his staff up to the ready and started to defend himself. After a bit, and several taps, he started to get a feel, and try to take the offensive. Martin had advised him not to take it passive, but to fight well. It would help him get the respect of her wolf and *might* make it possible for him to walk out of the ring. Many of the pack had shared details of bouts and training they had with her, and how she was a hard instructor, but she wasn't without care. He had completely forgotten it was being watched by others in the pack.

Brook was grinning, circling Steve. Seeing holes in his defence, she would tap him enough to bruise, but not to harm him. It was her favourite way to train and especially when she had a punishment to administer. She didn't need to tell Steve what he did wrong or what could have happened. She had her friends who were not enforcers do it for her over the week, and all of it had seemed to just build his dread of this punishment fight nicely.

Taking a tap to a calf, Steve winced, but tried to stay on the offence, and trying to speed up the movements. Brook seemed to just prowl and play with him. Tapping him on the bicep, then the thigh, before getting a good one to his rear, she smiled at his glare.

Steve was starting to get flustered. Every attempt to hit her was being blocked. She looked like she was dancing and wasn't having to try too hard, while he was having to work all out.

Making the mirrored moves she tapped him on the other side, before taunting him, "Come on, harder! I haven't even worked up a sweat, I'm barely warmed up!"

She swept his feet from under him, causing him to land on his bruised rear, and getting a couple of taps to his body when he didn't defend himself, "You can't let your guard down!" Brook replied, stepping back to let him get up, before laying into him again. Tapping him lightly, she added a bruise to a cheek, and then another to each thigh and calf.

"I've had seven-year-old pups who have more skills than you! You need to train more!" Brook taunted. She had a feral grin to her face, enjoying the fun. Steve was starting to pant and make mistakes. He tripped over his staff, blocking a low strike, landing on his already bruised rear, but this time blocking the taps aimed for his body.

"Good, you kept your guard up," Brook commented as she again backed off to let him get up and continued with her work at covering him with bruises. By the time Steve collapsed and groaned laying there, begging for her to stop.

Adam gave her a mind touch, *Enough; you beat him. Anything more is just cruel, and the lesson won't stick. Right now, it will stick well, and he won't forget.* He could feel she was just moving with the staff, almost in a meditative state, not really thinking. Her wolf was happy to share their displeasure in a physical method, and beyond that wasn't too concerned.

Looking down at him just lay there gasping, his hand limp, she had to agree; he was completely worn out, and he'd be feeling it for a few days, which had been her plan all along. She leaned over, "And that concludes today's punishment. Make sure you remember the lesson, or it will be worse next time." Everyone else who had been there to watch dispersed, some grumbling how it had been so one-sided, others enjoying the fight anyways.

Steve nodded, "Yes, Second Brook," he answered formally, "I'll make sure I heed the knowledge and suggestions of senior packmates from now on." He panted as he lay there, wondering how long they would mind if he stayed there, as he didn't even have the energy to roll over.

Brook softened her face, and glancing at a clock, "You have two hours till dinner. I suggest you use the time to soak in hot water." With that she turned and headed to her mate.

Steve nodded, and groaned as he tried again, and this time was successful to roll over, then get to his hands and knees, then crawled painfully out of the circle, to Martin who helped him stand, "Come, I'll help you." Martin complained, shaking his head, "You couldn't even land a single tap on her. It cost me twenty for that! Remind me not to bet against Adam or Brook. Together, they are even worse!" He added, as he slowly guided Steve out the door to take him to the hot spring in the greenhouse. There was a cold water shower there, which Martin was going to have him use; nobody liked relaxing in someone's sweat or worse. It also worked to keep stuff from being tracked into the pool.

*****

Adam smiled and opened his arms to his mate, his wolf forward in his mind checking her over, as she came up to him, "Feel better?" He asked, as Martin and Steve left, leaving them alone since the rest of the pack had already left.

Brook grinned, "Much. My wolf doesn't have the urge to leave teeth marks in his flesh anymore. What are we doing for the afternoon?" She asked.

"Since the Turn is complete, I was hoping you could start teaching me to shift to Were?" Adam asked, hope in his eyes.

Brook laughed and nodded, "It's better to learn it outside." Leading him up to the main floor, she grabbed a couple of blankets, and took him outside. They headed to a tiny clearing, where it was completely silent.

"To shift to Were, you need to bring your wolf up as if you are going to shift but need to get him to agree to sharing your body, then guide it. Some never are able to talk their wolf into sharing, and don't get it." Brook didn't say that those who didn't almost never rose higher than Delta rank in the pack, as if they didn't have the dominance and self respect to hold equal footing with their wolf, there were usually other areas of less self-control as well. She reminded him of the other parts of how to do the change, and other suggestions.

Adam nodded and sat on the spread-out blanket on the snow, after pulling his clothes off. Pulling another blanket around his shoulders, as the wind was brisk, even if it felt like it was much warmer than it should have been this time of year. He didn't realise that if he had been a human, it would have felt like ice, as he hadn't bothered looking at a thermometer. He thought it might be just slightly below freezing, not the -10°C it was, before adding the windchill which was more than a brisk breeze. It was much harder to freeze a werewolf's skin, so it was extremely rare for a werewolf to get frostbite.

Looking inward, Adam decided to discuss it with his wolf, *You willing to share a body?* He asked, not sure how to put his request in words, he sent him an image of what he wanted to do.

Yes, even shared, it would let me be out more Came the response, after he had thought about it for a while.

Calling his wolf forward, he tried to put what Brook had instructed into practice. He could feel himself shifting, and he was working hard to hold onto his human mind, and to get his wolf to share.

Opening his eyes, he could see he had a muzzle, and holding up a paw, he could see he had an opposable thumb, and respectable retractable claws. The blanket felt too warm, so he shrugged it off.

Trying to speak, just came out as animal sounds. Switching to mind-speak, *Let's try it again: So, how do I look?* Adam asked, *Did we do it?* Some he had heard had worked out how to speak, but he'd work on it later.

Brook smiled and nodded. Reaching behind her, she pulled out his camera and took a few shots.

Handing it over, Adam dropped his lower jaw in a wolf grin, both halves liked the way they looked. The camera being dwarfed in his hands, as he looked at the back screen. They had the same markings; black fur with dark brown and grey marking and highlights, just in a shape which stood on its hind paws or could bend over and run on all fours easily, if they really wanted. The camera felt small in his paws, and he handled it gingerly, not wanting to damage his D7100, even though he had ordered the Nikon D500 with a grip for when it released in a couple months, as a step up to a pro-level crop sensor camera. Once he had it, he planned on starting to upgrade his lenses too. He had ordered the 'kit' which was the 24-120mm f/4 lens with the camera, as it was a fairly high-end lens and was better than the one he had currently. It would even work with the full-frame when it came out, too. He had looked at some rumour sites and was considering the next 800-series camera.

Standing up, he handed back the camera, wanting to explore this body. He stood about eight or nine feet tall, when he stood straight, but it felt better to not stretch straight, as it felt wobbly, instead having his legs a bit bent, his tail a counterbalance.

Now, the tall height of the ceilings make sense; they were designed for Weres to not hit their heads, and to be comfortable.

The weather felt pleasant, and the wind barely gave ruffles to his fur. His senses were the best of both worlds: the eyesight was the excellence of the human form; being in wolf it wasn't quite as good as a human, and was positioned lower, but the night vision was better. He suspected it would be as good as his wolf in the dark. His hearing was better than both, probably from the larger ears; he could hear the feet of the wolves in the forest, and even both his and Brook's heartbeats. He could smell that Jess had been by recently; probably dropping off the camera. From the wind, he could smell who was patrolling upwind of them. He could smell the animals which were in the area, too. He took in the forest; he felt a part of it; it was where he was meant to be.

This form just felt *right* to him. As if he had been waiting all his life to explore it and feel this way. The cold weather was no hindrance to his thick double layered fur, being far better than any coat the humans made. The wind was felt ruffling his guard hairs but didn't chill him at all. If he had to choose one word for the weather, it would be 'comfortable'.

He heard Brook shifting, and turning, she was in her Were form. She pulled him in and nuzzled his cheek, before stepping back, and pulling out two steel rods. *Wooden staffs don't work for this form, even a gentle hit will crack the wood, solid steel rods are the only thing which can stand up to our force.* Brook informed him, passing one rod to him. *Let's do some moves, so you can get a feel for this form.*

The steel rod, he had seen them in the staff racks, and when lifting them, were quite heavy. He had been told they were twenty-five kilograms. As a human, that much weight he could lift only for short times, and once turned, even in human form, he felt it. In this form, it felt lighter than the wooden staffs which they normally used.

Holding it in the ready position, Brook started slow, as they went through the basic moves, before having him do the matching offensive moves. The first few hits clanged loudly, as he found he didn't need as much force, and he had much more speed. He had to use finesse much more than his power.

After an hour, Brook called a halt, *It's nearly dinner time. I know you would want to try to just hunt, but we have to organise for the weekend. We need to plan the run, since we are going to be taking not just our pups, but quite a few low ranked, it will be slower, and less risky.*

Adam heaved a sigh, *OK. After this weekend, I do want to try it out some more.* Feeling for his ring, as had become habit, he found it tight in his fur. He was glad she had gotten him a longer one, so it fit his Were form, and the complex looping kept the excess away when it wasn't needed, to keep it fitting well.

Gathering up the blankets and the rest of the stuff, Brook filled Adam's arms with the blankets and the staffs, as he didn't need to watch his strength with them and kept her paw on the camera.

Adam paced forward, with Brook following, heading off back to the pack house. Even though he was only walking, or well what felt like walking, it was as fast as full out running as a human. As Brook had said, it was quickly becoming a comfortable shape. He just needed to learn his strength and how much force to use. Reaching the door, he commented, *I'll let you get the door, for once. I'd probably take the handle—if not the door—right off.*

Brook panted some laughter, as she opened the doors, and led the way into their room, before shifting back and pulling on some clean clothes.

Adam followed her lead in dressing and matched her in the soft, stretchy capris and t-shirt.

Heading to dinner, Alpha Gareth gave them a list of people who were going with them to Longview. He had made arrangement with the Alpha there, as their resources were stretched to the limits; all the rooms including the Omega's barracks and visitor's wing were full and, in some cases, they were doubling—and even tripling—up in the beds.

It would nearly double the length of time to do the run, but their personal property—the few who had any—was being shipped by a couple trucks, and they got the nice run there. A few had decided to take the trucks, but most had preferred to take the run when the choice was offered. It saved them from having to send a bus with everyone, which was the other option which nobody wanted when offered. Even at the slower pace, it would take them the same, or maybe even less, time to run it than it took the trucks to travel on the roads there. Most had shuddered at the thought of another long bus ride. They preferred to run it, even if they would be exhausted by the time they arrived.

The trucks themselves were owned by Longview. They had used them to bring medical supplies for the take down, and thankfully had not been needed, and were instead used to replenish their supplies when Longview declined the offer to have them returned.

Adam thanked the Alpha and pocketed the report. "Forty-Five are joining us on the run. Another five are riding back in the trucks." Adam told the table, as he and Brook joined in, "Most are Thetas, but there are six who have been returned to Beta and ten to Delta."

Turning to Jess and Joshua, "I'm going to have you two do the Tail Run for the trip, and have Toby and Robin run towards the middle. The Betas and Deltas will be spaced around the outside." Both nodded, as the arrangement sounded good. They had been working on their Delta training, as with their parents now being Seconds, they were a bit of a target, so would need some skills to defend themselves till help could come. They would also have seniority so needed the skills to deal with it, and this gave them some good experience. Even the few who had complained about them trying for Delta had been silenced when the ones they were helping were elevated to Seconds, as Seconds having Delta-ranked helpers was more normal in their mind.

Adam smiled. He was looking forward to seeing his sister and mother. He both hated and loved the fact he was a bit away from his family, as it limited how often he could see them. Some, like his grandmother, he doubted he would have much to do with, but he did miss his mother and sister.

*****

After dinner, Adam and Brook decided due to the numbers they were responsible for, they were going to carry a bit more weapons; both felt if they planned for the worst case, it wouldn't likely happen. If it did happen, they would be ready for it.

It didn't take them long to get their packs ready. Adam grinned and moved Brook to the bed with a lustful look, and whispered in her ear, "We have some time now, and nothing needs to be done. Seeing you trounce Steve made me want you all over again."

Giving her a good kiss on her Mating Scar, she growled lustfully, "Show me how much you want me." Both could smell how much each wanted the other. Their clothes quickly were taken off, as if they weren't out of the way, they would be rendered into rags.

Eventually, they went to sleep, well sated.

*****

Waking the next morning, Adam rolled over and grinned at his sleeping Mate, again feeling how lucky he was to have her. Kissing her softly to wake her up, "Time to get up for breakfast, so we can get everyone organised for the run."

Brook grinned and nodded. Rolling out of the bed, she grinned and tossed a robe at Adam's head as he got up as well. He grabbed it out of the air and pulled it on, knowing they were shifting after eating. He didn't even think about how much better his hand-eye coordination was compared to when he was human.

Breakfast was, as usual, a mostly quiet meal and was quickly over. Adam was glad for it, as he preferred to have quiet when he was waking up.

Heading back to their rooms, they were met by their pups in their room, with their packs. The four quickly shifted, and Adam and Brook checked the fit of the packs, and confirmed they had everything they wanted, as this was the first long run with them. All four had their personal IDs set in the shoulder pocket, so they could be easily identified.

Adam and Brook shouldered their packs and checked to make sure their gear was set. Brook had presented Adam with a blade which matched hers, one which was designed to fit her Were, and now that he had his Were form, he needed a blade for it. Brook had received it the week before, but until he finished turning, and had his Were, it wouldn't fit him. She had ordered it when she was in the city, that first week after mating but had waited to present it. The pack didn't have a Blacksmith, and there was no way she could afford to get one from a Weapons master. Also, usually the weapons masters had years, if not decades, of waiting before it would be ready. She had ordered it from another pack which had a smith and had called in several pack favours — with the Alpha's approval — to have it done as soon as it could. Both slid them in the designed pocket which paralleled their spine. On the other side of their spine-pad, was their bow and quiver pocket. Both pockets could be easily accessed in either Were or human form and was out of the way in Wolf.

Walking out the door, they closed up their room after their pups. Heading out the front door, Adam counted heads, and found everyone was there. Most had already shifted to wolf. A couple had packs, but most were just sending the few belongings they were keeping, or the clothes they were taking.

Nodding at the waiting drivers, they headed off the access road, heading out. Even driving at highway speeds, they wouldn't beat the wolves, even going at the slower Theta speed. Adam looked over, and saw he was the last to shift, as Brook howled a call for the start of the run. Adam grinned at her, as he quickly sent a text on his phone to let Hank know they were starting their run before he tucked it into a waterproof pocket, and nodding for Brook to start out. Brook knew the trail, so she was leading the run. But they had some wolves scent-mark the trail ahead of them, so they wouldn't get lost. He was responsible for keeping an overall watch to make sure everyone made it; he would be ranging outside the group all the way there.

Both packs knew the trail they were using and had patrols to keep it clear. Adam looked over the pack, as everyone headed out. Everyone was in position, and he did another headcount, to ensure they hadn't left anyone behind. As Jess and Joshua headed on the trail, he nodded to Gareth who had stepped out to see them off, before shifting and taking off after them.

Even encumbered with his load of the pictures, frame, weapons, and his camera gear, he still was faster than the pace which Brook was setting. He ranged around, being a scout for them, coming up one side, ranging ahead before coming back the other side. Once they got halfway there, they'd be outside the area Brook knew, and would have to use the scent-marks on the trail left by the Longview scouts.

A couple hours into the run, they stopped for a half hour break at a creek. They were about a third of the way there. Some of the Thetas, flopped out, and panted, but most were not too tired. The seniors had a quick discussion with Adam and Brook, and they decided to slow the pace a bit, as they didn't want anyone run into the ground. Charlie was bouncing around, not even that exercised, as he had been forced to get even faster and stronger to keep up with Adam. He had ordered him to stay with Brook, as he was much slower than they were and worked well to set the pace.

It was only Adam's second pack run, and as they had Thetas and weren't going to a fight, like they had done on the other one, Adam was more just having fun. The serious side of being in charge of their protection aside, it was mostly a fun trip. He was enjoying the work. He did wish he could stop and take pictures, but promised himself he'd do it on the return, as it was just their family then.

All too soon for the out of shape Thetas, but nearly too long of a wait for the seniors, they started running again. Adam did another head-count, and again all were there; they didn't want to leave any behind and unprotected.

Even with the seriousness, Jess and Joshua were having a great time, and traded off keeping an eye on their back trail; making sure they weren't being followed and being the sweeper and making sure none dropped back without them knowing. When Adam realised they were doing it, he gave them praise, as it was an advanced skill which Deltas were taught, and they were doing it right.

An hour after the break, Adam saw some were starting to lag, and called for Brook to stop at the next stream for another water break, and for the group to catch up.

We're heading out of the territory which I know, and it is about time for us to switch as well, Came the reply.

Sending a wordless acknowledgement, he finished the loop, and scouted ahead for some water. Quickly, he found a water source ahead which they would have to cross. Seeing they would be getting wet, he looked for anything to let them cross the water dry-foot, and nothing was for several hundred metres in either direction, so they'd have to swim it.

Discussing it with his wolf, it would be better to swim after they take the break, so they could warm up while continuing the run. Their fur would keep them warm.

Brook let out a howl of, *"Where are you?"* To home in on Adam.

Adam replied with a howl of, *"I'm here!"*

They traded howls a few more times before she came upon him beside the best spot to get across; the water was shallow and didn't have much current here, but still would get some bellies wet. Him and Brook were large enough they would just get wet paws.

We're taking a bit of a break here before continuing on. Adam commented.

Across the water, a twig snapped. Immediately everyone was alert and on guard. A couple of humans stepped out. One had weathered skin and white hair, the other was much younger. The older one quickly pointed his gun at the ground and grabbed his companion's and did the same, before both bent to place them on the ground, and spread their hands, showing they were empty, and making sure not to stare at any in the eyes, calling out "sı̃ktogéja" or "wolf" in the local native tongue, with a respectful tone, with a look of awe on his face.

Brook thought she recognised the older one as being an Elder from the native reserve they were skirting, she had only met him once at the Longview Pack several years before.

Adam's hearing could hear the discussion, with the older being confirmed as an Elder from the respect, but not the words. He wasn't too sure on what to do. Adam looked to Brook, and she nuzzled him, *It's OK. The older one knows about us. He's trying to get the younger one to head back to their camp.*

Very soon the younger one, picked up his gun, but kept it pointed to the ground and headed away from the water. The older one spoke spreading his arms, "Greetings, brothers and sisters. You honour us with your presence."

With a running leap, Brook jumped the water; stopping quickly, she shifted, "Hello, Elder." She greeted, a grin on her face, "We meet again."

The Elder looked dumbfounded and blinked. Adam took control and started to have the wolves start to cross. They would take a longer break and relax while they talked to the Elder.

He too took a running leap and crossed the water, before joining his mate and shifting. He bowed his head in respect to the elder.

The elder shook his head, and blinked a couple times, "Brook, isn't it?" He asked in English. "I don't think you have aged in the five years since we last met!"

Brook nodded, "This is my Mate, Adam." The comment about not aging was common from humans, and one they tried not to answer if they could. For now, she was ignoring it as if it wasn't said.

The Elder grinned, lighting up his face, "Greetings, and congratulations, you two," He seemed to know what Mates meant to them.

Adam nodded in acknowledgement. As Brook was in control, he was guarding her back, and keeping watch on their group as they crossed.

Watching the large number of wolves move across the water, "What's with the large number?" noticing both were armed, if not with guns, "And why doing so armed?"

Brook sighed and realised she would have to give a little detail to alleviate curiosity and not have wild thoughts abound, "We're helping some move packs." She told the elder, not wanting to tell him about fact it was from a pack being taken down. "We are taking them to the Longview Pack. As the strongest, we are responsible for their protection. With the large number, we decided to bring more tools to protect them with."

The Elder nodded sagely but showed a little concern. He wanted more information but knew they wouldn't tell him anything farther. He would later send a request to Hank privately to see if he would say anything further. Seeing their IDs, he noticed, "Second? You, Brook, have surely moved up in your Pack; congratulations."

Brook smiled shyly, "Thank you, Elder. Right now, we are still in training. We have yet to pass all our Trials, but our current Seconds are senior to several of our Elders. They are wanting to step down, so we will be soon inducted officially."

Seeing the pack seemingly impatient to be gone, "I see your pack wants to get going again. Come find me again, sometime, when we can chat, possibly share a meal?" the Elder commented.

Brook smiled, "Maybe in a few weeks. Right now is a busy time for us." Thinking for a minute, "Don't speak of what we have said to anyone, as it currently is being kept to those involved, for security reasons." Pulling out a card, "Here's my contact information; email me yours later, and I will stay in closer contact." She had thought about it after she left the last time. As contacts with the native elders were few, and it was better to have them, as they did have a rich history of being in tune with nature.

The elder took the card with reverence he would give to an eagle feather and stepped back, "You honour me; thank you." He replied, before saying a few words in his language, it sounded like a blessing or prayer, before picking up his gun and heading off into the bush the way the younger had.

Adam and Brook shifted, this time with Adam leading, and Brook scouting.

Adam didn't know why Brook showed her face, and shifted in front of the elder, although he seemed to already know what they were.

Brook filled him in, *They believe, because we can shift, we are basically spirits, and are revered. The elders know of us, and sometimes are even invited to events at the Packs. He was at one event I was at Longview Pack for several years ago with my parents. I was introduced to him then. Longview Pack has deep ties to the tribe, as both have been in the area for centuries. There are several werewolves who have family in the Ga-hna community* She used the names the natives used in their own languages, as a way to honour their beliefs. She had learned some of their language, too. Mostly it was names in their tongue, which she tried to honour. Her father had a sibling who had mated with them, but both had died shortly after she was born. They had been mated for centuries and had been together since from before treaties with the European settlers were signed.

Adam sighed mentally, as he led them along the scent-marked path, heading for the pack, *I hope you will share your knowledge of them; I have always admired the natives for their beliefs, but was never able to find much to learn about them.*

Brook sent him some love and a mental nuzzle, *We will do that, and I expect we will get an invite to visit the Elder at some point soon. We may

not have much family ties, but I think we have friendship. I will share what learning I have with you when we have some quiet time.
*****

Eventually they arrived at the Longview Pack's patrolled territory, and almost ran right into a patrol. The four wolves were standing in their way, blocking the way, and growling. Adam was standing between them and the rest of the group, as Brook finished her round and stalked up beside her mate.

We are here with your pack's express invitation. Ask Alpha Grant or Second Hank. Adam told the patrol, annoyed they were stopping them, *The patrols were supposed to know of us. This is an officially sanctioned Inter-Pack Movement.*

The leader growled louder, as he could feel the power radiating from both of the wolves they were facing, *Don't move, or we will attack, while I check into this.* He was bluffing, as his wolf just wanted to roll over and submit to the much more powerful wolf.

He called to Hank, and asked him if he had a moment, treating this as a minor issue, not the major one it would be. Hank replied he was a bit busy and would get back to him in a few hours, knowing they were expecting the new members any moment... who were behind schedule and was starting to organize a few patrols to head out to meet them.

The patrol leader commented smugly, *Second Hank is too busy to deal with you right now.*

Adam growled back, *I am Second Adam from MacLaren Pack, and we are expected. Either you get out of my way, or I will contact Hank myself, as this is a violation of Inter-Pack Treaty.*

The patrol leader backed up a step from the force of the sending, but wasn't going to back down, *I don't believe you or your group of rabble is from MacLaren, as they come as humans when members come to visit.*

Adam snarled at the blatant disrespect before deciding he had to go over this one's head. Since he had met Hank, he had his mental image and could send to him at this distance, *Hank, we are on your north-western border and have been stopped by a patrol which is saying you are 'too* *busy to deal with us', can I tear a couple strips off this disrespectful, poor excuse of a delta?** He asked innocently, but the under-flavour of annoyance and rage at the blatant disrespect was felt.

Chapter 5 – Arrival at Longview

Hank's reply was a mental snarl before a short message, *On my way.*

Adam shared his amusement the patrol was going to get it, as he sat on his haunches, and linked the patrol along with the rest of his group, *Hank has time for me. He's going to be here—* Hearing a fast wolf go through some bushes, *About now.*

Oh, this is going to be good! Exclaimed Wolf-Adam to his other half and their mate in savage pleasure; he wanted blood for the disrespect.

Hank smashed into the patrol leader, knocking him on his back, taking his throat in his jaws as he rumbled a dangerous growl, *Mark, you were told a pack of wolves was going to be coming this way and to guide them in. Not to stop them in their tracks and to treat them like you had a minor question about a lone wolf asking for entry. You are on report and are to go to your room to wait for the Alpha's decision on your punishment. Second Adam is wanting to tear strips off you for your disrespect, but out of good manners will wait for Alpha Grant's approval, as it is not his pack's territory; if it was Adam's pack territory, or in neutral land, he would be within his right to enforce the punishment instantly without asking.* Stepping off the wolf, who rolled back to his paws, and had his tail tucked, head lowered, and ears folded back in continued submission knowing he was very much in trouble, *Now, go.* Hank ordered. Very quickly the wolf ran off with his tail still tucked, before Hank turned to the gathered group, *Sorry you had to deal with him, he was against this opening of the pack, but was outvoted by the pack, and the vote wasn't even close. On behalf of Alphas Grant and Louise, I bid you welcome. Come, we will get you settled.*

Turning to the three remaining wolves of the patrol, *Get on with your patrol. Make sure something like this doesn't happen again.* Hank growled, leaving it in the open so the new wolves could see them getting chastised for not preventing the incident. They yelped an apology and ran off to continue their patrol. All were glad to escape without a punishment as well, but each expected to have a chat when they returned and checked in.

Hank moved to trot the rest of the way, personally escorting them in. Adam and Brook stayed at his side. Hank looked at the packs they had, as they didn't look like the packs they used when they were in wolf-shape, theirs were just dog packs; these seemed to be almost human packs. However, right now, his main concern was getting the new packmates settled.

Taking them to a side door, *We have this group house and the one beside it for you for the next couple of days, while we get you bonded to this pack, oaths done, and get you a final home. Unlike MacLaren, we have smaller cottages in our area which are shared with a few. These two are our guest houses. There is food already prepared and ready for you inside. There are a couple of wolves in each building to assist you. Any issues, ask to speak to me.* The wolves streamed in, neatly organising themselves between the two places, and found clothes inside for them. Looking off to the forest, *Your two trucks have just arrived at the gate and will be here shortly. They will be coming directly here.* Hank advised.

Turning to Adam and his family who had stayed outside, *You are coming with me, and I am hosting you myself.* Hank advised; hosting another pack's Seconds, even though they were still 'Acting' was a privilege only second to hosting an Elder or Alpha. He had been honoured when his Alpha had asked.

Adam wagged his tail, *Lead the way, friend.* He commented.

Leading him down a trail, they arrived at a reasonable sized place, and headed inside. Shifting, they smiled, as it looked like an old log cabin, but with reasonable amenities. Hank noticed two teen-pups, two who were looking to be young adults, and one which didn't shift. Frowning, he could smell hints of dog from the one which didn't shift, before remembering that Charlie was not a Were but was a wolfdog; even he had a pack, although from the smell it just had some tasty smelling dog food—none of the cheap dry brown chunks for him.

Hank smiled, "Can you tell me about those packs?" He could see all six had the packs, but the four younger ones had smaller ones, which fit their smaller size. All six seemed to be carrying weapons on them as well.

Brook laughed, unbuckling hers, "These are a pack invention. They fit all three forms and will adjust to fit them automatically. A wolf with their paws and jaws can put the pack on, although with some difficulty, and can easily take it off. We have some training to fight with the packs on, and have the ability to have some armouring installed, like Adam's and mine have, although it does add a fair amount to the weight. They also are used to carry our weapons, so when we shift from wolf, they are instantly available, but when wolf they don't hamper us."

Handing hers over so he could look at it after grabbing a shirt and shorts from the bag, "Each are individually fitted. If you make it to our pack, we could have one fitted for you. The size of the pack and number of pouches is due to duties and strength, that is why ours are larger and more extensive than our pups'."

Hank nodded, looking it over as they all got dressed, "I think I will see if I can do that. Would your pack be willing to part with the plans for them?"

Brook shook her head, "I doubt it. They are looking at selling them to other packs though. They will be pricey though; they are looking at a thousand each, and that is for a basic; this is an enhanced one. The Bow and Arrow quiver and the sword sheath are fitted to the pack and help form the spine of the pack. We have a design for two quivers instead, for those who don't want to carry a sword. Or it could be adapted to carry a polearm or even a firearm." She had checked out a couple of camping gear sites, and there were human packs for half that price. She could see half the price being the fact it could configure for multiple shapes.

Hank smiled, hiding his slight wince at the price which while high, he could understand it, "I am not surprised at that price. I do think if word gets out that you'd be having large-scale orders from packs wanting to outfit their members with them. I can say without asking the Alpha that we would be very much interested." Likely every enforcer, and anyone who did any sort of work where they needed to carry anything when shifting would be wanting one. Often, they just loaded a horse with packs, and had them follow, but that restricted them to areas where the horse could follow, and to the speed the horse could manage.

Adam nodded, "Well, they think they can do it just by sending in measurements, but they need the measurements in all three shapes. Mine, they needed to adjust, as I'm a little bulkier in my Were form than they designed it for. I know they are working on the website for online ordering; it will be one of the first Inter-pack network sites." Several pups had taken it on as a project for one of their classes and were enjoying the challenge of using one of the online store templates and making it work for them. Chris was helping make sure it followed the best-practices and teaching them about security.

Hank grinned when he heard about Adam having a Were, before he noticed he lacked a second bite scar for his turning, "So you have finished your Turn? Not surprised about that." From what he was hearing and had been rumoured, he had turned fast.

Handing Brook her pack back, "Come, I'll show you your room; you did ask for one single large room?" He asked in confirmation.

Adam nodded, "Yes, due to the attacks, our pups didn't want a separate room, and just want to stay with us."

Hank nodded, "Thought it might be something like that." He commented, as he opened a door. Inside was a nice suite, a bit smaller than their own room, and without the sitting area, and only a basic closet.

There was a bathroom which almost rivaled their own. "This is my own spare bedroom; I'll let you get refreshed. My Theta helpers will have the dinner ready in about a half hour."

Adam smiled his thanks and nodded.

"Now to talk to the Alpha about the disgraceful actions of that soon-to-be-former Delta." Hank commented quietly.

Adam growled, "My wolf does want to take a couple strips off him. He ignored what he was sensing for how dominant we were, and the fact we had ID visible which showed who we were, then put us off as if we were just a low ranked of no consequence."

Hank nodded, "I'll let Grant know. He may allow it; if it was up to me, I would. I'll let you know at dinner."

Adam smiled savagely in acknowledgement, before closing the door. He could hear the shower going, and decided to join in.

*****

Heading out for dinner, they all were led by their nose. Hank was the only one there with the spread of food, "My helpers are painfully shy, and rarely make an appearance to any guests. They prefer to be the unseen help mostly." He apologised. It was one of the reasons he had taken them under his wing when they had been pups, soon after mating. A couple of other pups thought that since they didn't say no, they didn't need to stop the teasing. It instantly stopped as soon as he showed up. They had got better, but the more senior the guest, the more they hid. He didn't stop them, and instead served his guests himself. Any who thought it beneath him to do it, he stated it was to make sure he knew how much work they did for him, and also to protect them from those who didn't value their work.

Adam grinned and sat down, "Just make sure you share our complements about the food. It smells excellent."

As they passed the food around, Hank decided to wait until after dinner for the work related, commented, "So, how was the run other than that idiot former patrol leader?"

Adam and Brook growled at the memory of the disrespect. Brook answered, "Well, we had to slow down a bit as their endurance and speed wasn't up to our standards, which was understandable when we thought about it, and was the main reason for our delay. We did cross paths up with an Íyãħé Nakoda Elder near Ga-hna. It happened to be one I had met here. We exchanged some words with him."

Hank nodded, "They are an interesting people and have such a rich history. We have helped them get their traditions and history back which the Europeans had tried to eradicate. Luckily, we have many from before they were forced onto the reserves and had education in their traditions and values outlawed. We have been helping them regain what they have lost, mainly through the elders who know of us. I personally feel it is right, regardless of the respect they show us." He hadn't thought of himself as one of them in a very long time, as their current culture is not even the same as what he had grown up with. They were forced to change, but now were trying to get some of their roots back while also somewhat living with the European-sourced white-man culture, especially all the technology which was in it now.

Adam sighed, "I wish the human schools taught as much about their traditions and beliefs as they do of the Europeans, but I learned almost nothing about them in schools. Their history and beliefs are as rich as the European conquerors. Much has been lost."

Hank smiled, "Us wolves, due to our much longer lifespan, have many who remember the time before the European humans started trying to change their ways. In fact, I am from there, and my Mate found me about the time the European Missionaries were first trying to convert them. We hid here and waited for some settlers, pretending to be a group of settlers when they started to move into the area. There are a few others who are from the Íyãħé Nakoda among us here. It has kept the bonds strong, and a sense of family. Once in a while, they invite us to join them on a hunt."

Brook nodded, "That was a similar story for our pack. Working with the natives and helping them. We don't have a community near us, unlike you, so we have lighter bonds with them. I did give the elder my contact information, so I'm hoping they will be wanting some more ties with us." Her uncle was the last one who had any sort of close contact with them at their pack but they hoped eventually for more. There were a few who looked native, as they had ancestors who came from them, but they also had some other darker skins including several of African heritage, who had been brought to the continent against their will. Nobody cared what skin colours were any more than they cared what colour their fur was.

The four pups let the adults chat, as they chatted among themselves. All four were not tired out, as it had not been a hard run, but the distance had made it a good workout.

"My mate would love to have discussed it with you," Hank replied, "But she is off at another pack visiting her sister, who I can't stand, so goes by herself. She left yesterday and won't be back for a week." The last time his mate's sister was here, it ended up being two different times they took their differences to the challenge circle to work it out, which the fights didn't do anything but mellow them both out enough to get through the visit without having either pack get involved. They decided to avoid each other as much as possible, and his mate agreed to travel without him. Often arranging her visits when there was something he couldn't get out of, so everyone could just blame it on him being Second.

Both Adam and Brook laughed, "I totally understand," Adam replied, "I too have relatives who I can't stand. My grandmother almost had her throat ripped out by my wolf for some comments at Christmas."

Hank thought back to when he first met them and shook his head, "I wouldn't have been able to keep that sort of control at only a week after first turning." He had spent months restricted to the pack after being turned, but seeing the report of the testing they did, and how Adam responded, he had worked extremely hard, and had earned the right to go out of the pack.

Adam grinned, "Part of it was, I was almost expecting something like that, and had made sure to keep Brook between me and my grandmother and had talked to my wolf that her opinions didn't matter and she had no control over what we did. I was able to keep control enough to get myself out of the room quick. It still took over an hour to calm down enough to return."

Hank just nodded, still impressed. He totally deserved the Second rank if he had that sort of self-control. He would not be surprised if he saw a note of them becoming alphas in the future. Quite frankly, he would bet money on them being ones eventually.

Turning to look over the pups, "Are you going to introduce me?" Hank asked, realising he didn't know them, and although two smelled of family bonds, and the other two of lighter bonds, he could see the love between all of them.

Adam looked guilty, "The young two are Toby and Robin. Robin's parents died in a rockslide, along with Toby's father, a couple of years ago. Toby's mother had to care for both, even though she was working through her grief. I had interacted with them a little, but when the wolf got into the pack house, the following night Robin wanted to spend the night. Toby came for comfort at breakfast. They both ended up spending most of the day and the following night with us. The next morning, their mother decided they needed to go back to where they were before, and when I confronted her about some changes, basically dumped them on me."

Brook sighed, "She changed after losing her mate. She has resisted any and all changes since then. She is one of four who refuse to have the network upgraded in their room. She protests and resists each and every change we do. The pups had been kept down as Theta, and already they are doing some Beta skilled tasks. I think giving them something to challenge themselves and the love and encouragement has worked wonders." As was not having the opportunities being blocked, to make it even harder for them to get the chance to learn more advanced skills.

The two younger pups looked down in embarrassment at all the praise, and .

Adam continued the introduction, "The other two are Jess and Joshua. They were assigned as our assistants, but just after the last full moon, I found out they had no close relatives living, and we decided to invite them into our family. The formal bonds are being done at the next Full Moon Howl." Both beamed at them.

Hank grinned, "Welcome all four of you. I hope your stay is pleasant." Turning to Adam, "I know the trip is to visit with your human mother for her sixtieth birthday tomorrow. Giving her a surprise of four grandpups?" He was grinning at the end.

Adam nodded, "Yes." He tried to keep a straight face, but lost it and joined in on the laughing, "She has been asking for years for grandchildren, and even when I first introduced Brook to her, she asked for them. I just don't think she expected them like this. She is going to be sooo surprised!"

Brook continued as Adam was lost in laughter, "Since Adam's sister, Tara, knew about Toby and Robin, as she happened to come for a visit just after we took them in. She happened to even be there for the Full Moon Howl for the formal bonding. She met Jess and Joshua, and when they agreed, we let her know to add a couple more for the reservation. She was not surprised, as she felt they already looked up to us. She too is looking forward to the surprise. We have worked out a nice picture for her of us."

Adam gave Robin a look and nod. He scampered off to grab the picture from the pack.

"Talking about a Howl, we are having a special one day after tomorrow to welcome them. Any chance you could stay an extra night?" Hank asked hopefully. The Alpha had asked for them to be invited.

Adam looked at Brook, then the three pups which were there, and all nodded in agreement. Sending a thought to Robin, he also agreed. Being invited to another pack's Howl, let alone a special one was an honour which was rare. They would send a message to their pack letting them know they were staying another day later, as there was nothing they had to be back to the pack to deal with. "We would be honoured to stay for your Howl."

Coming back in with it assembled, Robin put the assembled picture frame on the table, so Hank could see. Hank's mouth dropped at the work and care taken in making it. "Wow." Was all he could say. The frame alone was a work of art, with some stencilled wolves in various poses burned into the rich pine wood around the pictures along with trails of pawprints. The pictures were well done and showed all of them in ways which just worked.

Adam was grinning, "I worked out the basics, and helped with the pictures. Robin and Toby got Jess and Joshua's pictures done for me, and added them into the group shot, so it is a group effort."

Once the dinner was cleared out, Hank pulled out some of the plans that Adam had sent, "Now, I had some questions about the network we are setting up between the packs..." He started. Jess and Joshua had offered to do the dishes, but listened in, and offered the occasional question or comment. What they were working on for the network idea was mostly over their heads. Both Toby and Robin were right in the middle and had been involved with the design of the plans. Adam had grinned and let them take over answering the questions, letting the pride of his pups show.

When they started to yawn, Hank wrapped it up. Commenting to Adam and Brook once the pups had headed to the bedroom to get ready for bed giving the three adults a little bit of time to discuss adult things, "I'm surprised you two are not worried about your jobs; all four of your pups are quite bright."

Adam just grinned, "If they do, that means I can find a new challenge, or something to do!" Getting Hank to laugh at his comment, "But seriously, being Seconds is a hard enough job, without having to do the day-to-day IT work. Erin is taking over the support and maintenance of everything computer related. Steve and Martin are dealing with the Security, and Toby is being their junior manager. As his skills develop and he finishes his training and education, he will take on more duties. Robin is working to take over the management of the IT, in general, and has started to be involved in mine and Brook's duties."

Smiling about the other two, "Jess and Joshua have decided to be our assistants, so as we start taking over more of the Second role, they will sometimes be our hands and feet, or taking details and knowing what they can deal with themselves or how soon we need to deal with it."

Remembering he also let him know, "Along with Toby, there is a she-pup called Sam who is also learning the security management side; both are already mostly managing the tech-related security under Martin and Chris. Lea, another pup, has already started being the Tech Instructor, while she finishes her education. She is already approved for Teacher continued education of whatever she wishes by the Alphas."

Hank shook his head amused, "It looks like you are already setting up for the next generation, more than a team within the pack." Or it could be they were getting ready to split the pack but wouldn't be till the pups were ready to step into a leadership role, and that would be minimum fifty years from now, due to the ages of the pups, so was of no concern for the moment.

Adam leaned back in his seat, "About that Delta," He asked, leading on, "My wolf is extremely upset, especially since you said he had his orders and chose to ignore them."

Hank grinned savagely, "He doesn't know it, but the Alpha has approved you giving the punishment after breakfast, in full view of the pack, and especially those you brought in. He will be demoted to Theta for at least a year, before he can start working to regain the seniority of being a Delta and will be told that if he messes up like that again, he'll be joining the Omegas. He was just recently appointed Patrol Leader, and it seems to have gone to his head." He apologised, "The Alpha said the fight would be as wolves, and anything less than a crippling injury is permissible."

Adam grinned savagely in reply, his wolf's bloodlust showing as his eyes shifted to his wolf, "Excellent. I hope this punishment will help him learn and be a better wolf."

Brook was also grinning as they stood up, both giving Hank a hug, before they headed into the room, to curl up with their pups. Toby and Robin were curled up in the middle of the bed, while Jess and Joshua were sitting on the edge of the bed waiting for them. Adam and Brook slipped in around Toby and Robin, and the other two curled up around them.

Charlie huffed his breath in disgust and curled up sulkily at the foot of the bed, as there wasn't any room for him at the top; the bed was big but fitting six was still a bit hard.

*****

The knock on the door in the morning woke them and got a growl from several throats, "Breakfast is on the table." Came Hank's voice, unperturbed about the warning in the growls, although he wasn't going to even try to open the door.

Adam and Brook got their pups ready, and out the door. All were starving and followed their noses to the dining room. As Charlie fell on a bowl put on the floor for him, each found a seat, but let Toby and Robin take their choices, then Jess and Joshua, before Adam, Brook and Hank selected their choices of the pancakes, sausage, French toast, sliced ham, and bacon.

There is a public punishment fight this morning. You are welcome to watch, Adam told his four pups over their bonds, while his mouth full of food.

Let me guess, that Scout Leader, for his handling of us? Came Toby's reply. At Adam's savage grin, he knew he was right, *Now who's providing the discipline?*

Adam's wolf-grin got larger, *I get to provide it, as the one most harmed by his actions. He not only disobeyed his orders and the pack's decision; he refused to accept my seniority and called my word into question.*

In effect, as we are here officially on behalf of the Pack, he disrespected our pack.

All four pups got a little pale; inter-pack politics was complex, which was why Elders normally dealt with it. Brook and Hank nodded, *His life could be forfeit for it, if it was demanded.* Hank reminded them, *Luckily, Adam is happy to use him as an example, and not do permanent harm.*

Adam differed; he knew his wolf had really coloured his view. As a human, he would not have ever thought about taking a life, except if they were directly and immediately threatening his, and there was no way to avoid it, *If he does offend me again in this way, I'm not sure I'd restrain myself.* He warned. He no longer was just there for himself; he had a pack, a family, and a mate to protect. He also had others who looked to him and his mate for protection, and he would protect them with his life, either by living for them or if needed, with his death. He also had to protect the secret of the werewolf at all costs. Now that he had finished turning, those laws and customs were now in full effect, he was now fully responsible for himself and his behaviour when among humans. *But my wolf agrees he's young, so should be given this* one *chance to redeem himself.*

Hank nodded looking serious, *I will make sure he doesn't repeat himself, as if he does it again to you, even the Alpha would not try to stop you.* He would be having that wolf doing the nastiest jobs for the next while. Even though he wasn't ranked as Omega, he would be getting the jobs as if he was in warning. That hopefully would smarten him up.

Adam finished up his breakfast and washed up. "So where is it being held?" He asked Hank.

"Out in front of the Alpha's cabin. You will want to wait on the porch with the Alphas, as the offended party." Hank replied, "Wait for the others, though. It would look better to go as a group, instead of ahead of the others."

Adam nodded, and pressed his wolf slightly, as he was the impatient one. In this case, appearance was a large thing, as most of this pack, if they knew of him, didn't know too much. Every time he came, he seemed to be a different person: first was as a new human with an injured mate, then as a Beta just after his first shift staying the night following a day with the family and first outing after being Turned, now as a seemingly seasoned wolf which has been given a task which usually went to an experienced and senior leader of the pack and representing the pack as a whole. Not to mention, he now was in the process of becoming the Second.

It didn't take long for the rest to be done. Wrapping an arm around Brook, he smiled and gave her a light kiss as they headed out the door. Hank led them on the short walk to where the crowd was already gathering. He let go of Brook's hand when they arrived, as they had discussed it; this part of the trip he had been in control, so he was dealing with the fallout.

Stepping onto the porch, he schooled his face to be mostly impassive. He did smile a greeting and nod at the Alphas who were waiting, giving a slight submission to them.

We'll sit down and meet your pups after this fight is dealt with. Grant sent.

It took a bit, but soon everyone was there, but the one being disciplined. The last to arrive was Mark, flanked by two wolves Adam felt were Betas. He stood below the porch, at the edge of a large, cleared circle of dirt looking dejected and kept his head down. That the two Betas didn't even need to have their hands on him was a thing in Mark's favour; he knew he had done wrong and needed to be punished so was not fighting the need to be brought for punishment. It showed he didn't blame others for his mistakes, Adam realised. As such, he hoped he would learn the lessons from the punishment well.

Grant gave a demanding howl and the gathered wolves were instantly silent and attentive, "We are here to deal with a major violation. Mark disregarded his orders and nearly caused an Inter-Pack incident." There was many gasps and surprise, while others nodded and looked angry, and the few in the know growled their agreement. Mark just looked upset and scared.

Grant howled again to get the attention, "He was ordered that if he came across the group from MacLaren Pack to immediately notify Hank our visitors had arrived and guide them to him. He had also been informed they were coming as wolves. He came across the group, lead by Acting-Second Adam." He nodded to Adam standing near him, "But decided to treat them as if they were just a pack of Lone Wolves who were coming unannounced and without permission. He requested Hank to come, without telling him it was the group we were expecting, and as someone would do, the unexpected was asked to be put off for a few hours, and Mark didn't bother saying anything." Grant took a breath, "That could have been something which could have been over-looked, and would be dealt with as a reprimand, but he decided to be belligerent with a Pack representative, ignored explicit orders to cover their arrival, and blocked their entry, which was approved by the pack as a whole." There was many nods in agreement, "And he further decided to question Adam's word, and as such the word of his Pack, and hurled insults which are not being repeated."

There was some angry muttering, and it took another howl from Grant to get the pack to settle, "We have had several confirmations of what happened, from those who are joining our pack and those who were in the Patrol. In addition, Mark hasn't challenged the truth of the reports either. In response, Acting-Second Adam has requested to be permitted to administer the physical part of the punishment; I have granted it. The rest of his punishment is he is stripped of his Delta rank and has been entered at the bottom of the Thetas. He will not be permitted to move from there for a year. In a year, he can start collecting the honours to be moved higher. If he breaks any more pack laws within the next decade, he will be reduced to Omega, and have at least a century as one to think about his actions." It went without saying, if he was made Omega, he would never be trusted again with a patrol leadership at all, let alone a position higher. Being trusted as an Enforcer would be nearly impossible, as all of Enforcers were trusted with the protection of the pack. Even now, it would be hard for him to regain the trust, and likely there would be those who would object to any promotion.

Alpha Grant gave Mark a very disappointed look, as he had felt he could go far in the pack, but now there is a good chance he would never get beyond a patrol leader in the pack, as there would be those who would not be willing to give him a second chance at even leading a patrol, even if he showed he would be much better with some maturity.

Many wolves had a look of grim satisfaction in the punishment. Getting a nod from Grant, Adam stepped up, "For the interfering of an Inter-Pack movement, for the disregarding of the will of the pack for personal interest, for the insult to MacLaren Pack, and for the disobeying the explicit orders of a superior wolf, I call Mark to the Challenge Circle, for a fight in wolf form."

Each of the charges Adam gave for Mark seemed to be a blow to him, making him wince. The last one was the largest, as Adam knew both packs used the same Pack Oath, and Mark's actions broke part of it. The insults to another pack had caused inter-pack wars, which had decimated one or both packs in the past. It could be construed to not protecting others in the pack, which was another part of the Pack Oath. The will of the pack was also a pack law and upholding them was a third part of the oath. For any of the three alone, he could be exiled as a Rogue, or even killed; he was getting off lightly. Inter-Pack movements like theirs had specific requirements, and although not a Pack Law, they were there to keep the peace. Both packs, Adam had found, followed Inter-Pack Treaty Rules as if they were their own, to the point of registering many of them *as* Pack Law. He hadn't yet learned that some of the Inter-Pack Treaty rules had to be entered in as laws, to ratify the Treaty membership.

Adam knew Mark had been mostly venting his frustration and not wanting an influx of new members to the pack. Since he was just barely an adult, Adam had decided to just give him a personal lesson that would hopefully stick more than words and provide him with a way to redeem himself without irreparable harm to his life and standing in his pack. Without a way to redeem himself, it would likely cause a major grudge, and given enough time, it could cause him to go rogue, and it would be a nasty affair for all involved. The reason, when he asked about it, he had got the patrol leader, was due to his parents continually lobbying for the chance. Even though he had the qualifications, he lacked the experience the pack normally made sure the wolf had before being given the responsibility.

Adam saw none who felt they could challenge what he said and the charges; if any had, he would have had to go into the details of why and the facts behind them to the other's satisfaction they were warranted or set them aside if they couldn't come to a consensus. If needed, they would have to do a Pack Trial, where all the facts and events would have to be gone over in detail by everyone involved, and any of those in the room could ask questions about the facts or ask for more details. Luckily, nobody called for more information on what was happening, allowing them to skip the formal trial. Stepping to the circle, he stripped and shifted to his wolf. Mark's face was white, as he was led to the other side, where he stripped and shifted.

If you surrender too soon, or don't give a good fight, I will have more punishment to deal out. I will give you a fair fight. I will tell you when you can surrender. Adam told the smaller wolf, who from his slightly large paws wasn't yet finished growing, showing he was still very young as he stepped into the ring. He had to be punished, but he had talked his wolf around to his view of one so young would be resentful if he had such a permanent mark of being made Omega or Rogue; he could recover and become a much better wolf for what he was doing, eventually.

Adam felt, if he was made an Omega at such a young age, he might go insane and become the worst kind of Rogue, and need to be put down for it, as an insane rogue attacked anything which came near it and was usually the cause of human attacks. Neither he nor his wolf wanted that to happen; his wolf decided a little leniency on the punishments now save one from that fate, and possibly others from a forced-turn or death was a better decision. His wolf even agreed that he could be a leader in the pack, if not for this mistaken belief of what he could do, which was from a lack of experience and maturity. He was happy with what had been decided, especially since he got to deal out physical part of the punishment.

Chapter 6 – Discipline

Moving forward, Adam stalked the light-grey furred wolf who seemed to take the punishment for what it's worth: punishment, but also a chance to not have it make the rest of his life a misery and disappointment.

Mark growled back at him for show, *I understand. Thank you for giving me the chance and not making me an Omega. I am honoured to try my luck against a Second.* If in the unlikely event Mark got Adam to submit, the punishments would be considered over, and the demotion cancelled. Nobody expected Mark to have a chance. It was a tradition which nobody even considered to change, of 'Might is Right', as for a Werewolf, strength was something which was needed by all. As Mark was the weaker, even a stalemate would be considered a victory to him. Adam could also decide at any point the challenge was complete, without a submission, or even decide to change his mind on the punishment from how the fight went.

Adam used it as a good challenge, and his wolf was happy to show off his skills. Mark yelped as Adam darted in and took a bite of his flank, not bothering with a stare-down for a while before the fight. It left behind a red mark, but wasn't deep; the yelp was partly shock and surprise from the suddenness of it. Adam went back to his circling, as Mark tried to keep facing him.

Adam darted and took a bite to the other flank, leaving another red spot. He kept it up as he lectured the wolf on his duties to his pack, and about what could have happened. He had been looking at their history, as knowing where you have been before you can know where you are going, especially the more seniors; he would rather learn from history instead of making the same mistakes.

For each bite, he had a lesson for the wolf. He told the public story behind the rules for the inter-pack movements, sharing several stories of where they were used to attack, and where they were used to ambush, and others where they were attacked by another pack while travelling and vulnerable. They should have been quickly escorted to safely within the pack's perimeter and protected as Guests.

For the disregarding the will of the pack, he shared stories which were about packs splintering or becoming ineffective, with many factions warring to the point they lost when small attacks happened. Or where because of differences, it caused other packs which had been friendly to become at war with them and cost many wolves their lives. In a couple cases, he had found the packs ceased to exist, as it shattered into factions and the wolves went their own ways, either from knowing they were weak, forced out by a different faction, or dying in a fight.

The story had been told by the former Second, who had tried to hold the pack together by staying neutral to all, but with the Alpha not bothering to stamp out the factions, he couldn't do enough to keep the pack together. He and those who supported him had found refuge in another pack when the Alpha was killed by a play for power by one faction, but the attacker lacked the ability to be Alpha, the Second refused to accept the leadership and left with many following him to the refuge of another pack, and the remains of the pack imploded within a year with few of those surviving.

If they were in human form, Mark would have been in tears, as he hadn't realised how his personal thoughts could have so negatively affected the pack as a whole; he loved his pack. He was sobbing at Adam over the mental link, who continued with his turning the grey fur into red with bites and scratches, which were not deep enough to debilitate, but were enough some might scar, or at least leave marks which would last years and were very painful now. He kept the stories about the insulting pack emissaries causing problems later, with less details. He did hit him hard with the ones about disobeying orders of superior wolves though but kept them to recent ones. Finishing off, he gave him the broad strokes about what Brook did to Steve for his issue; he didn't need to state what would happen for those where the bonds failed so soon after forming, as it was already known, and one of the reasons why so few humans were accepted into the packs without having mates.

Now, you can surrender, Adam told the very much chastised Mark. He instantly rolled on his back, with his tail tucked tightly to his belly, and whined his submission.

Mark had gotten in a few minor bites on Adam, and he was actually impressed he could connect. He stood over the young wolf, and took his neck in his jaws, and growled for a moment, *Don't forget the stories I gave you,* He commanded, pressing with his power.

As he backed off, he decided to put some balm on his mental wounds he caused, *You did well. I could see with experience you would have done fine; you were just pushed to be the leader too soon. Once the decade is over, and you are all clear, and have trouble advancing, come see me.* He could feel even his wolf was impressed how the near-pup held up to the punishment. There were some moves which impressed him and felt it was enough Mark should get a second chance. He just needed time to learn how to lead, and how to take commands better which would come from more time to mature and experience of his life.

Stepping out of the circle, Adam shifted back to human, as Brook came up and tended to his injuries, covering them with gauze pads; by the time they left to go back to their pack, they would just be healing scars.

Mark was lifted onto a stretcher and taken to medical, as his injuries, while minor, were numerous enough the healer wanted him in their medical section before he shifted back, as he might go into shock from blood loss. Hank had alerted them to Adam's plan, so they were ready for him. They would rather deal with a chastised wolf, than one which slowly goes insane from being forced so low so early in their life, and later when they hit the limit of what they could do and sank into depression.

Grant stepped back up, "The punishment has been administered. We will be having a special howl tomorrow night to introduce all the new members. Adam, Brook, and their pups have decided to stay an additional night and will be staying to represent MacLaren Pack."

The pack howled in celebration and welcome.

When it died down, Grant ended this meeting, and sent everyone on their way.

Grant nodded at Adam, as he pulled his clothes on, and Brook gathered their pups. Heading up, Hank and Charlie followed them into the Alpha's cabin, as Louise held the door for them.

Walking in, Alpha Louise guided them into their sitting room. Adam again introduced their pups.

After a round of hugs and greetings, they got down to business about the network. They hammered out much of the details which still needed to be agreed, and the framework for the formal agreement was ready.

Grant relaxed, "Now, I caught the edge of your sending to Mark, all through the fight, but not details. What were you telling him?" he asked, very curious. He could feel through the pack bonds that he had felt worse and worse over what he had done as the fight progressed.

Adam grinned, "I enjoy history, as knowing the mistakes of those before, keep you from making them again! I was telling him stories of those who made the same mistakes as what he was punished for and how they could cause whole packs to die, like…" Adam shared the specific stories which he had given. Grant and Louise started to grin, and even Hank had a smile.

"I think your punishment of a private lecture, while getting a public fight, and not giving him a long-term penalty will have us a much better wolf. One who thinks about the consequences of their actions, and not just about their own hide." Grant said. "I am going to have to talk with Gareth, so he can know what a special wolf he has in you."

Brook grinned, "I did something similar, gave a painful lesson but one which they would physically recover from. He was a new human member, so I just did it using a staff, and left bruises."

Adam laughed, "Martin—our Beta in charge of Pack Security, and the superior of the one Brook dealt with—told me while you were doing it, he would be telling stories to hammer home *why* he was being punished, and what *could* have happened, and what that wolf got for punishment and what they caused. I decided combining them would make a much more effective punishment, although I skipped what the other's punishment was."

Grant nodded, thoughtfully, "From the mental feelings I was getting, if he had been in human form, he would have been sobbing and unable to see from tears before you were halfway; I am certain he got the message."

Louise stood up, "I'm going to go check on him, and make sure there wasn't anything lingering from the mental part of the punishment that we don't want." She was in charge of their mental well being, and she realised she needed to have a chat with him, "We may need to change some education for them. Most are getting just a human education with some pack training. I can see that is not what they need and will need to make adjustments to incorporate some more wolf and pack classes."

Adam nodded, "From where I sit, most human education is about the individual, and lacks much of the cohesiveness of a pack, and the pack mentality. I could see that everything is geared towards the pack as a whole, instead of the wolf; a wolf could be sacrificed to protect the pack, and most would do it happily. I know I would."

Louise nodded and headed out the door. He had given both Alphas a great deal of food for thought.

*****

The drive into the city was fine but dealing with all the traffic and other drivers had Adam growling under his breath as he tried to do calming mental exercises. He remembered the bad drivers, but this seemed worse. Brook had told him that generally when entering another pack's territory, especially for senior wolves, they had to check in with the Alphas, so they had the visitor's scent, and were known.

In this case, Forest's Edge Pack, which while the city was within their territory, they didn't require visitors to do more than call to notify their entry into the pack, and Brook had pre-arranged it, since they weren't staying in their territory for the night and both packs were on good terms with the other. While Adam had been working his last week, Brook had met with one of the Betas, so they had her scent and knew she wasn't trespassing.

Brook sent him calming thoughts, *It's more of you are feeling your wolf, and your dominance is getting offended by them not being courteous to you. It's part of the reason I dislike driving in the city, as even I feel it too.*

Being able to put a name to it made Adam able to push past it, and calm his wolf, reminding him they were not wolves, and humans didn't think about others much, mostly about themselves; they were packs of one for the most part.

Reaching the steakhouse, Adam sighed with relief and parked. Tara and Sara were waiting for them by the door. Sara was wearing her service animal harness. When Charlie hopped out the back, Adam pulled his service dog harness on, and Charlie grumbled about it and the collar messing up his fur, mentally, but loud enough for Adam to pick up, even as he stood still to have it placed on him without a fight.

Tara smiled in greeting as they came up, "Mom's not here yet." She let them know, as she gave each a good hug, and welcomed Jess and Joshua to the family. Charlie and Sara gave their own greeting of bumping noses and a nuzzle.

Tara took them in to their table. Adam put the pups close to where Mary was sitting. Sara and Charlie crawled under the table to be out of the way, putting their heads in Adam's lap, begging for a scratch.

Tara stepped out and waited for their mother. She was hardly gone before she was back with her. She was very much surprised at all the people who were at her table.

"You told me you want grandchildren. I have adopted these four." Adam told her with a grin, "Happy birthday!"

She gave him a look, which he took to be 'are they like you?' He nodded and in a quiet voice as he hugged her, "They are members of our pack and can shift."

He introduced the four to her and she gave them each a hug, as she very much enjoyed the custom.

"This is a wonderful gift!" Mary exclaimed, leaking a couple of tears of joy. "So, when can I come visit?" Now that she had grandchildren, she wanted to get to know them, "Could I stay a week?" She asked as she gave him a tight hug which made him wince as it pulled one of his injuries.

Catching the wince, "What's wrong?"

Adam shook his head, "Had a major fight mid-week, then a disciplinary one this morning. I'm fine." He told her as they sat down.

Mary was shocked, "You did something bad and got in a fight?"

Adam laughed, realising her mistake, and told her in a much quieter voice, "Brook and I are now Acting-Seconds; we are learning to be the leaders of the pack under the Alphas."

Mary grinned, "If I have it right; if the Alphas were Picard, you are Riker?" she asked in confirmation, as she was a big Star Trek fan.

Adam grinned, "Yes, that would be a reasonable explanation. As for the fights, the big one was an inter-pack one; I can't go into details, but I was the one in charge of it, and led my pack in it. This morning, one of the Longview Pack..." He wasn't sure how to say what it was about, as she wouldn't understand their laws and beliefs, he simplified it, "Disobeyed orders, and also was very much disrespectful to me. He was going to be punished, and I requested to be the one to do it."

Mary looked confused, "But why a fight?"

Adam grinned, showing teeth, "We're wolves, discipline is mostly done with some sort of physical punishment. In this case, since the offences were when in wolf, the fight was as wolves. He got a few bites on me, while I disciplined him. I also gave him a good lecture, with some examples of how what he did could have had major impacts to his pack. I have been studying our history, so I had more than enough examples to use for the two hours we fought."

Mary shook her head, not liking violence but knowing her son now lived in a much different world now, one where violence was used to teach, and they could recover quickly from it, "I hope it was warranted."

Brook looked at her with a dead serious look in her face, "Three of the four charges he had laid had a death option, they were *that* serious; packs have gone to war over each one alone in the last five hundred years."

Adam nodded, "As I found out after the fact, he was not happy with some pack decisions, and it was his first time being in any leadership position. I took the option which would stick the most but would not affect his future beyond the next decade. Most of the options we had would have severely limited what he could do with his life. As it was me who was in the leadership role of the group which was offended and due to my rank, I could make the final decision, and our Alpha has already accepted the case as closed."

Mary went pale, but her colour came back at his explanation, and she nodded, "I don't really understand, but I know you have a totally different life now. I'll take your word for it."

Adam gave in to his wolf and decided to order a rare steak, instead of the medium he normally did.

He was surprised when their waiter arrived, and he could smell they were a Were; he knew there were some in the city, although the pack maintained their compound outside the city. The waiter could sense their seniority and gave deference which was due to them. When they had given their orders, under his breath, he asked for "Were-sized meals, for the four pups, Brook and myself, please. If possible, something for our dogs." The waiter grinned and gave him a knowing nod.

Mary had been looking more and more confused at the different signals Brook and Adam exchanged with the waiter.

Brook smiled, "He's Were, too. We could smell and sense it. He was just showing proper respect for our rank, which he could sense."

The manager came with the food, and Brook took the lead as she was closer to the end, as both could sense the Were in him. He smiled, and welcomed them, hoping they enjoyed their meal.

Finding out it was Adam and Tara's mother's birthday, he promised all desserts would be on the house, before leaving them to their meal.

The plates for the Weres had large slabs of meat on them, while Tara and Mary's were much smaller. Mary's eyes were wide, "Are you going to be able to eat that?" she asked, surprised at the size.

Adam burst out laughing, "Yes, and room for dessert. Our bodies have a much higher metabolism. This is a normal sized meal for us." He didn't bother saying they had a 'snack' before leaving the pack and might need another when they got back.

*****

Once the food was cleared away, including the desert, Adam grinned at Robin and Toby, who had the picture wrapped up between them. They pulled the picture frame up, "This is from all of us."

Mary nearly dropped it, not expecting the weight with the ease the boys moved it. Slowly she unwrapped it. Tara knew of it, but not what it looked like finished. Both gasped at the very beautiful, hand made frame, with stencilled wolves burned into the wood, before looking at the pictures.

Tara looked at Adam, "That group shot is different than the one I took when I was out."

Adam grinned, "It had to be altered to add Jess and Joshua into it. I love what you can do with a digital picture! Robin and Toby did it while I was busy. They also made the frame."

Mary had tears in her eyes, "Thank you so much. It is a very wonderful gift!" Turning to Adam and Brook, "Just getting grandchildren is a wonderful gift. I just wish you were closer."

Brook smiled, "You are always welcome at our home. Right now, we are full to the rafters, as we have most of another pack there, but they are mostly moving on to other packs soon, so will be gone within the week. We have a gathering at each full moon, and the next one, on the twenty second, we are officially adopting Jess and Joshua. You'd be welcome to join us for that part. We do a light night run as a pack, and you wouldn't be able to make it, as you don't have a wolf form."

Mary smiled, "I'd like that. Put me down as going."

Tara had been looking at her schedule for her work, "I'm going to be in the area again, so could make it as well! I think I could find my way there."

Adam grinned, "Excellent! You can drive mom, Tara, since you know where to park." She also had the pack ID to get into the hidden parkade.

*****

The next morning the six woke slowly; there was nothing planned till the evening, so they just cuddled, bonding together. By mid morning though, they were up. Borrowing some practice weapons, they took the time for a training practice session. All six had a good workout by the time arrived for lunch.

After a filling meal, they relaxed, and several pulled out their computers to check on what was going on back at the pack. Adam smiled, as he held up the cards for the manager at the steakhouse, passing one to Hank, "You have to try that place next time you're in town, they are an excellent place, and serve were-sized if asked."

Hank looked at the card, "Beta? They have a Beta running that place?" He would have expected a Delta at most to be there. He knew of it but hadn't ever been there. Adam wasn't the first to make the suggestion.

Adam shrugged, "I was surprised too. When asked, they have two private rooms, and they use it to host their inter-pack events. It's located in a well-connected city, so it allows for easy travel which doesn't need to be hidden. They use it to contact other groups, too. All the staff there are Were. They have a Beta to make sure there is someone there who has the skills and authority to deal with most issues."

Adam grinned and turned to Brook, "That's another qualification we have now! Three separate packs with contacts."

Brook shook her head, "You really want to qualify as quickly as you can." She stated, amused.

Adam just grinned back at her in reply.

Hank stared at him in surprise, "What have you already qualified?"

Adam had to think, ticking them off, "Well, wolf-run, wolf fight, weapons: staff, sword, and bow—both long and crossbow. Trainer status on staff and crossbow. We split the leadership of the attack on Shadowed River, so we both qualified. I just need the time to sit the testing for the Laws, both pack and inter-pack. I know the history of *five* Inter-Pack Treaty rules, not just the three required, and now have my required three contacts." Grinning at Hank, "The inter-pack negotiations are with you on the network. And the disciplinary action I just did, I need you, your Alphas, or an Elder to make an official report on it, please."

Brook continued, "Waiting to spring for the other two runs. He just needs to be tested on scent tracking as well, and he's qualified at the trainer."

Hank was amused and added up the time, "When did you sleep? It took me almost a decade to fully qualify! Wait, you have already qualified on wolf-run?"

Adam and Brook grinned and nodded, "We both did." Adam confirmed, "On ten centimetres of lightly packed snow. We had been just doing a personal test, just to see how much farther we had to go, but I mind-linked everyone to make sure we didn't run into anyone on the trail, and an Elder decided to time it. When it was realised many of the normal trail officials were out doing their own training, they were able to spread them out enough to make it an official run."

Hank was astounded, "How long?" He asked, expecting them to adjust the time for the conditions.

"Eighty-Five minutes on a full one-fifty trail." Came Brook's response with well-deserved pride.

Hank's jaw dropped and hung there; he was stunned and it took him several minutes to break out of his shock. "I only qualified the run on clear and dry trail. And on my *third* try!" He eventually exclaimed once his mind re-engaged. His personal best was about that time as well! He was starting to think they may be just learning to eventually have their own Pack. Their skills were already at or above what most Seconds had, with most having decades if not centuries to gain their skills; they had barely been given the title, and their experience was less than a year.

Brook grinned, "Adam wanted to catch the white wolf who broke into our pack house and terrorized a couple under us. He had escaped him once, and he definitely didn't want it to happen again. I wanted to be there to help, so I pushed myself to get faster too. Until that run, we had never really run full out alone, so didn't know how fast we were." Looking over at the four pups, "Mostly, we have run with them. All four would qualify the Delta test, and Toby and Robin the Beta."

Hank could just shake his head. "Are any of age to be tested officially?" he asked.

"We are testing for Delta this spring," Joshua answered, pride in his voice, "I think the Betas have been conspiring, as I just got word as we left which we now have the required fifteen who report to us to qualify as a Deltas. We had been placed in the lead of the main Safe room before the attack, so it was the last parts, other than the Human run."

Hank nearly fell out of his seat from laughing so hard. The rest just stared in shock.

Adam just shook his head and with a smile on his face, turned back to his laptop, which was connected back to his PC using a secure tunnel, so he could check his e-mail.

Once Hank calmed down, Brook decided to give the other bombshell, "All four of our pups were considered *Theta* before we got our paws on them. It looks like Toby and Robin, along with their Born-*Delta* girlfriends, will be qualified as Beta when they are of age."

This time Hank did fall out of his seat in surprise, and just sit there blinking for a bit on the floor. Shaking his head, he stood up, "Now that is a surprise: Qualifying at *Beta* with only adoptive parents at that level! I know we have rarely accepted Deltas from the Theta, and almost never Betas, but I'm thinking we may want to see if we can qualify some higher. We have been having not enough who do well in the higher positions, or are pushed too fast, Mark for example."

Brook nodded, "What we started just before Alpha Ralph split from our parent pack, was at the qualifications Spring Trials, all were permitted to test for whatever they wished. There was no spot which was for what their parents were at, so everyone was at the same level. If they didn't meet their parent's level, they were not penalised, and were just trained at the level they did qualify at. According to records, we did loose quite a few members who took their family to another pack when their child was given a lower rank because they failed to meet the higher qualifications and refused to still promote them. Many of the parents were ones who refused to show they had the qualifications to hold their ranks, and they opposed the changes which could have had them reduced in rank." The parents had not been forced to test, as they had the rank from before the changes and the decision was to not force the changes, but they could not change to another position which needed a rank without testing for it.

Hank nodded, "I was able to talk Alpha Grant into letting me and my mate test for Beta, and eventually qualify for Second, as I threatened to request a pack transfer if he didn't. We did have a few pack members who left when I did qualify and then was accepted into the rank, in protest, but I like the idea: allowing for those with the skills but born low to float to the top, and those who lack them but born high to sink to the level they are skilled at. I will discuss it within the pack, after talking to the Alphas, to see how many would like the changes in the rules."

Silence reigned as each did their own thing, and Hank thought it over, or privately talked to the alphas about it. "How do you deal with getting the training for those who are Theta?" Hank said into the stillness.

"We make sure all pups are informed they can get additional help and training on the weekend. Also, all the instructors keep an eye out for those who they feel would do well with the additional help and encourage them to go to it. Also, we don't allow the pups to have ranks. They are ranked 'pup' till they are mid-teens, and don't require any ranks till they are of age. It doesn't keep them from using their parents rank as their rank but does cut down on the stratification of the pack." Brook replied. She had helped quite a few move up, or to encourage those who she felt didn't have the temperament to be leaders to do other tasks, or not to aspire to a leadership role, but to do a skill they liked instead.

"But some parents still put roadblocks and feel that blood should determine your rank," Toby commented, remembering how his mother had not wanted them to aspire to be more than Theta and often gave them work to do when the extra training was scheduled, so they could not attend to get ahead. Brook and others had given up some of their personal time to run special classes for them and a few others, so they could get the training, but it was spotty, not steady as they really needed and now were getting.

Brook nodded, "Just so, but if they come to an instructor's attention, they might be able to get them the help, as long as the pup aspires and works hard." Thinking about before and after they took them in, "But having the disapproval of a parent, and not having them care about your education does often hinder their advancement."

Closing out his laptop, and putting it back into its waterproof, padded case, Adam stretched, "Time to get ready for the evening."

Chapter 7 – Group Introduction

Adam and his family stayed to the side, as it wasn't really their party; it was for those joining the pack. He was only there to represent his pack and although honoured, the releasing pack was not required, especially since they were never officially part of their pack, since they didn't have pack bonds and they had never given any oath for joining.

The Alphas and the new members had been working non-stop since the lunch the day before to get the pack bonds completed. It takes about four to six hours for the pack bonds to settle in the mind and headaches to go away. Even doing them in batches, and both Alphas bringing them in at the same time, it took the alphas almost to dawn to get them all joined.

The Alphas stood on the porch, which apparently was used as a stage for pack gatherings. Alpha Louise gave a demanding howl, and the gathered pack instantly was quiet. "We are here to welcome new pack members!" She began; she had to stop as there was a loud howl to greet them and welcome them to the pack. She had them line up and introduced them all to the pack by name. When she was done, she smiled and led the howl of greeting.

"Let's show them how we party and welcome them to the pack!" Louise called out, getting a cheer. Each of the newcomers, Hank had told them, had been given a pack member to help them settle in, which were about the same age and rank as the member joining. Adam led his family towards the food, being much more interested in what was there than in mingling first.

Heading over to the nearest table, the wolf serving the food, they nodded their head with a respectful, "Second," To both Adam and Brook as they were handed steaks which were nearly raw, as their wolves loved them. Adam had tried a bite of a medium, and had to agree, that the rare tasted better now; the medium had tasted very over done.

Taking the plates with a respectful thanks, they gathered the sides they wanted, before sitting at one of the tables they just set up. Keeping an eye on the rest of his family, as they had spread out a bit, seeing that they were representing their pack, Adam chatted with the other wolves who came to speak with him. Some were the wolves who came in with them and wanted to thank him for getting them in safe and sound. Others were wolves he didn't know and wanted to meet the new Second of a powerful neighbour. At Brook's suggestion, he didn't tell them he had been turned, but didn't deny it if they asked about it. Most knew he had been turned, and since their own second had been turned long ago, they were not too surprised. Most either didn't know or had forgotten it had taken their Second much, much longer to reach the skills Adam already showed. The Elders noticed but kept quiet, they would discuss how both Adam and Brook were getting more powerful physically, and how they agreed they wouldn't stay Seconds for long.

Several young Betas came up and chatted for a bit. Knowing they needed to have one contact in their pack, he had asked Hank, and found out they had the same requirement. He had passed out some of his cards to his pups, as had Brook; they had just gotten the first batch of cards with their new title just before they left, and Brook had just packed them both. Several asked for them, and he passed them out as he discussed interests with them.

Lucas came over for a bit. They chatted about the photography, and he showed him a picture he had taken of the picture before the pups wrapped it. He was speechless for the care and work which went into it. He smiled when he was told who it was for.

Adam had been getting some of Lucas' pictures in the e-mails they exchanged. Both had very different styles and interests in photos, so it was always interesting to chat about it. They didn't chat too long, as there seemed to be quite a few who wanted to chat with the new Second and find out what one of their closest neighbour was up to.

Finding out they had accepted him as a human mate was not surprising, but the fact they accepted two humans into the pack was surprising. The occasional human was permitted, but rarely was there a second in a decade, let alone at the same time.

Those coming to see him brought him refills for his meal, so he didn't need to get up. Once fed though, he mingled with the pack. Mostly they discussed lighter topics, and he refused to discuss "what if" about the punishment; the case was closed for the pack, and his own Alpha had decided to leave it totally in his hands, as it happened in another pack's territory, and that pack's Alphas accepted the judgment and punishment. If he did anything with Mark, it was between the two of them.

One wolf later in the evening came up to him, and after trading a hug and sniff, the wolf took a second good sniff before giving a nasty growl, "Where is she?" he demanded.

Adam growled back in warning, at the blatant disrespect, "I have no idea on what you are talking about."

"My mate! You have her smell on you!"

Adam shook his head, "I have been touched by most of your pack today alone, you will need to be more specific, and we can do it civilly." He was clamping down on his wolf, who wanted to attack for the disrespect. Since it involved a mate, he was giving him some leeway.

The wolf closed his eyes and took several deep breaths to calm down. Opening them, he had almost a pleading look, "She is not of this pack, I know that. May I?" He begged, wanting another smell.

Adam nodded as his own mate came over along with Alpha Grant, to investigate the disturbance. The wolf leaned forward and sniffed again.

"Female... human... late twenties" He commented, before taking a long sniff, and opening his eyes wide, "Your own personal scent is very close. You have a sister?" His eyes were hopeful, and clearly showed more respect.

Adam started chuckling, before laughing outright. Everyone around him was staring at him, other than Brook, who had picked up what was in his mind and was chuckling at the irony.

Once Adam got control and caught his breath, he smiled at the wolf, and nodded, "I do have a sister. She is twenty-seven. We were just together last night for our mother's birthday." It was a bit surprising her scent was still on him. Turning to the alpha, who had a concerned look to his face, "My sister and mother know what we are, and both are already cleared by my pack. Rest of my family doesn't know."

Turning back to the wolf, "She had commented about all the good-looking guys at my pack but didn't ask for any introductions. I did catch her looking wistful last night at Brook and I."

Both the wolf and Alpha Grant looked relieved. Some humans couldn't stand the fact of them and would reject their mates; the rejected wolf sometimes got so depressed they suicided. Finding another mate did happen from time to time, but usually those were at least a century later, long after the human had passed away.

The wolf realised he hadn't even given his name, "I'm Ryan," he introduced himself, his eyes lit with hope, "Any chance of wrangling an introduction? Or at least her phone number?"

Adam smiled, "I'll see what I can do. I'll have to ask her for it." He commented before pulling out his phone. He would never give out information for a person to another.

I have a wolf here who is very interested in your scent on me. He is nearly begging for your number. Can I give it to him? Adam texted his sister.

The reply came back almost instantly, *YES!!! A wolf asking for me? Why didn't they see me when I was there? When can I come next? What's his name?* Came the rapid-fire messages from Tara.

Adam laughed at the reply, *I'm still at Longview Pack, he's a member here. Had been asked to stay another day for some wolf stuff. Heading home tomorrow morning. His name is Ryan.* He replied. He texted her a couple more times, about how to come in, and to let him know if there were any issues, so he could deal with it.

Adam passed Ryan his sister's phone number, staring him down, "Now, you treat my sister well and with respect and we won't have any trouble. I do know she hasn't had a steady boyfriend for years but does have some cats."

Ryan gulped visibly, before nodding, and showing respect, as he quickly sent her a message, "Then it's good I like animals."

"Does she have any protection?" Alpha Grant asked. If she had a wolf-mate, she would need some. It pleased him, as it would give the two packs even tighter bonds.

Adam nodded, "She has one of our 'dogs." He commented, looking at Charlie, who was leaning against his leg, "Although hers is much smaller, and just the size of a small Mastiff."

Alpha Grant nodded, pleased that Adam had already arranged for some protection for one he was already considering a pack member.

"Alpha, can she come visit? She is free tomorrow afternoon." Ryan asked quietly, trying to not beg.

"Yes. Tell her to plan on either spending the night, or you are going with her." He replied, instantly. Ryan knew if she asked, she would be allowed to bring her pets. He was not going to keep those two apart, as it was looking almost like they could be mates. Turning to Adam, "Pack ID?"

Adam smiled, "Yes, got her MacLaren ID when she was last at our pack."

Alpha Grant turned to Ryan, "You get to inform the guards to let her in and she has MacLaren Family ID. If she is your mate, also get her one of our IDs."

"Yes, Alpha. I will let security know first thing tomorrow." Ryan replied, happy.

The Alpha smiled, amused on how this was turning out, and nodded as he wandered off.

Adam wrapped an arm around Brook, pulling her close, "So Ryan, tell me about yourself," He asked as he moved to sit down at one of the tables left at the side, pulling a curious Brook down onto his lap.

Ryan sat near, and his wolf was very respectful of the senior wolf, who might become a bond-brother, "I'm a Delta, and I work with the Pack's horses. We use them to patrol the areas which humans could see, so they don't see wolves, but we can patrol faster than on foot as humans. And much quieter than on an ATV."

Adam grinned, "My sister is horse crazy, so make sure you introduce her to them. I'll let you find out most about her yourself, other than she does have some food allergies right now."

Ryan nodded, "We breed the horses, and expose them to the wolves right from birth. That has them learning the wolves protect them from other predators and won't harm them. That and the fact they have learned some of our body language, which we can direct them when as wolves."

Adam nodded, "My pack does dogs; they actually can take linked messages, and since they smell of Were a bit, they are a good deterrent for rogues." He wanted to share more details, as he knew Sara was very good protection for his sister. He couldn't as it was a pack secret, "We train them to carry a pack, and we have a pack which is good in all three of our forms, and we can even fight in them, if needed, as long as they were loaded correctly."

Ryan nodded but looked a bit sceptical at the idea of a pack fitting all three forms.

"Adam took out the neck of a Beta as a wolf which attempted to ambush us, and the force of his attack had the body take out two others while wearing his, all before they could recover from the first attack." Brook replied, "They are designed to be a weapon support, so you can go wolf, and still have your weapons with you, but not impede you, even with a long run; we and our pups wore ours for the trip here."

Ryan nodded, now seeing how it could work, "Do you share with other packs?" He would love to have one, if it was possible.

"We are currently working on a way to make them without needing someone there. Currently, someone would need to come to the shop to get fitted personally for the pack."

Ryan smiled, "If I have a chance, I will come see you for one." If he could get one, he would; it didn't matter what the cost was.

Adam grinned, "They seem to be catching on; everyone we talk to wants one!"

Adam and Brook continued to chat with him for a while; Adam making sure he could trust Ryan with his sister, Brook to make sure Adam didn't do anything to him and to see him from another side; she had never seen him as a protective brother.

Eventually, Adam decided he would probably be a good fit for his sister. His wolf still wanted to see them together, but they didn't have time to stick around, as they needed to get back. He knew she would keep him on his toes if they were mates. It would help her with her health issues, even just from the Mating, as it tended to reduce some allergies and if she decides to be Turned, it would eliminate them totally.

Brook thought Ryan was sweet, in a naïve way. Finding out he had not even really had a girlfriend, as he had been waiting for his mate, she knew he was very much looking forward to this. She could tell he'd care for her if they were mates. She smiled, as Adam's sister had been texting back and forth with her as they chatted. It sounded like they were looking forward to the meeting.

At one point, Brook linked Louise, and made sure she'd keep an eye on her bond-sister, as she had come to really care for her; she was the sister she never had. She did hope she decided to turn, as they'd have even more in common then, and she would be able to defend herself much better, not to mention the much longer life she would have as a Wolf. Partly, she didn't want to have Adam lose his sister.

*****

Late into the night, Hank came up to him, "Soon we are going to be heading to our pack fire, as a time for us to bond as a pack."

Adam nodded, reading between the lines, "And you don't want any outsiders there. I understand." He replied, patting his shoulder, "There is one wolf I want to talk to, and it would be better to do it alone." Especially since he had to also have a chat with his parents after they confronted him, blaming him for the demotion.

Hank smiled, "Thanks." Knowing who he'd want to see, "If you want, I'll slip Mark to my place, so you can have a private word with him."

Adam nodded and headed to let the rest of his family know. He was surprised they had been invited to as much. New members joining was typically a time for the pack to come together without any outsiders. That was part of the reason they hadn't planned to stay for the introduction and was silently glad to have not been called out.

As the pack headed to the fire, they quietly slipped off to Hank's place, for a quiet evening.

Adam had slipped away first, and Hank showed Mark in. Adam took him to the living room and had asked his family to let him have a private word.

Mark was looking petrified.

Adam was quick to reassure him, "Mostly, I wanted to check up on you. I am not going to be giving out any more punishments, and even my wolf is satisfied with what you have already received. You were upset about the influx of new members. Both Hank and I feel you were pushed too fast into the leadership role, and if we had not been running behind schedule, your pack's most experienced patrol would have been the one to guide us in."

Adam gave him a friendly hug, as he looked much more relaxed, "I do know from my pack's side your case is closed, and even Alpha Gareth, when I spoke to him, agreed."

Mark looked down, "But how am I going to stay totally out of trouble for a decade?"

Adam shook his head, "That wasn't what your punishment was: if you don't break any Pack Laws, I talked to Grant about it, and mostly it is the big ones you need to stay clean with. I have spoken to the other wolves who were on your team and the supervisors; you have good potential. Even my wolf noticed it, and he thinks mostly in the 'now' and doesn't really plan much ahead or care much about what happened and has been dealt with already. I think being reduced and needing to take the time to climb back up will help you mature before being in the lead." His parents seemed to have been infected with an idea that they needed to push him forward, instead of letting those who trained him do so.

Mark nodded, feeling as if some of the weight was off his shoulders.

"Well, you will be at the bottom for the next year; just hold it together." Adam reassured him, before handing him one of his cards, "If you need help, or someone outside the pack to make a comment, let me know. Study hard, so you not only know the laws but how your pack interprets the inter-pack ones. There is one pack law which brings the inter-pack ones in as if they are your pack's. Hank let me know to have you talk to him directly if you have questions. He knows how it is to need to fight his way up. Your Elders would also be able to help."

Mark looked almost happy and nodded.

Adam smiled, "Now, your pack is having a fire gathering, off to it. Maybe you'll find some friends in the new wolves. The Betas and Deltas especially know how a single mistake can ruin their lives. If you ask nicely, in a year or two, they may be able to share their stories with you. Right now, it is very raw for them, and they wouldn't." Holding up a hand as he saw Mark open his mouth to speak, "I can't tell them, they are sealed pack records, and are their stories to tell." The Alphas had decided to just give them a fresh start.

Mark nodded, clutching the card as if it was a lifeline, "Thank you so much for caring about me. I'm sorry with the way I acted." Adam pulled him in for a good hug, before guiding him to the door, "Hank and Lucas are two I know well here; both would be willing to help you, with anything they could."

Mark tucked the card into a covered pocket and nodded, before heading off to the fire at a run.

Brook slipped up behind him, and wrapped her arms around him, "I hope he does well and doesn't mess up."

Adam hugged her arms tight, "I really hope so too. I plan on keeping informed on him. Once he matures a bit, he'll be a good wolf." Even his wolf agreed with it.

*****

After a quiet evening, and a good sleep, they were up in time for breakfast. Hank was still sleeping so they decided to make breakfast. Hank wandered in, yawning, just as they finished up making the pancakes and sausage.

Adam smiled, "Just have a seat. You have been so good to us, so we decided to treat you today."

Hank smiled back, "It's nice not needing to do anything except eat."

Brook sat a plate in front of Hank, as they finished up making the food, "We thought a good meal would work best before heading home. This was a good trip but looking forward to getting back."

Adam grinned, "We're all more powerful, so the run won't take all day, like the trip here. I'm expecting about four hours, not counting any breaks we take along the way."

Hank just shook his head, and started eating the food, *It's nice to not need to make a meal, just to eat it.* he commented, getting a laugh as the rest sat down with their food. Remembering his manners, *Thank you for this; it is a nice surprise.*

Adam nodded, *You're welcome; it's the least we could do for you putting up with us.*

They chatted over nothing about work, and the three adults involved the four pups, so they weren't feeling left out.

Once they were done eating, Adam and Brook washed the dishes, while the pups got everything else ready to go, coming out, wearing their packs, and Jess and Joshua each carrying one of their parent's packs in their mouth, already shifted for the run. Charlie had his own pack strapped on too.

Adam and Brook smiled their thanks, took their packs, quickly stripped, and stuffing the clothes into their packs. Strapping it on was watched by Hank who smiled at the ingenious harness which kept the connectors out of the way but allowed for adjustment or easy release.

Both shifted quickly to wolf and wagged their tails in thanks as Hank opened the door. "I hope to see you soon," Hank called as the seven of them headed out at a slow run which they could keep up the entire time.

*****

If it wasn't for Adam doing several stops to shift so he could take pictures, the trip would have taken only three hours. Brook got annoyed enough she threatened to leave him behind if he did any more 'picture stops' as they passed into their territory. All four pups growled in agreement. Adam whined and agreed to no more stops; the rest he could do at his leisure as they were within the pack's territory and patrol boundary.

As it was, it ended up taking an extra hour and a half, and they were just making the lunch mealtime, otherwise it would have just been the between-meal buffet, which was kept refreshed around the clock, and was made of stuff which didn't readily get warm or cold, and could be left out for a few hours without any issue.

Reaching the pack house, the four pups sprinted off to their rooms to shift and get dressed for lunch. Brook stayed with Adam and growled to get him to go faster, as she was hungry! When Adam realised what she wanted, he sped up, as he didn't want her mad at him for missing lunch entirely.

Making the tail end of lunch, they just made it in before the kitchen shut down, so they could clean before they started prepping for dinner. As they had made it for the meal and got the last of the hot pork chops which had been offered, Brook just growled at Adam, but once she was fed, wasn't going to be too annoyed at him.

Adam had grabbed their mail, what little they got. Some was thank-you notes about the fights, a few were bills for the equipment purchases, and he forwarded them to be paid, after making sure they were what he was expecting and not some sort of scam. There were some companies who thought it was good to make an 'advertisement' for their service which looked like a bill for the service to try to trick people into signing up. One was one which would transfer the website domain name registration to them, and they charged several times more than the norms for it.

Sitting down for some food, *We have our weekly meeting with the Alpha tomorrow morning. He doesn't want to wait till next week.* Adam commented to Brook, as he started eating; he would have been fine just going and chasing some rabbits on the way in, but their chefs had a way of making the food taste good. His wolf let out a mental growl of enjoyment of the food in agreement. They changed the spices, so even if they were the same meat, they had been done differently and had different flavours.

Chasing and killing our own food is nice, but we have much more important things to do with our time; like dealing with the white wolf. Wolf-Adam agreed, reminding him they had the invaders still in lock up.

What's the plans for this afternoon? Brook asked, *I think I want a bit of a nap, then a soak.*

I am going to see what the email and other messages have, but a soak after sounds nice, head up to our hot springs? Adam replied as they handed in their dishes with a thanks, taking a fresh travel mug of coffee. He had disliked the drink as a human but needed caffeine sometimes. Now he disliked pop, as he could taste all the chemicals it was made from. He did notice he was developing a taste for coffee, or at least getting used to it.

He didn't try to wrap his arm around his mate, as he liked to, since he could still feel she was a bit annoyed at him and didn't want to push her. Adam hoped the nap would put her in a better frame of mind.

They headed back to their room, and Brook pulled him down for a kiss before heading to bed for her nap. She never slept the best at strange places, especially when there was those who were looking to her for protection. Charlie wiggled over and curled up with her; he had come for a nap right after eating as the run was a hard one for him. She pulled Charlie close and cuddled, since her mate was doing other stuff.

Adam didn't have too many e-mails, but several were time-sensitive, and he dealt with them. He smiled, as he had got much fewer e-mails. He cancelled a few more mailing lists, and closed his accounts on a few sites he no longer had any interest in; he had plenty of friends here, no to mention a Mate and pups.

He did check in with Martin about Duncan and Keanna. They were doing better and had moved back to their room. Looking for the bonds to them, he realised he didn't have any special bond anymore, and checking with Martin, it seemed he had fully taken them on, and under his wing. It was understandable as from his discussions with other Betas which had those looking to them; the bonds did grow and fade over time, when they weren't the strong pack and close family ones. His wolf wasn't too surprised with how much time they were spending with Security.

As Brook woke up, he finished his computer work. Putting it into 'sleep' mode, since he didn't use it much, and he wanted to conserve power.

Adam could feel she was feeling much better for some food and rest. Leaning over, he gave her a kiss, and smiled, "Time for a good soak?"

Brook nodded with a smile, "That feels like something to do!" Watching Adam strip and shift to his Were form commented, "Wanting to try it out more I take it?"

Adam wagged his large tail, and quietly barked agreement, very much enjoying the shape. His wolf was revelling in the shared shape and the ability of using weapons while keeping the sharp teeth and claws.

Brook grinned, moved off the bed, and shifted to her Were as well. From the fact they stood digitigrade, and the heel was in the air, they stood close a metre taller than in their human forms, and both were well muscled. Brook got the doors as they headed out. Adam hadn't had a chance to compare, but Brook knew they would be much larger than most of the other pack in this form, as rank and power helped make their Were form larger.

Dropping down to all fours once they were outside, Brook took off, with Adam quickly catching up. Charlie had decided he needed to sleep and stayed behind when Adam told him where they were going and he could stay.

At points they stopped, and Brook worked with Adam to refine his skills, so he could learn the new shape and its abilities and limitations. It was slower than the wolf, partly due to the larger size, but was still much faster than human form could be. He could jump nearly three metres straight up in the air, which really surprised him. With a running start, he could reach five metres. The fur coat was very nice too; it blended into shadows in all but the brightest light.

Eventually they reached the hot springs and slipped in. They shifting back to human once in the water, as there was an icy north wind blowing, but in the water it didn't matter; it was nice and warm.

Brook curled up, leaning against her mate, "What were you going to do if we missed lunch?" she asked.

"My wolf was planning on hunting rabbits for everyone, or doing a hunt for a deer," He replied, truthfully, "He likes providing for the family."

Brook smiled, "At least you were thinking about it."

Adam laughed, "Even he couldn't understand all the stops. I just love taking mountain pictures!"

Brook pulled his head down to her and gave him a kiss, "At least you did stop when asked."

Adam was surprised, but kissed her back, as they cuddled and enjoyed the hot water and the quiet except for the sound of the wind and water. He didn't bother mentioning he had been worried he would get bit if he didn't!

Chapter 8 – Preparing

After relaxing and enjoying the time with his mate, Adam decided they needed to figure out what to do now, "I noticed our bond to Duncan and Keanna has faded." He stated, wanting her opinion.

"It happens. I wonder if they have another now to look to." Brook replied, having also noticed.

"Martin has them. I checked with him." Adam replied, "Is it normal?"

Brook nodded, "Yes. It happens from time to time, as jobs or tasks move to different positions, then have others they get close to and trust more. As we change our duties, and those who support us change, they may look to their new supervisor. Just never abandon one under our care, as that would look to the rest of the pack as they are not worthy of care and they did something wrong."

It relieved Adam, he thought it may have been his inability to protect them. He took a moment to think on the warning she had told him; if they turned their back one someone, after they had been in their care, he could see how it would have others wonder why they were being punished. He made a mental promise to not do it. He couldn't think of any good reason to why any deserved to abandoned in that way.

Sighing, Adam turned inward, to discuss with his wolf on how to deal with the white wolf.

We can take him. I think we should take him down in a fight. Wolf-Adam growled, very much wanting to be the one who killed him.

I'll agree to that, as long as it isn't a tear-him-to-pieces fight. Not sure I could handle it. Human-Adam replied, sharing a savage pleasure from his wolf, but knowing he didn't want a blood bath.

Tearing him to pieces is satisfying but is sooooo messy! As much as I want to do it, I understand and agree that tearing him apart doesn't solve anything which a quick kill doesn't as well.

Adam chuckled at his wolf, as he had already found he was a very fastidious wolf and hated getting covered in blood.

"What are you amused about?" Brook asked curiously.

"My wolf agreed to a quick death of the white wolf instead of tearing him apart, all because he doesn't want to get blood in his fur. He also agrees a quick death solves it just as well." Adam replied, chuckling.

Brook laughed and shook her head, "I have to agree, getting the blood out of fur is a pain, and a quick death, while less satisfying would be better."

Adam nodded, "At this point, I think if I was to tear him apart, it would stay with me for a very long time."

Sitting back and just relaxing with his mate, he could feel her pulling him mentally close, and he let her, as he pulled her on his lap to cuddle her body. He could feel a couple of minds approach as their wolves came forward to join the mental cuddle.

This is nice, came Wolf-Brook's mind-voice, **We need to do this more** she begged.

I agree said Wolf-Adam, seeming to nuzzle both human minds, as all four minds relaxed and shared thoughts and feelings. They agreed to not keep secrets, as keeping it open was better.

*****

The next morning, they joined their friends. Most had wondered where they were at supper. They got some playful teasing over disappearing as soon as they could and not coming back till late. Adam and Brook had decided to spend the time together, and had just hunted as wolves, and ate a couple of rabbits for dinner. They just got a smile from both in response to the teasing.

Catching up, he found they had finished doing the networking in the pack house, and lacking any work, Erin had given the techs a week to relax and just do the support. Adam agreed and suggested seeing if any of the outbuildings needed some network ports, or if they should just have the Wi-Fi there. Adam didn't need to be involved now everything was working and going well.

Adam turned next to Chris, who grinned, "The first scan has been done." He told Adam, but added to the rest as, other than Erin and Aurora, they looked confused, "I had asked Adam for permission to have a third-party security group try to break in, to test the security, and then generate a report when they were done." He turned back to Adam, "The report is in, and we were good, for a new network. But there is some more work to be done. Some of the changes are to how the servers were set up to isolate anything which is internet accessible physically from the internal network, so even if someone got in, they couldn't jump to the internal network." He stated, "I have already started coordinating with Erin and Aurora."

Adam smiled and nodded, "Just do what is needed. Send me a short report on Friday of what has been done, what you are still working on, what still needs to be done, and what we can't change." He'd review it on the weekend for the weekly meeting with the Alpha.

The agreement for the MacLaren/Longview network link was being finalized above his level, and Hank had all the details needed for it, till it was ready for them to activate the link and start testing, it didn't require him at all. The amusing part was getting the paperwork done for the passports, which they would need once they decided to start getting the entire network up and running. It likely would mean lots of travel for him and Brook. They also had to get permission from each pack before going. The fact they were Seconds now would also likely mean more travel representing the pack.

Adam had already planned out the expansion. Well, more of where to place the main hub site's approximate locations. He planned a second in eastern Canada and a third in southern US, and possibly more elsewhere in the US. It would allow for redundancy. Once the second was online and all the bugs worked out, the rest would be easy to do, since they would then have everything set up.

Once they finished the breakfast, Adam and Brook had to hustle, as they were late to their meeting with the Alpha.

Knocking on Gareth's office open door, "Sorry we're late. We were getting caught up with the others over breakfast." Adam offered.

Gareth looked up from the document he was working on the laptop on his desk, looking a little surprised, "Is it time already?" Before grinning, "I guess we both lost track of time. Not a big deal." Walking over to the couches as Adam and Brook sat down, "So how was the trip from your view?"

Adam shared a look with Brook, and she started, "Well, on the way out we ran into an Íyãhé Nakoda Elder near Ga-hna which I knew from a pack event at Longview years ago and had a short chat with him. He invited us to visit him and said maybe in a few weeks."

Gareth smiled at her, "Excellent, I have been trying to find a way to get communications with them, as they are down the middle between our two packs. I didn't know you had met them before, or I would have asked you to stay in contact years ago!"

Adam took up the narrative, "The other thing of major note was Mark's blocking the arrival, but you know about *that*."

Gareth became serious, "Yes, Grant and I shared several calls about it and the work you did. I am impressed on how you handled it. Not only did you keep your heads about it when the offences happened, but when you worked out the punishments, it was something which followed the spirit of the laws and was tempered with the circumstances. I liked the fact you told him what could have happened by following just the letter of the law, and how much worse it could be for the pack."

Adam smiled, "My wolf was impressed with his fighting skills, and if he manages to stay clear for the next decade, would be willing to help him, if he needs it. We feel he was pushed to lead before he was ready. His parents leaned on the one who makes the patrol teams to have him lead a patrol, and they just had the bad timing to give in when we were going to be there. If we hadn't been running late, mostly due to some wolves not having the expected endurance, we would have been on the expected schedule, and their most senior patrol would have met us, not the most junior. I'm thinking that in time, he could be a very valuable wolf and could go far."

Gareth gave him a very satisfied smile, "Good. I am having the issue declared closed. The elders have discussed it, and from the reports from the Longview Pack's Alphas and Elders, it counts as both a wolf fight and punishment. Adding in the pack fight and the two at the pack take-down, which is your four."

Adam grinned and nodded; he was one step closer to being fully qualified. It felt like he was checking off a list of tasks for a training course.

Gareth smiled, "To help you, you two are going to jointly lead the next Howl's hunt, be ready."

Adam and Brook nodded. Both their wolves had perked up at that, as it was a great honour.

"One last thing happened while I was there," Adam started, before pausing for some effect, "It seems that my sister is also a Wolf-Mate." He lost the fight to keep a straight face and grinned at the Alpha.

Gareth was shocked into laughing out loud. Adam just sat back and waited for their Alpha to catch their breath. Eventually he did, with tears in his eyes from the amusement of that, "Are you sure?"

Adam nodded, "At the special howl, Ryan, a Delta, was greeting me when his wolf came forward and demanded his mate. Once he calmed down, we were able to determine it wasn't a wolf in the pack who had touched me, but a human. The age he could smell from the scent and the fact it was close to my personal scent had it likely it was my sister."

Gareth nodded, for Adam to continue, "Well, I texted my sister, if she was ok with me passing her number to Ryan. She was fine, and they got together just after we got back here. This morning, I had a message he was her mate, and she was going to sell her place and move into

Longview pack. She hasn't decided about her work, but the pack is fairly convenient to them still. I haven't asked if they've mated yet, and if she is formally joining their pack. I will do it the next time we talk."

Gareth shook his head, "You are just full of good luck for us! This will just work to strengthen the bonds between the two packs!"

Adam was amused, "I was going to ask if my sister and mother could come for the first part of the next Howl, but this throws a big issue; my sister was going to be driving, so we'll have to see what's going to go on. I'll let you know what the plans are on next Monday."

Gareth nodded sharply, making the topic done. "How's the network coming along?" he asked, starting the next item in his mental list of what needed to be discussed.

"I have to finish the formal agreement. That's my plan for today and will pass it to the pack lawyers to be turned from notes of specific items agreed upon to the full agreement for signing. I'll have it to them by the end of the day and have them pass it right to you." Adam replied.

"Sounds like a good plan." Gareth agreed, "I should have it within a couple weeks then."

"I have Chris in charge of configuring this end of the network and planning for the eventual global network." Adam commented, "I have an idea for hiding some of the data we are doing, by offering internet services to those in the valley, and offering some server space for others. I would need several wolves able to interact with humans for the internet provider, but it would also be a reasonable revenue stream, as well."

Gareth nodded, "I'll think about them."

They discussed other minor details and Gareth brought them up to speed on the other projects the wolves were doing.

The meeting didn't end till the Alpha's stomach startled all three, and they realised it was already lunch time.

Laughing, they ended the meeting before they missed the meal. Heading to the dining room, chatting amicably about the travel conditions between the packs, Gareth realised, it was going to be generally easier to move as wolves between them. Some areas had human hunters, but he'd have to check a map. He thought the majority would be reserve or areas controlled by known allied with the packs and didn't allow human hunters. There was a couple of roads which had to be crossed, but they were forestry roads, so generally saw light traffic. As always, there were human poachers who didn't follow the laws, or Rogue Weres, but that is what Enforcers were for.

*****

During the afternoon, Adam and Brook worked on finalizing what was needed in the agreement, including many contingencies, from a simple malware getting into a computer, to hackers trying to get in, to the government attempting to seize the servers.

The last was very unlikely but could happen. They had all the servers set up in such a way which all the data would be erased if they are started without specific electronic keys being available. Those keys were in seemingly unrelated systems, and any wolf could easily render them in pieces and unusable.

He had Steve working on a system which would hide in the background as a backup measure where if it wasn't on the correct network, it would wipe the server.

They fired the information in an e-mail to the lawyers.

"Well, done just in time for dinner!" Brook commented, leaning back for a moment before they got up to head off. Both were a bit stiff, but less so since they now had a couple of nice ergonomic chairs, even if they were a bit pricy, it was worth it. Both had decided to pay for them out of their own money, instead of the general pack funds. Half joking, he added a message to the back of the chair, *Personally paid for by Adam and Brook, not pack property. If this chair is taken, you will be billed for it personally* and listed the price they paid for it, which he had initially balked at paying and had regretted the purchase until he had sat in it, and adjusted it, at which point he thought it was a good purchase. He doubted they would be taken with the note.

*****

After a dinner to meet up with their friends, Adam and Brook ended up curling up together, enjoying their alone time. The next morning, they were up at their normal before breakfast time.

They peeked their heads into their pup's rooms, they were gone, but from the scents, not by much. Adam frowned as they also checked Jess and Joshua's room, and also found it empty.

"Maybe they beat us down to the gym?" Brook asked.

Adam nodded, as they padded silently across the entry and down the stairs, continuously training to hone their stealth.

Arriving at the door, they crept in, and grinned as not only their six students, but several other pups were training under the gaze of Martin, who gave them a nod as they came in, not stopping the drill.

As they were past what was being taught and due to the limitation of space, Brook decided to do some advanced hand-to-hand skills with Adam; little tricks she knew but hadn't taught him yet.

*****

At breakfast, Adam sported a bruised cheek and Brook one just above her knee. Both were chipper, as they chatted with Sam and Lea this morning. Toby, Robin, Jess, and Joshua were also spread around their table, as they were heading to their range to work on some bows and crossbows for the morning.

As they left, Martin stopped them and pulled them aside, "Toby and Robin are almost at the level to be certified for hand-to-hand as trainers. Not much below that on the staffs right now. We normally don't certify them till they are of age, but we are short trainers on both those skills, especially for the pups."

Adam smiled and nodded, "We noticed that this morning with them keeping an eye on those around them."

Brook thought then asked, "You are looking for approval?" She realised what he was asking for, as she had done it a couple times to parents.

Martin looked relieved and nodded, "Right away for hand-to-hand, and for when they are ready for staff." Getting permission from the parents to have them certified early sometimes was an issue, or one where the parents tried to push too hard seeing how far ahead they were.

Brook looked to Adam and felt his agreement, "We're fine with it. They're not there yet for the bow and crossbow, but they seem to be getting better. Let us know of any other pups you think should join the training; we can do an advanced level for the pups if needed."

Adam grinned, "I have been delegating as much as I can of the tech duties, giving Chris and Aurora much of the server-side, and Erin the computer. Mostly, so I can start learning the Alpha skills to be Second, and because working with computers is so repetitive and boring!" Stopping and thinking for a minute; it was completely different than how he used to be! Before he could have sat in front of a computer all day without problem, "I think my wolf has really changed what I'm into and my interests."

Brook laughed, "It is known to happen. It shows you are integrating your wolf well into your mind, and as Second, it is a very good thing, it's also probably why you are able to pick up the fighting skills so fast."

Martin looked relieved, "I'll have to check with the Alphas for approval first, but it should be fine. Your pups were the ones who invited others to do the early training with them, after asking me right after the attack. The ones who have stuck around at this point are the ones which really want to learn; most are children of Thetas, and most seem to have some skills beyond what Thetas usually have. That includes Jess and Joshua." The ones he had asked to not bother showing up were the ones who decided they didn't need to work, but just liked how they could brag they were training with the Head Enforcer. Two, he had to threaten to have their goofing off count negatively towards their Enforcer application, and they hadn't shown up after that. Both he knew were thinking of applying, but were years away and a fair bit below the maturity he required.

Adam grinned, "I expect Jess and Joshua will pass the Delta exams. I found out after the attack, they took my order to get Chris and Steve to the saferoom to be a sweep for stragglers; they organised a quick sweep of the building with about thirty Deltas and Thetas. They actually found pairs of Thetas who had ignored the alarm and… well, were together. Even with having to bodily take them down, they were clear and the saferoom locked down within the normal window. I have already put in a commendation with the Alphas." He smiled wirily, "Being their parent, they don't get anything, but it does mean they can use it as a validation for their ranking."

Martin grinned, "I knew they came in with a large group, but not they had led a *sweep*. That alone would qualify them for all three parts of the Leadership trials. You sure know how to pick them out for help." He made a mental note to keep an eye out for what they are doing, as if he had known what they did, his notice of it would have earned them money, formal recognition before the pack, and/or some sort of special privilege or service. Some just collected them as future favours for a certain level of role, which they could even trade to other members, with approval from whoever is in the role currently.

Brook laughed, "Jess and Joshua were assigned to us when Adam moved in, we didn't choose them." She shook her head, "I would have had them under my protection, if I had known how hard they worked and they didn't have anyone looking out for them." She had never bothered gathering a Team, as she only ever expected to be a Trainer and had been mostly satisfied with it, as it helped contribute to the pack, but also left her with time for her own desires. For the Thetas, she had never had any which she felt anything special for, until these two. All the Thetas knew she liked and supported them all, so she had them occasionally asking for help, and she helped where she could, or arranged for others to help if she couldn't. Being Seconds, she was keeping an eye out for another who either needed their direct protection or was one who would do well with them, since their two seemed destined for a higher place.

*****

During the training over the next while, both Brook and Adam watched the six pups. Jess and Joshua looked ready to qualify, while Toby and Robin were spending half their time working with Lea and

Sam, adjusting them to be better. All six just needed to work on their own to get better and didn't need them to do much more. Adam and Brook worked with the harder targets, to get even better. Each target was only size of a palm and were at different angles.

Adam was using a recurve bow, while Brook was using a longbow. Both were challenging each other in a friendly competition of one shooting and the other working to match the shot. They had fun trying to make hard shots to trip each other up. Most they were able to make and those they missed, were missed only by a small margin.

By time lunch came around, they were all missing shots, and they called an end to it.

Heading in for lunch, Adam pulled Robin and Lea aside, wrapping an arm around each, "You're going to be working more with Chris and Erin now. We've been switching to doing more Second's duties now."

Both nodded, leaning into Adam's embrace as they walked towards the pack house, "We were expecting it to happen." Robin commented, "Thanks for letting us know. Can we still come to you for questions, or if we finish the work?"

Adam nodded, "Yes, you can." He replied, giving them a squeeze.

After a while of walking silently, enjoying the clean, cold winter air and the quiet, Adam commented, "So, Lea, you are enjoying the new room?"

Lea grinned, "Yes. I love it, even if I share it with Robin—I mean Sam." She cringed at the mistake, thinking he would make them split up.

Adam just laughed, "Brook and I thought you might share with your boyfriends," He teased, "We have no problem with you doing so. We expected you would; I take it you curl up together in one bed?"

Both Lea and Robin were blushing hard as they shyly nodded. Adam smiled, "Talk to Jess and Joshua if you want to replace the bunkbeds with a larger one; they can help arrange it."

Both nodded and blushed more, before Adam continued, "Having someone to curl up with is nice, and we both have no problems with it."

Even if they didn't remove the bunkbeds, they were larger than the human ones, and he thought they were a Full, if not Queen size.

*****

Lunch was a nice meal, enjoyed among friends. Brook and Adam spent the afternoon working on some backed up paperwork for the Alphas, and some involved the other packs. They were starting to take over the duties which the outgoing Seconds were not able to do or were becoming slow at them. Much of the paperwork had to be put into the computer. The Seconds had a hard time seeing the screen, and the typing was not very easy for them, so it fell to their replacements. Most of the work was of sensitive nature, so they could not use the tech-pups for it, and they were having to figure out what was too sensitive and what they could pass on.

The pups were quite happy to have important jobs of taking all the old paperwork and putting it into a computer form. Not only was the job itself important, they got to play with scanners and software to take the document and make it into something which was text and not just a picture of the text. Then they got to leave a permanent mark by making sure the documents were correct and with placing their digital signature on it as the one to digitize it, or the one who inspected another's work.

After the digital documents were confirmed as correct by a second check by a different person, once a week, they got to use the shredder! Many were being groomed to do sensitive tasks when they were older, so they had a special class which dealt with how to deal with sensitive or classified information. Adam had worked with Martin and a couple teachers to set up the objectives and let those who knew it work out the details. It was on how to determine if they can say anything, what sort of information could be given out to who, how to tell what sort of classification the document should have, and who to take it to if it has the wrong classification.

The Alphas quite liked it, Some would become the staff who supported the Alphas and the Elders, others would be those who managed the documents day to day, and others would work in other areas to keep their eyes out or be contacts for the secured documents in their area, so the Betas and Deltas could have someone trusted who could handle their sensitive documents, or to read over highly secure ones and pass on what they personally had a need to know.

They were being given extra physical training as well, so they could defend themselves as needed. Adam and Brook were waiting for the time they were qualified and could turn over the large amount of their paperwork to the pups as well. They had enough to keep them busy for years. There were old, archived records from the migration from their old pack in Scotland in the 1500s, and even a few records from before the trip which had survived the journey. It was enough to keep the pups busy for decades, which they all knew and were happy they had a position which helped the pack for as long as they wanted it.

*****

Dinner came not a moment too soon for Adam, as he saved the last document, and closed everything up, "Going to need to do something active tonight." He complained as they headed for the dining room, "I'm stiff!"

Brook laughed, "How about some more Were training?"

Adam grinned back at her as they lined up, "That sounds good!"

Sitting down at their table, they noticed the Alphas come in with Duncan and Keanna. They gave a short howl to get everyone's attention. Those getting their food stopped and turned to them.

"After dinner, we have an execution of the first of the attackers. David, from the Nameless Pack, had filed a false statement that Duncan had attacked him unprovoked. In fact, he was drunk and had attempted to rape Keanna when she refused him."

He had to stop as a loud, vicious snarl went through the pack. Duncan was standing tall, and Keanna was wrapped in his arms looking surprised. She looked very startled the pack was upset on their behalf. Many looked ready to attack the one who attacked them themselves.

Holding a hand got nothing, so Alpha Gareth had to howl to quiet everyone down, "Calm down." He ordered, pressing his power on the pack, "Duncan came to her defence and fought off the wolf. They were going to be both kicked out with nothing for the charge 'Unprovoked attack of a superior' and used for tracking practice till they were caught, then killed."

He had to again hold his hand against the feelings of the pack, "They snuck out and a heavy spring blizzard was the only reason they were able to escape and seek refuge here. Duncan requested a trial by tooth and claw for the attack on his mate and the false statement. I have granted it."

Gareth thought this would be going down as a story in a century, once those closest to it had recovered, and be a sealed record until they had passed, "As this was also the catalyst of the pack's downfall, it should remind everyone to always tell the truth, and never give false claim, even if you are at fault and in the wrong."

Gareth let his eyes sweep the room, seeing a thoughtful look on everyone's face, "That is all, enjoy your meal." He called, dismissing the attention and sitting down for his own meal of a raw steak, which he tore to pieces, because thinking about one of his wolves being attacked, even if it happened before they joined the pack, worked even him and his mate up. There was no way David was walking out of the ring. He had seen Duncan's skills at his training, and he looked to be excelling at them. He had heard from the trainers his motivation was to be able to better protect his mate. The trainers respected it and helped him learn the skills to do so, as best he could.

The whole pack seemed to be hurrying through the meal, not wanting to miss this, and to be there to support the wronged party. Both had become treasured members, even if they felt they didn't deserve being kicked out of their original pack. What talk went on was about it and the fact that such a small thing had escalated to the point of causing the downfall of an entire pack. Many of the facts of the chain of events were known publicly. It was also the refusal of the pack to allow members to leave which was the key decision which led to the pack being taken down.

*****

Adam and Brook moved to stand right behind Keanna and Duncan, along with Martin. The Alphas were on the other side of the dirt-floored ring which was in a clearing halfway between the caves containing those they had captured and the pack house.

Gareth nodded when the trickle of pack members ended, and he saw everyone who could make it was there. "Bring out the prisoner." He called out into the silence loudly. It was so quiet they could hear the echoes of his command.

Chapter 9 – Shouldn't Lie...

The crowd parted to allow David to pass, flanked by two guards in Were form. Many of the pack growled as he passed, showing their displeasure at his actions. It was a stark reminder to Adam of how different in some ways the perspective of a werewolf was from that of a human. In Canada, the humans had abolished capital punishment in 1976, other than for the military, which still had it available for some crimes until 1998. This was the first time he was seeing it, and what shocked him the most was when he had realised it, he was actually looking forward to it, even though he knew it was going to result in the death of a sentient being. This was completely at odds with his upbringing and human morals as he had been taught and was another thing which made clear to him, he wasn't human any longer. But his wolf totally was against allowing someone who's actions knowingly caused others to die, and even worse, the actions also caused his pack to be declared Rogue and thus the death of it.

David seemed to not care and ignored those in the pack around him. He stopped at the edge of the circle, and the pack quieted down.

The Alphas stepped forward, "We are gathered here to have a Trial by Tooth and Claw of David of the now Nameless Rogue Pack against Duncan of MacLaren Pack, who is also fighting on behalf of his mate Keanna. The charges against the Nameless Rogue Pack member are Attempted Rape of a Mated Wolf, and then Giving a False Report." The pack howled their approval of the reasons, with none there opposed or questioning it. Gareth looked at David, who looked belligerent, then at Duncan and nodded, "This is a fight to the death or submission. Begin."

Duncan stepped forward and into the ring and nodded at the alpha. David took a few moments before he did as well. Adam and Martin moved forward to flank Keanna, while Brook guarded her back, showing without words they supported her in whatever the outcome was. The would also be there to make sure she didn't interfere with the challenge in any way.

The rules which governed their fighting circle hadn't changed in over a millennia and were shared by all the packs they knew and knew of. If you refused to enter or left the ring under your own power, you forfeit the challenge and would just be killed. If you ended up outside the ring not of your power, you had to quickly re-enter to not have it count as a forfeit. It was hand-to-hand, unless it was stated to be a weapons fight, but with no restrictions given, they could use any shape they wanted. Nobody could enter the ring until the fight was over, as it was considering helping a side, and helping from outside was also prohibited. In both cases, it would earn the helper an instant title of Rogue as it was a breach of the fight laws and customs, and any watching were permitted to put them to death, if the other fighter hadn't already done so.

David started hurling insults at Duncan, who just seemed to stand there and wait as he ignored the taunts. The rest of the pack could hear the insults and the growls grew till the ground and air seemed to vibrate with the sound.

Suddenly, David lunged towards Duncan, moving fast enough many missed his start. Duncan was ready and tossed him over his hip and into the ground, where he rolled to the edge of the ring.

David snarled and tried the move again, and again was tossed nearly out of the ring.

Duncan just waited for David to come to him.

Good for him, let the enemy tire himself out in the attack. He loses nothing with the pack, while David can't seem to wait. Brook commented to her mate silently.

Adam could see that, *How long do these fights generally last?* he asked.

From seconds, to nearly a half hour. Extremely rare to go more than that, but the record I know about is nearly an hour, but the first third they stared at each other. Came the reply.

So, it is better to just wait for an opening to deliver an attack. Adam worked out, *It seems whoever coached Duncan had it right.* His wolf was watching out their eyes and was enjoying it.

David tried a third time and this time, David landed with a loud hit which many in the pack winced at, as it had to hurt.

It took a couple of minutes for him to get up, but he did. He started shifting to his Were and snarled. Duncan had shifted at the same time and snarled back.

You are just an Unranked. You can't defeat me, David commented in open, refusing to believe he had been already knocked down three times. Quite a few of the pack laughed; many Thetas in their pack could defeat a Delta, especially when they were fighting like he was. Many Thetas in the pack could see how the rogue was lacking many skills they had to learn. In many cases, it helped them with their confidence; they had the skills to help themselves until an Enforcer could reach them.

I have been promoted to Delta and have been training. Came Duncan's calm response, as he crouched as if to spring at David.

David could take it no more and rushed Duncan. Duncan stepped out of the way at the last minute but grabbed his tail as he passed, and with a quick slash of his other paw before David could respond, severed it with his razor-sharp claw before shoving David away, as he screamed at the sudden pain went from a pulled tail to a severed one.

Duncan calmly padded over to the edge closest to his mate and handed the tail to her, with a savage grin, *Here, I told you I would get you his tail as a present.*

Keanna openly grinned and nodded, taking the tail and stroking it, as the pack roared with laughter. Many had said something similar in anger, but he actually did it. The Elders traded a knowing look; it likely would become a pack legend now, how they had defeated the one who attacked their mate and gave his tail to her. Likely it would be passed as a warning to those who might think of rape, as no wolf wanted to have their tail removed. It wasn't something which would regenerate, and in their wolf form, they would also be missing their tail. If this action helped prevent the attacks in the future, it would be good.

The elders traded thoughts, while they outwardly just watched impartially, knowing this action of actually removing the tail and giving it to the harmed mate would make the rounds to other packs, and might even become a legend.

Duncan stepped to the middle and waited for David to come back up. He came with a flurry of paws and opened several nasty lacerations on Duncan, as he tried desperately to save his life. He seemed to stagger back, and Keanna screamed, as David came for her mate. It took all three to restrain her.

As David went to strike again, Duncan grabbed one paw and deflected the other, bending the one limb till it snapped and David screamed out in pain again as Duncan again pushed, this time tripping him, so he landed on his broken arm.

This is getting nasty, Adam commented to his mate, wincing as Duncan did the mirror move and broke David's other arm. It showed to him clearly a difference from humans, and how they responded.

Yes, but it allows him and his wolf to work out the aggression and pain from what was done to him and his mate. Look at Keanna, it is almost therapeutic to her. Brook commented; glad they didn't see this side of them often. Most were just short fights to take down the offender, not to cause them pain before they died. Martin was who they looked to, and the Alphas were also there, so it wasn't their place to say anything to Duncan.

Adam glanced over, and she had a look of relief and even a little of pleasure, as her mate nearly tore the other wolf apart. Turning back, he was just in time to see Duncan take a nasty bit to a leg, before jumping and landing on David's; the snap audible even to those in the back as the thigh bones snapped from the pressure, and David screeched like a dying animal.

I want his fur for a rug! And I don't mean figuratively. Duncan said as he looked in the pain filled eyes of the beaten wolf which seemed to just beg for death, before twisting his neck to put him out of his misery.

Duncan then stepped out of the ring and was immediately swarmed by medical staff who quickly put pressure bandages on the worst of the bites and lacerations, as his mate came to him, still clutching the tail. As a couple of others went to move the body, Duncan turned, *I did mean it; I want his skin for a rug, at least for a bit, for what he did. Not only did he attack my mate when she refused him, but then lied about the fact when I forced him off her, forcing us to run for our lives, thinking we'd be killed and forcing us to constantly need to hide and look over our shoulders—* Getting more and more emotions in his sending's before he was cut off.

ENOUGH! Commanded Alpha Maria, surprising everyone to silence and still. She was usually the gentle alpha; the one you went to for a hug, not the one who made the hard orders, *We get the picture. Do as he requested. Skin and then tan the hide. Do the same for the tail.* She ordered them, before taking a breath, before continuing calmly, "He also, from his actions, caused an inter-pack war. Then ignored a pack takedown, even after the remaining leader was killed in a fair fight, he still went to attack another, and when confronted, lied about even knowing Duncan and Keanna. As such, he is without honour and died a rogue. The rest of the remains are to be buried in an unmarked grave.. Maybe next time he will act better." She stopped to let it sink in before dismissing everyone, "That is all for this evening." She didn't bother saying this action was a warning to those who would lie and not fight honourably. She didn't believe there were any in MacLaren, but if there were, those who could contemplate rape would not listen to her words, so she saved her breath, but she was watching for it, always watching.

As Adam and Brook turned to head in with the rest, *Not for you two. We need a chat.* Came Maria's mind-voice.

They nodded and waited for many to leave before heading over to the Alphas, "You wished to talk to us?" Adam asked.

Maria glared at Adam, "Did you know Duncan would do that?"

Adam shook his head, "No, I didn't. He also looks to Martin, not us, now. They both do. It started when they began staying in the Security Centre following the attack."

Maria nodded, "OK, I will chat with Martin. I understand his thoughts, but turning a wolf into a rug is not nice." She shuddered. "I hope you aren't thinking of doing that too."

Adam shook his head, "A nice quick death for the white wolf, who still refuses to give us his name."

Gareth growled as he joined them, "He has refused to give us that, but has given other details about the pack, and what he was up to. He just refuses to give us any details about him personally." He had an idea who it was, but lacking any proof was keeping it quiet.

Adam's cell went off, and checking the name, announced, "It's Mark, the Second from the Arctic Shadow Pack." And at Gareth's nod, answered the phone.

"How's it going Mark?" He greeted.

"It has been a hard week, but we finally found the Wolfsbane. There is a keg full of the stuff, which is pretending to be beer." Was the reply. *"Luckily, we found the records about it, and where it was hidden, and we didn't try to drink it."*

Adam looked over at the Alphas, who would have heard what was said. They looked alarmed at the quantity. "One minute, I have the Alphas right here." He told Mark, putting his phone on mute, looking at them for direction.

"Go. Take Evan as he's trained to drive the LAV." Gareth started, then paused for a moment, "Take Toby and Sam for a ride along."

Maybe if the pups noticed those in security got to do interesting trips, they could get more interested. As it was, there was only a handful who were under a century old as Enforcers, and he wanted more, or it would start to be an issue in another century. Many had flocked to construction, or other physical jobs which were safer in the last few decades. With the number of Enforcers the pack had, the levels needed to be selected had risen far above the requirements, but as applicants dropped, so had the level needed, even if few had noticed. Now, if they even were close to meeting the base requirements, they would get into the training, where as long as they were diligent, would pass.

Adam nodded at Brook, as he started to run towards the bunker they kept the LAVs in, "I'm personally on my way, *as we planned*. In an armoured *SUV*." This was one reason they, like the enforcers, they always kept their packs close. He ordered Charlie to stay behind, as 8 hours in a LAV was not something he wanted to make him do for a simple pickup.

"*Right, Armoured* SUV," Mark replied, taking the hint, "*See you in a few hours.*"

Reaching the bunker, Adam entered the codes to get in and started prepping the vehicle.

He had just started the vehicle and moved to make sure they had the right restraint straps to carry the keg when the others ran up panting.

Evan smiled and unlocked the weapon's locker at the back, pulling out three assault rifles, clipped two into the racks in the crew area and the other into the one in the driver's area, before going to the ammo locker, removed already loaded magazines. He passed Adam and Brook four magazines each and taking the same, "From the amount of wolfsbane, we can't be too careful." He instructed, as it wasn't normal to have that much firepower outside of a major inter-pack battle, nor were the rifles legal in Canada. They rarely had them out of the hidden lockers. It also meant they had to make their own ammo, or work with other packs to smuggle it in.

Adam was stunned. He had just started to be trained to use the weapon, but nodded, as he moved to help the two wide-eyed pups stow their packs and get strapped in. Passing them his pack, "It should be a boring trip, but just in case something happens." Both nodded.

Evan came to the door again and passed each a handgun in a holster, "Just in case." He added, as he passed them even to the pups. He then passed two loaded clips to each as well, one was already clipped to his own hip, "Strap in. Brook will close up and then we'll be off." He advised.

"Do we need to trade off?" Adam asked.

Evan shook his head, "Just got up in time for supper and the show. I'm good. The Shadowed River pack house?" He asked, forgetting they were now *nameless*.

Adam nodded, "The *Nameless Rogue* pack house." He reminded him, as he strapped in beside the pups. They heard Evan climb into the driver's compartment, as Adam showed them the headsets, so they could talk, and it would protect their hearing as they drove. Adam looked at the pups and shook his head, not having wanted to have them deal with guns, but could see why it was needed. He loaded the handgun and showed the pups how to do it, before clipping the gun's holder to his hip, having already tucked the spare into his pack's pocket. The rig pulled forward a bit then stopped, and Brook was quickly in the door, and quickly closed and secured the hatch, throwing the compartment nearly into darkness and leaving just a strip of red LED lights lighting the compartment. He noticed she also had a gun strapped to her hip.

Once Brook sat and pulled the harness tight, Adam called for Evan to head out. "The first part is bumpy and a bit rough," He warned the pups, as the LAV rumbled down the trail to the road, as Brook pulled on another headset.

They were bounced around while on the trail, but the pups felt like it was just a ride and had fun. They 'awwed' as it levelled out and the engine sound changed, as they were on the road.

Adam settled down and leaned back against the headrest. They had replaced the padding in the seats to take it from painful to reasonably comfy. He told the others to relax as the drive was about four hours, due to the roads. He leaned back and dozed, having his wolf come up and keep watch.

*****

Arriving, the change in the pitch of the engine woke Adam up. Looking around, he noticed the other three were awake as well.

"Adam, Brook, it appears we have a problem," Evan reported.

"What sort of problem?" He asked, unstrapping so he could slip his pack on, pulling a gun down and attaching it to the harness, then loading the magazine and checking the other three were in the front of his vest.

"There appears to be three unknown SUVs are here as well. One, from the look, is even armoured." Came the reply, "I'm going to park with your hatch as close to the door as I can."

"OK. I'll check with Mark," Adam replied, grabbing a handle in the roof. He gave Brook a look as the LAV lurched into reverse and moved closer. She nodded and started getting ready too.

Looking at the pups, "Packs on, but belt back in. May have to go fast." Adam warned, getting nods in reply.

Mark? What's going on? Adam sent; he hopped the little contact was enough for his wolf to get his mental scent to directly link him.

We had three separate groups decide to try for the wolfsbane; and they took the bait of SUVs. We let them in, then took them down. Area is secure, come to the Alpha's office. Came the reassuring response.

Something still didn't feel right, and he shared a wordless thought with both Evan and Brook. Reluctantly, "If anyone enters that door except us, shoot." He advised, showing how serious of a situation they were in, and how much trust the Alpha had in them. Both nodded and pulled the guns out of the holsters, keeping them pointed at the ground as they had been taught.

They heard Evan pop his hatch and give them a mental *Clear* Before they released the hatch. Adam raced for the door and entered, checking to make sure it was clear.

There was one wolf there. He immediately lowered his weapon, "I'm to take you to Mark." Was the response.

Brook had quickly joined him but there was some gunfire and she had a hole in the side of the pack. *Hit the armour; I'm fine.* She advised at his glance, already shifting to her Were, and leaving the rags of her clothes behind.

Mark, was there a wolf to greet us inside? He asked as he expected to be greeted by Mark, not another, and he couldn't place the pack-smell; it wasn't Arctic Shadow. Nor was it Shadowed River, or any other pack he knew.

Ambush, Came the quick warning before the mind link went silent.

Ambush! Adam warned his packmates, as he moved to take out the wolf.

Brook moved to close the door behind them, *Evan, call the pack, tell them there was an ambush, get the other LAVs on their way! Have them call Arctic Shadow and get them to send help too. Toby, secure the hatch then pull the red handle down.* She ordered. The extra handle would lock the door, so it couldn't be opened from the outside. *When we get back, you will need to release the door from the inside; red handle first.*

Adam had shifted to Were, shredding his clothes in the process as his pack adjusted to fit his larger size, as he swatted the gun as the wolf tried to bring it up, snapping his support strap and tossing it into a wall, before using the other paw to swat his head, hoping to just knock him out.

Growling, he looked at the sprawled wolf, and hearing him still breathing nodded, and pulled out some cuffs to secure him. *We have to stay secure for four hours till we have reinforcements.* He complained as he strapped the wolf's gun to Brook's pack and handed her his ammo; they weren't going to leave anything which could be found, even if he was unlikely to get free.

Cradling the gun like a toy, he reached up and loosened the strap for his sword and knives. He liked the quiet of the edged weapons over the noise of a gun, but in this case, they were going for speed, and a gun could take out someone much faster from a distance than even his bow and arrow. He would have to shift back to human to use his bow; it just wasn't sized for his Were, nor did it fit his clawed paws. He made a mental note to get one which he could.

As he started to move, Brook kept an eye behind them, watching for more attackers. His repeated attempts to contact Mark went unanswered, *I think Mark has been knocked out,* He didn't want to think about what else could be why they couldn't contact him.

Both padded silently as they worked towards the Alpha's office, to see if that was where Mark actually was, or if he called the clear under duress.

*****

Twice before reaching the Alpha's wing, they took out the sentries. The first ones they were able to take out while he wasn't looking and secure him with just a bump to the head, but the second they had to shoot, as he saw them first.

Reaching the door to the Alpha's wing, there were four wolves guarding it.

How did you want to do this? Adam asked Brook, not really wanting to just kill them off.

We have no choice Brook replied, having seen it through his eyes, *There is no cover to get close to them to take them out. They will have felt the death so already be on guard. We both need to take two out fast.* She didn't like the wanton taking of life, especially not knowing if they were an enemy or not, but it had to be done.

Adam nodded, and moved to take sight of them; they were alert and watching, but hadn't seen them, *Got the two on the left*

Brook gave a silent mental acknowledgement, *Ready... Go!* she called, as they both quickly took out the fighters with single shots to the head.

They quickly padded forward, with Adam pulling a door open, and letting Brook take the lead, as he now watched their backs. Noticing several wolves tied up and gagged, laying down, he couldn't tell if they were just knocked out or worse. They moved in and took the two guards before they could respond, knocking them out, having put their weapons down. They grabbed cuffs and secured them.

Heading into the inner office, Adam saw one wolf with knife to a knocked out Mark's neck. As he entered his wolf took control and pulled the trigger, killing the wolf instantly, before he even realised they were there and weren't going to respond to their demands.

Coming close to Mark, he was able to hear him breathing and still having a pulse.

Alpha, Adam called, knowing he needed to update his pack, now they had a minute, *We had a nasty ambush here. Four alive and five dead attackers so far. Arctic Shadow wolves were bound up and knocked out. Second Mark was knocked out and had a knife to his throat. That wolf is not an issue. We are going to wait and protect them till reinforcements arrive, or they recover, before trying to find the Wolfsbane.*

Good work. ETA is three hours. I was able to contact some of the wolves who work in the police, and they are giving the LAVs and a SUV a police escort to your location. The Ambulance is with them. Anyone in need of immediate attention? Gareth quickly replied.

Adam glanced at Brook, as she brought the Arctic Shadow pack members inside the room, and using her claws broke the human-grade cuffs, and removed the tape from their mouths. She shook her head.

Not so far from our allies. Not too concerned yet on the attackers. Seeing the cut on Mark's neck, but the fact it had already stopped bleeding, wasn't concerned, *Nothing which a wolf can't handle without help, anyways.* he amended. From the bumps, they all probably had concussions, but they just needed down time to recover from it, as long as they woke up.

Good. Keep me apprised. If you find the wolfsbane, send it out right away in the LAV and we'll pick you up in another vehicle if needed.

Spending the next few minutes checking in with Evan and reassuring the two pups they were safe there, and no, they couldn't move out of the LAV to help. Adam went and gathered the first wolf who was to "escort" them in and the other who was still living. He put them in the outer office with the others they had taken alive, making sure their bonds were tight.

*****

What felt like several hours later, but likely was only one, Adam stopped his pacing when he heard a groan from Mark. Being a senior wolf, he expected his recuperation to be better than the others.

Adam moved close, but still out of reach, as he didn't know how Mark would react. He was glad he was prudent, as Mark came up swinging, and growling.

Careful, they knocked you out. Adam commented. *We need to know - where's the Wolfsbane?*

Mark blinked and shook his head, before holding it in his hands, groaning, "It's here They weren't able to make me give it to them before you arrived, once they gave up saying they were here for you. I thought we had them contained, but they somehow overpowered my wolves. In the safe behind me. Seven, Twenty-Five, Thirty, Fifteen." He sat up and leaned against the wall.

Adam moved to the safe and opened it. There was a stainless-steel beer keg inside. It was labelled as beer, but someone had written over it 'Wolfsbane'. He quickly grabbed it, passing Mark his gun, *Guard the door, those of your pack are in here. There are four of the attackers alive outside the door, bound up. We had killed five, including one who had a knife to your neck as we came in.*

Brook nodded, and started moving forward, leading the way, as they rushed to get it secured. This was enough to kill every werewolf on the continent and have some left over. Depending on the kind, for humans it might make them a little sick to being lethal, but any amount would kill a werewolf for sure. The run through the halls seemed to take forever, and seemed to stretch much longer. Both were expecting to have others try to ambush them.

Get ready to open the door, we have it. Brook called the pups.

Evan, head out as soon as we have it secured, we're waiting for the reinforcements. Adam called, following their orders. He silently was wishing Charlie was there to guard his back.

They received agreements from those waiting.

They reached the door and saw the LAV still in place, they rushed down. They called to have the pups open the door, and Adam piled in. Sam waiting with the straps ready; it was the work of seconds to secure it down.

Strap in now. Adam told Toby and Sam, jumping out. Both raced to get in the nearest seat as he slammed the hatch shut and secured the hatch from the outside handle. *You two are responsible to make sure it arrives safely.*

Go, go, go! Brook called, and then both had to duck their heads as the LAV sped off, sending rock flying as Evan floored it. Both headed back to deal with another wait for the reinforcements and to guard the other wolves.

Getting back towards the room, *Barrel is out and safe. We're coming back,* Adam called out in warning. He had pulled his sword out, deciding it was the best to have it in his paw. His wolf revelled in the fact it had been made just for them. It was a very big, very sharp, and very strong claw!

Arriving back in the outer office, Mark was sitting beside the one who had Mark with a knife, "We have a problem; this was one of mine." Mark commented passing the rifle back.

Adam stayed in his Were form, putting away his sword as he accepted the gun, as the weapon was almost too powerful for him in his normal shape to shoot reliably, *What is it? That was the one we had to shoot to prevent you from having your neck cut.*

Mark looked bleak, *This one is one of my pack.* He answered, *He was the one leading the prisoners to the cells as well. We now know what happened. I hope you trust those with the Wolfsbane.*

Adam strapped the gun back to his harness, and nodded, *The driver is a close personal friend of Brook and myself, and the other two are our pups. I would trust all of them with our lives.*

Brook came over still in the powerful Were form, *Just talked to Gareth, and having him personally receive it. Also, I let the pups know to not open the door till he's there to personally take it.*

Mark seemed to droop with a sigh, "That is good. Now, we just have to wait for rest of my pack to wake up." He walked back into the inner office and checked on them.

Adam sat backwards on a chair; being in Were with a tail, made it hard to sit in a chair designed for a human, not to mention they felt like they were made for pups not adults. *Our other LAVs and some other vehicles should be here within an hour or two; they have a police escort. They are some of our top fighters and will be here to help. Alpha Gareth notified your Alpha of the situation.*

Mark winced then sighed, "Well, I've probably bungled this job enough that I'm going to be demoted back to Beta. I let a packmate defect and cause problems for two packs. Especially since it involved Wolfsbane!" It didn't matter if he had defected before; he hadn't found him before he caused problems.

Adam winced in sympathy, *Ouch. I didn't realise they would be so harsh. If I did, I would have tried to keep it to just my pack. When you called an ambush and then went silent, we started moving and had it relayed back, so more could start immediately.*

Mark nodded sadly, "Yea, depends on how he takes it, since I am in my first decade as Second. May get demoted more or even suspended, even though I didn't get to pick those who came." Davis was one who he would never have had on a critical event, as there were enough times he was found to just barely do the job well enough to not get reprimanded. Likely, from his defection, he would be declared rogue and buried.

Adam sent a thought to Brook, who agreed with him, *If it gets bad enough, talk to us, and we'll put in a word with our Alpha for a pack *transfer.* Brook told him, *We don't take failure where you couldn't control it for demotion. You didn't know you had a traitor with you, or in a moment of trust, you were beaten, and you didn't get to choose them.*

Mark looked thoughtful and took a bit before replying, "I may just do that. I still am going to want to come and get a pack from you. They didn't get the Wolfsbane because I changed the code to the vault when I secured the wolfsbane in there. Since only I knew what it was, it is going to help my case." If he had lost the wolfsbane, he would likely himself would have been looking at a punishment of being declared rogue, and the best would be to be kicked out as a loner. He started to think about how to protect the others of his pack, as he watched over them.

The rest of his pack started to moan and wake up. They seemed to mostly just have bumps on the back of their heads, showing they had been taken unaware. Adam had a thought, *How many of your pack arrived here?* He asked Mark.

Twenty Five, why? Came the perplexed reply.

Counting heads, *Including you and the traitor, there are sixteen here* Adam replied, *That leaves nine unaccounted for.*

Chapter 10 – Problems

What!? Mark exclaimed, counting heads himself, before giving a mental groan, *This is much worse than I thought* It looked less likely he'd be able to hold onto being Beta.

Brook, let Gareth know we have nine from Arctic Shadow who are unaccounted for. Have the reinforcements and Evan be on high alert. Getting wordless surprise and agreement, he noticed Mark over at one of the dead looking them over.

This is very bad... I know this Beta; he is from Night Depths Pack. As are others. Mark replied, looking scared, *I hope it isn't this pack all over again,* Moving to another, *This one I knew, she had tried to seduce me at a pack gathering. I thought I recognised her just before they knocked me out.*

Brook exclaimed, and gave a growl, pulling her mate into the talk as she called Gareth, *This just went from bad to worse Mark has identified several of the dead wolves as members of Night Depths Pack*

Gareth seemed distracted for a minute before replying, *I just got an ultimatum from that pack to return the Wolfsbane. Apparently, they supplied it. Keep a watch out for further violations of the Inter-Pack Treaty. Night Depths pack never joined the treaty, unlike Shadowed River who paid lip-service to it, and as such isn't trusted. We can't touch them, unless they attack on our territory.* It felt like they were put on hold for a minute, *Reinforcements were advised and will be there in forty-five minutes. Evan now has a police escort back, so we should have them here in a *couple hours. He did say there was small arms fire as he left the pack area, so some are still out there.* There was also a silent thought tagging along of Gareth putting the pack to higher watch level, even if it wasn't a lock-down.

Moving to the other three bodies, Mark called out, *One more Night, and from the scents, the last was a Lone Wolf.* Moving to the living, *Two are Night and the other two are Lone's*

Adam flicked an ear in acknowledgement, and passed it on to Brook and the Alpha, before moving the Lone wolves away from the two of Night Depths. *I want to talk to these two first, and separately. We have forty-five minutes till the reinforcements arrive.*

Mark flicked his ear as he asked, *How many are coming?*

Twenty-four in the two LAVs, not sure on the other vehicles. Each of the LAVs were designed to carry a military section of twelve. It was a tight fit, as they didn't usually carry more than six at a time so they could shift to Were, but this time, the Alpha had sent the max he could. Hearing some of the wolves were waking up, Adam nodded, *You need to go deal with them. We need them to help do a new search when the reinforcements arrive. There was some gunfire as the LAV left.*

Mark grinned, "Got two sets of keys so far. I think they are for the three outside." As he came over to Adam, who was crouched beside the two lone wolves. Frisking them, "Found the third," he called, pulling up some keys on a neck lanyard.

Adam grinned, holding out a paw, *I'll hang onto that one. Depending on what they say, I might let these two go. Lone wolves have a hard enough time surviving, without taking their vehicle too. From their responses when attacked, they were reluctant to kill, which is how we were able to take them alive.*

Mark nodded and handed over the keys. Adam tucked them into a pocket on the front of his harness, while Mark looked on enviously, "I still really want one of those packs," he commented.

Adam panted a canine laugh, *Come back with us to our pack and we will get you one; we did promise you that we would.*

Mark smiled and headed off to see his wolves. Brook soon came out and joined him in the outer office, giving him a nuzzle as they watched the door and the wolves they captured.

They wanted to see what the lone wolves said. They would not make any decision about them until they did.

*****

*Second Adam, we're just pulling up at the front door. No gunfire so far, where are you?** Came Randy's mind-voice, nearly startling them. **We have the ambulance and the police vehicles at the edge of the property. Do you need them?** The human police were setting up a perimeter and limiting access to keep any humans who were unaware from entering. Parks officials had also been told to close specific trails in the area, for 'bears' but had been hinted there was a dangerous fugitive who was suspected in the area and they didn't want to have the public alarmed.

We're in the Alpha's office. Brook will guide you in. No medical needed, just have a bunch with nasty headaches and possible concussions. Adam replied, as Brook headed out the door, **I want sixteen to come in, with the rest secure the perimeter as you want. I'm going to pair them with the Arctic Shadow wolves and do a room by room sweep of the place. One is going to keep an eye on the prisoners.**

Yes sir.

Adam let Mark know, so his wolves could get ready. Very shortly, Mark's wolves came out, and Brook returned with their wolves. They nodded their submission to the two Seconds who were waiting. All had shifted to Were-form for their senses, strength, and speed. Each of the wolves from his pack wore their pack, with the armoured vest, and several carried an armoured vest which fit a Were and adjusted to fit all sizes well. The vests were quickly handed the Arctic Shadow wolves and shown how to strap them on. It would protect them from any attacks, and the high collar would help deflect attempts at the neck. It would also clearly identify those who Mark had cleared and were still under his command.

Pair up. Adam ordered. Everyone could feel he was stronger than Mark, so he had the combined seniority and authority, especially with Mark not challenging it. Very quickly they paired up, with one solid black furred wolf left, *Jesse, you're with me.*

She nodded and moved to stand near him, glad to get to work with the Second.

The rest of you are doing a re-clear of the entire building. If you find any wolves, dead or alive, they are to be brought back here. We have nine unaccounted for from Arctic Shadow who may be friend or foe, so be careful. Also, we have five from Night Depths. They refuse to agree to the Inter-Pack Treaty, so are to be treated as foes, but I want them taken alive and as unharmed as possible. Got it? Adam ordered, as Brook came to stand beside him.

There came a chorus of, "Yes sir!" from them.

Three pairs are to work to clear a hall, one pair on each side and one which stays in the hall and will handle any you find. Go. There was momentary confusion and some trading of partners, but they quickly scampered off to sweep the building. He didn't need to tell any of them this was basically a battle condition.

Adam put a paw on Jesse's shoulder, *You have the tough job. If they find anyone, you need frisk them all, make sure they are all secure, and then keep an eye on them. Brook, Mark, and I will be using the inner office to ask questions of them one by one. Think you can do that?*

Jesse nodded. Some of the males thought it was a nasty job of babysitting, but it was a very important one of great trust, as it was one which could mean a loss of untold intel and could either make friends or enemies. It also was dangerous. If one got free, it could be their death before they could warn another. She had no issues with it, and it was one where she would be working under the direct notice of the new Seconds.

Adam led the way with his paw still on Jesse's shoulder, *These two are Lone Wolves, we think.* motioning to the two close to him, *Those *two are Night Depths,** he motioned to the two closer to the bodies which had been laid out with respect.

Jesse started growling and nearly snarling. Her parents had moved to MacLaren from Night Depths as a protest over some of the policies they had. The stories she had heard were not nice.

Adam looked started, **What's that for?** he asked. He wanted them in good condition, if possible.

My parents left in protest from Night Depths over some actions of the leadership. They weren't the only ones. Was the comment, along with a couple of memories of scars she had seen on her parents for years growing up.

Adam blinked and nodded, **Just keep your claws and teeth to yourself over them, you can growl all you want, as long as you do your job.**

Jesse nodded and was going to act like the professional she was, her wolf still making a quiet growl heard. She would do her job and show the Seconds she was valuable. She was in the pool and had bet that within three decades Adam and Brook would have a pack of their own. If she did her job right, she could be a Founding Member of a pack, something very few ever had the honour of. If she did it bad, it could mean they might hold it against her and deny her joining.

One of the lone wolves was starting to wake up; the one who had greeted them at the door.

Brook picked the wolf up and moved them to the inner room, followed by Mark, as Adam nodded to Jesse before following them and closing the door.

Brook placed them on a comfortable chair, his hands still bound behind his back. If they tried shifting, they would dislocate both shoulder joints, if not also break bones, as wolf's shoulders didn't have the range of movement human ones did.

The senior wolves sat in chairs around him, watching the lone wolf like prey as he woke up. The wolf thrashed a little, before he realised he were bound up.

We have a few questions for you. I'm Adam, this is my mate, Brook, and friend Mark, who I think you know. Adam started. He decided not to tell their ranks, as it would both put him as a Lone Wolf at ease and a little shaky, since they all three would seem to radiate power and seniority. His nose would tell him Mark was a different pack than the other two.

Lone wolves rejected the protection and support which came from being part of a pack, some for the desire to be alone, others from a desire to not have to listen to anyone else. Some packs refused to do any support of any of the Loners. They usually wanted to live on their own, without leaders who could tell them what to do, but the consequence was they didn't get the protection.

MacLaren would help a Lone wolf who requested assistance, but usually there was some sort of payment demanded, which could be a number of hours of work, or just money. Sometimes it was nothing but was rare, and often when the Loner was way down on their luck. More often, it was something cheap and covered the time and effort at what it cost the pack. But the pack would only intervene when requested; no request and they were hands-off, since it was what they wanted.

The lone wolf seemed to look one to another, before the will to fight coming out of them and they slumping in defeat, knowing he couldn't fight anyone let along all three, "I had no choice! They threatened to kill my mate and pups!" He blurted out without being asked anything, seeming to try to explain his actions.

All three of them blinked and froze. They were not expecting this. Quickly discussing it between them, they would take a different route. All Weres would do anything for their mate and any pups under their care. Even Adam already was feeling it.

Adam sat down and relaxed, as the other two did as well, *Who is 'they'?* Adam asked calmly.

The wolf shook his head, "I don't know. I have been living between Arctic Shadow and Shadowed River packs in the neutral territory for the last fifty years. I know they were a pack, but they refused to even tell me their pack name. They just wanted you two dead for disrupting their ally and wanted the wolfsbane back. I was to take you to Mark, who would hand over the wolfsbane then the six of their pack would attack and get the wolfsbane back."

You said six from Night Depths pack? Mark interrupted.

The wolf nodded looking at Mark, "There was six from that pack, ten from yours, and two loners. Other than one from your pack, the rest either had threats or something else holding them to go against your pack."

One is still free! We only have five! Mark exclaimed. All three shared a thought. Mark and Brook notified the wolves patrolling there was one more Enemy, and the rest had been coerced to go against them. That made it a little harder, as they wanted to take them alive, but it also opened up the option for whatever force was required, as they should have asked for help from the Alpha or at least the Second there.

Turning back to the wolf, *Where is your family now?* Mark, asked. He was turning out to have just been in the wrong place and with a family.

His shoulders slumped, "Locked into our basement. There are two of that pack who took over the house and they give them only minimal food. They haven't let me see them since they took me, and other than my mate bond, I don't know how they are."

Mark spoke to his alpha, and quickly got a response: there were ten additional wolves being sent and should be there soon. Knowing two, he contacted them and found out they were already in the neutral area, so had them hide but stay there.

Spying a map rolled up, he grabbed it and with a sweep of his arm, cleared the desk, *Where is your place?*

Pointing to a spot, after taking a while to locate himself on the map, "There."

Mark gave a feral grin, *I have ten wolves as reinforcements almost right there. We'll get them to safety.*

Looking at the map, Adam nodded; there was a road which went almost there. *Get them to the road; I'll have an armoured SUV head there to get them away.*

Mark nodded, *Letting my wolves know...* he advised the two, as Adam had an SUV redirected.

They'll be in position in under an hour. Adam advised.

They turned back to the wolf, *I have wolves who happen to be close; they will get them out and Adam has a vehicle which will pick them up.* Mark told him.

They will be taken to MacLaren as our guests, and you will join them as soon as we can. Brook told him, having just talked to the Alphas, and worked out that part.

The wolf blinked a few times staring at them, before breaking down in sobs, "Thank you, thank you, thank you." He blubbered, nearly incoherent in relief.

All three nodded, *What is your name, and what else can you tell us?* Adam asked.

"I'm Dante. I don't know much more, as they didn't want to tell us anything. I think they expected you to kill me." He slumped.

Adam discussed it with the others, and released his cuffs, *For your information, it is Night Depths Pack who has your family. The wolfsbane has already been taken away and it will be destroyed.*

Dante put his face in his hands and groaned, "Why them? Why did it have to be them?"

Lone wolves steered clear of that pack, because they were the only pack in the area who agree to the Inter-Pack Treaty. For that alone, other packs didn't interact with them, so they had a habit of taking rogues who were still mostly sane, and in the last few decades, any Lone wolves they could get their paws on and forced them into their pack. Few escaped alive.

The packs around them had standing agreements to help any and all wolves to escape them, and even provide sanctuary for the individual pack members who renounce their membership in Night Depths pack.

Lone wolves were helped to relocate and get a fresh start outside the reach of Night Depths Pack. Reading the agreement, Brook had found there was also a mutual assistance clause in the case of being attacked. In the seventy-some years since the regional agreement was made and most of the packs signed it, Night Depths had been isolated with few packs wanting anything to do with them. She passed the memories to her mate, since she doubted he knew it already.

At this point, they couldn't join, as there were enough major violations which couldn't be overlooked. If they were to sign, it would be signing the death of the pack. The last attempt fifty years ago, where they were offered amnesty to that point, was rejected by the killing of the emissaries. That was when the agreement for the mutual assistance clause was amended to the agreement. A note which was signed by all members at that point was Night Depths was to be considered an Enemy Pack and taken down if possible was added.

The packs had decided a Were War was not something they wanted, as Night Depths had ties to some packs in Russia who were quite powerful, especially during the Cold War time. None had felt a need to change afterwards, so all the packs waited for Night Depths to attack before they would take them down as a response to the attack, and not be considered the aggressor. Since then, they had been mostly silent. Most packs would help individuals as long as they broke the bonds from the pack, as then they could be treated as lone wolves.

*****

Brook guided him out of the office and to a couch, letting Jesse know he too had been affected by Night Depths, but was being trusted. Dante just lay back and relaxed.

Let us know when the other lone wolf wakes up. Brook asked Jesse.

Heading back in, Adam and Mark pulled her into their conversation, Adam sent her his memories of what had been said. They were discussing how they could deal with the nearly rogue pack. The only thing which was keeping it from being taken down at this point was the tradition of each pack being autonomous, and not attacked without reason.

Along with their strong ties which could spark a Were War, they were waiting for them to attack.

We can be prepared, but we can't be the aggressors; we must wait for them to attack first. Looking at Adam and remembering what happened with Shadowed River, *Or well, trespassing and showing intent to attack first.* Brook slid in. She doubted the sensors would give them a surprise counter-attack again, and instead would just be there as one more way to detect the incursion at the edge of the territory instead of further in.

Adam nodded, *I agree, and since we have the wolfsbane and they have given us the ultimatum, it is likely they will attack us. As much as I don't want to lose anyone else, we are the best set up to repulse the attack with the minimal losses.*

Other Lone is waking up, and the two others are as well Came Jesse's call, putting a hold on the discussion.

Mark went and gathered the wolf putting him in the chair, *Careful, from the scent, he is nearly a feral rogue; he didn't smell like that before.* He stood behind the wolf, ready to restrain him, if needed.

The wolf shook then was suddenly awake, finding his arms bound up he snarled, "Release me, or you will be sorry!"

Adam just pretended to be relaxed and carefree, *Why should we do that? From your scents, you have no pack, and no mate. Also, you should not have been in a pack house. If you answer our questions, we may release you, or even offer sanctuary.*

Adam got another snarled growl, "I am a member of the Night Depths Pack. Release me so I can fulfil my orders."

Brook took Adam's hint and looked relaxed as if they were sitting around the fire pit and chatting, *That's strange, this pack area was the Shadowed River Pack territory, we are quite a ways away from what is claimed as Night Depths territory. What are your orders?*

A loud growl was heard, "Female, don't speak to me. You should be in the kitchen making food. l I'm hungry."

Adam nearly lost it and attacked, giving out a loud snarl as his jaws snapped a finger-width from the wolf's nose, *You don't talk to my mate that way. Answer her question: What are your orders?*

The wolf seemed to pale for a moment, as he was hit with the strength and anger radiating off Adam, before he got his composure back, "You don't scare me," He bluffed; he had nearly peed himself.

Linking the other two, they decided they weren't going to get anything from him, and not wanting to have him try to escape, Mark swatted his head to knock him out for transport down to the pack for the interrogators to deal with; that was one thing he didn't want to think of. The best he could see this wolf getting was a quick death.

Mark dragged him away, placing him beside the dead, *He says he's a Night Depth,* He told Jesse, *He's also almost rogue, too.* Getting a nod of understanding. Reaching into her pack, she pulled out the heavier restraints they had, and added them before removing the rope he had been tied up with.

Taking the one who was awake, he lifted him to standing, and guided them back into the office. The wolf was slow and limping but didn't fight or even give a protest.

He slumped into the seat, looking at his lap, "Just kill me now. I failed; the wolves are free and the wolfsbane is lost. That alone has signed my death warrant. The fact I am captured alive means it will be a painful one, so just kill me." He begged.

How about we don't kill you and offer you asylum or safe passage? Brook asked gently, *All you would need to do is break your pack bond.*

The wolf looked to Mark, "I didn't harm any of your pack, and tried to prevent others hurting them. Do you want me dead? We have been told other packs would rather kill us than look at us."

Mark shook his head, *I would never kill a wolf from Night Depths pack who is willing to learn the right way and had treated others with respect like you did. If I was an Alpha, I would accept you into my pack, but I'm not and my Alpha doesn't accept Night Depths. At most, I could offer safe passage through our territory, under escort.*

Our pack would accept you and has accepted others from your pack in the past. We would be willing to offer you a fresh start. Adam offered, already checking with the Alphas for approval.

The wolf started crying, before shuddering and passing out. Mark bent down and sniffed his neck, *He's fine, and I think you have his answer; he now lacks a pack scent. This is normal when a pack bond is snapped like this. He had to make it in his mind that he was not part of the pack and get the agreement from his wolf to snap the bond.* He bent down and released his restraints, and moved him to a soft couch, *You will need to take care of him, as he will need help till new pack bond can be made. If he had always been in that pack, suddenly not having pack bonds will be similar to losing a mate, but not as bad. He was willing to trust his safety to us.*

Brook and Adam shared a wince and would make sure he also went back with the first vehicle. Adam let Gareth know he accepted their terms and had already broken the pack bond. He was surprised to say the least and would deal with him when he arrived.

Adam went and gathered the last one. He fought the bonds, and he had the stench of fear. He tried to be gentle, but with his thrashing and being uncooperative, ended up carrying him into the inner office. On seeing the packmate not moving started fighting more, and the fear scent got stronger.

Adam dropped him into the seat, and Mark secured him.

"I'm not going to tell you anything! You killed Danny!" he yelled, fighting his bonds.

Is this Danny? Adam asked pointing at the wolf they had put on the couch in the corner, not having got to the point of getting his name.

"Yes! I can't feel him in the pack bonds anymore."

Adam released him from the chair, and carried him over putting him down near him, *He broke the pack bonds himself. He's just passed out in reaction to it. He'll recover. He was offered help if he left. Listen for his breath and heartbeat, he still lives,* Adam told him gently.

The wolf bent down as best he could, still being cuffed behind his back. He visibly calmed down and let his breath out in a sigh, when he realised he was still living before walking himself back to the chair and slumping into it. "We were told you couldn't break the pack bonds, only the Alpha could, and it would kill us instantly if we tried. We had been told other packs hated us and would kill on sight. So far you have treated us well, under the circumstances."

Mark crouched down near him, *It sounds like you were lied to. You can break your bond, as long as both the human and the wolf wish it. It is similar to having a mate die, and often, like Danny, causes you to pass out from the stress. It could do the same to you if the Alpha did it suddenly.*

We know you are going to face execution for your failure, if you return to your pack. Brook replied, Seeing he was being better, reached down and released his cuffs, *We are willing to extend the same offer to you of asylum and maybe even membership in MacLaren Pack, or at least safe passage to another pack of your choice, if you break the pack bonds.*

The wolf rubbed his wrists, as he thought it over, "I'm Leon. How do I know you will not hurt me while I'm out?"

Adam breathed out a sigh, *Well, Leon, you will just have to trust us; we haven't harmed you when we knocked you out the first time. What does your wolf say?*

Leon looked at him with hope and even trust in his eyes, "He says we can trust you and wants to be free of our pack. I'll do it." He said, before closing his eyes, and not much later, they had to grab him before he fell out of the chair. Adam laid him down on a thick rug which Brook placed down near Danny.

*****

The three senior wolves decided they needed some rest and organized so Adam took the first shift, Mark the next, then Brook took the third. The two not on duty curled up and went to sleep, while Adam headed out of the office, to check on the others out there. He saw Dante was awake and sitting up. He crouched down beside him, *Not able to sleep?* he asked gently.

Dante shook his head, "There's fighting above my family, but it seems to be quieting down." He replied before seeming to listen then a big grin lit up his face as he threw himself at Adam and only his fast reflexes keeping him from being taken down, as he started sobbing on Adam's furry shoulder, "Thank you, thank you." He kept sobbing.

Mark glanced in, having felt his surprise, but was just amused, *I guess he heard; his family is safe and being escorted away from the house. Two wolves are staying to protect it from looting, the other eight are headed here once they get the four to the vehicle.*

Adam flicked an ear back as comment, before just letting the wolf calm himself. "Wish I still had my keys." Dante sighed after a while.

Adam reached into his harness pocket, *These keys?* he asked, like a conjurer.

Dante grabbed them, "Yes! I want to leave and meet with my family!"

Adam nodded, *Yes, and I want you to take Danny and Leon with you; they have broken their pack bonds and may join my pack. You and your family are welcome to join as well.*

Chapter 11 – New Pack Members

Dante nodded, "I can do that. Tell them to come."

Adam looked as sheepish as a wolf can, *They are sleeping off the snapping of their pack bond. They should be up around dawn. Can you wait till then?*

Dante nodded, "If you have food?" He begged.

Adam panted some laughter, reached into a pocket, and pulled out an energy bar, and offered it, *Unless you want a MRE, I just have more of these.*

Dante shuddered at the thought of MREs and took the bar, "This should be good till we arrive at your pack."

Adam nodded, *Ask for some food when you arrive, and the chefs would make you something, or there is a buffet which is kept going all day and night.*

Dante curled back up on the couch, "Well, I'm going to get some more sleep before morning." His family was safe, and soon they would be reunited under the protection of a pack. His family was in the vehicle, with an Enforcer, heading to the pack.

Adam nodded and checked around the outside, taking the reports as they finished clearing the building. They had found three unconscious wolves in the lower level and from the multiple hits they would be out for a while, and two more in the lockup, pissed off they had been betrayed.

Randy, is the outside clear? Adam called, having had left him with the outside to clear.

*I was just about to inform you. We just had a firefight when we stumbled across where the wolves had been holed up. One dead Night Depths, two seriously injured Arctic Shadows, two unharmed but petrified Arctic Shadows. The two injured were just found and we are taking them to the ambulance. *

I have three who need to get medical attention, as they appear to have a bad concussion. Adam replied thinking fast, *I'm just going to send the three in one of the captured SUVs with the ambulance. They are going to be leaving here shortly.*

He quickly went and shook Mark awake, getting one of the keys. The group leader was almost at the door when he passed him the key and told them they were convoying with the ambulance. The three injured were being carried down the hall, and Adam just nodded. Mark was at his shoulder and mentally checked them off his list of missing.

The two who had been locked up, came in behind and knelt down in front of them, "We betrayed the pack." One said, the other was just white, knowing their pack's rules for what they did.

Mark looked at them, *I want to know why you did it* Adam took a step back, as this was mostly internal to their pack, he was going to watch, and maybe advise Mark, but was not going to interfere. *Cody?*

Cody sighed, "Davis told me the ones we captured were being released. I challenged him and he knocked me over the head. I came to just as his pack," He nodded his head at Adam, "Came to release us."

Turning to the other, *Charles?* Mark prompted.

"When Cody was hit, I decided something was up, but before I could even send you a warning, I too was hit."

Mark sighed and looked to Adam for his input, he didn't know how to handle this, as he had just been promoted as well, when the old Second died protecting some pups on a run, and the Alpha had said this was his trial; with how bungled it was, there was no way to keep the position.

They didn't disobey orders, and when an order they believed was forged came, decided to check on it first, and were knocked out before they could alert you. I suspect it was the same for the other three.

Mark nodded, *You were following orders, and were betrayed by your Beta. I will take the ownership of that. Relax in the office here, Second Brook is asleep in the inner office so keep it down.*

The two other wolves were escorted to them. Adam dismissed their escort with a nod, as they as well submitted to their highest ranking here, thinking they were about to be killed for their failures. Both reeked of fear.

Mark just gave them a look and they started babbling.

"Davis gave us orders to attack any vehicle or person. When you were knocked out, we realised it wasn't right, as I recognised Adam and Brook, and this being a correct pickup. We were threatened and stuffed in a cave by Kane and Benji. We were told that if we called out, we would be killed. We saw Kane and Benji get shot by a wolf after an argument, before they were taken out by a MacLaren."

Mark growled to Adam, *I think these two were also duped. Seems a good thing Davis is dead, as he'd be getting much pain before he was killed if not.* No pack liked a traitor. And on top of that, one who was dealing in wolfsbane.

Adam nodded, *I just let Alpha Gareth know there is inbound injured, and they were questionable, and to hold all five in the secure isolation rooms. He told me it wasn't the first time they had wolves come in and they weren't sure if they were friend or foe. They'll be ready for them.* Letting out a yawn, *Both parts of me are tired, so we're going to go curl up with Brook, you handle things for the next few hours, or hold them till Brook's up.*

Getting a nod, Adam let Mark know the two former Night's were going with the one Lone back to MacLaren as soon as they woke up, and to have Randy assign them an escort and navigator to get them there.

Yawning again as the long day and night caught up to him, he headed to the inner office and had barely enough energy to pull off his harness and pack before he snuggled against his mate and went to sleep.

*****

Brook shook Adam awake gently, later in the morning. She had shifted to human, "Time to get up."

Adam yawned and nodded getting up, and shifting down to human, pulling on some shorts, foregoing a shirt. It would allow his wolf to continue slumbering in his mind, so at least one was fully rested. It was one downside to the Were-form, it tired out both minds, leaving neither fresh to guard their body after an extended stay in it, which was the only reason he didn't spend all the time he could in it. If he needed to shift fast, he didn't want to waste another shirt. "Anything going on?" he asked.

Brook shook her head, "All quiet. We need to discuss the plans then get back. Randy can coordinate the control. We're taking over here."

Adam nodded and stretched, before pulling his pack on and securing the harness.

Looking around, he saw Danny and Leon were no longer there and walking out, Dante was also gone. "The three head out already?" Adam asked his mate.

"They left at first light, a couple of hours ago," Mark commented, walking over to them. "I've organised the dead. Davis got buried for betraying his pack, the five Night Depths were just following their pack, so were burned. Your pack is tending the fires to make sure there is nothing left. They'll scatter the ashes on the wind." He shook his head at all the death. Some was being collected to be returned to the pack. He had let them know to make sure it was put in the Urn of Remembrance before they left and let him know how it went. He almost expected the Alpha to refuse to let them be added, so had asked for a second portion for himself. He would beg whatever pack he ended up in to accept them. Since they died under his command, it was the least he could do to see they were remembered by a pack and not forgotten.

Brook took over the updating, "We have the updated orders: Randy is taking over with his wolves. We will be taking the SUVs back, along with one of the LAVs, shortly. Many of the Arctic Shadows are already heading home. The rest will be shortly."

Mark sighed, shoulders slumping, "For my role, I've already been demoted to *Delta*. Through Brook, I've arranged a meeting with your Alpha for a pack transfer." He had even been stripped of his Enforcer designation.

Adam pulled him in and gave him a hug without thinking, "It sounds like your Alpha is blaming you for it."

Mark leaned into the hug, "Yes, but it was also to protect the others from censure as well. The Alpha is one who mostly cares about results. If I let the others take the fall as well, I could have stayed a Beta, but when so far it seems they were knocked out before they could report, it seems they shouldn't be held accountable." Getting a glint, "But I do want to hear what Kane and Benji say; they may have had something to do about it. I'm thinking the other three were duped but will need to hear their side. The four others have already gone back with most of the others and will be getting further training on how to prevent it from happening again. The rest are handing over to your packmates and getting a meal before heading back."

Brook smiled, "Happier news: both the two former Night's and the Lone family are considering joining the pack. We sent some wolves to help pack their place up, and they will be moving into the pack's territory for now. They decided to take an outlying cottage. As we are their sponsors, we have to be there for their final decision and swearing in." She understood them not feeling safe in their current place and wanting to at least move, which Gareth had promised the pack would help them do.

The feeling of having new pack members join was one of the happiest feelings he felt, only second to feeling the mate bond settle in, bonding with the pups, and joining with his wolf-mind. Adam just gave a nod.

Brook looked around at the old paint, badly patched holes, and warped doorframes, "I was considering if this place could be refurbished, but from much of the condition, it has not been well maintained and had weak construction from the beginning. If it wasn't for the mountains in the way, it would have major borders with ours. I'm thinking we should discuss it with the Alpha, to hang onto the territory, which is why I suggested taking over the guarding of it."

Mark led Adam to a makeshift canteen, had him sit down, got him a big plate of food, "I could hear your stomach growling!"

Adam gave a small playful growl at the teasing and started to wolf the food down. A busy night awake would leave anyone hungry! With their Were-metabolism being higher than a human's, he was very hungry. To him, it seemed like being in Were form ate energy even faster than being in Human or Wolf. Mark brought him another plate, before he could get up. Nodding his thanks, he grabbed it after taking the last of the food off the first.

Once he was done eating, he stood up, as his dishes were whisked away by a helpful Theta who had come with the latest forces, and Mark guided him out the front door. Brook was waiting there for them, along with a few other wolves, chatting with Randy and Jesse. The one near-rogue Lone wolf was escorted and secured in one of the SUVs, which had been configured for prisoner transport.

Jesse was heading back with them. Since she had got a good sleep and was rested, she would be driving. Brook grinned at Jesse, as they took the two front seats, making Adam and Mark sit in the back.

Shrugging as he did his seatbelt up, "Fine with me, I can nap on the way back!" Adam commented, as they headed out. He wiggled a bit to get comfy.

Both Jess and Brook laughed, and Mark just commented, "Sounds like a plan!" in agreement.

Both of them had dealt with the issues over the night and let Brook rest. She was welcome to have female time with Jesse on the way back while they got more rest.

Adam had asked his wolf to nudge them when they were just pulling into the parkade but was startled when Brook squirted the window hard right by his head as she did the mandatory wash. He could hear her chuckling in her mind over it. He grumbled for a moment, while he stretched, feeling fairly rested, if a little stiff. His wolf had also been startled awake by the spray; it seems his wolf had slept too.

Brook hopped back in after hitting the release for the inner door, to let them into the parkade. The fact every vehicle was washed before entering really kept the dust and dirt down in the parkade and allowed for an inspection. Since this was one of the two SUVs from the Lone wolves they confiscated, they had to go all the way down to the third level to park in one of the few unassigned spots.

Hopping out, all four had a good stretch session, after being cooped up for several hours. Adam came up behind Jesse when she was done and gave her a good hug, "Thanks for the smooth ride back! I think I slept the whole way!" he commented as Brook came over with a smirk.

"You two were sure snoring up a storm." She commented.

Mark just shared a smile with Adam. Both knew to just let her be right, "I did get a nice rest, to catch up for my missed sleep from last night! Thank you."

They all laughed as they headed up the stairs to the first level and the tunnel back. They chatted as they jogged the tunnel; the three alternating a sprint ahead to open the isolation doors for the rest, just to get some exercise. As Mark didn't have an ID yet, he couldn't get the doors.

Reaching the building, Adam and Brook got Mark a temporary visitor ID. While they waited for that to be done, they chatted with the guard on duty and picked up the latest pack gossip. Once Jesse had checked in, she headed off on her own. She had been given a day off for the overnight work.

Charlie came barrelling down and nearly took out Adam, he was so happy. Adam had to stop and take a few minutes to calm him down and reassure him before he could be introduced to Mark.

They told him the public information about their 'dogs, as they took him for his informal meeting with the Alpha. Being so senior, he was brought right in. The walk took twice as long, as there were many of the pack who wanted to hug the, still Acting in name only, Seconds and welcome them back.

Jess met them just outside the Alpha's wing and took Adam and Brook's packs from them, for repair in Brook's case, then cleaning and refill, so they were ready for next time. She passed them some clean clothes for all three, and they ducked into the Alpha's meeting room to change, tucking the dirty clothes into a hamper bag Jess had left Adam would toss them in their laundry basket when they had a chance.

Knocking on Alpha Gareth's open door, they walked in, before Adam and Brook took a step to the side. Mark moved to sit at the desk as the Alpha looked up, "One minute, checking some budgeting". He commented, as they took seats. Charlie lay down beside Adam, not wanting him out of his sight. Adam had left him behind as they were supposed to just do a pickup and cooped up for eight hours with barely a bathroom break was not kind to him. If they knew they were going to stay and have to fight, they would have taken him with them, regardless of the issues it caused.

Mark was a bit nervous, but the fact the Seconds supported him helped. Even though they were still Acting-Seconds for another couple months, they seemed to exude as much confidence and seniority as the Alpha did, but they did defer to him.

Gareth looked up when his mate walked in. All three stood in respect, and accepted hugs, before Maria sat down in a seat beside her mate.

Gareth turned his computer monitor away, and started without any preamble, "Brook told me your pack is demoting you from Second to Delta for your loss of control of the situation, and you would like to transfer packs. I want to hear your side, Mark." He stated, leaning back, and taking his mate's hand in his.

Mark took a deep breath, "Well, I would have been demoted to just Beta, but I was looking out for the others. Twenty-three were knocked out, and two were brought here with serious injuries. Most are just getting a slight seniority reduction, but there were four who were going to be dropped to Omega in all but name. It wasn't going to be fair for them to have that because of one Beta who had defected. As we weren't able to take him alive, and I was still living," he turned slightly to Adam and Brook, before turning back to the Alphas, "Thanks to these two, they were taking the fall. I was the leader for the assignment, so I should take the heat not those who were just doing their job and got in the way."

Gareth shared a nod with his mate, and grinned, "Then Arctic Shadow's loss is our gain." He was protecting his packmates and taking all the blame on himself. Both him and his mate thought it was a good reason, even if they didn't agree with demotion for the failure of the taskdue to something outside of his control, since he was still on the trial period for the role.

Pulling his phone close, he grinned at Adam, "Lea taught me how to access my contacts in here this morning!" As he pulled up the entry for the direct call to the Alpha of Arctic Shadow, turning it to speaker mode. She had also helped him get the few direct numbers he called often into it. The rest he could do himself as he had time, but it wasn't a priority.

"Rufus. I take it you have Mark there, Gareth?" Came the booming voice from the phone.

"Yes," Gareth replied, "We have decided to accept his pack transfer. How do you want to do this?"

The transfer between packs was touchy, as the wolf could snap his bond with the agreement of his wolf, as could the Alpha with any of his pack members, but it was painful for both. To the Alpha, it was the same as if they died, but to the member, the loss of the pack bonds usually knocked them out from a half hour to a day. The snapping of the bond reverberated to the rest of the pack and could be felt by all. Releasing a pack member with both in agreement was much gentler, and although it was felt by the other members, it was just a ripple rather than a large wave.

"Mark?" Rufus asked, making sure he was there.

"Yes, Alpha?" Mark asked.

"Do you wish to leave the Arctic Shadow Pack, and go your own way?" Rufus asked. Everyone could hear he didn't really want to release him, but knew he had no choice; a wolf could decide to leave the pack when he wished, it was one of their oldest laws. He had always run the pack where even the Alpha wasn't above the laws.

"Yes, Alpha; I wish to leave the Arctic Shadow Pack." Mark said, tears running down his face, knowing he was leaving his family and friends behind.

"Then I release you and consider your oaths fulfilled." Rufus said with a sigh, "You will be considered a Friend of the Pack and will still be welcome to visit here."

"Thank you, Alpha Rufus." Mark said with feeling, and all could hear the loneliness in his voice; he had no pack for the first time in his life. He was grateful he was being permitted to visit the pack still. Some Alphas banned wolves who left from even communicating with their former packmates.

Adam had his arms wrapped around him before he realised he had started moving, giving Mark some comfort.

After a while, Mark moved, and Adam returned to standing beside Brook, as the witnesses. Gareth and Maria moved to stand in front of Mark, each putting a hand on his shoulder, "Do you wish to join the MacLaren Pack?" Gareth started. The oaths were the same, but this time, Adam didn't have to catch him, he had only to steady him, as he caught his balance, and they could hear and feel the welcome from the pack, as everyone felt the new pack bonds form. They sat him back down, as Adam lifted the temp ID's lanyard from his neck and placed a permanent one showing his rank as Beta, which was why it took them longer to make IDs.

Mark sat there with tears of pain and loss turned to joy for a bit, before wiping his eyes and catching his breath, "I don't want to go through that ever again; that was painful! It felt like part of me was ripped out!"

"I've heard it feels to some extent similar to loosing a mate," Maria commented softly, "Which is why we decided to do it now and have you a Lone Wolf for as short as we could.

Glancing down at the ID, "Beta?" Mark commented, "I don't deserve this."

Gareth raised a hand, forestalling any further objections, "You do. We need strong wolves like you. You were quite willing to give up your position and rank just to protect the wolves under you, even when the reasoning behind that demotion was not fair to you. I had called and discussed it with Rufus before this meeting. He has to wait for some of the elders to pass before he can change his pack laws to not ignore circumstances, and he privately agrees it was not fair, even if it was your trial as Second. There are just too many powerful members who felt you failed in your duty to the pack, and to change it would cause the pack to dissolve into chaos. It was why he didn't try to entice you to stay. He wanted to give you a chance to stay at the rank you deserve, not the one which he would be forced to leave you at for at least several decades and possibly make you become disgruntled." The rule about demotion for failure was one which was even written so the Alpha couldn't use the 'Alpha Law' to override. Rufus had been trying to change it for decades, but the elders kept the pack from letting him change it.

Nodding to Adam and Brook, after a minute or two to let it sink in, he continued, "I can't offer you the same position again, as that one is filled. I can offer you a good position. For now, you are part of Adam and Brook's support staff. You will help them transition into the Second role. Right now, we don't have a free Beta suite, so we have you in one of the auxiliary rooms in the Senior Beta's wing. Once the outgoing Seconds move into the vacant Elder's room, and Adam and Brook move into the Seconds' suite, we will move you into the one they currently are in."

Mark nodded, ducking his head in respect, "Yes, Alpha." He replied, seeing already how he would be valued. He expected Adam and Brook to have their own pack, so if he kept up his skills, he might even wrangle Second when they split.

"Did you need anything from Arctic Shadow?" Maria asked, "We have you covered for the week with clothes already. You will be given time next week to go up to pack and get your property from the previous pack, if you wish."

Mark shook his head, "Daniel and Kyle owe me. I didn't report they were petrified but conscious. I just said they were unable to tell me, so they got off easy and know it. I'm going to see if I can have them do the packing, and if they can bring everything down. I'll call them later."

Joshua walked in, "You called, Alpha?" He asked respectfully.

Gareth nodded, "Show Mark here to the room I had you prepare this morning."

Joshua nodded, "Yes, Alpha."

Adam stopped them for a moment, "Gareth, should we get him a laptop?"

Gareth smiled, "Good idea!" he said in agreement.

Adam turned to Joshua, "Help him sign out one of the spare laptops. A high-end one. I'll get him the software later. Once he's settled, show him around the public areas of the pack house."

Mark was surprised, but before he could ask any questions, Joshua ushered him out of the office, and Adam and Brook sat back down.

Gareth leaned back, "I have the basic overview of what happened from the wolf who came back with the three this morning, it seemed that you had a busy night. Why don't you give me what happened from your sides?"

The discussion was long as they had to discuss every detail. Gareth let them know the medical lab was working to develop a way to break the wolfsbane down and render it inert. Most of it was currently locked in an ultra-secure vault, inside the saferoom. The lab had only small samples of it, and the lab's security was almost that of the saferoom's. It seemed the way it had been made it would turn into a gas fairly easily, instead of breaking down, as they expected, so was taking much longer to figure out how to dispose of it.

At the end the Alphas sat back, "Well, it seems Night Depths is going to be pissed with us; not only did we get the wolfsbane, but they lost nine members, which doesn't even include the three lone wolves. It's good the pack is at heightened alert. We have frequent patrols on a random schedule, and more watching the cameras. I know from experience that death and the snapping the bonds the way Danny and Leon did feel almost the same to the pack unless you are looking for it."

Danny and Leon were led into the office by a Theta wolf Adam didn't remember the name of. Both were looking much better. Both had a chance to get a shower and fresh clothes. They were looking much happier as well.

"Danny, Leon, welcome." Alpha Gareth greeted them with a hug, before the other three in the room did the same. "I have discussed it with Adam and Brook, and they are willing to stand as sponsors for you. From what I have seen, they have an Alpha's ability to judge nearly on a moment's notice a person's ability." Taking a breath to look at his mate, "From our discussion this morning, we agree with them. Are you still wanting to join this pack?"

Both could barely speak as they nodded; they were overcome with emotion. Both could feel the happiness around them and how the pack worked together for the betterment of all and had decided they wanted to stay for the protection it represented. Both hated the chasm in their mind from not having a pack.

*****

After they have been brought into the pack and had been escorted to rest before the introduction, Dante and his family were shown in, and the parents gave their oaths to join the pack, with a second oath to stand in for the three pups, so they could be brought in. The oldest being only ten, was too young to bind to any formal oaths; they would give theirs on their twentieth birthday, as did all the pups born into the pack. The parents were also expected to teach their pups how to act, and what the rules were.

By the time they had recovered, it was almost dinner time. As they had several new people, the chefs had fired up the barbecues and had been making food for the pack to welcome them. They were very much surprised at how happy the pack was to get new members. Danny commented Night Depths didn't even do the greeting, let alone a greeting party. He liked it, as it gave a chance for everyone to come together in a relaxed environment and meet the new wolves. Adam was chatting with Dante's oldest pup, as the pup was curious about why he had Charlie, when Jake came up for a hug and wanting to meet the new pup. After introducing him, Jake grabbed his hand and scampered off to show his new friend around.

Dante had seen it, "He's already making friends, excellent." He commented to Adam as he came up to him, giving a friendly gentle shoulder bump. At Night Depths, he would never have done that to a Beta, let alone the Second, as they would take it as an attack, and at best he would have been beaten. Here he could see it was considered an affectionate contact.

Adam smiled, "They know to stay close, and not to go past the treeline without an adult. If they do, they are restricted to the pack house for a week. All the adults keep an eye on the pups at gatherings like this, as they are the future. Jake is one I'm keeping an eye on, and he's very responsible for his age."

Dante looked relieved, "That's good, hope he keeps my son out of trouble."

Chapter 12 – Tests

The next morning Adam knocked on the door to the room Mark had been given, and just got a sleepy growl in response. *I guess you're not wanting breakfast.* Adam commented privately to him. He hadn't even counted to five in his head when he heard a thud of him getting up.

Less than a minute later, a sleepy Mark opened the door, "How can you be awake at such an hour?" He grumbled, as they headed for breakfast. Brook fell into step with them as they left the wing.

Mark made a beeline for the coffee pot. Everyone could see there would be a fight if he didn't get some, moved out of his way with respect, but clearly amused. One even handed him a fresh over-sized mug of it with a smile before pouring himself another, and the sheer look of bliss he had when he took the first sips had Adam nearly laughing out loud. Several there chuckled or made amusing comments.

After making his selections from the buffet line, he made his way over to Adam's normal table. Sitting down with their friends. He took a taste of the sausage and gave a moan of pleasure, "I haven't had sausage like this in years!"

The table laughed, "This is a normal breakfast," Adam commented, amused.

"You have some excellent chefs here," Mark commented, "I don't know how you stay fit."

"We exercise and go for long runs. It's also healthy food. To keep our costs down, we grow much of it ourselves, and we arrange with another pack to supply us the meat and we have a slaughterhouse in town. We don't have much pastureland here to deal with cattle." Brook replied. "Don't eat too heavy; we're checking out your physical training this morning."

Mark nodded, "With who?"

"Us, of course." Adam said before grinning, seeing some colour drain from his face. "Come on, we're not that bad! You have to be tested to make sure you are up to this pack's standards." He commented with a smile.

Jess sat down beside Adam and leaned into a cuddle he gave her in greeting, "Could be worse; they could be disciplining you."

Steve shuddered, "I had to *crawl* out of the ring after a round of staff with Brook!"

Brook gave a feral grin, "And I was going easy on you, since you're human." She laughed when Steve shuddered again, as again he made a mental promise to never give her a chance at getting him into a ring again.

Joshua sat beside Mark, "At another pack, Adam disciplined a wolf and nearly had him in tears just from the stories he told!"

Mark shook his head, "I heard of that one. Our—well, Arctic Shadow's—Elders were talking about it non-stop, and how it was such a novel way, especially for how it happened; doing the physical punishment while telling him how similar actions had caused packs serious harm." He shook his head. "That Mark is still going to have issues." They had talked about it, even though he was out doing the work at another location.

Adam smiled, "More of, I think he's going to think before he decides to do something. He was on his first patrol as a lead, and he only got it because his parents had been leaning on the ones that set the patrols." He grinned at Brook, "I more enjoyed the discussion I had with his parents when they thought to yell at me for bringing the charges to their son when we stayed to the group introduction."

Adam brought those listening into a mental rapport and shared the memories. Since it was done in full view of the entire pack, he didn't think it wrong with sharing it, nor did his mate. Brook was amused at the thoughts as they came in.

~~~ At the Longview Pack's Group Introduction ~~~

A pair of wolves approached, who he could tell from their look, and if the scent which the light breeze brought his way was to be believed, were Mark's parents. They appeared to be in their late 30s, if they were human, so would be likely at least a century, if not more.

"You," The female started, pointing a finger at him. He could feel she had less seniority than him, even before the promotion. They were mid-ranked Beta, at best.

"Me!" Adam commented in a mocking tone, amused. His wolf was growling at the disrespect but subsided when he read what his human was thinking of doing to them. They were partly to blame for it was their actions which put their son in the position he was not ready for, but as their son was an adult, they could not be responsible for his actions, even if they were the cause of him being pushed into the position.

"How dare you force my son to be demoted like that! You are just a guest here." She started, ignoring his stated rank. Other wolves seemed to be taking sides, but he noticed there were many who seemed to think he was in the right. Others were just looking amused at her.

Adam let her spout off about it, but when she started to run out of items and started to get into insults about him personally, and insinuated about him exaggerating the issue, he snarled. That stopped her in place, as she felt his power, and backed up into the protective embrace of her mate, Adam didn't move nor could she bring her eyes up to meet his, as he stared at her. Others who were watching moved away from her. Disrespecting a guest was not a good thing, and feeling his power, they were having second thoughts about supporting her, as upsetting a very senior wolf just was not done.
~~~

"First, in the interfering, he made us stop and wait." Adam growled, "He knew we were coming and had his orders on what to do. I could have taken it upon myself and attacked him and his patrol then and there, and it would have been my right. If forced, I had the license to kill any who were in the way or interfered with the movement, being the lead of the movement. I decided to not do it then and there. I know of four cases in the last century alone where it was done. I also know of two cases where being held up caused the death of all the wolves on the movement. In one case, it also caused a pack war." They were many centuries ago, but the rules were there to prevent them from being repeated. It was also why the actions which the leaders of the movement were authorized to use to protect those under them were so loose and often near limitless.

He could see her pale. Pack wars were rare, but very bad for both packs. Wolves like her son tended not to survive, as they lacked the experience to know when to retreat or the advanced skills to survive, and tended to think they were immortal. He also had been senior enough ranked where he would have been in the first wave of fighters sent, regardless of his inexperience.

"Second, the Inter-Pack Treaty rules guiding the movements were registered as Pack Laws. They are in the sections which all Deltas and above have the right to enforce, even to the death. He could have been attacked and killed by his patrol second for breaking it. If Hank wished, he could have bitten down, not just gripped him when he arrived."

She got paler and shrank back more, she wasn't able to back down now, as her mind was starting to get wrapped up in what could have happened. Even she knew the laws.

"Didn't you teach him that the pack's will is more important than his personal thoughts? If you did, it didn't stick. He had decided his belief that the pack was better served by not adding the new members, when the majority wanted it and the Alpha made the decision to accept them. If I was a member of your pack, I could have hauled him before the Alpha for that alone. For ignoring the will of the pack or of the Alpha, he could have been declared Rogue or Lone Wolf and kicked out."

Adam let the message sink in, for a few minutes, with wolves around them nodding about it in agreement, as he led her down the trail of thought he wanted her to visit. Some of the new members were coming over, as more became aware of what was happening. He was saying the worst case, not bothering with other and much more common punishments were given.

"The disobeying of a superior wolf is another for in this case it could have been an instant death sentence. He should have known it, and known he needed to obey explicit orders which were given, which were to notify Hank as to our arrival *and* to guide us into the pack without stopping us; he failed to explicitly state the first and failed in the second."

She was nearly in tears realising how many times he had his life on the line, and how Adam was basically letting him off easy.

"The last one of giving comments which were insults, and calling my word into question. The sort he gave have started *five* pack wars in the last millennia. Be glad I decided to look deeper and not take them more than a frustrated, young adult. I was within my right as a Beta, let alone an Acting-Second to demand his life, if not to declare war and take out as many wolves as I could." Being an Acting-Second, his word was beyond reproach. It was disrespecting not just him, but his pack. By calling him a liar now about what happened, she was saying he was without honour, and by extension the pack as a whole, as they supported him in a senior role.

She was now in tears, but she was still listening. He could tell it was getting through to her about the trouble her son could have been in, and she was lucky to still have him alive, lucky to have him still a member of the pack, and very lucky to not have any sort of permanent mark on his record. She was lucky he wasn't calling for her to be punished. He could tell she hadn't thought about her being punished, but would later, once she had time to think about what he said.

Fixing a glare on her, she dropped her eyes, feeling the power held in check just by the strength of will, "The root cause of all this was your pushing for him to be placed in command of a patrol. Those in the leadership knew he wasn't ready. He needed more time to learn his place in the pack and to gain experience before being placed in such a position of trust." He lowered his voice, "I have talked to the leaders, and there was a nomination for him to The Academy."

The Academy, they all knew, was an inter-pack training course for promising Weres—and not just Werewolves—and it was where MacLaren's Next-Alphas were currently training. Most Delta-ranked who went would get further training at the pack for senior roles, or even could look to be bumped up to Beta due to their skills and knowing how to use them best. Many ended up in the lead of an area, if not eventually Seconds. Some even left their packs and founded their own as Alphas. All were highly respected within their packs, as there were very few who got to go, they only had 150 students from around the world at any time and was a two-year program. Any who graduated, if they ever wanted to move packs, many packs at times would work hard to entice them with privileges often reserved for those far above their level. Most packs gave the members they sent some extras, so they would not be interested in leaving.

After letting it sink in, Adam looked at her sadly, and told her quietly, "He no longer qualifies now he has this stain on his record. At best, they might consider him in a century, but with how many applications they get, it is unlikely he would be accepted then with the stain." Rarely did a pack send one which was much more than halfway through their second century, so it was unlikely the pack would support his application. Most sent wolves in their first century or early second, so they had enough time to use the skills and pass it onto others in the pack. Adam released her from the glare, "There is nothing I could have done to help with that one. He is going to have to work extra hard on his own to learn the skills or get under the wing of one who is willing to overlook this single instance and train him."

Even Mark's father was looking upset at the last part; not realising he had been nominated for the program. They had been trying to help him get ahead, but in doing so had badly damaged his chances of advancement now. Their current Alpha had been sent to the program, when he was the Next-Alpha, so he could learn the skills taught there. Even though he had only been nominated, each pack only got to nominate two in a yea. The nomination application had a cost as well, and they had only a one in fifty chance of going to the next round of qualifications, being he was a Delta. As a Theta, without the stain, it was one in five hundred at best who went to a second level qualification test. Often, Thetas were brought with a senior as their helper, and got training that way.

Knowing now was when to hit them, "From now on, let those who have the experience leading do the leading. If they ask for your opinion, you can give it, but don't push them till they give in for it. Let him find his place at his own time. It will be better for everyone. Don't ruin your son's life any farther by trying to push him for duties he is not ready for just because you think he's entitled to it."

Adam turned away and caught the eyes of a very proud Brook and nods of agreement from many others, including the Alphas. The parents would hopefully learn from how they had not helped their pup, but actually harmed his chances to get ahead by trying to push him up, before the trainers felt he was ready.

~~~~~

Adam waited for the wolves to be released by the memory. Mark was the lastand shook his head, "Ouch. Was that Mark aware of the nomination?"

"I believe he was. I know he was, by the time I chatted with him later in the night. I do think he is still a promising wolf. He just neededs to learn more, and get to the point he is living his pack oaths." The elders of his pack had arranged with Longview's Elders to keep him informed how he was doing quietly, "He's being given a course of pack history and put to tasks to explore the reasons behind the laws with their
~~~~~

pack elders. They have other plans to help him mature and be better. He might need a pack transfer to be able to excel, but we'll see once his punishment is complete in a decade or so."

Finishing his breakfast, "I'm going for a quick run. Mark, you need to change into some light training clothes, and prepare for a good workout. Meet Brook and I down in the gym in thirty minutes."

Getting a nod, Adam left the dining hall at a trot with Charlie hard on his heels.

*****

Adam jogged into the gym, saw a few friends at the side to watch, came up and watched as Brook and Mark finished their warmup sparring. Mark turned to him, and he quickly turned it into a test to see how good he was at hand to hand. After nearly an hour of trading moves, Adam was smiling, as he could see their newest member was good. At a mental request to his mate, she tossed Mark a staff, and came forward. Adam backed up and let her do that part; she was still better than him, but it seemed to get by a smaller margin every time they worked out together.

Adam called a halt when he could see both making mistakes, handing each a water bottle, as he drank from a third.

Mark was grinning, "That was fun! What is next?"

Leading him over to the racks at the side, "Swords. Pick a training sword." Adam offered, picking up his favourite, which was almost the same as his live one.

Stepping in, Mark shook his head, "I don't know how you are so skilled this fast." As he moved to the guard position, taking the first swing, as Adam just laughed. Both took a good bout, but in the end, Mark won by a slim margin.

Seeing it was almost lunch, they released him, so he could change and get a shower. They quickly wrote a note for the Alphas, about the half of the qualifications they tested. Since it was starting to snow, they couldn't do the distance weapon qualifications. Lunch was a nice meal, as Mark entertained them with stories from his old pack which had the whole table laughing.

After lunch, Adam and Brook used the downtime to have a chat with Mark in their suite, to discuss some of the pack secrets. While they were doing that, Adam loaded Mark's laptop with the software he would need. The one secret which surprised him the most was the real story behind their dogs.

"I can understand why they started the program; this was one of the first packs in the area." Mark commented.

Brook shook her head, "Longview was here before us. We were the second; although they are on the other side of the mountains and there are only three passes within a close range of here, the ability for us to meet is limited. Other packs, including Night Depths and Shadowed River had scouts in the area within a few years, so we needed the additional noses on the patrols before we really got settled in."

Mark looked at her, but nodded, "I forgot they have been here longer. Arctic Shadow doesn't have much contact with them."

"They have also maintained their contacts with the natives. Their Second, Hank, was from the group which is now on a reserve at the edge of their territory. They are helping them recover much of their heritage now that the other humans have stopped trying to stomp on them."

Mark nodded, "Back to the dogs, who gets them?"

Brook smiled, "We do anyone who is human related to the pack, so if a mate is a human, as Adam was, they get one, as then they can choose when or if they want to be Turned. Their immediate family is offered one. As are any humans who join the pack. We also look for some deserving human children in the surrounding communities, or use them as service dogs. Although for that we tend to use the dumber ones, as they are still more intelligent than a typical dog. They take two to four weeks to do the six-month course. We do also do some cross-breeding of some regular dogs, and those usually are close enough to regular dogs that those are given to regular service dog groups."

Mark smiled, "How smart are ones like Charlie?" he asked, looking at him asleep on the floor, as Adam used him as a footstool.

Brook grinned, "Not only he is one of the larger ones, he has the skills to function on his own with simple commands, like 'patrol and report unusual' or guarding duties, where the one guarding or a designated can determine who is friendly and can approach. Those are trained in how to try to deter those not permitted and when to escalate. Their mental bonds allow them to receive commands from those in wolf form. The ones like Charlie can even be used in combat situations, but we try to not use them more than guarding the back of a fighter."

"Charlie was with me when Shadowed River attacked us. He kept those from attacking me from the back and let me know when there was one flanking me." Adam commented.

"Do wolves ever get paired?" Mark asked.

"You want one of your own," Adam teased, amused before continuing seriously, "Most don't bother or want one. It is like having a perpetual pup in your care, one you need to watch out for and care for. With humans, it's more of them being stronger and able to be protection for them. You would need to talk to an Alpha for permission. Once you bond, it is similar to a mate-bond, and they will be with you till the death of one of you."

Brook smiled, "No, their death won't kill you, but it does affect you; it is really like they become your pup from the way they bond to you. They have an eighty to one-hundred year lifespan. It's also more they choose you, than you pick one out."

Mark nodded, "OK, I'll talk to the Alphas about permission." He also was going to chat with the others to see if he actually wanted one or not.

"You get it, and we will go with you to their area."
*****

They moved to other topics of discussion about what duties they were going to have him do. The Arctic Shadow pack had some tech and computers, but Mark had been astonished how much Adam had wired up the pack, and his future plans.

"I can see how this would bring us closer, globally. It would open up means of communication, like what happened with the human communities over the last forty years." Mark said, getting caught up in Adam's dream, as much as Brook had already become.

"But we will be using the lessons learned by the humans over those forty years to make it better and even more secure. We won't be limited by legacy issues and groups which don't want to have changes and will also be doing it totally without the controls the governments, especially the US, have." Adam stated, dreaming big, "It will totally be redundant and allow for no single pack, even this one, to dictate terms or make the decisions without the agreements of the other groups. Another is all communication will be encrypted, and as such would not be able to be monitored, even basic communications."

"The biggest thing is to get other packs to agree to it." Mark said after a good moment's thought.

Adam nodded in agreement, "Longview is already being the first trial. They are currently getting their network set up so they can be the first link. We're using the company I worked for as a supplier right now. My contract and the other packs are becoming one of their larger customers for new equipment. I'm still not wanting to have any more humans come in. We have already picked up a couple as pack members." The new owner was a large US-based tech company, since they had recently bought out the company he had worked under, as the owners had wanted to slow down and start stepping back. So far, they hadn't made any changes, but he was totally keeping an eye out for them.

The discussion turned to the two humans who had recently joined the pack and Mark laughed, "I heard the story from them. It makes it more interesting they decided to give up nearly everything to stay here, especially when the only other humans are mated to wolves, so they already have a slightly different view. Steve's Dunstan does seem to be too smart for his own good."

Both Adam and Brook laughed hard, "Steve is a bit hard-headed and doesn't like to listen much, so they are a match. Dunstan is steady when needed."

They discussed various topics and the differences between the pack. Adam did a bit of a tutorial on the laptop, handing it over, including some of the higher management systems. The alarms for the security system could be monitored and would enable access to the cameras in that area during the alert, otherwise he would have to use one of the computers in the security office, because the access and restrictions had been finalised.

Jess poked her head in, "Dad, are you three needing us to grab you food, or are you going to join the pack for dinner?"

Adam glanced at the clock on the wall, surprised, "Lost track of the time; we're mostly just chatting now."

Mark was confused, "Jess is your daughter? I thought she and Joshua were the two who took care of you."

Adam smiled, as he wrapped an arm around Jess as they headed out for dinner, "When I first came, that is what it was. Brook and I came to really care for them, and when I found out they had no close relatives and were actually not even twenty yet—they turn twenty in the spring—we decided to ask if they wanted to join our family."

Mark sniffed with a frown, but as he opened his mouth, Jess answered it for him, "The formal is being done at the next Full Moon Howl. I don't mind the wait."

Brook chimed in, "We also have a couple other younger pups who we adopted, and we are now watching their girlfriends," Before adding silently, *We both think they are mates, so we decided to let them stay together, where we can watch them. Don't tell anyone; until they are of age and are sure about it, we are letting them find it out on their own.*

Mark nodded in agreement to the silent request, smiling, "It sounds like you are well on the way to having a good family.

Adam had to let Jess go to give a hug to a few young pups who were begging for hugs, as they reached the dining room, "And we seem to have become the favourite of many of the pups. Doesn't hurt we organise a pup-evening to play occasionally."

Mark nodded, smelling an enticing scent as they entered the dining hall, and realised it wasn't the food; his mate was here. Letting out a low growl, the wolves got out of his way till he found out the male who the scent belonged to. The other male had stopped eating and started sniffing the air as he got close. When they touched, both could feel the bond and were quickly kissing, oblivious of the pack starting a joyful howl, as they realised they were witnessing a finding of mates.

Adam and Brook had followed to make sure nothing untoward happened, gathered the two up, and took them to a small meeting room. Jess had grabbed the food from the table, quickly made up a plate for Mark, and was right behind her parents as they left, carrying the food for them.

Stepping out, they closed the door quietly. Adam didn't even think they noticed they had been moved; they were so much enthralled in each other.

Gareth came out of the Alpha wing, "I could feel the finding of mates in the bonds..." He said leading, expecting them to know who had found their mates.

Adam grinned, "Mark and Ben."

Gareth stared before starting to chuckle which became a full belly laugh, "I always thought Ben went that way, no matter how hard he tried to hide it. He never seemed to really care for the females in that way."

The wolves had no prejudice against same-sex mating. They were much more rare than heterosexual mates but were still considered natural. They allowed for the pair to be a way for orphans to find a new home, or to have couples be there when the pup's parents were busy, and the pup needed an adult. It was also thought of as population control, so they didn't grow too fast.

Adam and Brook had smiles on their faces, as the gossip seemed to be centred around those two today. Ben had been away visiting some relatives in their source pack for the last month and had just arrived in time for the meal. The whole pack thought it was a good idea for a party. There was much amusement running around how his mate had shown up while he was away, when part of his reason for travelling was the fact he was searching for his mate.

Before the end of the meal, Alpha Gareth gave a mental nudge to Adam and Brook's mind, *Before I forget again; are you up to dealing with the white wolf tomorrow?*

Adam replied with an affirmative, *Still given nothing?*

We have nothing personal, Gareth confirmed, *But we do have a fountain of knowledge from him on the pack, contacts, and details. He just refused to talk about himself.*

I'm ready to deal with him; I'm thinking a quick fast death. I'm at a loss if we should bury or burn, though Adam replied, *I'm thinking of deciding on how he acts when he hears his fate.*

*****

They were eventually able to extract Mark and Ben from the room and get them involved in the spontaneous party. That Ben was the Head Chef was something amusing. The feeding of the pack was one of the most important things to his mind.

It was late when the party broke up. Adam had taken the two aside and given them a week off, although he expected Ben to be in the kitchen a fair amount still, to get to know each other without distraction. He did give them a heads up about the fun the next afternoon, Mark turned thoughtful and agreed to be there to Ben's surprise with a thoughtful look on his face.

*****

The next morning Gareth announced the execution, and the buzz was if it was going to be like Duncan's fight. With an arctic-cold storm blowing in, many outdoor activities were reduced or cancelled, and many were either lounging on the grass in the greenhouse, or in the hot springs. Adam and Brook were relaxing with many of the pups in one of the lounges. Adam was telling some old events he had read about in some of the old documents, embellishing them into a story. He not only had all the pups, but even many of the adults enthralled in his story. He had changed names, and only the elders knew who the stories were about. Even they had to smile at how he described them, especially since he was basically staying true to their memories of the person and event, even if he hadn't known them.

All too soon, it was time for lunch. Due to the nasty weather, the fight had been moved into the gym. The lunch was again buzzing with thoughts on how it was going to go. Brook and Adam exchanged smiles, about the fact he planned on giving the wolf a quick end, if he could. There were too many weapons at close hand if he was to ignore the rules.

Adam made sure to have only a light meal, so it wasn't going to cause him problems with him trying to digest a meal while he fought. He had arranged for more food after.

Stepping into the ring, he waited for the wolf, doing his warmup stretches and moves, as most of the pack moved to good spots to watch. Mark and his mate were holding hands up close to the front. Mark looked expectant.

Chapter 13 – Justice is Best Served Cold

As soon as he was led into the room, there was growls coming from the white wolf as two in their Were form were forced to nearly drag him into the room and to the circle. He was wearing a basic plain t-shirt and shorts. They were cheaper and easier to provide than prisoner coveralls. With the fact they tended to tear them when shifting, and those in custody tended not to care about the clothes provided, they preferred to go cheap. Mostly, they bought bolts of fabric and made their own, since that made less waves in human circles.

Adam stood and watched as the wolf shook off the guards, and stood there in human form, "Well, are you going to at least tell us your name?" Adam asked in a curious voice.

"No. You don't deserve to know my name." Was the growled answer.

"Carl. His name is Carl." Was Mark's soft reply.

Many turned to him in surprise. Adam glanced his way, but quickly turned back to the wolf, to prevent an attack while he was distracted.

"You're here now? Did Arctic Shadow decide to kick you out too?" Was Carl's reply, oozing scorn and satisfaction.

"No, I left because I wanted to." Mark replied, some pain evident in his voice, even if he didn't explain, the pack could tell it wasn't all his choice.

That's my brother. He was kicked out of Arctic Shadow as a Rogue Wolf when he tried to force some changes on the pack, which were similar to what Shadowed River had done. We haven't spoken in over a century, and I didn't even know where he had gone, or if he was even still alive for the last half of it. Mark sent to Adam and Brook. *I was hoping it wasn't him. I won't beg for his life, as what he did and how he acted, death is warranted. I would ask to be permitted to burn the body.* The last part was nearly pleading. He deserved death, but he wanted to morn for the loss of his brother.

Granted; his body is yours. Adam said after a short discussion with his mate and wolf, and eventually the Alphas. His offences warranted death, but the burying was something he could forego, as he was mostly just following his Alpha's orders. It was those orders which put him in conflict with this Pack.

"Well, Carl. Did you want to hear the decision of this pack?" Adam asked.

"Don't bother. I know what you decided: to kill me as painfully as you could, rip my tail off, and then to skin me and bury my broken bones." Came the belligerent response, "That is what you had done to David."

Adam sighed, "I admit Duncan went a bit far, pushing the limits of what is acceptable, but the charges and what happened was different in his case." He wasn't surprised word of what happened had reached even their prisoner. Standing tall, he decided to give the charges anyway. It would show they were not going out of their way to make charges, "Carl, you are charged with entering a pack territory without leave or treaty, with entering a pack's territory, and pack house for malicious intent, terrorising two wolves of another pack, and attempting to kidnap two wolves of another pack. It has been decided on a Trial of Tooth and Claws, with me carrying it out. When you are killed, your *brother* Mark has requested your body for burning." He had to stop, as there was to much noise from those watching. Some were astonished and other against the permitting of the rites.

"SILENCE" Adam roared, the sound echoing in the training room, a deep growl backing it as he pressed mentally on the pack who were there. Many moved to step back or submit to him from the force. "If there are any who challenge the *charges,* they can speak. If you are just thinking the punishment is too lenient, that is my decision." He stated firmly, and the pack was mostly quiet, other than some muttering he decided to ignore, as it was just about the punishment. His patience was wearing thin, as he could feel many were wanting blood over the pack bonds and seeing he wasn't going to give them a bloodbath, were disappointed. The fact he was a brother of a new pack member surprised everyone, and they started to chat about it, forgetting they were witnessing justice, not to chat about it.

"I have granted Mark's request to be permitted to burn your body when you die; as long as it's an honourable fight. If you want a quick death, that is your decision, and I am willing to grant it, if you wish." Adam said after taking a deep breath and working to calm down. Fighting while angry he knew wasn't a good way to fight.

Carl looked shocked and looked between Mark and Adam, "You still care about me, brother?" He asked quietly. "Even though we haven't been together for almost a century?"

Mark had tears in his eyes and Ben had his arms around him, "You are my brother, I still love you, even if I have to agree your punishment for your actions requires your death." Those around him could feel how torn he was; he knew his brother had turned to the bad, and for his actions deserved the sentence, but wished he could save his brother all the same.

Looking to Adam, he nodded, "I'm not going to submit to a quick death, but if you promise you won't humiliate me like Duncan did to David, I would prefer a nice clean fight to go out with some of my honour intact. I never did like those orders, but he was my Alpha; I had to obey. I didn't want to be killed for wanting to leave." He hadn't known the pack did it, and had only learned about them after he joined, and by then it was too late. He had felt any who wanted to leave should be allowed; those were often the weakest links in the pack, as they didn't want to be part of the pack.

Adam grinned ferally, getting what he wanted: a good fair, clean fight, "Agreed; I prefer the saying 'Justice is Best Served Cold'. So far, I have found it much more satisfying in the long run than seeking revenge while angry. A proper fight: if you win, you will be released as a Lone Wolf to go your own way, cleared of all the charges, and if I win, you will be dead, and your body will be turned over to your brother for cremation."

Wolf-Adam snorted at the thought of losing the fight. He was really looking forward to this fight. He was almost their equal normally, but practice is needed constantly to stay in peak form, and their opponent has been not given it since they caught him.

The guards stepped out of the circle quickly, leaving just Adam and Carl inside it. Both started to move and watched the other with an intensity. They circled each other several times, trying to gauge each other's strengths.

Adam just watched patiently, he was not going to respond to the feints and aborted moves. He did stay in his relaxed fighting position and waited for Carl to attack in earnest.

After several minutes of trying to get Adam to attack or even respond, Carl growled and attacked with some furious moves. His moves failed to get inside Adam's guard, but some moves were close. He kept striking out with his bare hands and Adam kept deflecting the strikes, while Adam started to attack; his strikes were mostly blocked, but occasionally made contact. Adam was still grinning, as this felt like a nice workout, not a hard fight, but Carl was growling, frustrated as none of his best moves were getting through.

The fight went on long enough the most impatient wolves were starting to growl under their breath; it looked more like a good training bout, even though both were going full out. The experienced Enforcers were watching closely, as they could tell it was a fight with two who had similar levels of skill.

Moving back, Carl shifted to his white-furred Were form. Adam followed, shifting, and going to his black-furred wolf, with the brown and grey marking flashing in the light as he moved. He was a good ten centimetres taller than Carl. Adam waited for him to get over his surprise, as he was slightly wagging his tail; he was enjoying the fight! Both parts of Adam were amused on the surprise of their opponent, as he realised who he was facing.

You! Carl growled, realising something suddenly, looking at Adam's fur, and realised why his scent was somewhat familiar to him.

Me? Adam asked, mockingly. He had a feeling he just realised this wasn't their first encounter, but their fourth!

You are the one who keeps stopping me! Carl replied shocked, as he attacked, nearly missing the paw which returned the attacked, just getting an arm up in time to block it.

Yes, it was me. I stopped you from taking two who were under my protection, Adam growled in savage satisfaction, *Yes, it was me who nearly caught you as I chased you from the pack territory,* He was trying to not get worked up over remembered what had happened, *And it was me and my mate who chased you at the fight, and made you crash into trees.* He remembered with savage satisfaction the successful ending of that chase. He had to work hard to keep a level head, and keep his wolf contained, so they didn't make mistakes.

Carl growled, showing more feral, as his wolf wanted to take over and attack the one who he realised had bested him several times already: he had chased them from their prey and out the window, then chased them at full speed far out of the territory, forcing them to use strength they hadn't realised they had, and to use all his skills to hide the trail, and it took finding a small cave to hide in to escape and finally chased them at the fight, he winced at the remembered hits to his shoulders and head. His shoulders were still tender, as they had nearly been broken and had deep bone bruises. This wolf was the reason he had been sitting in the cold and damp cave for who knows how long.

The time it took Human-Carl to grip his wolf better letting Adam grip his and stay calm, knowing they would need their wits to win this fight now that he was enraged.

Carl seemed to blur his paws as he attacked in earnest. Adam took several hits and roared in pain. Taking a chance, he barrelled into the white wolf, head tucked, taking him down to the floor, but taking two deep slashes in exchange. Carl was not expecting that, so lay there stunned for the moment with his wind knocked out, which was all Adam needed to take Carl's neck in his jaws. He fought for a moment, before relaxing in defeat, realising that without ripping the jaws out of his neck, he wasn't getting free until Adam released him.

Carl looking to his brother, *I'm glad to see you one last time, Mark. Goodbye.* He said to his brother.

Do it. Carl demanded, speaking just to Adam, *Thank you for a good fight.* He knew he had lost, and with that, his life was now over. It had been a good fight. He closed his eyes in defeat, knowing at least his body would be treated with honour and respect. Adam bit down hard, carrying out the sentence, and giving him the death as quick as he could by breaking his neck.

Standing up, Adam moved out to his mate. Mark had fallen to his knees, sobbing over his brother's body, petting his head fur as he said his goodbyes to a brother who he hadn't ever expected to see again, as his mate rubbed his back. The rest of the wolves were dispersing quietly, as two brought a stretcher to take the body to be prepared to be burned once the storm ended.

"Let's get those slashes checked out," Brook told Adam, guiding him out the door and down the underground hall to the medical area as she wrapped an arm around him as his reaction set in. *I already passed it onto Gareth that the two were brothers. He said he wasn't too surprised that our captive was Carl; he knew of his expulsion and he was made a Rogue.*

Adam let her guide him, as the injuries were starting to really sting, and his legs were starting to feel weak, as the adrenalin began to fade. *I can also see why he refused to give us personal information; him being declared rogue would have been grounds for an instant death and maybe even a burial.* he sighed, *I wish we could have saved such a strong wolf,*

If he could have changed how he thought, he would have been proud to have such a strong wolf in his pack. He mourned the needless loss of life, let alone such a strong wolf.

*****

Leaving the medical centre, he grumbled and winced at the slight pulling of the stitches. He had been ordered to stay in his Were form till morning, then stay wolf for the next day.

Brook was amused, as he had been ordered to take it easy for the next week or two. Some of the injuries were worse than they looked at first glance and were down to the bone.

Heading into the dining room, Brook helped Adam get his food, his forepaws being clumsier with the delicate tasks. She did get him a good helping of meat.

Sitting down at their table, and Adam working to eat as the rest kept glancing over, *Due to the placement of the injuries, I have to stay in this form till morning, as shifting could make them worse.* Adam told those there. Seeing Mark and his mate had joined them, Mark still looking pained but eating slowly, *After dinner, we need to have a meeting with the Alpha.* he told them. Both blanched a bit before nodding.

*****

Both looked a little anxious over what was going to be said as they were led to the Alpha's office. Gareth followed them in, closing the door behind them, and leaning against it. Mark and Ben sat slumped on the couch, as Adam and Brook leaned against the desk, arms crossed. It looked comical, with Adam as a Were and Brook as human and much shorter.

"Now, what is it about that white wolf being your brother?" Gareth asked.

Mark ducked his head, "Carl and I were born to the Arctic Shadow Pack, about a century and a half ago. He had ideas which because we were pure white fur, we should be treated special. That some rules shouldn't apply to white-furred wolves, and we should be given defer- ence. The Alphas didn't like it, and gave him several warnings, then reprimands for refusing to treat others with respect and for ignoring the rules, before finally demoting him to Theta, where he still tried to push ideas, through his friends, about how wolves should treat the Thetas. He still thought he should be Beta and white-furred wolves were special and 'pure'. It came to a head when he picked a fight with the Alpha when we were fifty over some changes he wanted, and the Alpha refused to consider or even put them to the pack for consideration. The Alpha exiled as he was not willing to continue to have him not conform to the pack rules and refusing to show respect for those who were senior to him in rank following his demotion. The fact he tried to cheat several times during the fight, was what had him branded him a Rogue and kicked out of the pack."

Mark sighed and had to wipe his eyes and take a deep breath before continuing, "I was not able to talk to him after that, but tried to keep track of him, through security, as a 'dangerous wolf', but lost track of him fifty years ago, which was about the time I think he made it into Shadowed River, and I started to hear comments about the pack having a very fast white-furred new member. I had tried to find out if he was the wolf, but when I checked with the pack back then, they refused to discuss if he was or wasn't a member. I had no idea he was the white wolf until I saw him. Every time I heard of a white wolf, I thought about him, and hoped to catch up with him." He hadn't had time to see if it was him.

Gareth sighed, "I knew of Carl, knew he was considered 'the fastest white werewolf' had tried to push the Alpha to do something with a fight, and after the fight was kicked out as a Rogue. No other details were given, just it was an 'internal pack matter.' I thought it was him but lacked confirmation. As it is, there was nothing we could have been done to prevent his execution; the two he harmed demanded he die. They wanted him buried in pieces for what he did, but we decided it wasn't warranted. We were getting as much information out of him which we could before his sentence was carried out." He stopped there, and let it sink in, before fixing Mark with a hard stare, "There had better never be something like that again, or I will have to make a painful example of you." He growled, showing his disapproval, letting it also be felt over the bonds, "Let someone know so we can resolve the concerns *before* we are at the challenge circle."

"Yes, Alpha." Mark said quietly, cringing a bit as the disapproval bit into his mind, "I don't know of any others of my family who has been exiled. If I have any information, I will pass it on." Gareth had more presence and felt far scarier than Rufus ever did, and he was just getting a private reprimand so wasn't too upset! It wasn't like he had much time since he had just joined the pack, and then found his mate.

Adam gave a mental sigh, *He was a strong wolf, and wish he didn't think that way, as we could have used another strong wolf in this pack.*

Gareth laughed, "Although he might have challenged you for your position."

Adam snorted, **Doubtful.** His wolf replied for them both, the fight proved he wasn't as good as them, **Although he would keep me on my toes, and make sure I stay the best I can, or he might have a chance.**

Gareth laughed, seeing the shaved and stitched spots, "I do see he got you good,"

Adam nodded, *Yes, he was really good. A few went all the way to the bone! Some are in bad spots, so I have to stay this way till morning then a day as a wolf, so they heal well. After that, I have two days of human, and no training or fighting for a week!* The last was almost a whine, as he had come to enjoy the training.

Everyone else but Brook winced, "Ouch," Was all Gareth said for several moments, "It sounded like you had a good fight."

Adam nodded, *Better put me on the 'injured' list, as I'm going to use the time once I'm human to catch up on my paperwork, so it won't go to waste. Mark can do the physical work till the Howl. I was able to get the healers to agree to let me lead the hunt, as long as I followed their directions to the letter till then.* He was impressed at the hard bargain they drove. Both halves had agreed the honour of leading the hunt was worth not being able to even go for a good run till just before then, and they warned it was only if they agreed he had healed enough.

"I can?" came the startled reply from Mark. He was very much surprised to be placed in such a position of trust already. The training of the pups was a high honour, especially since these were mainly Adam and Brook's pups and their friends.

Gareth nodded, "Yup, you can." He said, confirming Adam's appointment of his relief while he obeyed the Healers, "Monday afternoon, and Thursday morning he takes a class of advanced training for the pups. These are his own, and several others who are ahead of their age-mates."

Mark smiled, "Sounds like fun. I always enjoyed training the pups."

Brook grinned, "Don't forget the Friday evening run."

Mark groaned, "How long?"

Gareth grinned, "They use the official one-fifty trail usually. It's a good workout."

Mark winced, "I hope I can match your pups! If they were anything like Adam and Brook, they would be fast!"

Brook laughed, "They have run it at Beta speed, and Jess and Joshua have done so at Delta. Usually, we run it at the Delta, so they can stay together. But I have been pushing it faster, to try to get Jess and Joshua even faster."

Gareth laughed at Mark's face, "You're dismissed, and take your mate with you! Go have an evening to yourselves. You probably want to stay inside, though. The storm is still raging and isn't expected to clear till tomorrow afternoon. The Elders will help with the cremation once the storm ends." The wolf wasn't a member, so it wouldn't be a pack event. Few would turn up, with most there to support those giving their good-byes.

Continuing to chuckle, Gareth nodded to Adam and Brook before heading off to enjoy his evening as well.

Adam lead the way with his mate back to their room, *I'd say let's go soak in the hot spring, but I'm supposed to keep the injuries dry.* He complained, as he flopped on the pad at the base of the couch, *Throw in a movie, and we'll cuddle.* He could sit on the couch in his current form, but not cuddle, which is all he could do currently; healer's orders.

*****

The next week was very annoying for Adam, as he couldn't do many of the items in his normal schedule. The morning meeting went on as normal, even though by then he had shifted to wolf, and had just flopped across his mate's lap when she sat down on the couch. The meeting was fairly brief, and they mostly discussed the other groups, as they had a meeting on what they had done when they got back. He got a bit of a tease at the fire, but he just ribbed right back he was following the healer's orders, just to prove he was *one* wolf which could and would; he didn't say he was doing it so they would clear him for leading the Howl hunt. He had negotiated to get the minimal restrictions possible for the least time possible, but he would follow their directions to the best of his abilities without putting the pack at risk. It seems he impressed the Healers as they had agreed.

He could tell most of the wolves were quite proud he was in their pack and enjoyed the time to sit and chat around the fire. Several passed him hot dog wieners and other chunks of meat, as he relaxed on the sand around the fire, leaning against Brook's legs, belly being warmed by the fire. He finally could see why dogs loved to do it.

As soon as he shifted back to human, he called his sister to see how she was doing as he had been too busy to take the time to call her. She had been gushing over her love of Ryan. Adam was happy she had someone who cared about her. Once she had finished talking about him, Tara started in on the horses, which had Adam chuckling over her comments. He confirmed she was joining the pack, and their mother was going to stay there instead of going to MacLaren at the next full moon. He had no problem with it, especially with Adam and Brook leading the Pack Hunt. He did invite her and her mate to come to the next one, and to see if their mother could, or to arrange another date to come over.

He didn't bother asking if she was going to Turn, as it was a personal choice, and one which shouldn't be influenced by anyone. He did comment, "If you want to know some details about my change, let me know." They then chatted quite a while about various things, but before they started discussing stuff which shouldn't be talk about over an unsecured phone, he called an end. He would call back when they had the secure link up and running.

*****

Thursday, he was permitted to shift, but as the injuries still hadn't fully healed, he had been ordered to take it easy and keep them dry. The restrictions included a list of things he reluctantly agreed to not do.

Growling with frustration he flopped back on the bed, not sure of what to do; he couldn't train and couldn't relax in some hot water. Pulling out his e-reader, he decided to catch up on some of his stories and was astonished on how far behind he was on some of them. He wondered if he would get caught up on all of them, or if he would have to make more time before he lost all awareness as he fell into the story.

*****

Brook lifted the e-reader right out of his hands; he hadn't even realised she was in the room.

"Are you just going to lay here and read?" she asked, amused. "I have stood here for ten minutes, and you didn't even look up once!"

Adam reached for the device, nearly whining, "I have nothing to do, I have *all* the paperwork done, I have delegated enough I have no duties to do with the tech, and I am not allowed yet to do any training, including going for a run, or have a nice soak! I haven't got caught up with my stories, yet!"

Passing it back to him as she crawled onto the bed to cuddle up against him, it being middle of the afternoon, "Well, I just did a good run, so I'm going to have a nap here." Laying her head in his lap, she went to sleep, as he used one hand to stroke her hair as he continued to read with a smile on his face. Both knew how good stories could trap you in another world.

*****

By the weekend, the healers had declared him fit and cleared him for his activities. It seemed he had impressed them by following all their orders, and not trying to find loopholes in them. Letting out a whoop, he raced back to his room to strip and shift to his wolf. Both of them wanted a good hard run. *Taking a loop of the one-fifty.* He called to Brook, as he trotted out the door, using his warmup pace.

Charlie whined when he tried to follow, and checking with his wolf, they agreed to take it easy, and run at Charlie's pace, *Come, we'll run fast,* Adam told him. It would keep him to the 'easy run' the healers wanted him to do before the Howl.

Charlie took off, with Adam pacing beside him. Charlie knew the route, except he sometimes wanted to take shortcuts or cut across the switchback portions. Adam made sure to keep him on the trail, as some of the areas were a bit sensitive. It ended up taking a bit over the time a Delta had to qualify at, and they both weren't overly pushing it.

Coming into the room after doing a cooldown, Adam's tail was wagging. He was fit and ready to go for the full moon in a couple of days. Brook grinned and placed bowls of cool water down for them. Both Adam and Charlie headed for one and started drinking.

"How was the run?" She asked as she checked the healing scars, making sure none had opened back up.

It Was nice to get out and stretch my legs after several days of doing almost nothing. Adam replied to Brook's question, *Looking forward to leading the Full Moon Hunt!*

Brook nodded, "It's a great honour." She agreed.

*****

Adam and Brook stood grinning at the Moon Howl ceremony. They had all four pups standing with them. He was surprised it had been less than a month since he had asked if Jess and Joshua wanted to join their family, so much had happened. They were waiting for the Alphas to arrive, so the ceremony could start.

All six of them were quite happy, Adam's wolf was nearly bounding around in happiness in his mind, much to the amusement to the human half.

The Alphas came out right on time and howled to catch everyone's attention.

Chapter 14 – Moon Howl

The Alpha's howl quickly gathered everyone's attention.

"Once again, it's the full moon. We have a couple of items first. As you all know, Adam and Brook decided to accept Jess and Joshua, when they found out their parents were no longer among us."

There was a howl, which was both joyful, including caring for the two, and sadness in remembering the lost wolves. Most of the pack knew what happened. With the knowledge Adam and Brook had taken them under their wings, had brought them into the discussion of the rest of the pack. The fact they were seeming to be skilled much farther than their Theta status was really shaking up those who felt the rank of their birth parents specified their ranks. Adam had heard some of the comments, and really was trying to change it, with the Alphas' full approval and support.

Adam and Brook stepped forward with Jess and Joshua between them to stand before the Alphas. Both Jess and Joshua were beaming, but still had tears running down their faces, they were so happy to be getting new parents, even if they were just about to become adults and officially didn't need them.

"Does anyone have any concerns or reasons why these pups cannot be taken in by Adam and Brook?" Alpha Maria called out over the gathered pack.

There was silence. Those who thought there was too much of a difference of ranks decided to stay silent with the way Adam seemed to know who they were, and seemed to give them a personal glare, daring them to comment on their taking in the two pups. None realised they were the same ones who commented about his other pups for the same reason.

After a minute of waiting, Maria nodded, closing the topic, "I am calling it closed with unanimous consent by the pack. I accept they are suitable, and they have been already acting as their parents for well over a month." There were many smiles and nods, but they were respectfully quiet. Adam and Brook had seemed to care for them right from the day he moved in. The fact none were willing to give any sort of complaint meant it could never be brought up again by anyone who was here.

Turning to Jess, Maria followed the same traditional sayings, "Do you wish to be bonded as the pup to Adam and Brook, to follow them as if they caused your body's creation?"

Jess could barely speak, she was so happy, "Yes," she said quietly with tears running down her face. "They are like the parents I always wished mine were like."

"So be it." Maria said, smiling broadly.

Adam and Brook moved and touched foreheads to Jess, also with good grins. Both steadied Jess when she stumbled as the bonds formed before she blinked a few times and straightened up. Toby and Robin moved to hug her and stand at her side while they repeated the ceremony with Joshua, handing her the drink to help kill her headache.

There was a loud howl from the pack celebrating the joining when Joshua stepped back and was handed the drink. Most of the Thetas and even some of the Deltas they were working with had found them to be very hard workers and were working hard to expand their skills in their expanding duties.

Gareth motioned after a bit for quiet as Adam and his family stepped back, "We also have several new members who have recently joined us. Mark will be functioning as Adam and Brook's assistant. He had been demoted for failing to control the cleanup at what was the Shadowed River's pack house. He decided to come here to the gain of our pack."

There was a growl about the demotion. Most of the pack knew of it already, and almost all had thought what happened could happen to anyone. You need to trust your pack to be loyal, and to do their job to the best of their ability, not be looking over your shoulder for the few traitors. They had gotten an introduction so didn't need to be introduced tonight. Still, after the growl, there was a happy howl for them in celebration.

Gareth smiled, "We are also doing the investiture of Adam and Brook as the Seconds. They will be taking over the job officially, following the Spring Trials." There was a loud howl for the announcement. Everyone already knew they would be very good for the pack, but there were rumours and speculation floating around about them being Alpha Material. Gareth ignored the several betting pools he officially didn't know about which were trying to guess *when*, with very few willing to bet for them to stay Seconds. Most common bet was for when Brook turned a Century. A couple who had seen them fight had been given good odds for within the decade of having their own pack.

Brook, then Adam stepped forward and gave the pack their oaths as Seconds. Mostly, it was just a formality but was one tradition most of the pack liked. Also, the oath wasn't given to the Alpha, but to the pack as a whole, showing they were there for the pack, not for whoever was the current leader.

"Another announcement," Gareth said after a bit to capture the pack's attention again, "Adam and Brook will be leading the hunt tonight—" The rest of what he wanted to say was lost as there was a very loud howl. All knew it was a great honour to be given the hunt to lead. It seemed for once, few actually had learned of it, as many were surprised.

Gareth smiled and nodded to Adam to give the last announcement. He stepped forward, grinning, "Many of you met my sister at the last howl." Many nodded. They had chatted with her, and many liked her. "Apparently, she also has a wolf-mate, in a Delta at Longview Pack!" Another howl, as all new mates were always celebrated; this would also strengthen the bonds between the two packs. She had been well liked when she had come to the other party, and the fact she was Adam's sister was another factor. Almost all the pack were quite happy he had joined them, as he was giving a fresh breeze to the pack, while working to learn and fit in. Most of his changes were minor things which helped the pack be much stronger, and he only did changes after trying out the current way for a while, so he knew how it was done. Most suggestions or questions about a different way, just had never been thought of; if they had, they would have already been implemented.

Gareth smiled when the howl died down, "With the announcements out of the way; Let the Moon Howl begin!" He called out and starting the Howl. It was extra joyful with the new wolves, the adoptions, and the promotion to Second to celebrate.

They had occasionally scared hikers in the area with the loud howling, but the local forestry officials knew of them, and the complaints and reports just disappeared from their desk. They knew they would not attack any human without provocation. Often, if there was a new official, they arranged for them to visit the pack at a howl night, so they could see they were just celebrating a full moon and not starting a hunt for a human and were not the savage beasts which many stories made them out to be. Many poachers did find themselves hunted and turned in, in good condition with the irrefutable facts for prosecution after a long night many said of being chased by animals after losing their weapons. Most times if they commented on that, they were just laughed at, and told to stop being afraid of the dark. Most of them were never seen again in the area hunting. If they were, they made sure they were hunting legally and had all the details right, and still often were jumping at shadows.

All eight up on the deck stepped down and joined in the pack. Adam, Brook, and their pups got lots of congratulations and hugs from the pack, as all could see how much they had already bonded, even without the close mental bonds.

The chefs had outdone themselves, trying a new recipe for the meat, and the food disappeared quickly. Many of the mates of the wolves who he had led in the various fights, who hadn't fought alongside their mate, came up and thanked him personally for bringing their mates back. Some, like Adam and Brook, were partners in everything, and stayed together, even when fighting. Others had different duties, or one was not as strong or interested in fighting, so stayed back. The pack accepted both ways, and when both were Enforcers, tried to keep them together.

Many others had ideas or suggestions. With them being Seconds, it made them much more approachable than the Alphas at times, especially for the lower wolves. The fact both didn't really use their powers, except when they were absolutely needed was one thing many liked. The fact Adam was willing to stand up for the Thetas and even the Omegas, made them fear his power much less.

There were the usual squabbles over the last of the food, but most didn't pay attention to it. If a pup or a female who was pregnant or nursing usually came up and took the last bits while, usually males, fought, leaving the winner nothing as a prize, much to the amusement to those watching. None would prevent a pup or a female caring for one the leftovers. Eventually, everyone headed off to the fire pit, where a large bonfire had already been started.

*****

It's time Gareth commented to Adam and Brook. Although they didn't know, he had been watching them on a couple of their own personal hunts and was astonished how fast Adam had picked up the skills; he was ready to have the honour of leading the pack in the hunt. He had ideas for what to use the pair for, so he didn't have to worry about them trying to take his position in a few decades. He was working with the elders from several packs to finalise the plans.

He was glad to have a break and wanted to see how they would work with the majority of the pack's adults. They would be watching and be there at the end, but it was much less work than leading the hunt. It was close to a holiday for him and his mate.

*****

It's time Adam and Brook heard. Ending their current conversation, they moved off and stripped before shifting. Shaking their fur to settle it, they let out a loud howl to call the pack to the hunt. Both Alphas soon came up and joined the howl. After a few minutes they stopped howling the call to hunt, letting more of the wolves come running. After a while when most of the pack was there, Adam and Brook started another howl, this time the call of the start of the hunt. It was quickly picked up by the rest of the pack, and they together sang the fact of being a pack and hunting together.

Adam pulled on his mate and his wolf's knowledge to organise the hunt. Brook had helped organise major hunts, but never a pack-wide one. It was a perfectly clear night, so the moonlight made it seem easy for them to move. They quickly moved to pick up the trail of the elk, tracking it through the forest.

Brook worked to guide the ambush team, getting them hidden into place to catch the animals, while Adam coordinated the part which was going to chase the elk into the ambush. Mostly she knew what to do, it was just many more than was normal.

Between the two of them, they decided which ones in the herd to cull. There was an overabundance of elk in the area, and they were doing what any pack would do: cut them down. The forestry office had even called them and asked them to take out a few. They had approved for up to ten to be taken down tonight, which was a very large number for one night. It pissed the human hunters off as they were always just told the local pack had taken some out and there was no need for them to 'manage' the animals. Especially since this was way beyond what would normally be the human's elk season. Those same hunters would then try to start talk about an 'over abundance of wolves' taking out 'their' elk. Their view was quickly refuted by the numbers of wolves, not mentioning the werewolves, and the fact the hunters had tried to get open season on the elk[Pointing out they just didn't like how the wolves were the ones managing the elk population usually worked to have the hunter ridiculed and shunned into obscurity.

The werewolves decided they would take down: one young one which looked sick, two with a broken hoof—probably from slipping on an icy rock, three which were clearly old, and the older male who was past his prime.

Most human hunters would want to take out the majestic male leading the herd or one of the half dozen large females which were in prime condition, and most of those were. The herd needed those to survive and prosper. They would prosper all the better with them culling the weakest from the herd. That sort of hunting had made Adam upset, even as a human; the taking for a trophy, disgusted him. He didn't have a problem with hunters in general and had no issues with them. As wolves, they helped the herd by taking the weakest, none of the animals were wasted; what wasn't eaten was used for other purposes or left for the scavengers to pick over. Already there were quite a few owls following them, which Brook noticed. If it was day, the crows and ravens would be the ones following.

They passed on the targets to all the wolves, with the knowledge of if they found a couple others which were sick or injured, they could also take them down.

Adam barked the go to those with him, and they started to make noise with short barks and howls. Some moved in on the sides as well, funnelling the Elk to Brook and her team. Adam's wolf was given most of the control, as he normally did on hunts, but his human part stayed forward to learn. The human half had trouble actually giving control over, instead of the wolf just pulling control away and him not really fighting it, but it was getting easier with every time he did it. When he had discussed it with the Elders, they let him know sometimes those turned took decades before they could even permit the wolf half any control without a fight, so he was doing well.

The seven animals would not make a full meal for their entire pack, but it was not needed, as they had all fed well at the barbeque. This hunt was to renew and strengthen pack bonds, to let their wolves out to have a feeding themselves, and to help manage the animals to keep them healthy and strong.

The herd was quickly moving in the direction they wanted them to move. Brook had asked him to not try the most dangerous job of actually taking an animal down. Since he was still new, and after a discussion with Brook and his wolf, he decided it was for the best, as there would be other hunts. If it was just deer, it would have been fine, but being elk, which outweighed even them, was another matter.

As they reached the hidden catch wolves, they had found two others which were limping badly as they were forced to run. It appeared a cougar had got its claws into them, but they had fought free. The gouges from its claws were getting badly infected now. They were barely able to maintain a three-legged run and were quickly taken down by several wolves each before they got close to the ambush. With their immune system and gut able to process the sick animals safely, they didn't worry about the infections the elk had.

The other two injured were taken down not too much later, and the rest were taken by those doing the ambush. The rest were allowed to escape and would be just that much more wary of wolves in the future.

By the time the snow blown into the air from the escaping animals settled, they had all those they wanted down. One wolf had a paw smashed from being stepped on by a hoof, and another had a glancing blow from a kick. It was good it wasn't a direct hit, as that could have been fatal. As it was, he had a broken rib. After grabbing a chunk, both had trotted slowly back to the pack house for treatment. They would be out for a while.

Injuries during the pack hunt were normal. The two wolves would likely get some ribbing from their friends, but it would be all forgotten by the time the next moon night came around.

Adam let his wolf dive into the nearest, after those who had actually taken it down had taken their choices. His wolf kept a wary eye out for the Alphas, as they could now decide they wanted a portion of this one, and they would have to submit. As it was, they had settled on another animal, so he was able to get his choice.

Brook had made her own choice and was also happily eating. She had helped to take that animal down herself but hadn't actually delivered the killing blow.

After a while they let out a joyful howl of success.. They got their meat, only two wolves were injured, and they would make a full recovery.

*****

There was basically nothing left by morning, just some bones, and the hides. Many of the bones had been broken open for the marrow as well. Several owls had also dined on the meat. Adam saw a Great Horned and a Snowy Owl himself come in and take some of the meat.

They saved the hides, by having the first ones skinning it back with claws, so they could use the leather. The hairs being hollow meant they would over time break and fall out, so they usually didn't use them for rugs or throws. The pack had maintained the skills for natural brain tanning, so it would take quite a few weeks for the skins to be ready. It was something Adam wanted to learn, but it would be when things had calmed down.

Adam woke up snuggled down against his mate, lifted his head from her shoulders, and gave a good yawn before stretching his body out and giving his fur a shake to get rid of the snow which had fallen in the early morning while they slept. Even his wolf was disgusted with how much blood was still in his fur; their entire front legs, chest, and muzzle were caked in it. Some of the blood dislodged from the shake, sending the bits flying.

Looking around, most of the pack which was still there were similarly covered. Jess and Joshua were curled up near them. They had helped scout the animals but had stayed back in the actual hunt. Also, near them was Mark and the others who looked to them and had been involved.

Brook had started to wake up when he moved off her and followed his thought, *It's what happens when you are eating fresh meat.* She commented amused, as she stood up and shook her own blood-caked fur, *Come, lets go wash much of it out before heading back.*

Adam nodded his wolf-head and followed her to a stream which was rushing through some rocks and was only iced over at the edges. Both waded chest-deep in the cold water and braced themselves in the flow. The water tugged at their matted fur. They even at times held their breath and ducked their heads under to wash their muzzles and head.

Climbing out, Adam was cold and felt a bit cleaner. Shaking the several pounds of water out of his fur, he gave a mental sigh, before licking his mate on the nose, and bolting off towards their room to finish up cleaning, once he had hands and some good soap.

Both gave a good friendly race back, just to be running.
*****

Once they finished a good hot shower to get rid of everything, they flopped down in their room and relaxed. They ended up cuddling, and each reading their own book. Nothing was planned for the morning, and nobody, other than those doing the patrols, was going to be doing much this morning, so it surprised them when there was a knock at the door.

When Adam called for them to enter, not feeling the want to move from their seat, and put down his e-reader, they were surprised when Jake came barrelling in and pounced on Adam before the door even had a chance to close.

"What's this about?" He asked the pup who was nearly strangling him with how tight he was clinging to him, while he shuddered a bit.

"Had a nightmare and Mommy is on patrol." Came the muffled response.

Adam cuddled the young pup, "You're safe." He reassured him. His wolf was whining in the back of his mind, wanting to help the pup, but knowing there was no real way to do anything about a bad dream.

Eventually the pup relaxed his grip and curled up in Adam's lap and fell back asleep.

Brook had curled up with him on the couch and was reading, amused. Now that Jake was asleep, he pulled back out his e-reader, knowing his presence would comfort the pup and help him sleep. The more senior they got, the more the pups had been coming to them for help and support.

Anything planned after lunch? Adam asked silently to not disturb Jake.

Nothing really. We could do some training, or just stay here Brook replied.

When did we last do a Pup time? Adam asked. His wolf perked up at the thought; he loved to play with the little pups.

A couple of weeks ago, I think. Brook answered after taking a moment to think, *You want to play with the pups again, don't you?*

Adam grinned over at her, *Both of us do.* He confirmed. His wolf was nearly bouncing in his mind, wanting to play.

Brook let out a sigh, *I guess we could* she said, playing a put-out mate, before grinning at the look Adam was giving her, knowing she enjoyed playing with the pups as well.

Jess, Joshua? Are either of you around the pack house yet? Adam called.

He got a wordless sleepy complaint from Jess, which faded back off to sleep. But got a chipper, *What did you need, Dad?* From Joshua.

Please check the board and see if anything is scheduled for this afternoon. I'm thinking of some pup time. Adam replied.

A few minutes later, Joshua replied, *There's nothing booked; most are probably still recovering from the full moon.* he hesitated for a few moments, *But you're not going to like this: there is a winter storm coming in and should be here early afternoon.* He warned.

Adam sighed, and silently discussed it with his mate, *I take it the gym is open?* He asked; they may have to stay inside and play. The adults could handle the storm, but the pups, especially the smaller ones, would be chilled too fast.

Yes. Want me to book it? Joshua asked.

Yes, please. Let the pups know, and I'll announce it at lunch. We'll let the parents rest and relax without their pups bugging them.

Brook nudged him, *Are you trying to make yourself very popular with the parents of young pups?* She commented, amusement flavouring her tone, *Taking the pups off their hands for an afternoon in the gym on a day they can't go outside.*

Adam pretended to look offended, but was amused, *What do you think?* He protested, before giving it up, *We have a bunch of very good pups. Of course, I like to be with them. If it makes me popular with the parents of the pups by giving them a few hours without needing to worry about them, all the better.*

They chatted the rest of the morning away, and even watched a movie, all without Jake waking up. Every time Adam tried to move him, he clung all the tighter to him. They ended up giving up on trying to unwrap the pup from Adam and let him sleep. If he needed the security of the Second to sleep, so be it.

Stroking Jake's head, to wake him up, "Time to wake up, it's almost lunch time." Adam said softly.

Don't care. Wanna sleep. Came the sleepy comment.

"That's nice," Adam started, amused, "But I'm hungry and would like to go to lunch. You are welcome to join us."

Jake finally opened his eyes, and asked, "You won't make me sit with the other pups?"

Adam frowned at the feelings he could sense behind the simple comment, but tried to hide it from the pup, "That is what I said." He replied gently.

Brook gave him a look and nodded; she had noticed it too.

Chapter 15 – Time with the Pups

Adam growled in his mind, *I think he's being bullied. We need to keep a watch for it. I hate bullies.* He commented to Brook. His wolf was growling as well, thinking that putting down a pack mate could cause problems later.

Brook mentally tried to sooth her mate, as getting upset would just tip off the bullies. She knew it would just make them pick on him more when they weren't watching. The four they had dealt with had not been aware they had been watched but had mostly been working to change their ways. It seemed their punishment had sunk in, and they didn't want more, so hadn't even been pushing around others their age let alone the weaker pups. They had definitely tried to stay out of their way and not call attention to themselves.

Brook held the doors as they walked into the dining room. Adam still carrying the clinging pup.

Could you get us a plate of food, please? Adam asked his mate, as she held the door into the dining room. There were not too many there, and most were still looking tired. The run and hunt had been long and exhausting for many in the pack, even though they had kept it slow for them. It amused his wolf, and he thought many wolves needed to exercise more.

Getting a nod from her, as he headed off to their normal table. Jake finally let go as they sat down across from a yawning Mark, who had just finished a night shift which he had volunteered for. He also subscribed to the idea of the leaders doing the worst shifts, so they could show they knew how they went. The 2am to 8am shift after a full moon was definitely not one many liked. Usually there were a few who volunteered for it, as there was a pay bonus for it. Brook placed the plates of French Toast and sausage on the table for both of them, along with a similar one for herself, before sitting on the other side of Jake.

I'm glad for the increase of strength the changes gave me; I would not have been able to carry him so easily as a human Adam joked to Mark and Brook, as he helped Jake with the choices of fruit on the table, then with the syrup, before he ate. Keeping a discrete eye on the pup table, he could see a few glares pointed their way, which he ignored.

Seeing the room had started to fill once they had mostly finished, Adam stood and howled to call everyone's attention. Once it got quiet, he smiled, "I know many are still not fully awake, but with the bad weather moving in this afternoon, I am taking over the gym for a puppy play time this afternoon. All pups, and those who want to play with them are welcome to come down. Those parents who want to go sleep some more are welcome to drop them off and they will be brought to the dinner meal. That is all."

He grinned as he sat back down, to eat his slice of pie for dessert, seeing the excited face of many of the pups. He quickly finished his food, and headed for the door, Jake trotting at his side. There were already a couple of parents waiting for him in the gym.

One gave him a hug and a tired smile in thanks before leaving their pups to his care as they yawned.

Adam's wolf was whining; he wanted out to play! He quickly stripped and shifted to his wolf after placing his pack by the door, keeping some control, but letting his wolf get the pleasure of the play time.

As the pups trickled in, many grinned and gave him a good hug around the neck before also shifting to play. Mark stood by the door, having followed them down, with a spreading grin on his face.

Brook watched before bumping Mark's shoulder, "Didn't your old pack do pup play times?"

Mark shook his head, "Nothing like this. Occasionally a parent would watch two or three others, but no general play time for all the pups, and *never* from the seniors offering it." He thought back and wished he had thought of doing them with his previous pack. He could see how much pleasure the pups got, and he felt it would make the most senior much more approachable, as they would associate good things with them from a young age, not just punishments and orders.

Adam glanced from where he was play fighting with several pups, mostly using his paws to roll them over when they tried to run into him, *You are welcome to join in and play* He offered, *I bet your wolf is begging to come out and play with the little ones,* He teased, before turning back to them and laying down, as several had started climbing on him. Several of the littlest ones yelped in happiness, as they started using his large wolf body as a jungle gym and playing over him. A couple others were playfully trying to catch his wagging tail.

Jake seemed to be having fun, but there was one or two which kept trying to make him fight. He wasn't going to step in unless it got out of hand. He needed to learn to hold his own, but Adam still kept an eye on him.

Adam was nosing a pup playfully, when he heard a pained yelp, and looked over. A brown and white furred pup was bowling Jake over, stiffed legged, seeming to want to do more than play-fight, but Jake wasn't having anything to do with him. Jake let out another yelp as the other wolf bit him on the flank.

Shaking the pups off, Adam stood up and walked over, with everyone starting to notice the fighting. Several of the little pups whined or gave a mental, *Aww,* As he stood up, from their play.

Stepping behind the pup, as he prepared to attack again, Adam grasped him by his scruff, and lifted him partly up, his own tail held straight up in authority. The pup was too large for him to lift all the way off the ground, but the front paws came off the ground, and when the pup started squirming in his grasp, a chest-deep growl stilled him instantly.

You know fights are not permitted in the playtime, Skylar. Adam growled, leaving the speech open to everyone in the area.

Skylar had his ears back and his tail tucked, knowing he was caught, *We were just playing* He tried to explain.

That was not playing, nor did Jake want to play-fight with you. Adam growled, *I'm very disappointed with your actions. I am going to have to think up a punishment for you. Till supper you are to be within a body length of me. Step out of line before the punishment is complete, and you will have a much worse punishment.*

Yes, sir. Came the quiet reply, as the pup remembered the punishment his brother and his three friends got. He had been still eating and had missed it. Since then, they had been no fun to try to be with, as they refused to do anything but train, or play amongst themselves. His mind was still smarting as well from the mental slap of disappointment ringing through it. The only thing which would have hurt more would have been the Alpha's disappointment and disapproval.

Releasing the chastised pup, with his tail still tucked against his belly, and ears back. Adam wandered back over to the little pups, Skylar following. Laying back down slowly among the little pups, Skylar just stood to the side.

Putting his head down to sniff and nuzzle a pup in front of him, *Well, don't just stand there like a statue, you are going to let the little ones play over you.* Adam commented in amusement. Watching out of the corner of his eye, he saw the shock before Skylar lay down without a word. The little pups barked and yelped a storm thinking it was great fun; they had two bigger wolves to play with now! Skylar was about the same size as Jake but was still much bigger than the little pups.

Brook had been keeping her amusement to herself as Adam told the pup to stay with him, and to let the little pups play over him. After a bit she started laughing in his mind, *Skylar has never liked to be around the little pups. Having to let them play over him is a punishment all in *its own!** She commented before her mirth took over, as she fell over in stitches as she watched the expression on the pup's face.

She was teaching some pups coordination, on a small track of rocks set in concrete which was covered in a soft sand. The object was to only step on the stones, not the sand. They ranged on the easy trail of which were over a foot across and not too far apart, to ones which were the size of a pup's paw and were spaced far apart. Additionally, they were colour coded, and for additional challenge, was to use only one colour. It also helped them to consciously control where their hind-paws were placed, instead of just not caring. In hunting, it was needed, so they could make sure their hind-paws were just as quiet as their forepaws. As they advanced, they learned to climb ladders in the wolf form, which was part of the obstacle courses.

Several had stopped and were just staring at her, as she stood up and nodded for them to continue. It was a key skill which she felt all wolves needed, as it gave them a better coordination of their movements through knowledge of where each paw was at all times. There were several longer stretches outside, some which took a gallop for a wolf to have the inertia to move from stone to stone.

Adam gave her a mental growl, but when he watched Skylar lay his head down and the pained look he had, had to give a mental chuckle at it, *Well, any ideas for his punishment? Thinking of having him help the littlest pups for a week or two since he doesn't care for them.*

Adam's wolf sent both a picture of the pups as human being helped by Skylar, with a very pained look to his face, and they both started laughing mentally. If he wasn't already laying down, he would have fallen over in amusement.

*I don't know... that seems almost cruel.** Brook commented when they were able to stop, *I think four days should be enough time.**
*****

All too soon for the amusement of both Brook and Adam, but way, way too long for Skylar, it was dinner time. Standing up, Adam headed for his clothes and shifted. Stepping out he gave a short howl to catch everyone's attention, "It's time to shift and head upstairs for dinner."

Seeing several which had fallen asleep and were curled up around him; one pup was even curled up on Mark's back, Adam smiled at his mate, and turned to Skylar, a gleam in his eye, "Keep an eye on the sleeping pups, and I will have someone bring you a plate of food. You are free for the evening when they are all gone. Come see me at breakfast. Think about why you are being punished and why we have that rule." His wolf was howling laughter in his mind at how he was dealing with the pup. He needed some special lessons, and maybe being forced to be with those young pups will help him get it.

"Yes, sir." Came the quiet and subdued response, as Skylar sat down beside the pile of the sleeping pups. Several moved in their sleep to press against him.

Adam turned and smiled as Jess came down with a tray of food, "Brook asked me to bring this down?" She commented, stopping in front of him, at the foot of the stairs, as it seemed to not be for him.

Giving a grin and a nod, "I have a naughty pup watching those who are still asleep, they're in the gym." Adam commented, with a feral grin, "He doesn't like the little pups, and was forcing Jake to fight, so part of his punishment is to watch them."

Jess shook her head, "You think of the worst punishments which fit the crime." She said with a grin, before heading into the gym with the tray, so Skylar could eat too. She quickly came out as Adam waited.

Wrapping an arm around her, Adam walked with her up to the dining room, "Now we can eat! Even though mostly I played jungle-gym for the littlest, I'm starving!" He said with a laugh.

*****

Four days later, after dinner, Adam sat down in a small meeting room with Skylar, "So, what was I punishing you for?" Adam asked a much subdued and tired pup. The normal caregivers had loved the fact of being given near free reign on his duties for the four days and had used him for the most active and exhausting duties which he could be given; some jobs they didn't give him as they were not suited for his size. They also had him dealing with the clingiest pups. The reports from the end he was starting to enjoy being with the little pups.

Bending his head down, "I broke the rule of no fighting during the playtime." Came Skylar's quiet answer.

"Do you know why that is a rule?" Adam asked calmly, sitting back. He much preferred to make sure the lesson he had tried to teach had been learned, instead of just they got a punishment and not understand the *why*.

Skylar sighed, "I couldn't think why, but I did apologise to Jake. We have play-fought after that, and he even thanked me for the fun."

Adam smiled, as he did have the report back on it. "The reason you got in trouble is you went beyond play, since he didn't want to play fight. When it goes beyond play, it is no longer fun for the one who isn't winning. The play time is for bonding and to give the parents time without their pup underfoot. When it is no longer fun, what does it do?" He was trying to lead the pup to the answer, so he learned it, rather than just lectured at. Skylar was a smart pup he had been told.

Skylar hung his head, "It would make them not want to play any more."

Adam nodded, "Yes. And what can it lead to?"

Skylar almost looked like he wanted to hide, "It could divide the pack?" From the answer, he sounded like he was nearly in tears.

Adam moved and gathered the pup in his arms. It seemed the talk allowed the pup to understand what could happen if they didn't change. From what he had heard from others of Skyler, was he sometimes pushed too far, but was usually a good pup. "Yes, if it was left too long. I hope you learned your lesson. Since Jake was still playing after, there shouldn't be any lasting split. I am calling this punishment over."

Skylar broke down and cried, when he realised it could have harmed the pack. No healthy wolf wanted to harm their pack and would feel bad if they negatively affected it, even accidentally. Adam held and comforted the pup, knowing the reasoning behind why he was punished had sunk in, and he would not do it again.

It took a while, but eventually Skylar pulled away. Adam let him go after a final hug, sitting back in his chair.

Skylar still refused to meet Adam's eyes, "May I go, Second Adam?" he asked.

Adam smiled, "Yes, go enjoy your freedom. Remember, if you need help, any of the senior wolves, myself and even the Alphas are there to help you. We are all a pack together."

Skylar nodded and was out the door as fast as he could.

Heading out himself, after straightening the room up, Adam, caught up with his mate in their room, giving her a kiss, "All done. I think he's going to be very good now."

Brook grinned, "I'm glad. I wonder what he thinks of the little pups now he's had four days of being forced with them."

Adam laughed, "The last reports showed he seemed to be enjoying helping the pups and was almost attached to the clingiest ones. What I want to see is if he takes up their instructor's offer to have him stay on and help them more. It would give him a position which is very much in need." What nobody had told the pup, was if he did stay on, since it wasn't a punishment any longer, he would be paid for the time, as it would count as a job for the pack.

Brook smiled, "And one which does give a fair amount of prestige for the skills needed. Nothing is more important than the little ones." Also, for how valued the pups were, it paid a good wage. After giving him another kiss, she pulled him to their room, "I feel like a nice run, just us two." Jess and Joshua had taken Charlie for a long run that afternoon, as he was slightly faster than them, it was a good workout for all three to tell Charlie to run full out and they chased him.

Charlie was flopped out as flat as an exhausted canine could be on the bed asleep. He barely opened his eyes when Adam came in and lacked the energy to even flop his tail in a wag. Adam petted his head for a moment, as Charlie closed his eyes and went back to sleep. Adam sensed he would be out for all night.

Adam smiled, "That sounds like a nice Saturday night." He replied, giving her a kiss before stripping to shift to his wolf. He gave her a good nuzzle, then lead the way out the door.

*****

Adam and Brook wandered back in Monday morning, after spending the entire day and two nights before out, just renewing their bonds and cuddling together, mostly as wolves. They did take some time to go and visit the wolves guarding what had been the now Nameless Pack's territory. Most of them were young single wolves, with a couple seniors to supervise. All were honoured to have them come and do a personal inspection, showing their duties were important to the pack. Charlie had joined them the first morning, after realising they weren't back, and he wanted to be with Adam. He followed his bond to find his person.

They were waiting for the heavy equipment and to get the permits to start pulling down the building. They had found major structural issues and didn't want to keep it. A few storage containers had been brought in, and they were already pulling everything which wasn't fixed down. Some bins were scheduled to arrive that week, so they could sort out the materials for recycling.

They had a quick shower together, then joined their friends for breakfast. They were teased for disappearing, as Toby and Robin cuddled up to them. They just smiled back and refused to describe their time alone together.

Following having a good meal they headed down to the Alpha's office, knocking on the open door.

Alpha Gareth looked up from his papers and smiled, "Well, I see you have been settling in this last week. I loved your punishment for that pup. I got the note about them fighting, have anything to add?"

Brook started chuckling, as Adam smiled and answered back, "Well, it seemed appropriate, as he had made some bad choices, and I decided he needed to get over being uncomfortable with the little pups. Even if he didn't, it would be even more of a punishment. The other part was he needed to learn was if he bullied those who didn't want to play-fight, it was actually fighting, and could cause rifts of mistrust in the pack. His own imagination took it from there."

Gareth had his smile getting bigger with everything which he said, "I think you have it exactly right. His punishment and the decisions were exactly what was needed to nip that thought and get him corrected before it became an issue." Shaking his head, "That sort of decision is one which a seasoned Second would make, after years of service; not the weeks you have had." He didn't add it was also a skill needed to be an Alpha.

Adam's wolf just preened under the compliments and refused to utter a comment to his human on it, which was unusual; he usually was giving nearly a continuous commentary on the actions and commenting on his thoughts before they did anything.

Gareth laughed when Adam blushed, and Brook looked pleased, "If I didn't know better, I'd think you had designs on my position."

Human-Adam was startled, his wolf was chuckling, but was giving a gentle negative, "I've just got a talkative wolf which seems to be giving me good advice, and I am trusting intuition on what to say when he doesn't tell me directly what I generally I should do or say. When you said taking your position, he chuckled but indicated he wasn't. I always feel a very good amount of respect towards you from him. I don't think he wants to ever challenge you for the position."

Gareth nodded and agreed silently; his own wolf was quiet on it, but was very comfortable with the two, he didn't feel at all challenged for his position from them. As his wolf had no problem with them, and didn't feel threatened from them, he wasn't going to look into it further.

"How's the network link going?" Gareth asked. The network was still their project, even if they had handed over much of the day-to-day and the details to others as they got busier with the Second's work. They still were setting the direction. Once the first few were connected, it would likely take on a life of its own, and after the other few initial hub sites were linked, it would not need him involved at all to continue it.

"Longview is getting their servers set up and getting a fibre link installed. They found they need to rebuild their entire network, as the current setup is too old even to be supported for upgrading." He had found out their core network was a token ring, which was ancient in network terms, and was easier and cheaper to just rebuild from scratch. "They had a snag on the feed of some human permits they had to get. They should be ready to test in about a week." Adam replied without hesitation, still a little miffed on the slipping of the timeline. It was understandable, but he wanted to be able to chat with his sister. Until that link was up, they wouldn't be able to chat about any of the changes, unless he travelled to see her, and he was busy enough even taking a day to see her would be a bit hard. When quiet time, like the last weekend came up, he really wanted to spend it with his mate, and taking part of it to go to the other territory for an inspection with her allow for both. They currently didn't have a reason to go to Long View Pack. With their rank, they would need to pre-arrange the visit with the Alpha. It was a downside of gaining higher ranking Adam had found.

Adam grinned, "Their tech sounded positively gleeful when he called to tell me they had to fully rebuild it. I have Chris working with them to make sure it is set up correctly and as secure as possible. He says we are all ready at this end for the link as soon as it's ready at their end."

Gareth nodded, liking where they were on the plan. "Once they are online and you know the details, I have four other packs in the area which are interested. I have other packs farther away enquiring on it as well."

Adam grinned, "In that case, I need to work and finalise the details on the expansion plans. I have a few key sites which would need to be built first, I'll get you the general locations once I finalise it, so we can start negotiations for links. I'm planning a network where all the local packs link into a main site with one or two backups pre-configured, and those main sites interconnect and link with each other." He needed to look up where the main global internet trunks were located, as those would be the best places for the packs to have the main sites too.

Gareth nodded, his eyes a little glazed, "I don't need the details! Lea has been a big help in helping me learn how to use the computers, but I don't need to know how it works. Just tell me what packs I need to get you a contact at, and I will see about getting you them."

Both Adam and Brook laughed, "I'm learning, but still some of what he says he has to explain, and it gives me headaches," Brook told their Alpha, amused at the look on his face, knowing she had worn exactly the same expression several times.

Gareth smiled a bit, before sobering up as they continued their updates. Gareth was starting to give them more tasks to do, as they started to take more of the Second's traditional duties. The discipline and day to day work of watching the pack was one he was quite happy he no longer needed to do, since the old seconds were unable to do so. The good thing was there were only minor issues, and they were ones he had been forced to let slide, as he didn't have the time to deal with them.

The pack had started to learn Adam and Brook were being quite inventive on their punishments, and were tailored to each individual infraction to the likes and dislikes of the offender and their abilities. The kitchen staff were quite happy when they got help with the dishes, as were the Thetas in the laundry. Both areas were favourites for minor infractions, and with the kitchen, being forced to scrub pots while smelling the cooking food was almost a torture in itself! Those on punishment didn't get samples or treats which those who worked in the kitchen received. Others were forced to clean the common bathrooms with varying sized brushes due to the level of the offence. Others got garbage duties, which included taking the bags to the bear-rated bins by the main garage, often being ordered to walk them instead of loading them in the Argo.

"I am getting a fair bit of amusement from the comments and complaints I'm getting for what you give for punishments. I mostly just give them the option they can challenge you, or me if they dislike it, and most just go and deal with it; when I suggest what I'd have given, most decide to take your punishment." Gareth commented, after they had reviewed the reports from those who supervised the punishments, "Sadly, the number of complaints I have been receiving have lessened." He sighed theatrically, getting a chuckle from the two. It was amusing to watch the others try to not do the punishment, to not wanting what he would give them instead. He knew them better, so often knew the punishments they would dislike more, or would give them more time than Adam or Brook had set.

"We have been giving out fewer punishments, and they have been toeing the line more, noticing we aren't letting as much slide. Some I have just pulled aside the first time for a lecture and sent a feeling of disappointment at them. I think just that has worked wonders, too." Adam commented, "I am trying for where the more senior wolves know what sort of jobs the Thetas have to do, and in a pinch can help them out. It allows for the senior wolves to be more grateful for the fact there are those who do jobs they find distasteful."

Gareth nodded, "I think you are doing a wonderful job. It is going to be a long-term, and I think the oldest will pass out of the pack before some learn that lesson."

Adam and Brook nodded in agreement to his statement, as they shared it. They had found the oldest were often of the thought any and all change was bad, as they had been through enough changes already.

Gareth leaned back, "Our last item is what to do with the Nameless Pack's territory. It is far enough away it isn't feasible to permanently attach it to our territory, even if we take the neutral area between the two territories, which is large enough for *another* pack. The current pack house there and most of the existing structures are not salvageable and we are working to get them torn down, as you know."

Getting a nod from the two, Gareth continued, "You have any ideas for what we should do for that territory?"

Adam looked at Brook, and both grinned, as they had been thinking they would be asked. Brook nodded at Adam, as he had some very nice ideas which he could share.

Chapter 16 – Meetings & Training

Adam nodded at his mate's wordless comment, "Well, since this pack will be splitting within the next century, I was thinking it would make it be a ready built place for them to go. It would give them a bit of continuity and would allow for a slow transition. It would also give us the choice for either a sub-pack to just stay there, still with your ultimate control, or for a separate allied control by another Alpha."

Gareth nodded with a smile; it was along the lines of his own thoughts. The Inter-Pack Treaty clearly gave them first choice on if they wanted to keep the territory or start a new pack there. They also had the rights to pass control to another of their choice. Or they could just release the territory, and it become free territory for the first to have a presence to take control of it.

"I did not like the look of the pack house that was there," Adam continued, "As it seemed very impersonal, and more a barrack than a home. I do prefer the idea of a pack house, rather than scattering everyone to different houses. For one thing, it is easier to keep everyone together and closer knit, especially having communal rather than individual meals."

Gareth grinned, "I take it you would like to be in control of it?" He asked mildly, when the thought occurred to him, back when he had them lead the fight to clear it out, his wolf had sat up and was all for it. Since meeting Adam, Brook had grown and expanded her abilities, from being just a trainer and mid-level Beta, and she had flourished with skills which matched Adam's. He was starting to feel something from them, a hidden power which almost felt like an Alpha; he was going to need to speak to the elders about it. Shaking his head from his wool gathering, he listened to Adam's answer.

"My wolf wants this, saying it would fit more of our potential. I was more than happy just being the Beta in charge of the technology. I never expected to even get that high of position." Taking Brook's hand, "I would have been happy just being a Theta wolf with my mate, everything else is just more than I ever expected to get."

Taking a deep breath before he continued, "I would be honoured to learn to be in control and eventually be the Alpha, but can we take a long road approach to it, please?" Adam felt that without his wolf helping to keep his head up, they would have already drowned under all the work and the needs of those who looked to him.

Turning to Brook, as her thoughts were something which was required too, Gareth nodded.

Brook took a deep breath, "I would be honoured, but too have been feeling a bit overwhelmed, like my mate. I have been leaning on my wolf much more often since meeting my mate than ever before. I have been learning all I can, including studying the laws with Adam, so we both not only know them, but also know the reasoning behind them and why they exist, to keep the spirit of the law, more than the just the words. I too would ask for a long road approach to it. My wolf also has said similar things about fulfilling our potential."

Gareth nodded, "I was noticing that. The big difference between the Second and the Alpha is the Second only does the big decisions when the Alpha is away, and they can defer some to when the Alphas are back. The skills which are needed are almost the same for both roles. Both need to be able to make the hard decisions but also be there to comfort those who need it, and to work together with the rest of the pack to keep everyone happy. Many of the abilities of the Alpha are more from experience than anything, and it is something which you can only gain with time." It also took the talent of thinking of others before themselves, but it was one thing they would have to learn for themselves. From what he had seen, they were already starting to do it. Some of the skills of an Alpha were an Alpha-only secret, so they would not be told, unless/until they became an Alpha. Some elders knew it, so if the worst happened to a pack, they could be taught. But in these days, there were other Alphas who could be mentors too.

Both Adam and Brook looked relieved, then Gareth dropped the big surprise, "I am thinking, and this is with the approval of the elders. We will be having you take control of the new territory, but as Seconds, and have it as a sub-pack with you reporting to me. That way, you can get the experience, and we get the population relief. I'm thinking within a century you will gain the skills to elevate you to Alphas, and give you the autonomy and separate the control of your pack. By then, I think we will have enough members to fully support two packs independently."

Both couldn't have been more surprised; their mouths were hanging open, and their eyes were blank. Reaching behind him, he grabbed a camera and took a picture of their expressions, as he chuckled. It was even more funny than he had expected, and his mate had the thought to have a camera ready. He sat there and waited for them to collect their wits and decided to hold off the rest of what tasks he was going to have them do till later. Let the decision settle in, especially since it was such a big one.

Eventually they got it together, and both nodded and closed their mouths. "This is a totally unexpected and great honour you are bestowing on us." Brook stated softly, "Thank you." Adam was still looking very much shocked and surprised, more than Brook.

Gareth smiled, "You are welcome. I can now tell you that Grant and Louise had been worried about you wanting to take over, following the punishment you did there. It showed a flash of the leadership skills of a great alpha. They actually recommended to me for you to take control of that territory, or I'd need to watch out for my position in under a century. I want to work with you and to train you so you two more than just occasionally show the ability but can be ones which other packs look to for guidance. You two are quite a bit too young to be taken seriously for the Alpha position, from the point of view of many of the Alphas, but with time, will have the skills and experience to be even better than me." Standing up, it forced the other two to stand as well, as a show of respect, especially for what he had offered. "Now, I had put it around we will be making an announcement at the beginning of lunch, which is now. I don't think we can even try to keep it from the pack, so I'm not even going to try."

He had put their names forward for the next year's Academy, with Longview, and even Arctic Shadow's formal support of their application, as he had discussed it with Rufus as well. He too had noticed the two from the reports of the others at their debriefing of what happened and was concerned there would be issues if they weren't challenged. The Alpha Track which he had forwarded them for, last accepted a Turned Wolf two centuries before, but they needed the Spring Trial qualifications to finish the application before they would reply. Since there were only a few pairs accepted in a year globally, it was one of the highly contested training programs, but with three formal approvals, and if they already pass the Trials at Alpha level, they will almost certainly get in. He hoped they would have fun, but he had heard from one wolf, who's comment had travelled and almost became a review—and a warning—of the program, where after the training from the Alpha stream, even the elite human forces training was easy.

It did also mean he would not have their skills for the two years they were gone training, as currently it was out in Russia. By then, his pups would be back from their own stint, as they were graduating at the spring equinox, and be back in time for the spring trials, where they would show they met all the skills needed to be confirmed as Next Alpha.

As they walked out, Brook had a thought, "Alpha, as we will be running the sub pack, who are you going to have as *your* Seconds?"

Gareth smiled, "I have been considering offering it to Mark and Ben. Both have been tasked with some duties which show Mark was getting some of the skills, and Ben has always had reports of flashes that way and is why he is the Head Chef."

Brook nodded, with a sly grin as they walked out of his office, "Darn, I was wanting to ask Ben to come with us." She would have loved to ask Lupita, but she tossed a cleaver in the direction of the last Alpha who made the request to join their pack as their head Chef, and even offered for them to only be answerable to him directly. The cleaver had shaved a piece of his beard off before imbedding itself in the wall, and her warning of she hit what she tossed it at. Since then, word seems to have spread, as she hadn't had any offers since.

Gareth laughed, "He was one I would not have wanted to lose. Maybe ask him to train one of his staff to be yours? Maybe make a list of who you want to go with you; I would prefer not to lose any of the heads of departments, but we can see." Maria was waiting for them at the door to the dining room, and smiled in greeting, before opening the doors.

The pack got quiet quickly as the four filed into the room, and all eyes turned to watch them. It had been passed around there was a major announcement happening. Wolves being curious, nearly everyone who didn't have duties elsewhere was in the room. It was packed, with nearly every seat being filled, and even some extra benches and tables which weren't usually used had to be brought out. There were others who took a later or earlier meal and were standing around the outside of the room as well.

Gareth smiled at the attentive pack, "I see everyone wanted to hear the news. It has been discussed as to what is to happen to the territory of what was recently taken under our control. The Inter-Pack Treaty states we, as the pack which took the largest offences which caused their downfall, get to decide what happens. As our pack is getting nearly too large, it was decided we are going to use it as space for eventually starting a new pack." He had to hold his hand up to quiet the pack down, as they were wondering who would be there and who would stay here.

"The process to set up a new pack is being hampered with the fact we cannot reuse the existing structures. This is going to take a while to deal with, and nothing will be finalized for decades. We have the time, so we are not going to rush and make it happen. We build for the long term, and that takes time and planning." Gareth smiled at all the nods he was seeing as the pack agreed with him.

The pack's engineers and architect had started the basic design work before they had even made the final decision to take down the old pack house, having already seen how it was going, and were going hard at it already, with basic designs, which could be modified to fit the final location when it was decided. They had said they had initially just started doing it as a fun project as they didn't have much work, but when it was brought forward to Maria, she had instantly approved them to continue and to make a design.

"Adam and Brook will be leading this sub-pack—" Gareth had to stop there, as he was drowned out by a very loud and very joyful howl from the pack. It took several minutes before they calmed down enough to continue. He didn't even bother wasting his breath to calm them faster.

"As I was saying, Adam and Brook will be leading this sub-pack. They are young but show flashes of the skills of an Alpha." Many of the older members of the pack nodded, not just the Elders, who smiled, as they had seen them too, "Once they are more experienced, in a century, we are looking at officially splitting the pack, and they will become the new Alphas of their pack." There was stunned silence for a few moments before the pack again burst out in joyful howls. Some of it was pleasure for the new Alphas-to-be, as already Adam and Brook were well loved and respected. A few others had guessed early, had taken bets with great odds, and now stood to collect some profit.

New packs were formed maybe once in a lifetime. Their pack had been taking in lots of lone wolves over its life, and had many pups, so they had gained a large number that way. It was nearly unheard of a pack expanding as fast as theirs had. In the lifetime of the elders whose parents had decided to move their families to the split, they had gone from a new pack to one which was already looking at needing to split again. Gareth made a mental note to see if the history books showed if it had happened this fast before. He thought they may be setting a new history mark of how fast they were growing, but with how the world was getting, with much fewer dying, he had heard from others their packs were growing too. They had just started a little earlier and larger than some of the others.

I hate major announcements, they take so long! Gareth sighed mentally to the three standing with him, as they waited for the pack to settle down. He got mental chuckles back from them.

"Making a new pack is not something we can do at any speed. We will be starting the process this summer to find out who would want to move to the new pack." Smiling and giving a nod at Adam and Brook, so they could say something.

Adam took his mate's hand in a tight grip and feeling he was way out of his league; he had never wanted to be a leader! He was sure those around him could smell his nerves. Taking a deep breath, and getting the support from his wolf, "I know many would want to come see us with suggestions. Take a week and make them well thought out before sending them. Please either use the new e-mail system," He got a chuckle as many still were only using written notes, "Or drop us a regular note, and we will be taking suggestions. I have a few in mind who I would like to take, and some who Alpha Gareth has already told me I can't take," He got a laugh in reply, "We will be approaching them over the next few weeks to ask them. The plans are still early, and most of the existing structures are not fit to use, so are being demolished. We will be working on plans for new ones. Input from packmates will definitely be valued and considered. It may even cover something we miss!" He got the laugh he was going for at the end as he stepped back.

The last he hadn't been outright told, but he was going to fight to get most of his own plans which were starting to form in his mind to actually happen, but they could deal with them later.

Stepping away, the pack erupted in one last howl, and then was noisy as they got their food. The whole pack was very much excited for the news.

Sitting down, they were congratulated by their friends, Mark looked a little sad, sitting across from them, *Why so glum?* Adam asked, concerned.

I have just started settling in here, and don't want to move again, especially closer to Arctic Shadow. He commented honestly, expecting since he was considered part of Adam and Brook's team, he would be moving. The way he had been treated at the end had soured him to his old pack. He still chatted with his friends but had no interest to return for a visit; they could come here. He knew Alpha Rufus had named him a Pack Friend, but until they changed the policy which there seemed to be no energy to change, of holding a wolf accountable for something they couldn't control just because it happened while they were under their orders, he wasn't going there. He had told the Alpha that in one email.

Well, good news for you then; you and your mate are two whom I have been told already I cannot have. Beyond that, you will need to speak to Gareth about it. Adam commented, as he dug into his lunch. Mark perked up, and smiled, as it seemed his new Alpha had plans for him.

Adam and Brook let the noise go around them. They were still in shock over the decision they would eventually be the Alphas for the new pack! It was a huge honour, one they were both not sure they deserved, one they never really aspired to be. *OK,* Brook had to revise the thought at a snort from her wolf, *but what wolf pup didn't daydream of being the Alpha of their own pack?* It just was one dream she never thought she would see come true. By the time she was fifteen, she had given up the dream and had just tried to be the best wolf she could be.

Some were giving suggestions on ideas, and they were shaking their heads, saying, "We said work them out then send them in next week. We want thought out ideas, not just quick suggestions."

Once they were done eating, they traded a glance and quickly headed out to get changed for their training. Grabbing their bows and a quiver each, they quickly let those training with them know they were heading for the far training area, where it should be quieter and needed more effort to get to them. Both had a wish for quiet while they trained.

*****

Adam and Brook smiled as they had got in some good training time in addition to helping their normal six pups. All of them gave them a good hug when they met up and gave their own congratulations, but then were worked hard. Both thought about their key positions. They needed someone to be their Seconds, even if they would still be officially ranked as Beta, then needed medical, security, food... the list was endless.

Walking into their room, with all six pups still with them, Adam turned to Jess and Joshua, "I want you two to talk to the Thetas under you, see who would be interested in joining us, and who wants to stay here. In both areas, there will be lots of room for advancement, here because of those leaving, and in our group because it is just forming. We will start discussing it this summer; I want the word spread that those who are Theta but are showing promise in the next few years at the trials will be given the chance to get the training to qualify for a higher rank and skills for roles in the new pack." Both nodded.

He was wanting to see how they would do being the head of the Thetas, having been there, they would understand the feelings of them the best, but would be able to give them a good responsibility which reflected their skills.

Toby and Robin were still too young to qualify but would be old enough before they moved.

Gareth, Adam called, as they relaxed before heading off to dinner, *If you are taking Mark and Ben as your Seconds when we move to take the new pack, I'm thinking we should just stay in our rooms for when William and Joan move out of the Seconds' suite. I think also getting them started training with us would be better.* He wanted the transition to be as smooth as possible but was trying to think the best for both packs.

Stopping for a moment, he realised he was already thinking of the sub pack as *his own pack*, not as a sub-pack. It startled him, but the thought felt right, and even his wolf agreed with it.

Brook followed his thoughts, and cuddled against him as she chuckled, *In everything but name, it will be ours. It's just that Alphas who are under a century rarely are listened to or given respect. By protecting us from that, it lets us get the experience, and allow time for more of the pack to decide which group they wanted to be with in the end. Also, to find the best fit for everyone.*

I like that idea, Gareth replied, *It saves on everyone having to move twice. Have them come see me after dinner tonight. I plan on leaving Ben more in the kitchen and have Mark more of the official person. You are already starting to think like an Alpha! I'm glad we have a role for you which is going to allow you to have enough scope for your skills.* Well, without needing to challenge him for Alpha of this pack.

Adam sent wordless agreement back, and passed on the message for Mark, before settling back to the discussion with their four pups, Sam, and Lea.

Martin, after dinner, would you be free for a chat? Brook called out, having a thought of her own. From the way Toby and Sam had been acting, they felt like leadership material, but she wanted Martin's thoughts first.

She got an amused reply, *I was planning on going to the campfire, but I could give you a few minutes before that.*

It shouldn't take too long; we can head over together after.

They continued to discuss ideas for how to organise their pack, and share thoughts of who they should take. From the amount of work, they were thinking it would be at least four or five years before they could move into the new buildings, but they could easily get the plans started now. Most people were not going to be told till the summer, as he wanted to see how everyone did at the spring trials, as there may be some who did better at them but hadn't come to his notice before.

"Do pass it around: we will be watching the trials for an eye on who to request for the move. I want to see how everyone performs under stress." Brook commented, knowing many didn't bother attending the Trials, unless they were wanting to change rank. Many, like herself, didn't realise how much better she was, and the fact she could qualify higher, now she was looking to qualify for the Alpha level and should be able to do it easily.

*****

Brook smiled and led Martin out the door of the dining room, "I'm not sure how much more of the congratulations I can stand!" She complained to her oldest friend. He just laughed as they headed to one of the small meeting rooms. Adam knew what she was asking, but they didn't both need to be there. While she didn't generally work as a patroller, as she had been more valuable as a trainer, she had trained as one and had worked as one for a bit. Before she had found her mate, she had occasionally helped with the patrols if they were short last minute. Right now, since Adam had yet to have the time to train to have the skills of how to do a patrol, she had stepped back from it. The skills for it were on the list in her head of what she was teaching him when they could fit it in with all their other duties.

Flopping in one of the chairs and leaning back, Martin asked, "So, what were you wanting to ask?"

"Adam and I were wondering about your thoughts about Toby and Sam; do you think they would be good candidates for doing your job in the new pack?"

Martin sat there and thought for quite a bit with his eyes closed, nearly to the point if she couldn't see him tapping his fingers to a beat only he knew, she would have thought he had gone to sleep, before opening them, "For how young they are, and the fact I've had them only for a short time, I'd have to say 'maybe'. That said, since it is going to several years before they would even be able to qualify for the job, I'd say almost for sure they would be able to handle doing it when they come of age. I will work with them, but I would also want one of the older wolves to be an advisor for them, even then."

Brook smiled, "Yes, that's what I'm thinking of too. They can be trained for the next few years, and we wanted to not even inadvertently have something like what we saw at Longview, where one is pushed too soon, which is why Adam's not here. I would like them trained for it but use your judgment; if they can't handle it for any reason, let us know. Do get them some mentors who would be moving with them to the new pack, so they are not without experienced resources."

Martin grinned, "That is understood. I will keep that in mind. I take it you two want to be mostly hands-off for the training?"

"Yes." Brook agreed, "If you think there is something we can do, let us know, and we can do it, otherwise we'll let you do it, as you can look at it objectively, instead of us hovering or of bias for them, or working them too hard. Just keep us informed on how they are doing. Adam also asked if you would be the one to find out those who would work with them for the security forces. You know them better, so would be the best to decide, and to find out who would even want to move." She didn't want to be the cause of an issue like what they had to deal with at Longview.

Martin nodded, "I can do that. I'll even see if we can start a 'junior' program, and take those as young as fifteen, with their parent's consent, for training. That would let me find those young ones who may be a better fit to move. I'm going to be watching the junior trials, to see who's best." The junior trials were testing and a way to assess the younger pack members, and to get them used to the spring trials format of testing. Some were offered special training if they showed skills. It was also a good way to build comradery and do skill assessments for advancement. It also got them used to the way the pack tested, so they knew what to expect when they came of age. "I'll have it passed around that for the next few years we will be looking at the trials as a way to find those with skills to fill positions in the new pack and as replacements here and will be looking at fifteen and up. I hope you don't just limit yourself to the younger. I understand for the top positions you have favourites, but if I find someone better?"

"If you do, put them forward, as if we could have a leader on each shift, and run four shifts, would definitely be the best. Eventually, we would like to do that; maybe before we retire..." She commented, thinking very much long-term and for a pack which would definitely outlive the people in the roles at the start.

Standing up, they walked out together, arms wrapped around each other's waist. Adam met them as they exited the building, and joined them, holding Brook's hand. Both he and Brook knew their bond was good, and that none of her friends would ever come between them, so he wasn't worried about showing affection with other males. It being a cold night, Adam shivered, and when they got to the fire, he stripped and shivered as he shifted to his Were form with a sigh, *Warm...* He commented to Brook, his sending fuzzy with warm feelings, and just got a giggle in reply.

When he sat down, she hopped in his lap, and he wrapped his furred arms around her, *Warm...* She commented back, *Love you, my heated blanket* She teased.

Again, they were treated to more congratulations, but when the third suggestion was given and asked to wait for the week, they decided to stop giving them. Many had questions for their ideas of how it was going to be structured.

We are going to be going on ability more than anything else Adam told them, *I plan on using the Trials to find those with the abilities to do tasks, I am thinking they will be expanded, but not sure yet. Skills like stealth in moving would be one skill. I plan on also doing job skills but will allow for others to try new skills. I don't want to prevent those from trying something new. I want different levels of skill, so not everyone tries to move at the same time.*

"Another," Brook added, "For the next century, as we will be one pack, there will the ability to switch between them easily. So, there is nothing which anyone actually has to decide any time soon. Nobody is going to be making any decision for four or five years, as that is what we are expecting before the new Pack House will be ready to go. We haven't even taken the current down yet! We still need to plan and build it, then deal with the furnishings."

Starting next week, we will be accepting requests for suggestions for the property, including wishes. We will review them and see what we can do. I do know we will have a greenhouse like we have here, and some sort of hot pool. The security will be tighter than it is now here. I want to be able to prevent what happened with Duncan and Keanna from being possible there. But enough of the future! This time is for us to relax! Someone pass me a mug of something tasty, please! He got the laugh he wanted, but also passed an oversized mug with some hot apple cider, he lowered an ear in thanks. The handle was large enough to fit his paw, and was slightly different shaped to handle his muzzle, for him to sip at it. They passed a human-mug to Brook as well, getting a smile of thanks.

Everyone started to have fun singing and laughing at stories and jokes like a normal Monday night. He howled to the songs, enjoying how his wolf had much better musical abilities, and made the songs sound so much better. All night long, Adam had people curling up against him and stroking his soft fur. That made his wolf very happy, as happy as having the pack around him content.

Chapter 17 – Chat Time

Thursday broke bright sunlight, after more than a week of gloomy grey skies. Adam groaned and tried to roll over, but he couldn't move without rolling on top of someone. Using his nose, he not only smelled the expected Charlie and Brook, but also Jess, Joshua, Toby, Robin, *and* Jake! Opening his eyes, he smiled. He was on his back, with Brook snuggled on one side, and Joshua on the other. Jake was laying as a wolf on top of the blankets on top of him, keeping him from being able to roll over. Turning his head, he could see the other three snuggled up behind Brook. Charlie had been pushed to the foot of the bed, where the canine was using his blanket covered leg as a pillow. The large bed was feeling a bit cramped, and as usually happened when he had so many in the bed, he was thinking they needed a bigger bed.

Stretching a bit, he wrapped his arm tighter around Joshua and Brook, and closed his eyes, and dozed back off with a smile waiting for the others to wake.

He had nearly fallen back to sleep when Brook started to stir. He pulled her close for a kiss, then let her go, "Morning!" He called out.

Joshua rolled on his back and stretched, before smiling, "Morning" He called back.

Brook just grumbled; often she didn't want to get up, especially if their pups were curled up with them, "Let me know when it's lunchtime. Not getting up till then." Sliding her head into Adam's armpit to block out the morning light streaming into the room.

Joshua laughed as he rolled out of bed and with a smile headed back to his room to get ready for the day. Jess was not far behind. Both had plenty of duties they needed to do daily and didn't want to cause issues with not having them get done.

With his now free arm, he started to stroke Jake's head and back, to slowly wake him up. He did in canine fashion; yawning and rolling to his side to stretch all four paws out. Blinking sleepily, *Do I have to get up?* He whined.

Yes, you do. I can't get up until you do. You have classes to get to, and if you don't, you won't make it to breakfast and will go hungry. Adam commented. He wouldn't actually go hungry, as there was always food out for those who missed meals, as a hungry wolf was a cranky wolf, and a cranky wolf was one which was dangerous and on a short fuse. The food just wasn't as fresh nor hot; it was stuff which sat for hours well without problems.

Jake grumbled but did hop off the bed and used the dog door in the bottom of nearly every door, as no adult would begrudge a pup from coming for comfort.

Three left. Human-Adam commented to his wolf who just panted laughter in his mind. It wasn't the first time he had to do all the work to get everyone out of his bed before he could get up.

"Toby, Robin; time to get up for breakfast. We have training this morning."

Both grumbled too but got up and headed off. He knew they liked the quiet workouts they did, instead of the general ones the pups normally had, since there were a few who had no interest in learning and disrupted the class occasionally.

Charlie had woken up with all the movement but wasn't moving much. He'd get up as soon as he was up. He disliked being out of sight of Adam for any length of time.

Moving his arm to stroke Brook's back, "I have everyone else up; it's time to get up."

"Yes, you made the bed cold." Brook grumbled with a slight growl, "Still not wanting to get up."

Adam sighed, slipping free, "Fine, stay in bed. *I'm* going to training. I still feel that I can't slack off at all. I've only had a few months of training, even if I can beat any wolf when I really put my mind to it, so far, other than the Alphas. Even with him, it seems that all which is keeping me from winning is experience and a better body-memory. Both those just need training."

Brook pretended to sleep, but listened to his comment, knowing when he got *that* tone it was important, as he sounded like an Elder giving a lecture. She sighed and didn't want to get up, even though her wolf wanted the training too. They were not quite matching Adam anymore, which was irking her, but as her wolf kept nagging her, she needed to train more to get better. "Alright, I'll get up. I want us to be training with Martin or one of the Alphas though.", She told him, as she slid bonelessly out of the bed headfirst onto the heated wood floor as if the weight of the blankets was too much for her to lift, and gravity was too much for her to even sit up, before stretching and finally standing up.

Adam wrapped an arm around her in a quick hug and gave a peck to her lips, as they headed into their closet to get clean clothes.

*****

Over the next two weeks, they got the Longview pack network connected and tested. Every free moment both of them were working out with the best fighters the pack had, working to hone their skills, and not just in human shape but in wolf and Were too. They hadn't heard anything from the Night Depths Pack but had captured three scouts who had quickly surrendered and asked for asylum. Two had moved on to Longview Pack, and one had moved to the Forest's Edge Pack, which was Northwest of the city and was located right at the edge of where the forested foothills met the prairie.

Both had passed on they were getting ready for an attack. With the scouts not returning, the Alpha was telling everyone they were being killed. Neither knew when the attack was planned, nor where it would start. They had found out there were only fifty fighters, as they kept all the females locked up and had only male fighters. MacLaren could field three times that number easily. With the full moon being on the following Tuesday, the senior wolves had thought it would be when they'd attack. Most wolves enjoyed the moon hunt, but they had decided to have just the main pack one, and not allow the after-hunts, as it would be easy to pick them off then.

Once the network had the security checks, he was finally doing a video chat with his sister. It would allow them to have semi-regular chats.

*****

"Hi Tara!" Adam greeted as the video call was connected, seeing his sister visible.

"Hi! I see you finally have it working." She was impressed at the quality, and it was from a little camera above the monitor. Her brother always seemed to know how to make the computer work well.

Adam chuckled, "It was up four days ago, we just had to test it to make sure it was totally secure."

Waving her hand as if she didn't, he could go on for hours about how the technology worked, "I don't need details. Just knowing we can chat without issues is enough." One thing hadn't changed; he still talked lots about tech, more than she could stand.

"Not only chat, e-mail between the two and phone calls are also connected through the secure network." Adam corrected. "How's Ryan?" He asked, changing the topic, seeing her eyes glaze, before she could say something.

Tara got a dreamy look to her eyes, "He's perfect. More than I ever thought possible. He's been showing me the territory on horseback. I've even been assigned a horse, and when possible I take care of her too. At first, she wasn't too sure about Sara, but they are now best buddies." She didn't comment, but both were out having a gallop around the horse paddock. It seemed to her that after being Mated, her abilities with the wolfdog had grown. It had startled her the first time the dog had spoken to her in her mind using actual words. Now, with a bare thought, she could tell where and what Sara was up to and didn't even think about it.

Adam didn't need to ask if they had mated, as he could see part of the mating bite, and it made his wolf happy that she too had someone to watch out for her and would be there for when she needed it, beyond him. The changes caused by the mating would help lessen or even resolve her allergies. He could see she too didn't need to have glasses, as it had been resolved as well.

"Are you considering turning?" Adam asked, curious. He'd support her whatever her decision was and was just curious on which way she was leaning.

"I haven't decided. What do you suggest?" Tara asked. She liked the idea of being able to shift but wasn't too sure on if she would like it having a creature able to follow her every thought and it living in her mind.

Adam shook his head, "I cannot give a suggestion for that sort of decision. I will support it whatever way you go but can't offer advice. One thing to keep in mind, a 'No' can always become a 'Yes'; it's just once turned, you will be stuck with a wolf in your mind. You need to make it totally on your own. I can answer questions about my experience if you want. Another you may want to talk to is Hank. He was turned a century and a half ago."

Tara stared, "He was *Turned*?" she asked, incredulously, "He seems so much the wolf." A very scary wolf at times, too.

Adam laughed at the look on her face, "Yes, he was, so he'd be able to answer the questions; if not, he would know who to point you to. Just be ready to be down for a week or two and being limited to the pack's territory for weeks to months afterward. My turn was extremely fast, so double the time for the average turn."

She sighed, "That is what I'm worried about. I'm thinking about it. My Mating hasn't totally finished, yet." She didn't like the time being down for the start of the turn, even with her mate watching. That was the one stumbling part. She was still trying to decide if it was worth the risk or not.

They discussed a few of her concerns there.

"Have you joined the pack?" he asked.

She nodded, "I did. Still getting used to all the mental bonds, but it does feel nice to know I have others to trust and who care. I don't know how you can bear being the top wolf. It's way too much responsibility for me."

Adam smiled, "Luckily, we are doing a transition, so we are slowly taking over the duties, so we're getting used to it. I'm starting to get used to it." He didn't add his wolf was being a help, as she wouldn't understand until she had one of her own. It was very rare a mated human would not eventually decide to be turned, just some took many decades to decide. Others, the first major illness put them over. The biggest thing was they had to totally want it, or there could be resentment or issues between them and their wolf, causing control issues.

Tara nodded, "So now that we have this link up, I was curious on your plans for the future."

Adam smiled, "Eventually, I want a global network, so all the packs can communicate freely. First a regional network, then continent. Test and secure at each step, so we make sure nobody can get into it."

Tara was impressed, "Wow; that is ambitious."

Adam grinned, "I know, but it is the long term goal. I want to get another couple packs going, then work on developing another main site, and connecting it next then start hooking the packs in that area to that one, with me totally hands-off. At that point, I could go and share it with packs in key areas to make and support the major locations, so no one pack is in control of the entire network, only their part."

Chris knew of his vision, and with Adam being given more and more leadership duties, Chris was taking more and more of the technical side of how to turn the dream into reality, since he had many more skills in doing it as well. He had been helping with the issues getting the first link up, too.

Tara smiled, "How long have you been working on this?"

Adam grinned, "I had a thought of how I'd make the internet, if I was to do so, for years and when I was given the chance to connect this pack, I had an idea and refined the idea before taking it to the Alphas and the Elders. What they could understand, they liked so I got approval. At that point they started getting contact with other packs to see who's interested. So far everyone is. Never before have the elders been able to communicate sensitive things except those which they could drive to."

Tara shook her head, "That's enough on that! Don't drown me in knowledge!"

Adam laughed and nodded. Sobering up, he asked, "I have a young wolf I would like you to keep an eye on, if you could?"

"It's Mark, right?" She had sat down with her mate and had found out what happened, because when they had been together for their mother's birthday, she had been concerned about Adam's injuries.

Adam nodded, "I take it you got the full story."

She looked a little upset, "As much as the pack itself knows. You had a fight, you won, and if he was in human shape, he would have been in tears when you were done. What did you do to him which riled him up?" From what her mate told her, the fact he didn't leave any permanent injury or scars, let alone kill him, her mate had said showed Adam was using a large amount of restraint.

Adam moved forward, "I don't want you to tell anyone but your mate. This is an Alpha Order, make sure he knows that too." He wanted to see if it worked over the link.

She dropped her head, and intoned "Yes, Alpha." Shaking her head as she raised it, "What was that?" She asked. She felt the command in a way she had never felt before. He was pushing the boundaries of the Alpha Order by doing it to his sister, who was in another pack. The fact those Alphas were the ones who told him to keep it quiet would make it right. He disliked having to use the Alpha Powers, which he was just starting to learn how to use and needed the practice. He had accidentally done his first to one of the pack. Luckily, Maria was nearby and noticed. She immediately had both him and Brook trained how to use it, and more importantly, how to not have it triggered.

Adam grinned and ducked his head, "Thanks for letting me test it. That is also under the Alpha Order. An Alpha Order is an order which works only for your pack usually, but with our blood bond, it lets me do it with you and through you to your mate. Only Alphas can use it. It is an order you can't get around. If you try to tell someone other than your mate or tell him other than over the bonds, you will be unable to speak."

"That's goo— wait, you're a Second not an Alpha." How could he be using an Alpha Command, unless he was an Alpha, but how could a pack have two Alphas?

"We are keeping it low key till both Brook, and I turn a century; ask your mate about it. I will tell you more later." He wasn't sure he wanted to tell anyone he was a reincarnation of the pack's old Alpha, Alpha Gareth's grandfather. Taking a breath with her nod, going back to the first topic, "This is under the Alpha Order. I told Mark what the maximums were with stories which happened in recent history. Several caused major pack damage, including several pack wars."

She went white. Her mouth moved, but she didn't say anything. She had heard a bit of pack wars, and they sounded worse than any human war she ever had heard about.

"From the investigation, he had been promoted at his parent's insistence, against the senior enforcer's thoughts of him not being ready yet. It turned out they were right. He was against the influx of members and didn't understand he couldn't prevent it. For that alone, I could have killed the entire patrol. I didn't and called in Hank. I still think with more experience he would be a very good wolf. I also had a chat with his parents about it, and I think it stuck there too."

She smiled, "That sounds like you are giving him a break."

Adam nodded, "Yes, once he's done the limited duty in a decade, I'm going to look at giving him a second chance, if he doesn't get it there." Stopping for a second and he took a breath, "He could do with a friend, though. From what I've heard from Hank, he's been abandoned by his friends."

Tara smiled, "You were always one looking out for the underdog. Now, what was that about the Alpha?" They both loved these long rambling chats, and both had booked a good amount time for doing it.

"It appears my wolf remembered some of his last life, which was Ralph, Gareth's grandfather. Also, I seem to have been getting skills at an astonishing rate, and it seems I inherited his fighting style. I've been training with Gareth to get the experience, and not just half-remembered skills."

"Sounds like you have found the perfect place for yourself." Tara commented, impressed.

Adam grinned at his sister, "Yes. I love my new life as a wolf. It's more of what you do for the pack than personal achievements; it is quite refreshing. I have always felt good helping others but it just seemed those with less morals were the ones who got ahead while those who cared were stomped on so often that many stopped trying. With wolves, everyone works towards a common goal of having a relaxing pack."

Tara blinked, and Adam waited while she had a thoughtful look on her face as she worked through it, "I had wondered about some differences which I had seen, but you are right; nobody thinks for their own betterment but for that of the pack." Taking a longer pause, "With how it's working, I agree it's nice. Everyone cares for the others around them."

Adam nodded, "It's also the fact that if one is really upset it can affect others and then the pack as a whole. Which is why generally packmates look out for the other." Moving to sit up straight, "The last part on the differences between Humans and Wolves is not under the Alpha Order, and this is the end of the Alpha Order."

"Yes Alpha," Tara intoned automatically.

Adam sighed, looking at the time, "Got to go. I have some work I need to do."

They took a few minutes to say goodbye, before they hung up. Adam's wolf enjoyed the time talking to Tara. Even though she wasn't a wolf, he considered her a sibling. He was very happy she now had not only Sara but now a Mate—even if he was only Delta ranked—to help keep her safe.

Heading out, Brook nearly pounced on them, giving them a good kiss; his wolf was still forward. He let out a contented growl as he returned the kiss.

"So, enjoy your chat with your sister?" She asked with a grin.

"Yes, I was able to catch up with her," he commended, *We shared a bit more details on Mark's discipline under an Alpha Order – it works over the video conference correctly.*

Brook nuzzled Adam, *That's not a fun memory. How much did you tell her?* She knew mates share all, and he wouldn't have forced her to keep it from her mate.

I told her I told him stories about what could have happened. I didn't tell her about the special training he lost out on. Both had been very sad for him when they found that out, as Longview couldn't put another name forward nor did they get the application fee back, so they lost out on it. The few who knew his name had been the one put forward were keeping quiet, so it wouldn't make him even more upset. Most never found out unless they were accepted to go.

Brook smiled, "That's good. Come, we have a planning session with the Alphas and Rein." They were discussing what they wanted for their pack, and how they wanted the building laid out. They had finally got the land surveys back, so they could figure out where the best spots to locate the buildings.

*****

Coming out of the meeting, Adam and Brook were grinning, "I love the fact we got basically everything we wanted, and then some! It sounds like we will have a place similar to this but a slightly different layout. The living spaces were similar but were not retrofitted for the security, but was designed in. It was nice that the engineers and architects were there too, so we could get most of the details hammered out."

They had decided on secured and isolated escape stairs which led right to outside the bunker that was the safe room. They had a fire exit for the unlikely fact of a fire in the building, to meet with the human fire codes. The doors and walls around the fire stairs far exceeded the fire codes, as they were rated to protect from an enraged werewolf and to protect them on the way to the safe room. They hoped it never needed to be tested. They even had horizontal isolation doors at each level which could be sealed behind the last one as they descended if the penetration was at a higher level.

Most of the buildings had been designed so they could have easy upgrades or changes without affecting the overall structure. All areas were well insulated, to minimize sound, especially between living spaces.

To save room, they had decided the entry hall would double as the dining room, the gym was bigger, but actually was in a separate building, as they wanted the space to have more training when the weather was bad. The medical and security areas were part of the outer part of the safe room, so they could make sure the non-fighters got to safety, and stand between them and the attackers, if they got that far. The kitchen was also designed to be a secondary safe area, from the way the Chefs refused to leave their domain when the alarms rang, it was better to just have them stay there. All the buildings were being connected by tunnels. They were deep enough in the mountains they could be isolated and need to come and go by air or take several hours through avalanche areas as wolves. They had found they had some places at the edge of the human areas, and often came and went from there.

The pack house was planned to be in a place which actually had a very good view of a pocket valley with a lake, which they planned to have a secret backup safe room, and a nice mountain view off the other side. They were going to have to cut a new access trail into the site, but virgin forest around the site was going to be nice and would hide the building well. There were natural hot and cold springs in the area, so it would allow for easy hot pools and clean water. They didn't need to try to get a drilling rig to get them a water well. They had a little larger senior Beta/Second wing, as they had worked out how the pack was going to be divided and determined the ranks it contained, so they needed it to be a bit larger. Currently, heads of positions were a mix of senior and mid-level Betas, and they wanted to bring them up to be equal in rank and seniority for similar level of work and supervision.

He had accepted a pod layout for the senior members, since the senior wolves tended to be surrounded with some favourites which helped them in their duties, and in turn, the senior looked after the juniors. Giving them each a room, with a shared bathroom between pairs of bedrooms, then a shared gathering space for the team to relax was one of the requests made by the pack already.

The plan was for it to look like a rustic cabin inside, but with plenty of space for pictures and other artwork. Outside, they were going to blend it in with the enviroment as much as possible. Power was going to be from wind and solar, mainly. All had given into Adam's wish for it to be as green as possible, as their wolves liked having minimal impact.

The meeting had run late, so they had a working lunch then dinner, as all wanted the buildings ready to start the ground-breaking as soon as the ground was the soft enough. It was far enough from the existing structures the teardown wouldn't affect the construction, and they would get the access trail in right away. They wanted a presence in the area before another group could even think about trying to take it over.

Walking into their room, he smiled and pulled her in for a kiss, "I'm thinking we should do a paw print of all the founding members in concrete or a resin and have them around the main room."

Brook stood stock still before a slow grin which turned into a big grin, "I love that idea! It would give a legacy for the pack. Tint them in one colour, but then all who join afterwards tint to another colour and change it every century."

Adam smiled, "Showing when they joined." He answered, before giving her a good kiss. They were alone for once. Even Charlie had scampered off somewhere, bored about halfway through the meeting. Reaching with his mind, he could sense Charlie chasing rabbits, just to be running.

Brook nuzzled Adam, "So, what's up with Tara?" She had adopted her as a sister which she never had and was interested.

Adam smiled, "Well, she Mated." He had to pause for Brook's expected squeal of happiness before continuing, "And has been settling in, having joined the pack. She hasn't decided if she is going to be Turned, yet." Adam hoped she would agree sooner than later, but it was totally up to her. Most humans eventually decided they wanted to share the other half of their Mate's life, but some took decades to decide. By law and tradition, he couldn't push her; she had to decide totally on her own. Part of it was as if it wasn't totally agreed, it could end up reacting like a Forced Turn, and those are harder on the body.

*****

Monday morning, Brook and Adam were grinning and chuckling over a joke of their friends as they headed for their meeting. Knocking on the open door's frame before entering and closing the door, they worked at sobering up.

"You two are extra chipper this morning." Gareth commented as he moved to the couch.

"Just some jokes at breakfast," Brook explained.

"OK, first, the architects took your drawings and details and worked out a layout of the facilities for your approval." He told them, as he pulled out a topographical map which had the building outlines on it. Both Adam and Brook leaned forward to look over it well. There didn't seem to be any changes from what the meeting had done, just with a finalized spacing. They had also worked in the mechanical and communications rooms, and the other storage areas to fill in the holes in the layout.

Attached was an estimated picture from where the Alpha's master bedroom would be; a nice panoramic view to the east, overlooking the water. Any buildings on that side were lower and would be contoured to appear to be small hills. The pack house was the only building which was planned to be more than a single story tall above ground.

Signing off on the document, they worked their way through the floor-by-floor plan of the pack house. The kitchen was about the same size as MacLaren's and they had gotten the details of how she wanted it laid out from Lupita, when she had requested to be on the list for the new pack, bringing out desert right to them later in the lunch. She was a large, stocky female. Without shifting from human, he had once seen her shift an entire frozen cow carcass in the freezer, before starting to chop off the parts they needed for their next meal. He smiled at how forward she was and had the memory. Her signature was clearly over the kitchen area, with a back door which went straight into the living area for what would be her Team. There was also a staircase down to below the kitchen, which had a second refrigerator, freezer, and food storage area. All three were huge and designed so they could have several months worth of food on hand or could buy in bulk. The engineers had also put in a good loading dock for it, even if it had a bit of a tunnel, as it was not against the house.

~~~~~

Lupita plunked the tray down with some fresh cinnamon buns on the table. Each was drizzled with icing and maple syrup and steamed gently; there was enough for everyone there. Lupita told Adam and Brook the reason for them; a bribe, "I want to be on the list for the new pack. I talked to Ben, and he thinks I could be the Head Chef."

If you don't accept, you'll be in the doghouse. Brook told him with a picture of him in a very basic wooden doghouse which barely fit his wolf shape, with a collar on his neck attached to a short chain which ended at steel post in the ground. Since they could not get Ben, getting Lupita was the next best thing. Her deserts were the rave of not only the pack, but every single one of their guests. Ben trusted her to take over his duties when he was unable, on the rare occasion. While the kitchen didn't run very formal, it was clearly accepted she was his Second.
~~~~~

With this sort of bribe, I almost want to say 'I'll think about it' to see what other tasty treats we would get. Adam teased Brook.

He got a mental growl and a glare in response. "We were planning on asking you. Accepted." Brook told Lupita, before Adam could reply. They had discussed who they would want, but they thought she wouldn't want to move, as she had been offered a position by many packs as the Head Chef before and had declined it. To the point of brandishing a carving knife as she described why she wasn't accepting an offer from one Alpha, when they pushed. A couple had not only offered her Head Chef, but basically her position would have ranked on par with the Second and would only have answered to the Alpha, along with a large salary and control of the menu and food budget. She was not asking for any conditions or details for them to have her both would realise later. It seemed there were a few who were just waiting for a split to get their promotion from not just her but several others who were the second in duties, and had not accepted promotions to other packs or other duties.

Adam just smiled, "I hope you do make some more tasty treats occasionally," As he munched on the fresh treat with the look of bliss on his face. Giving her a sober look, "Do talk to Ben about learning the executive duties, so you have some experience. Also find out which kitchen staff would want to move, and work with Ben to find out how to split it and get everyone trained for their new duties."

She laughed, "I already have been doing some, so he can have time with his new mate. This will give him a reason to give me more duties, which will get me the experience. Several of the staff are interested. I'll get the list of who is wanting to come with me, and how I'd want *my* kitchen laid out to you."

~~~~~

Shaking his head to clear the memory, they finished reviewing the pack house, Gareth commented, "Once your buildings are done, I think we are going to borrow some ideas and renovate this place. Some of your ideas are very innovative. I suspect many of the Thetas are going
~~~~~

to be surprised at the amenities you are giving them, and the size of the rooms."

Adam smiled, "I thought so too. It shows them they are a valued part of the pack. That is why I had a couple of lounges put on each floor, instead of just down here." He tapped the main floor.

In the lower floor, he had a large tech area for higher end PC workstations, for gaming and photo editing, and other stuff with an oversized AC unit and room for large printers, scanners, and even a plotter. In addition, there was a photography lab, where camera gear could be stored securely. It even contained a good-sized darkroom with isolated ventilation, some stainless-steel sinks, and an emergency wash station which had an alarm which would sound in Medical. There were provisions for the computers in the tech area to have a linked water-cooling loop but hadn't done too much for it so far, as he wasn't sure what would be needed for it. He had it set up with a raised floor, so it would be easy to do changes in the future.

Eventually they finished reviewing the plans. Everyone sighed when they were done without the comments about paperwork, as all knew it was a downside of being at the top.

"I had Chris approach me. He was looking at being turned, and since he doesn't have a Mate, wanted us to bite him. I told him we would be willing do it, but he would have to get permission from you." Adam commented.

Gareth gave a firm nod, "Have him see me this afternoon. I'll make a decision, but we will need to hold off on the actual Turn until the Night Depths pack is dealt with."

"Reasonable." Adam replied and took a moment to let Chris know. It was not a "Yes", but Gareth always wanted to speak with the one being Turned and basically interview them to make sure they had thought the decision out well and had learned all the facts they could. Since they had been living with the pack for months and had fit in with the pack, it was almost a given Chris would get the approval.

"Last part before we go for lunch; we have neutralised about a quarter of the wolfsbane. The chemical reaction apparently is extremely dangerous in large quantities, so they are having to do it a little at a time. They said if they do it faster, it starts vaporizing the wolfsbane instead of reacting with it, and the deadly vapour lingers in the air for hours. We're glad they hadn't found that out. Only us, and the actual researchers know about what is happening, and we must keep it that way." The Alpha laced his words with his Alpha Order, to make absolutely sure it wouldn't be shared. He had already done it with their researchers.

"Yes, Alpha." They both intoned, and understood for the order, and didn't bother even trying to fight it, as they agreed with it.

"Now, Lunch!" Gareth cried out and headed for the door.

Chapter 18 – Fighting the Alpha

Just as Gareth put his hand on the door handle, the Attack alarm sounded, *Attack force on the western border. Twenty wolves are estimated. They were found by a sudden shift of wind by a patrol. They seem to have found where the border of the sensors are and they didn't alert us.* All four heard. Adam and Brook ran for their room to grab their packs, as they had a moment to do so. For once, they had left them behind in their room.

Hold sealing the pack house for ten minutes Gareth called Martin back, keeping the Seconds in the loop.

Attack teams, you have five minutes to gear and meet outside the front door. Alpha Maria called out, *Reserve force team leaders: contact Martin to get your team's station. Form up outside. Everyone needs full gear, as they may be using wolfsbane.*

Adam and Brook were outside and gathering their double team and racing for the border two minutes later, *Don't they know not to piss off hungry wolves?* Adam complained with a mental growl, *I am going to be very grumbly, and no rabbit will survive if they get close.*

Brook and the rest of their team growled in agreement.

Let's try to be civil and not be the aggressors, but don't show leniency either. Brook added, as they listened to the information from the patrols around. Charlie had seemed to pick up a dozen of the dogs as well, which were coming behind. All were almost his size, and Brook knew they would be a great help.

Martin, we have four Betas, six Enforcers, and twelve dogs in our team. We are already out of the pack house valley on the way to the gathered attack. Any new intel? Brook called out. Both knew Martin, as security chief, would stay behind and manage coordinating the teams from the security office. The Alphas would split up and take other groups, as would other Senior Betas.

Still doing a check on the approaches and the rest of the perimeter. All non-combatants and pups are secured. All pack members are accounted for. We're going to keep the normal heavy patrols running, as this is not their entire force. Rein and Mikan are on the way as well. Gareth is leaving in two with the remainder. Came the immediate reply.

Who's the lead of the patrol on-site? Adam called, jumping over the fallen trees and pressing through the deep snow.

Evan and Kuri. They have been able to gather a full force of ten there.

The others followed in his trail. After a half hour, he slipped to the side, letting Brook take the lead, so they weren't tired when they arrived.

Evan, Kuri? We have the first forces. Where are you? Brook called, once they were near the area.

We are just below the peak directly in front of you. You sure made good time. Came Kuri's reply, surprised they were making the time, even with the snow.

They slowed their speed for the climb up to save energy. Adam and Brook met with Kuri, while the rest panted as they recovered from the fast run.

Follow quickly and silently. Keep to the shadows. Kuri warned, as they followed the track to Evan up the ridge staying in the shadows, crawling through the snow at the top. Those still catching their breath stayed back but followed, trying to pant silently.

Evan gave a single tail-flop in greeting as they came up beside them. *Line up with the mountain peak directly ahead and straight below. I counted twenty-seven here.* He said in greeting.

They could see them down in the clearing below seeming to get ready, moving around without rushing.

After a short discussion between the four, *Twenty-seven have been seen here. It leaves almost half their known force unaccounted for.* Brook sent to Martin and the Alphas.

They have another force to the north! Came Martin's fast reply, *That's where the rest are; they just stepped into sensor range. Gareth, Rein, and Mikan are going to deal with them. I'm sending two patrols to help with you, and the cavalry is bogged down in soft snow, so is unusable.* The cavalry was their LAVs and the tank.

Adam sent him a wordless acknowledgement, as he pulled out binoculars, *We have Alpha Night here! This is the primary attack, that's the distraction!* He exclaimed to those with him and to Martin. Their procedures were, since the Alpha was leading another fight, everything would be relayed to Martin, who was coordinating from the Security office. So far, nobody knew what the Alpha's name was, and their pack all just called him 'Alpha Night'. They had been able to smuggle out a current picture of him, so it was a positive confirmation.

Copy, Alpha Night confirmed there. Was the quick reply.

Let's break up their plan here by taking out part of their force before they realise they are spotted. Brook told Adam.

Everyone with bows or crossbows: spread out along the ridge. Hold Fire for now. Adam called out. Two thirds started to move forward, each of the two groups had several white or silver furred wolves. Those moved into the exposed areas, as it was hard to see them against the fresh snow. They could see the force was alert, but still getting ready. It seemed they were waiting for MacLaren to commit their forces to the other attack, from his training.

Gareth wants to time our two counter-attacks at the same time to maximize the surprise and distraction. Martin relayed.

We copy. We plan on a first strike with arrows here from our observation ridge. Reading a surface thought of Brook's, Adam caught her eye and nodded, as he shifted to his Were, and pulled out his Were-sized bow and opened the quiver for it. *We're sending the dogs to take any who try to flee. Does Gareth want to deal with the Alpha?*

It took a long moment for Adam to relay the question, as Brook already started to direct the rest into positions, which included the two additional patrols who came up, each of four wolves and all had bows. They had enough bows that with two shots each they could target almost everyone there. They would either stay hidden unless attacked, or be ready to instantly attack.

He said 'You can have the challenge of fighting an unknown Alpha. It'll be good training for you.' Rumours has him not fighting cleanly, so be on your guard. Was Martin's reply. It was filled with an undertone of respect and shock. Alphas were the hardest to fight, as they needed to be tough enough to fend off all challenges which were tossed at them. It was the first time Gareth and Maria in his knowledge had delegated the attack of an Alpha to another. *Gareth also passed on he is two minutes from being ready, are you?*

Yes, we're ready. Brook called out, letting Adam have the honour of preparing to take out the Alpha. She would be right behind him and protect his back, along with Charlie. The rest would move in, and with the support of the dogs, would take out the rest. Currently, he had got slightly ahead of her in skills, so he could have the honour of taking the Alpha down. The fact he was a bit bulkier than her, as was normal for male wolves, meant he was better equipped to do so as well.

They relayed to prepare, *Make every shot count. Aim for kill shots where possible. The more we take out with arrows, the fewer to get close on us.* Adam informed their team, himself sighting on the Alpha. His wolf didn't care about honour, and right now just wanted the pack dead for the wolfsbane. Add in the attempt at a stealth attack, and they were hoping to have them removed before anything happened.

Counting down, they timed the attacks to happen at both sites simultaneously. *Fire!* Adam called out, as he released his shot at the Alpha, who seemed to realise just in time to get an arm up and take the first arrow in the forearm and the second missed, before Adam dropped his bow and started to bound down the ridge with the others right behind him.

Taking a quick count, they got six which appeared dead, eight who appeared to have major injuries and were out of the fight. They had just by that, taken out half the force. They now had the upper hand, even without counting the dogs.

Reaching the Alpha, as he started to bring his gun up as they came over the surprise of the attack, Adam swatted it across the barrel, bending it and tossing it out of his hands, and growled deeply. He yelped as a knife entered his side, before snarling at the wolf he hadn't noticed, and gave a backhand swing of his paw and sent him flying into a tree. Sliding down it, that wolf was out of the fight.

Putting his attention back to the Alpha, just in time to duck the swing of an axe aimed at his neck. Rolling away from a second swing, Adam pulled out his sword, and stalked forward growling more.

You are just a lowly turned wolf. The Alpha taunted, *I should just kill you and take Brook as my mate.* The comment about his mate was laced with lust and longing, as he could see she was a very good looking she-wolf. Her Were-form was large, well muscled, and could feel the mental strength from her, even if her breasts were small for his taste. He totally disregarded how Adam was clearly a match for her not only physically but also the mental presence.

Adam gripped his wolf from just jumping in, as their attacker seemed to expect. Both smiled inwardly at the roll of nausea and revulsion at the thought the Alpha wanted her rolled from Brook, as she made sure none of his pack interfered with the fight. It soothed both of their rage enough they could harness it to give them energy and an edge. He laughed at the Alpha, who stared at him in surprise, *I think if you finished me, you'd better have a pyre ready, as Brook would finish you *without a second thought. If you would rather fight her instead of me, I have no problem, but the same would apply.* He sent his love and respect for his mate, along with a thanks for the compliment to his mate, knowing the Alpha would be confused.

Coming up with his sword in his paw, Adam showed his teeth and growled menacingly. He had to keep moving and was just able to meet the Alpha's swings or move out of the way. He growled at the fact he couldn't get on the offensive.

What? Am I too much for you? The alpha taunted. He was feeling a bit alarmed. This turned-wolf was matching him an Alpha, from a long line of Alphas! He started to panic and swing more erratically the longer the fight stretched; it was already the longest fight in a decade! Most gave up or were taken out after two or three swings!

Adam did coolly notice the Alpha was tiring faster than him and starting to ooze the scent of panic, so he just watched for his opening while staying on the defensive. Everyone had commented about his endurance, so he didn't mind being defensive at first, and letting his opponent tire himself out, before using his greater endurance to eventually take advantage and win. Taking one opening, he sliced deep into the Alpha's arm, getting a satisfying roar of pain and surprise. The Alpha tried to fend him off, but the next strike was to one of his legs, causing that leg to buckle.

You will not take me alive! The Alpha declared as he fell, letting the axe blade fall on his neck, nearly cutting his head clean off from the weight and sharpness. He had known he had been defeated, and he couldn't handle the shame of being defeated by a Turned-Wolf, no matter how skilled.

Adam shook his head as the other wolves who were still alive let out a mournful howl and instantly gave up, throwing down their weapons, and kneeling or laying submissively, necks bared.

I take it you got the Alpha? Good job! Came the amused, comment from Gareth, startling Adam, *Everyone here just gave a mournful howl and submitted.* It also had an underlay of shocked surprise.

Brook came up with a pressure bandage and started working on the knife wound which he had nearly forgot about in the middle of things, but now was making itself known. He yelped as she cleaned it out with some water and disinfectant. She wrapped it with some vet-wrap; a product which was developed for veterinarians. It stuck to itself, but not to skin or fur. By the end, most of his chest and other parts of his body were covered in it. The injuries he hadn't noticed he had received made themselves known as Brook cleaned them out.

Yes. It seems he went for quick kills and lacked endurance and when he couldn't failed to quickly win, I just had to outwait him. Even with a knife wound, I outlasted him. He had taken out an Alpha who had killed other Alphas in challenges, and some who had two or three centuries of experience; so he was entitled to some bragging.

Adam could hear some crying, and as soon as Brook finished, they headed down to where it was. Kuri was weeping over one of their wolves. Adam knelt and softly placed a paw on Kuri's back, giving silent comfort. He knew Ali was nearly Kuri's littermate and was her yearmate. He knew Kuri had trained with her, and they had been in the same team from the first training till now. He wanted to cry too, as Ali was part of the group which had welcomed Adam when he first came. He could feel the distress as his mind relaxed its focus from the fight.

Did you have any loss there? He asked Gareth, his heart and mind heavy; this was the first loss under his direct orders. *We lost Ali.* He wanted to just break down and cry, but they needed to get all their prisoners back, then deal with the remaining pack. She may have moved with other friends mainly and took on many extra patrol shifts because she enjoyed being out in the forest as a wolf, but he had hung out with her a bit. She was very shy in large groups, but in training, she was a fighter and gave her all. He had heard she was totally dependable when out patrolling too and was known to see clues which had been missed by others at times.

Tyron, Came the sighed reply. *You and Brook will need to come see me when you get back. Martin is arranging some snowcats to get out to *you, but they are slow.* The snowcats had big, wide tracks designed to float on top of the snow, but they were not fast at all. A five-year-old pup could run as fast as they could go on fresh snow, where it was packed, they were fast. And the width made it tricky to go through the forested areas.

He couldn't hold it in any longer and tilted his wolfish head back and gave a low mournful howl for the lost packmate and friend. Most of the others from their pack, those who weren't keeping an eye on the Night Depths pack, joined in on the howl. Kuri joined in lowly, as shared grief did help. After a while he ended the call and most stopped quickly. Kuri had shifted to her Were and cradled her fallen near-sister to better howl out her grief, leaning into Adam and Brook's embrace.

Several of the totally cowed prisoners were recruited to carry their fallen alpha, or other packmates. Most took their duties without comment, although the one first asked to carry the alpha just said, "Let him rot where he fell. I am glad to see the last of him." And refused to carry the body, several called out agreement.

Exasperated, Adam called out, *I need a volunteer to carry your former alpha's body back. It doesn't mean he will be burned with full honours fitting a good Alpha, just we need to move away from here. This is too close to the human trails for my liking.*

One wolf came forward, "I would carry it for you, Alpha." As he bowed to him. To his mind, this dark-furred wolf who they had been told was a Turned-Wolf, which they had been taught were only fit to be Omegas, was much more of an Alpha than theirs had ever been. He genuinely seemed to care about all those around him. He even openly grieved for the loss of a single packmate, and a female at that. Their old Alpha never grieved with the pack, and often belittled a loss as their own fault. He also was as strong as their former Alpha, but had much greater endurance, showing he was better to lead them.

Adam nodded, *Thank you. I'm not an Alpha, yet. I'm just a Second in training*

The wolf shook his head, "According to our laws, since you killed the old Alpha, you are now our Alpha, Alpha." He stated respectfully but cringing slightly from habit. The old alpha would have back handed him for contradicting him, even if he was wrong. He would have given the swat before giving the correction, too.

Adam sighed as Brook chuckled in the back of his mind. *Alpha, it seems we may have an issue. It seems they have a law that because I killed their Alpha, I am now their Alpha.* He called to Gareth, trying to keep the whining from his voice, but unable to keep a silent *I'm not worthy for this* or *I'm not ready to be Alpha* from running through his head as he oversaw the cleaning of the fight, so no human would stumble onto it. He could already see their captives showing him respect and loyalty as they joined the MacLaren wolves in the cleanup, but often glancing back at him, some with awe in their eyes and others with hope. His wolf refused to let him dismiss them.

It took a while before Gareth responded with just a feeling of near hysterical laughter, and he seemed to still be laughing even as they grieved the two lost pack members, *It is the old, traditional, way. Before we got a better succession, the Second, or whoever wanted to lead the pack, had to fight the Alpha and win in a Pack Challenge. Usually, the Alpha fought to the death, unless they felt the other was worthy of being their successor, but the other often could submit and have everything go back to normal.* Gareth seemed to get control of his amusement, as his next response was much more even tempered, *They are all yours. We will discuss it when we are back. I will pass it on to your new members here, bring them to the pack house, and we will work out something for living arrangements for now.*

Adam just sighed, *I'm not ready to be an Alpha!* He whined to Brook who just laughed at him. *You do realise it also makes you their Alpha, my mate.* He told her. From the shocked look on her face, she hadn't realised she had also been elevated, if he was. Now it was her turn to be shocked and his to silently laugh at the look on her face, and her feeling she wasn't ready to be an Alpha.

Turning to the gathered wolves, most of the now-former Night Depths watching him as much as they could, with a bit of fear, wondering what he would do. *Since your laws state I am your Alpha, I have to introduce you to my Mate.* He reached an arm out, and Brook slid into it, *I am Adam, and this is Brook. I don't know how it was done before, but she is my equal and will lead at my side.* He said it firmly, and with the hard feeling, all there could tell he would take no dissent to it, *We will gather the rest of your former pack and find out what shall be done. If any don't wish to live by my rules, let me know before we form the pack bonds, as accepting the pack bonds means you accept our decisions and rules.*

There were quite a few who were looking startled, but none looked like they couldn't live with the Alpha's mate being their equal and an Alpha alongside him, *One key rule: all wolves, no matter if they are male or female, born or turned, are ranked by skills. I will see about using the MacLaren's Spring Trials to rank all of you, without any bias. We will discuss it later.* The pronouncement seemed to startle them even more and had many murmuring about it. Several were looking at him with startled respect, some with hope. A couple of the larger ones were now showing some fear. They could feel these orders were not something he would accept dissent for.

Conferring with Brook and both Alphas, after getting an accurate count of Night Depths before the attack. They figured out moving down the Omegas from the loft would give them more than enough room to house all of them, even if it was more of barrack-style, until his new pack house was ready.

It was passed to Martin to organise it and make sure there would be food for those they were bringing in. Many of them looked underfed to both Adam and Brook.

They decided to let two go back as runners and tell the pack to start getting ready to move. Adam and Brook were going to ride over to introduce themselves to the non-combatants and those who had stayed behind.

Just managing to keep up with his injuries, he stayed to the tail, till they met up with the snowcat. Everyone, including his mate, insisted he take the ride back. Growling under his breath, Adam finally gave in. He could see the respect in his new pack's members. Brook reminded him not to shift from his Were until the healers told him he could, as it could make the wound worse. The shifting pulled skin and muscles around, so when there was a cut, it could tear and make the injury much worse.

As he rested on the way back, he discussed names for the pack with Brook. They didn't want to use 'Shadowed River', as that pack no longer existed after being declared nameless and rogue. Thinking of the fact the valley was nearly untouched, as there was a major river blocking accessand steep cliffs on the "easy" ways, they settled on Wild Valley Pack.

Looking to the others in the snowcat as the engine purred as it floated over the deep snow taking them back to the pack house, most cringed when he looked at them. He mentally sighed, *We are working on a new pack house, as the MacLaren Pack is getting too big, so we are working to split.* He smiled as all those who were awake were listening with rapt attention, *I have already talked to Alphas Gareth and Maria. They have approved you having me as your Alpha, while we still reside at MacLaren. We are clearing an area out which will fit all of you, including those back at your current pack house.*

"Alpha?" One which was sporting an arrow to the arm asked hesitantly, and waited for Adam to nod before continuing, "I assume this new pack is going to be where the Shadowed River was from all the surveying of the valley." At another nod of confirmation, he leaned back with a happy sigh, "You found a most beautiful location to build. I am honoured at the chance to live there." Several others murmured agreements. Later, they would learn several had been scouts in the area, but all had pulled out as they started to patrol the areas more.

Adam lowered his ears in a blush and gave a wolfish smile, *We decided to call it Wild Valley Pack.*

If they weren't injured and many strapped in tight, there would have been some dancing. All had broad smiles on their faces, as they all liked the name.

As Adam was helped out, his wounds starting to hurt again, Brook ran up and shifted from her wolf to her Were, and slipped an arm around him, on his hurt side, *Lean on me.* She ordered him. He decided to not say a thing, as she helped him down to the medical. They immediately had him in a room and a healer checking him, "You missed your liver and kidneys by a small amount, but just nicked an artery; you'll be on your feet in an hour. Your Alpha Healing rates have kicked in. The others are not major, they just hit skin and muscles." The healer told them, as Brook shifted to human to not be in the way but be able to stay close to her mate.

Before he could leave after having finished treating the injuries, Brook stopped him, "What Alpha Healing rate?"

The healer shook his head, "I said too much as it is; talk to Alpha Gareth." He told them, before stepping out.

Brook crawled up on Adam's healthy side and cuddled him, as all knew having your mate helped speed healing. With mutual thoughts, they spent the time waiting for him to heal enough they could leave chatting about plans on how they wanted to run the pack. First, they agreed on was ability would determine roles, not birth. They decided they would add 'Pup' as a formal rank and for everyone who wasn't of age and hadn't passed a qualification test. It would be a spread of duties and tasks, with heavy on training and learning. Adam also like the idea of Junior rankings, but they needed to discuss it further before they would do them. He thought about also having it include the Theta duties, under supervision.

By the time they come of age, I want all pups to know what the Thetas do and have done at least a week with every duty, so that in a pinch all members could lend a paw to help with cleaning, cooking, or maintaining the property. Adam offered.

Brook took a bit to think, "I like that; it would let those who think they are too good to do the jobs know exactly how much work goes into doing them. It might get them to respect those who do them regularly. The fact it enables everyone to help when we have major events is good too." She grinned, "Also, I think the adults should have to do at least one week in a decade, as a refresher." She added, "Although for the cleaning those wouldn't be the dirtiest areas, save those for punishments."

Adam looked slyly, *And knowing which each detest the most would give us a nice punishment to give to those who step out of line, while not having to use the Omega for anything but the most grievous infractions. We have such long lives; I don't like the fact you really can't recover from it.*

Brook nodded in agreement. She felt exile as a lone wolf or even death with honour was better than being named Omega.

The healer slipped in, "I happened to overhear the last part of your discussion," He commented, as he checked Adam's wound, "I happen to agree. Punishments, when they are over, which don't leave lasting marks are best. I have seen too many who have been made Omegas, only for them to turn suicidal, thinking their lives are over. The more senior they were, the more likely they are to kill themselves instead of taking help." Nodding to himself, "OK, you can shift to human now,"

Adam closed his eyes and slid back to his human shape, the wound shrinking slightly, but starting to bleed slightly.

The healer quickly applied a dressing to it, and taped it into place, and gave it a boost to the healing, so it didn't need to be stitched, "OK, now keep it dry for the next day or so, till it's sealed. This sort of wound tends to heal from the inside out."

Adam smiled, "Thanks, now to chat with Gareth and then get the others."

Jess slipped in with some clothes and quick food which could be eaten with the hands. She wore an impish grin, "I thought I felt you shift, and thought you two might want something to wear, and need some food, since you missed lunch."

Adam pulled her in for a hug, "I can never say it enough, but thank you for taking such good care of us, even with your increasing duties. Don't ever think we are not appreciative, even if we don't say anything about it."

Jess blushed tomato red and didn't say anything, just wrapped her arms around him. Suddenly she pulled back, "Alpha? When did you become an Alpha?" She blurted out, startled. She could smell the difference in his scent, and checking the bonds, could feel it there too.

Brook just chuckled, as Adam sighed. She grabbed some of the food, leaving the explanation to her mate, "It seems that by killing the Night Depths' Alpha, I became their Alpha. We will be sharing it with the pack tonight at dinner. Feel free to pass it onto Joshua, Robin, Toby, Sam, and Lea; no others, and make sure they know not to pass it on either. Our Pack will be staying up in the loft." Adam explained; he still wasn't too sure how it happened.

"That... Is... Interesting" Jess said slowly. It was so way off from what she was expecting.

Brook pulled a thought from Adam's mind, "We think you and Joshua would be best to be the contact for the Thetas. Many, I suspect, are going to be very traumatized. That you are young and are the ones to take care of us, would mean you could bring their concerns, which they are too shy or afraid to bring to us themselves. Eventually, we would like you to be the head of the housekeeping, which is a Beta rank."

Jess just stood there, unable to think. Too many new ideas she had to digest all at once!

Brook grinned, turned her around and softly pushed her to the door, "Let it sink in, and go about your day!" Jess woodenly walked out the door and headed back to make sure all the cleaning had been done. Normally, she'd be training this afternoon, but due to the fight the schedule for today would be destroyed and none of the trainers would be doing any training, as they had almost all been involved with the fighting. Those who hadn't, had already headed out to replace the patrols who had been in the fights and were too tired to continue the patrols.

*****

The Healer took them on the rounds to see those who were in-jured—most were majorly honoured their Alpha personally came to check up on them, as their old Alpha had never come to see how they were in Medical and visited those of MacLaren as well. Afterwards, they went to chat with Gareth. He met them at the entry to the medical, hav-ing just finished his own rounds of the injured.

Holding up a hand, "Wait till we are in my office, much of what I'm going to tell you is for Alphas only."

Both nodded and used the short walk to get their thoughts in order.

Closing and locking the door behind the two, Gareth turned and smiled, "First, I want to pass on mine and Maria's congratulations, and welcome to the most exclusive club of being Alphas." He sat down on one couch, and Brook and Adam sat on the other. Adam winced as his injuries pulled a bit.

"First, while you are here, we will be in charge, and you will act like Seconds." Gareth told them, getting nods. They both expected and agreed to it, even their wolves didn't have an issue with submitting to the much more experienced Alpha.

"I know the healer let it slip your healing is increased, but the full story is, you can pull health and energy from the pack through the bonds, and you will be able to sense if there are problems. Also, the pack will sense you and can pull comfort from you." Gareth continued.

"Wait," Adam called out, "We haven't formed formal bonds with anyone yet!"

Gareth nodded, "Those who were at the fight would have had the tentative bonds formed, as they accepted you as their Alpha. They will last at most a week or so." He grinned, "As did those who you visited in Medical. They already consider you their Alpha, so even without the bonds, their minds are reaching out for you, and yours is accepting them." Both could feel their wolf agreeing with him, and a slight con-tent feeling of having members to lead, inspire, and to protect. He got serious, "You need to formalize and finalize the bonds before they fade, or it will greatly harm their trust in you."

Adam and Brook nodded, now understanding where the abilities came from, "I want to head out and gather the rest of the former Night Depths here *today* and discuss what to do with the fallen. Several wanted to just leave Night there to rot; I suspect he ruled through fear and intimidation. I want them to decide together his fate."

Gareth went a little pale, "I didn't realise it was that bad. He would have had his closest with him, so I'm still very surprised how fast they transferred allegiance. I'll leave that with you. I don't need to be involved. It's something for your pack to deal with. Just let me know what is decided."

Taking a breath, "Next, your bonds with the pack—once formalized—are closer to mate bonds. In the fact, there is no limitation on distance to mind-speak to anyone, or them with you. I personally only use it rarely, as some members travel just to get away from the tight pack bonds." He didn't bother mentioning that when Brook had been caught in the rockslide, he had felt it and had been trying to track her down to send help, even as Adam had got to her and had been taking her to somewhere they could call. "Another, you will not be able to travel for more than a month away from your pack, without the bonds starting to get painful. Think of winding an elastic around your finger then pulling it, it starts to dig in and leave it long enough, it will snap. If it happens, both you and your pack will be badly hurt."

Both paled and didn't want to cause that, "We'll be careful." Brook answered for both of them.

Gareth nodded, "I am here to give you some advice, but you two have to work out much on your own, and develop your own style of being Alphas. You will make mistakes, but as long as you are forward with your pack, they should forgive you."

Getting a nod of agreement from both, Gareth smiled, "Now, I assume you want to do the formal bonds tomorrow?"

Adam nodded decisively, "I want to show them they are valued, but also to have some sort of control over them, if they are out of line with what this pack's rules are."

Gareth grinned, "In that case, go get the rest of your pack. I have been told there was only forty who stayed behind. They stripped the pack of all the fighters to try to get the wolfsbane back. The pack had been told we were making weapons to use against them. Which, when we were shown to just be using arrows, made most just decide their alpha lied and give up. I have two busses and two trucks warming up for you, with drivers."

Both smiled their thanks and headed out of the office. Heading to the loft, both smiled as those who had come back with them came up to greet them. They were surprised when they were pulled in for hugs. The first couple tensing before relaxing in the hugs. There quickly formed a line for all to get a hug and comfort from the Alphas. Several broke down crying when they got the hug as it was the first time in a long time—first time ever for some—they had a friendly contact with the Alphas. All could feel how much both cared about them.

Once they were done, "I need four to come with us. We are going to get the rest of the pack. We have enough room here to fit you all up here." Adam requested.

"Alpha, where did the Deltas who were up here go?" One asked.

Adam shook his head, "This floor generally is used for our Omegas, and as overflow for guests. We currently have only two Omegas, and they happily moved to our Theta quarters, on the floor below."

That got a major noise, and everyone was startled. At the fact this space was what the Omegas got, they wondered what did the senior wolves get? Four stepped forward to stand behind their Alphas.

Raising a hand, Adam got instant silence, "We will be dealing with all the dead when we get back. As a pack, we will decide on their fate. I know many want the old Alpha to be left as carrion, but we don't do that here. I am willing to have him buried in an unmarked grave, but that decision is for everyone to decide. We'll see you when we are back with the rest of the pack."

Chapter 19 – From Ashes...

Reaching the pack was much faster than they thought it would be, as they could move on some clear highways most of the way. Since they were closer to the humans, they had to live more as humans, so they would find the new pack location refreshing. They could run around in their wolf or even Were forms without worrying about humans seeing them. It was one reason they chose that spot to build the new pack house at.

Pulling in, they stepped out of the bus, as a gun went off, hitting the ground several feet away. The largest of their escorts stepped forward placing himself between the shooter and their Alpha, clearly showing without words hc would bodily protect with his life, if necessary, "This is your new Alpha! Show him some respect! He wants to take you away to a place where the Omegas live like Deltas, and there is enough food for all!"

"Like hell he is! He's still a young pup! He's not even half a century!" Called out a female, who had a skirt which just barely covered her rear, a bare midriff, and a tacky-looking top which seemed to not be able to contain her breasts. Her hair was all done up in ringlets, her face was caked thickly in makeup, and her nails were even too long for Brook.

How can she walk in such high heels? They must be six inches! Brook asked her mate, her disgust for this bimbo showing clearly, as she moved to stand at Adam's shoulder. From the feelings she had got from the others, they weren't used to mated Alphas, so she was going to keep a backseat to Adam until they got back but wouldn't let anyone stomp on her rights once they had been told about them.

Adam growled at the implied insult, "I may be young, but I did take care of the one who called himself Alpha Night." Stepping closer to the female, he growled again, "And who are you?"

"Cindy." was the snapped reply.

Adam showed a feral grin, "Well, Cindy, since you are refusing to accept that I'm the Alpha, even with others telling you it, and you certainly felt his death. You have the choice of Challenging me here and now for being Alpha, or with leaving as a Lone wolf. You have one hour to decide."

Many were surprised he would be willing to accept a challenge for the pack from a *female*, let alone one who already attacked. Many were muttering about him being too lenient, as the old Alpha would have already killed her.

Adam coolly kept an eye out for the gun to start moving, so was able to duck the bullet aimed at his head. Many wolves around him growled. You couldn't just attack, and weapons were never permitted in a challenge without consent of both sides, and *never* a projectile weapon. Most wolves disliked using guns, as they were noisy and didn't require much for skills. They were basically a "death stick" which only the weak used, unless absolutely needed. They did recognise they were much faster than a bow.

Before she could realise she had missed, Adam had torn the gun out of her hand and wrapped a hand around her neck, "You just earned yourself an execution." Looking at the others, "What's the punishment for attacking the Alpha, according to your laws?"

A very elderly woman was helped forward, "I never thought to live to see the day the pack would be delivered from that demon." She said, bowing her head to him, "Alpha, according to the laws, *as they are currently written*, for an unprovoked attack, the person is to get a death of your choice then burial in an unmarked grave. In the past, they often just tossed the body out for animals to play with, after being tortured to death. If the Alpha was feeling vindictive, sometime they were tossed out alive but broken past the point of healing for a slow death from the animals and exposure."

"Unprovoked? He killed my Mate-to-be. I was taking vengeance!" Came Cindy's gasped reply.

The elder gave her a wilting look, "You cannot 'become' someone's mate. You either are or are not. Since you are not, you cannot claim mate-vengeance. Also, he had told you that you could challenge him for the pack, which is the same as a mate-challenge for an Alpha, and you decided on an unprovoked attack instead, while he waited for you to voice your decision. If you did it to any wolf, under those conditions, they have the right to instantly kill you."

"But—" Cindy started before Adam tightened his grip as his wolf pushed forward, wanting to just end this threat.

"Is there anyone who dissents from the decision on her death? Speak now!" Adam called out loudly; most of the pack seemed to be there. A few who looked to be her friends, as they were also wearing the same sort of outfit, seemed to start to want to speak, but at Adam's level look, they looked at their feet and refused to say anything.

While he waited, he discussed with Brook what form her death would be. Brook was all for ripping her to shreds while still alive for her attacks on her mate; leave it as a warning for others for unprovoked at-tacks would not be tolerated unless they wanted a very painful death. Brook conceded when he offered another death, which was a bit less messy.

"Since there is no dissent," Adam said taking on a formal tone, "I, Adam, Alpha of what remains of the Night Depths Pack, sentence you to death for refusing a succession of Alpha, for not once but for twice attacking me unprovoked and unchallenged with a gun, and for false claim of a mate." He loosened his hand, "Any last words?" he asked mildly.

She started to squirm and try to escape, "I refuse to accept your judg-ment! You are not my Alpha! You killed my mate! I demand vengeance!

I do not answer to you! You are lower than Omega; you were born a human!"

Releasing his hand, he struck with his other fist to her neck, crushing her throat. She fell to the ground writhing, trying to breath but unable to do so around the crushed trachea, "Then I also name you Rogue, for refusing a judgment by the Alpha." Wolf-Adam growled out, having decided on the death and had pushed his human aside to administer it, for the insults given to them. They were Alpha, not below Omega. He was incensed that although she wanted vengeance, she refused his human's offer of a Challenge fight and instead wanted just to kill an Alpha for the sole cause of winning a fight where their opponent chose to die.

The slow death his wolf had given her seemed almost too much to the human part of Adam, taking several minutes before he could even think, after realising what his had had done. Many of the pack nodded in agreement and had a look of savage pleasure, he decided to not do anything about it as she slowly died of suffocation. Giving her no more thought as the Pack needed him, he stepped past her, "When she is dead, load the body up. She will be buried as a rogue. I want everyone to be there for the farewell to the fallen. Alpha Gareth is waiting for us to be back." He told the two truck drivers and got a quiet, "Yes, Alpha."

He saw many with packs brimming with possessions, "As you have heard, I am Adam, and I defeated Alpha Night. He decided to die than live defeated. This is my Mate—" He said, wrapping an arm around Brook, pulling her close, "—Brook. She will be my equal and will rule by my side." He turned deadly serious, "She is also your Alpha." He told them with a slight growl, showing it was non-negotiable.

He saw many dubious faces, but the oldest looked happy, as did many of the females. "Gather what you need. We have enough bedding and basic clothes if you need. Also, you do not need to worry about food, there will be plenty for all. Tonight is for the fallen in the fights. All have been treated with respect. Tomorrow is for the living. We have two trucks, so there is plenty of room, if there is stuff you need to bring."

Looking at the shape of the building, with many cracked windows, shingles missing from the roof, and most of the rest curled, cracked, and covered in moss. With most of the snow melted away, he could tell there wasn't much insulation either. Parts of the siding were also falling off. A silent inquiry to his mate got a shudder; this was worse than the condition of the nameless' pack house. They weren't even going to look at the condition of the inside, as the building was in such a state of disrepair, it would be cheaper to replace than repair. From here they could smell, it hadn't been cleaned in a very long time, and there was a lack of working sanitation.

Several just moved forward to them, tentatively, with just having a backpack or bag of stuff, "This is all we have, Alphas," One said quietly, "We're Omegas."

Adam counted more than a dozen. "That's fine. I will be reviewing what you did to become Omegas over the next few weeks. When we took out the..." He paused momentarily, as they would not know the other pack was now nameless. "The other pack, we overturned most of them."

They looked at him with startled eyes, "We were told you kept less than a quarter and killed the rest!"

Adam sighed, "No, we killed as few as we could and only those who attacked. We did only keep less than a quarter, but several other packs accepted the others into them, Brook and I even escorted the group which went to Longview Pack ourselves." He didn't comment on the issues during that trip, since it didn't matter.

They looked relieved. "Come," Adam coaxed, "You can get on the bus with your bags. Relax."

Many smiled and all came for a hug from both of them before climbing on the bus. While some were not in tears, their eyes were bright while they held them back. They could already sense he would be a fair Alpha, and be there not just for the most senior, and treat the rest like slaves.

*****

Adam relaxed as the last of the stuff was loaded. Few had taken more than a bag or two. He remembered a comment from one of their scouts which had come back with them, *"Only the Alpha's chosen few had any sort of money for luxuries. Most had to save up for months to get anything more than a pallet on the floor."* He commented in an aside to a longer conversation. Adam sighed as he had then, before commenting to Brook, who was riding on the other bus, *We will be needing to be firm with those few who were the 'Alpha's favourites' but be gentle to the rest.*

One of the Elders had carried a large urn in their arms and refused to relinquish it to the care of anyone else. *The Pack Urn,* Brook commented with awe when she saw it. Pack Urns were never moved from the pack, except when the pack itself moved. That the Elder was bringing it showed that the pack was no longer at this location. Even he knew what that meant and assisted the Elder onto the bus, giving the respect the urn deserved. The urn would contain some ash from every member of the pack which had died, since it was started. He had the Shadowed River Urn hidden, instead of tossing all the ash to the wind, and destroying the Urn itself, as was normal when a pack was made nameless. The results from the decisions of the last Alpha weren't ones he was comfortable on giving to those who had died. He not only had the agreement of his wolf, but of his mate too. Some would be added to their own pack's now, and the same with Night Depths. Only then would the *nameless pack*'s urn be destroyed. He had confided in Gareth what he had done and had taken a bit to talk him around to his thought. Eventually, he had agreed, but on the condition the urn was destroyed soon.

Brook gave a frustrated growl in agreement, *I had a similar thought. From the look here, they may need our physical presence till we get the full bonds formed. Gareth had said we can comfort over the bonds, but for this, I think we need to give them our physical presence.*

He gave a wordless agreement.

Jess, Joshua? We're on the way back. You have about an hour. Get the loft set up for everyone to curl up together, we will be up there too. You and your sibs would be welcome to join us.

Jess gave a startled affirmative, and with Joshua, they quickly rounded up some help. How he said it, it sounded like they were worse than the few who had joined from the nameless pack, and their stories had made her cry at times.

Sitting back, Adam chatted with those around him. He had specifically sat in the middle of the bus so the most could sit close to him. Most asked him quiet questions, very few he refused to answer. Most were on his life before becoming a wolf, and to those he answered, "I'm no longer the person I was then." That Adam could no more turn into a wolf than he could lead a pack. That Adam was at best a Gamma, and more likely a Theta, for all his skills with computers.

They were surprised when they learned he had shifted for the first time at the Winter Solstice, seeing how much of a wolf he was. Even the elders showed some respect, one even commented they thought he had several decades as a wolf at least from how he moved and reacted. He wasn't going to say anything about his wolf remembering his previous incarnation, till after they were fully bonded to them. And then only to a very select few.

Driving up to the parking, there were several snowcats with skidded trailers, Adam stood up, "The pack house's access road is currently snowed in, so we have our snowcats to get you and your stuff to the pack house. Elders and pups, you just go to the snowcats, the rest of us will deal with unloading." He could sense Brook giving the same orders in the other bus. Both had been surprised at how few pups there were. There had been only fifteen pups, and five he'd consider elders, which had left fifteen who weren't omegas, Which was a few more than they had been told, but they weren't worrying about exact counts.

Several of the Elders smiled relieved at him; he was going to respect their age and ability.

There were a few who complained, but just a look silenced most, and a glare did the rest, when they objected to lifting and carrying. The few larger items were easily moved, then it was mostly bags of various sort which they just handed over. Those he felt deserved rewarding were given seats in the arctic cats. The rest he took down to the tunnel. Seeing how those who work hardest got rewarded, several smirked at the alarm on the face of those who tried to shirk the workload or only did as little as they could to not get a reprimand, but then tried to sneak into a seat in the snowcats, as they had been the Alpha's favourites.

Security was watching, and opened the doors for them, then met them with temporary IDs. Adam smiled, "These IDs are set to get you into the gym, and many other of the common area doors. Keep them with you at all times. We will get permanent ones with photos later this week." They would do them after they had the formal bonds and oaths, and it would be Wild Valley Pack ID.

Many stepped back as Charlie bounded up to Adam and whined as he leaned his head into his side. "This is Charlie, he may smell like sort of a Were, but he is not. They are intelligent, though. You will see many here, as we breed them; partly as cover for having a large number of 'wolves' and for an excuse for the fur on the furniture. All have basic service animal registration and training, and some go on to be seeing eye dogs or other service animals for select humans. Others are used to help with patrolling. This one chose me when I was first Mated, and still human, for my protection. I don't need him, but he is a handy companion, and he does watch my back generally in a fight, or in the last one, he led other dogs, to keep watch at the edge of the fight, and to guard any who went down. Come we'll get you settled."

Brook took the oldest Elders, and those who would have trouble with the stairs (there were a few she felt were ill, but not enough to make them go to medical) up the elevator, as Adam led them up the stairs. Many marvelled at the look of the place and all the mouldings. Several stopped to look at some.

Taking them to the top, he led them into the loft. Several kitchen staff were helping Jess and Joshua lay out a couple of tables of food.

Jess came over after she finished, "I thought everyone may want to relax up here, so got permission from the chefs and from the Alphas, we have two hours before the memorial services." She leaned into him and relaxed as Adam automatically wrapped his arm around her, her wolf was relaxing too, enjoying being held.

He smiled his thanks, "This is Jess, and Joshua is over there," Joshua waved as some looked, "They are two of the four Brook and I have adopted as our pups. I have two other pups which we keep an eye on, among others who look to us. If any of you have questions which you don't want to bring to me or Brook, Jess and Joshua will be around, as they are in charge of the cleaning and maintenance of this floor. The memorial service starts in two hours; it is also for the fallen from Night Depths. They gave their lives honourably for the pack." He might not like the alpha's decisions, but he wasn't going to treat the members as Rogues, unless they were greatly dishonourable.

Most of the senior wolves were very startled at the last. The fact he claimed two who were doing the menial duty of putting food out, and then they were told they were also in charge of the cleaning? Most didn't know what to think as it was so far out from what they expected a pup of the Alpha to be doing.

Many of the low wolves were looking contemplative, especially those who had said they were Omegas. Many went to go to the food, and at the first shoving, Adam went over to those senior wolves trying to force their way in and lifted them by their collars. They looked well fed, while those they pushed away didn't, "You now get to wait till everyone else is done getting their choice." Looking around everyone was watching, "I was going to hold off with the rules till tomorrow. When getting food, everyone is equal. You will be civil and let those already there get their choice. You will not force them away. Also, pups and pregnant females get their food first."

Adam sighed before starting to speak, "At the end of the memorial, there will be no longer a Night Depths Pack. Brook and I have a new pack, and a pack house similar to this one planned for where Shadowed River was. It will be called Wild Valley Pack. We will spend the day tomorrow discussing the rules and policies for the new pack. Any who feel they cannot live by them can either join another pack or go as a Lone Wolf with our blessing."

Brook came up with two jars of stones, one of dark one of light, and an empty metal jar as the last sat down with their food. Adam nodded, *Glad you found them* he told her, as it would make it easy. "We have Alpha Night's body still. As a Pack, I want the decision if he should be burned, or left in an unmarked grave to rot. One jar is full of light-coloured stones, the other has dark. Each are to take one of each, and then we will do the next part."

They were all curious enough they did as he asked. Most sat at the few tables, or on the couches, as Brook went around with the jars.

Once she was done, "Now I am letting you as a pack decide what happens to his body. It was your previous Alpha. I have listened to all the views which I could. A few have given they want his body cremated with honour for the protection he has given the pack over his life. Others wanted to leave him for the animals, which I cannot allow, as there are too many humans. I am not taking any more discussion. The two options you have, is dark: dishonourable burial in an unmarked grave known only to those who do the burial. The other is light for an honourable cremation. Joshua will come around with the jar for your vote. Put only *one* of the pieces in, the other we will collect later."

Once the votes were in, Adam cleared a large serving tray, and upturned the jar. It was almost pure dark. There were maybe a couple handfuls of lighter bits in it. "The pack has spoken. Once we are done the memorial service, I will need four volunteers. Two for each of the two bodies which need to be buried. We can deal with the honourable dead first. Finish your meal, I need to let Alpha Gareth know the result."

Stepping outside the door, Adam relaxed back against it and let his breath out in a sigh, *Alpha, the decision is in: Burial. There was only a very small number of dissenting. I did the light and dark stones, so there could be no complaint about fixing the vote. They are probably worse off than we ever suspected if they hated him that much in death. I am putting it to volunteers to do it.*

Adam took a deep breath, *I also had to kill one nastily when I arrived at the pack house and declare her rogue.* He decided to just open the memory of it to him.

Gareth took a bit to process the memory before he replied, *Looks like you did what was needed. Sometimes what is needed is not nice or tasteful. Saving her would have only had her thinking of revenge to get back at you. Eventually one or the other of you two would have killed the other, but others could have been hurt or killed in the meantime.* He tried to soothe him with the truth. He had seen it and had hoped Adam didn't need to, and didn't try to be lenient the next time one needed to be dealt with in the way he had this time.

Thanks. It went with what I felt. Just my upbringing as a human is a pain sometimes with, 'You need to keep everyone alive as long as possible', and if someone wants to die, there is something very wrong with them and they need to be protected from themselves. The wolf mentality is much simpler. He gave a mental sigh and a full body shake to clear his mind, before slipping back into the room.

Seeing most were done eating, he grabbed a bit of food which he could eat on the way; he would grab more before sleeping. "It's almost time. Finish up eating, the dishes get separated over here in the tubs, and the kitchen staff will get them cleaned overnight." Adam called out.

Many came over with their plates, while 'his headaches' as he was starting to think of them, left their plates and would have just headed out, if it wasn't the glare Adam levelled at them, "You just volunteered to wash the tables down once they are clear." He told them in a calm but firm voice, "Now go get your dishes. You are responsible for dirtying them, so you are responsible for making sure they reach the bins."

He held up a finger, "And if you say it is beneath you to put your own dishes in a tub for cleaning, you will be on kitchen duty for a week, *washing* the dishes." When that punishment was given, they didn't use the dishwasher, but instead had the one on punishment do *all* the dishes, as had been done before they had the convenience of a dishwasher. The kitchen staff had laughed the first time he turned someone over to them with the punishment. The one with the task of washing the large pots happily took control of them and kept them hard at work from right after breakfast, with a short lunch break, another for supper, then until it was time to go to bed.

They snapped their mouth shut, and they all scurried back to put their dishes away, "Plates in one tub, bowls in the second, cups in the third, and silverware in the fourth." He directed, "Good!" He praised as they followed the simple direction, "Now Jess has the cloths and the soapy water. She will be making sure you do it right."

A couple sighed, but looked half interested. The rest looked very put upon for being made to wash the tables. Glancing at the others, he grinned. There were looks of open amusement, amazement, and even some rubbing their eyes in disbelief as they did the work, *Maybe they are redeemable, after all.* Adam called silently to Brook, who was also watching them, *I still think we should use the plan of everyone learning what my mom called 'basic domestic skills' of washing and cleaning. Maybe then they won't think they can just leave it for others to put their dishes away for them.*

He murmured comment to some he felt were more responsible, telling them where to go for the memorial. Those who had formerly been of the pack were told their former pack was here, but he hadn't had time to tell them. He was trying to keep the surprises for the next day.

Brook offered to stay once about two thirds had left, letting him head down. As they hit the next floor down, he heard a squeal of, "Danny!" And an older female went running to the wolf they had given sanctuary to. With his eyes bright with tears, he ran to her and gave her a big hug.

Tears streaming down Danny's face, as Adam watched from the landing with a small smile on his face. He motioned for the rest to continue, and most did. A few stayed with him. The two talked quietly, before heading to the stairs.

"Thank you, thank you!" The female wept into Adam's shoulder, "I thought I had lost my son, but to find him happy and healthy here! Thank you!"

Adam patted her back softly, before moving away, "Come, we have to give the fallen a send off." He coaxed.

Turning to the mostly older women who had stopped to watch, "If your children were captured, many have been saved. Only a few had to be put to death. Some have move to other packs. I was going to deal with that tomorrow. We can see about getting communications with them, although most will not be secured, and if they want, we can arrange a meeting."

They nodded, most looking a bit hopeful, and moved with him. Danny and his mother had their hands tightly clasped, not wanting to lose each other, now they found each other again.

After they headed outside, Adam nodded to Gareth as the two packs kept a bit of a distance, but also kept glancing at one another curiously. Stepping up beside and little back, he let out a little sigh, waiting for Alpha Gareth.

Brook was almost right behind him as he stepped up. "I think that's everyone." She commented.

Gareth let out a demanding howl. Since Adam still considered himself part of his pack, some of the demand for quiet rolled through him and down the tentative links to those in his pack, "Today is a sad day. Due to a fight brought on by an Alpha who didn't treasure his pack, we have lost two of our own. Adam took down the Alpha, and by doing so since that pack followed the old ways of 'he who defeats the Alpha becomes the Alpha', he now has the survivors looking to him and Brook as Alphas."

Adam stepped forward, "Due to the MacLaren Pack finding out about both attacks before they could start, and the counterattack being successful, most of the losses was on what *was known as* Night Depths Pack. There are eighteen who were on that side who died. Also, the Night Depths Pack name died with their Alpha. Most are happy to see him buried."

There was nodding from his pack, but loud gasps and muttering from those in the MacLaren. If they lost either Alpha, they would fight all the harder and would demand an honourable cremation. Raising a hand, he got a respectful silence, "We lost Ali and Tyron from MacLaren, but the eighteen others were..." He read out the eighteen names slowly, as many grieved. As each name was read, the pyres were lit. Either family members or friends lit them. Once they were all lit, Adam stood tall, "From the ashes of these who we lost, we will build a new pack! We will build the Wild Valley Pack!"

Many howled in celebration at the nice pack name chosen for the new pack. *I want a handful of the ashes from each of the twenty we lost. I want to have half mixed in some of the mortar for the keystone, and some for a memorial.* He sent to Gareth, having come up with a fitting idea on the spot. *We will also need to start a new pack Urn. From what I have gathered, 'Alpha Night' didn't care about the dead. Their Pack Urn was maintained on the sly by the Elders and hidden from him.* Later, he would learn that Alpha Night thought the Urn destroyed. The Elders had been ordered to bring it to him, but they had instead brought one full of wood ash, which he then dumped out into a midden pit, and had the Urn crushed. He declared the dead were not to be honoured. It had caused the first fracturing of the pack, but most were unwilling to take their chances with leaving. Since then, the pack's elders had kept the urn hidden, and with the help of a few of the pack, had worked to get some of the ashes from members who had passed. The Alpha never turned up for the pyres of any pack member who died, and he didn't say any words of why they were not worthy of respect.

Gareth gave a mental nod, and silently passed it onto the elders, who were going to make sure the fires burned all night and hot enough to make the bodies ashes. The ashes of the fallen would help those who lived build a new life. *I will see to the new Pack Urn, and since the pack will also be an offshoot of us, I will instruct some of our ash be added as well.* This was pushing some of the plans way forward. *You will need to deal with the scattering and the planning of the memorial garden.*

Adam gave a mental nod, quite touched he would still be following many of their traditions for Pack Splits. It would give many of them a fresh start, but one where they still had ties to the past, and also to other packs for help. He had not been sure their split plans would be followed.

Many started breaking up and meeting the newcomers, unaware of the discussion by the Alphas.

Many stayed close to Adam, so it seemed he had a mass following him, as he mingled. Every so often he would pull several from both packs to chat and discuss various topics. He did give a big hug to Kuri who was weeping more over the loss of her friend. Evan had his arms wrapped around his mate as soon as Adam let go, and led her away, *Find me or Brook if she is still crying in the morning, we should be up in the loft.* He quietly offered Evan and got a grateful look and a nod in reply.

Many were heading off, a few asked about a bonfire, and Adam just sadly shook his head in negative, "There's one tomorrow, for the 'Howl'" He told them. Soon, many started to head in, even though most were not of the pack, they had been brought in, when their pack was.

Looking at how the pack who looked to them were staying fairly close, he was right; *We're staying with the pack,* He told Brook, *They need the comfort*. He got a grim nod in reply. Even those who tried to seem tough had tears in their eyes and looked skittish.

I'm going to see if we can have a nurse or healer, and all those still in Medical to come as well. She commented, before heading off. Adam quickly sent Charlie up to the loft, and a mental message to their six pups, although Jess and Joshua were basically not pups anymore, nor were Lea and Sam actually theirs, letting them know where they were.

He led everyone up the stairs to the loft. Those who couldn't make it, had some who carried them up; none wanted to be separated.

Most were subdued and followed Adam into the loft, where there were thick mattresses, all pressed together, with piles of blankets and pillows scattered, "I had this prepared this afternoon, as I knew most, if not all would not want to sleep alone." Charlie was already curled up in the middle, and most of the pups quickly joined him, with a couple using him as a pillow. The oldest pulled a couple blankets up to cover them, "Brook and I, and possibly some others, will be here as well." He saw Danny and Leon had joined them.

"Where is Alpha Brook?" One asked.

"She is seeing if she can arrange for those who are still in Medical to be brought up. It not only would help their mental state, but being with their pack, will help them heal faster." Adam told them, as more and more were moving to curl up on the beds. Some had moved a mattress slightly separate, but still in the vicinity.

Brook walked in at the head of a procession of medical staff, with the remaining members on mobile beds or gurneys. Most were slid down and had several packmates who made them comfortable, before curling up with them. A couple were on equipment which needed to be plugged in, and another on an IV drip. The healer who had treated him walked up and gave him a hug, "The worst showed improvement, just by coming in this room! This is a wonderful thing you are doing for them. I will be staying here to keep an eye on them, but it seems I may be able to get some sleep too."

Adam smiled and yawned, before finding Brook to curl up against her back. He didn't even feel others come curl up around them, nor pull a blanket over them. It had been a long day for all.

Chapter 20 – New Pack

The next morning Adam stretched and moved out of the mass of bodies, joining those in the showers. "Morning," He called out, as he moved to a vacant showerhead and started to wash.

A wolf moved up behind him, "Let me do your back and hair for you, Alpha" They offered.

Adam nodded, and was washing his chest, and he let them work on his long hair. By the time he was towelling off, many others were getting up too. He followed his nose to the food and headed for the breakfast. After putting a bowl for Charlie out of the way, he sat down in a seat with his own plate and ate, chatting with those around him. He decided to try to learn some things about them, but what most wanted to know was his ideas for the future.

Wolves trickled in as the smells from the pancakes, sausage, French toast, eggs, hash browns, ham, and bacon penetrated. There was even a small portable station the Chefs had put up if someone wanted to make their own omelet! There was also a toaster with a loaf of bread beside it, with butter and several jellies for toppings, a tub of various fruit, yogurt, and a tossed salad. Jugs of juice were sitting at one end with cups. Some were astonished at the layout of food. To Adam, this was a normal spread which you usually had to go to the main dining hall for. Once many were finishing up, Adam moved to one end of the hall, and gave a short howl.

Everyone was quickly quiet, "Now your bellies have been satisfied. I have had many of the same questions, so thought today would be best for a discussion and to answer your questions. First, yes this is the normal spread of food they serve at MacLaren; they just made more and brought it up because I asked. I am giving you today and tomorrow with food up here to get used to it, and the way MacLaren does things. After that, you will be expected to eat in the main dining hall on the first floor."

Waiting for the comments to die down, "Next, I know you were told that MacLaren killed most of the Shadowed River pack. The fact was, while the pack was named rogue and is now nameless, the members were mostly absorbed into many packs. If you have a friend from there, I will make time to find out where they are or what happened. I will warn you now, some did die, or were put down when they refused to submit, or the few who went rogue."

Before anyone could start with questions, "It has been the policies of the packs which were around the Night Depths Pack for decades, of if any scout who was taken alive, and hadn't killed, they were offered asylum, not death, if they broke their pack bond, which sadly, you were told was their death. I only have access to those recently we have dealt with, but the fact the policy has been in effect over a century means many may be living still who have been mourned as lost, like Danny and Leon. I can look them up, or we can have it passed on to see if any other packs have records." Many started weeping or talking there.

Adam talked quietly with Brook to let them digest the first parts.

Adam ended up needing to howl again to recapture everyone's attention, "Next, is how the pack will be organized: It doesn't matter what rank your parents or siblings had. Each of you will be tested personally and will earn your personal rank. Each year in the spring, MacLaren holds Spring Trials. They are to test the skill of pack members, which is then used for selecting the best for promoting to duties, especially the senior ones. They include: runs in all three forms, fighting skills, weapon skills, leadership skills, knowledge of the laws, not just the words, but knowing the meaning and even some history behind one. Knowledge of other packs in the area, tracking, and hunting are also tested. All require retesting periodically, so they can show they still meet the requirements for the rank and position. Not even the Alphas will be exempt from this."

Jess started passing out the first set of papers, which outlined the requirements for each level.

"You can try as many times as you wish, but you can only officially test once per year. Unofficial tests to see if you have the skills, are available and can be done as often as you arrange them. For runs ask around, and they can show you the main trial trails, which are a loop, starting and ending here, and are the set distances each level must run. To see where you stand, just have someone time it."

Holding a hand up, keep questions to the end, "Also, if you want training for skills, you are all welcome to them. Just let me know, and I can put you in contact with the trainers. If you are a trainer, come see me tomorrow after breakfast, and I will see about having you qualified right away for your skills, so you can go back to training. Usually the elders, with the help of specially trained wolves who are not competing that year for what they can't see, are those are who certify results."

"Pups are not eligible for the official trials, but they are allowed to do the training which they are able to do. Duties will sometimes require certain levels of skills before you can try for them as well. Now I'll take questions."

"What if we qualify at different levels for items?" Came the first question.

"Then you will be considered at the level of the weakest skill." Adam replied, "And if you are able to upgrade the skill, you could be increased in level. One thing which will be happening, once the pack starts having an income, each member will receive a stipend to share the wealth. The amount will depend on your ranking. The higher your rank; you could make more. There will also be other factors. Working for the pack, like a cook or staff to keep the place clean, will have a separate wage income, as well." Giving a feral smile, "If you are a problem, get in fights, or have to be disciplined, you could see it reduced or suspended as part of the punishment. The length would be based on the severity, but as the pack house hasn't even been built, there are no pack funds, right now. I will be gathering your old pack's funds and figuring it all out soon. Doing the Trials is optional, but you will be ranked as Theta and a non-fighter until you are formally qualified. Most positions within the pack will require passing the tests. Failing qualification re-tests can also reduce your ranking. Repeated failing may have you removed from the role."

"Any other questions?" Adam asked. Answering the questions tended to bring out ideas for the future. Most seemed to make sense.

*****

After answering questions for a while and they started to be unrelated to the ways they would be ranked, he turned the pack's attention to the laws and rules the pack would follow. He had made a booklet which he went over with them. The first was the section on the Inter-Pack Treaty. They spent a fairly long time on it, as many had been raised where there were no laws above the pack, they were sovereign. It took a while to show how it worked, and the fact it worked better, as it kept the Alphas honest to their peers and made the pack accountable to other packs. That he was able to show how it allowed packs to work together, and even for letting packs visit together in peace sold them on it.

They took a break for lunch, and for the pack to glance over the next section of laws on their own.

Since they had a chance to review it on their own, he mostly discussed it with them. A couple laws they even rewrote to be clearer to the spirit and less chance of being misused. One rule he had never liked was about flogging for minor infractions. They decided to completely remove; it was replaced by one where they got Theta chores instead. The length determined by how many offences and the severity. As this was being decided, the Thetas and Omegas were grinning, as were several of the few females. A few looked like they would rather be flogged than being forced to clean a bathroom, dishes, floors, shovel snow, cut the small amount of grass they would have, or any other duty they could think of. By supper time, they had gone through it all. Adam had pulled out his laptop to make the changes to his file immediately, so they were recorded how the pack wanted them. An updated version would be given to everyone the next day.

He had realised there were very few females in the pack, and when he had commented on it to Brook, she had grinned and told him it was good, since there were more in MacLaren than males. Adam hadn't really noticed, as his eyes were for his Mate alone, which amused her even more when he admitted it to her he hadn't noticed.

Adam stood up, "As it is the Full Moon, we will be having a barbecue outside. After that there is a bonfire, then a run and hunt. As we have so many wolves involved, we will be doing two hunts. There is a major surplus of Elk in the area, so we have two herds which we will be thinning for the human park service." Many smiled. "The older pups are welcome to come and help with the tracking," The four looked happy at that, "But the young ones will be brought back here, and there are a few who will care for them for the night." Several who were still too young to go on the hunt but old enough to not enjoy being left behind looked disappointed.

"We will also be doing the formal bonds tomorrow, as we don't have time today. Normally, the bonds are done before the introduction, but we have the tentative bonds. If there are any who don't think they can live with the rules we have worked on today. Please decide before we do the formal bonds. I will work with those to find them a new pack or let them go on their way as Lone Wolves."

"Scouts, just so you are aware, you may be asked to help survey the Night Depths territory. Right now, it has been absorbed into the outer area of the MacLaren and our Pack's territories. If you want to be a Lone Wolf, but stay in the territories, it may be arranged. You would still be expected to follow many of the rules but would also be given some limited protections."

He got a few thoughtful looks, but many looked eager to join formally. A few had complained about the laws, but most were the ones before they had been re-written. He was going to pass a copy of the changes to Gareth, as they were laws he liked the least and were some of the older ones still in use. Unlike humans, if the law was no longer relevant, it was removed, not just left there and just not enforced for decades.

"Let's go!" He called out, as there was nearly a stampede for the stairs. He smiled as even the older ones weren't forgotten, but many were cackling as they got piggy-back rides. About half of the former Alpha's favourites seemed to have settled down to the new normal and other than a gentle look, hadn't needed to be talked to. They had two which he was surprised were still living who were still bed-ridden and attended to by medical, each also had two packmates who promised to stay with them. One each had left, but promised to bring some of the food for them. *They are already starting to function how a pack should function, and not how it was under fear; just looking out for themselves. They realise helping others is not only supported but is encouraged* He said with a little awe of how fast it was coming together.

They brought up the rear and nodded as they met up with Gareth and Maria as they stepped off the stairs, as they shared greetings and headed out together. "I wonder if any will find mates today" Adam wondered out loud. The other three laughed.

"I wouldn't be surprised. I already have several females who I have caught eyeing them. Let's see how they do tonight; I suspect you will get some of my wolves running with you." Gareth commented. If he had some who found mates, he was planning on letting them switch immediately, as he had almost too many wolves to deal with. He felt the split couldn't come soon enough.

"I had a chat with Chris today, and I approved his Turn. At your leisure, schedule it with him. He also asked about moving to your pack, which only makes sense. With you turning him, it would make a bond with him, so he's yours."

Adam smiled, "I know he's been working hard at getting the layout of all the security done for the new pack. It looks like it will be even tighter secured than here! There seems to have been new sensors out which just recently hit the market, which can detect electrical energy, the way fish can. Those are not affected by rain or snow. I passed him the budget for the security, and he was nearly gleeful. He said he could do the 'need', 'want', and the 'nice to have' inside that budget, and still have cash left over for the future upgrades."

Gareth grinned, "Long-term investment at its best. We needed to reduce the amount of cash we have, anyways; I was getting concerned about tax audits." He had gifted Wild Valley part of MacLaren's money as starting capital and was providing more as a loan towards the building of their facilities and continuing to pay for removing the old. On top of it, MacLaren was paying the wages for many of those doing the work.

The werewolves had never subscribed to 'Trickle Down Economics' as the humans called the not requiring a company to increase wages as the economy grew, and instead giving the breaks to the rich with the thought that those company leaders would then be able to pay their employees more, instead of directly giving the workers the benefits. How well it worked was shown by how worker wages had been nearly stagnant since the 1970s, while the ownership's share had grown huge since then. The werewolves believed in equitable shares, so they often were paid much more than the humans for the same job. They also made sure they had enough workers to handle the work without overloading them, meaning they had enough to handle the work of a couple of wolves if they were not available for a day.

Adam nodded, "At last check on Sunday, he was almost ready for sign-off to order it all. Then we can spend the money. Until the new security office is built, it will be linked and they have worked out a way so even after, each office will serve as a backup of the other, with your approval?"

Gareth stopped and thought for a bit, "On that, I will need to think about it. It's not something we can decide now." He wanted to discuss it with the elders, and Martin before he did anything about it.

Adam nodded, "Nor is it something which can be done for months. Even then, it can always be turned off, and should be reviewed at least once a decade by both sides."

Adam's stomach grumbled, "Well, I guess it's time we got out there, and get the official part over with before we have a mutiny!" He hadn't had a chance to munch on anything, as most of his pack did during the afternoon.

They laughed as they opened the door. Many wolves got quiet as soon as they stepped out. Gareth's howl was almost not needed. "Here we are again. Tonight, we look to the future. With that, Adam is doing an introduction."

Adam stepped forward, "I'm going to try to do this as fast as I can, so keep howls of welcome and other noise to the end, so we can get to the food." *Form a line, and I'll just be calling out names as you come up.* he told his wolves, *Not doing ranks, so there is no order needed.*

He went through the about seventy names in about twenty minutes. He was surprised he could remember them all! As a human, he had trouble remembering the names of those who worked in the next room over from him! His wolf snickered at him for the thought.

"Now that is out of the way, *Now*, you can greet them," He called out, and there was a loud, welcoming howl from MacLaren. It brought tears to the eyes of some of the wolves; another pack was welcoming them, if not as one of them, as a branch of the pack!

The two packs started mingling, as the four watched, they saw and felt three different mates form. Each time it happened, a ripple of a howl was given out in celebration. Toby and Robin came up with plates for the four Alphas, "I thought you might want some of the fresh stuff." Toby demurred. All four gave their thanks, and almost as one used the railing for a table to eat at, as they watched the mingled packs. A couple small squabbles were heard, but the feeling from the bonds indicated they didn't need them to deal with the issue, and they soon ended.

"The minor squabbles actually show they are happy enough that minor issues they feel need to be dealt with." Maria said quietly, "If they are unhappy, the minor issues are not voiced, as their minds are on the larger issues. It is always better to let them sort them out themselves unless they bring them to you."

Brook had started to move to intervene, but relaxed, "That actually sounds good. It also means less work for us! If I knew the job was going to be this hard, I would have wanted to stay as just a pup trainer!"

It got a laugh from the older two, "But you feel called to lead, do you not?" Maria asked, and getting a nod, "Well, being the Alpha is more of a calling and a need, than a job. You would never feel fully satisfied as a trainer."

"I guess so; it feels right to be in charge." She sighed, "Why does life have to change so fast?" Brook complained. Thinking back, it was one reason she got annoyed; the very limited authority had started to irk her, even if she hadn't really noticed it at the time.

Adam laughed, "Be glad you are not human; this is the pace of a human life. Most live their lives out by seventy, if not sooner. I am using the slower pace to relax, but I do agree it does feel a bit rushed now. I do hope the other Alphas will at least give us some respect, even if we are young." He remembered the comments about some not giving respect to those under a century.

Gareth smiled, "The fact you won it in a battle, where the other Alpha attacked your pack, and then you honoured the defeated pack's laws and took up the mantle of the Alpha? Many will respect you for it. The fact you took out an Alpha which several of their packs lost theirs or nearly lost theirs to over the last century or two? It will get you noticed, and some will even fear your strength. I do know Grant and Louise will support you, and I suspect Rufus will. We will need to have an Alpha conference soon. I have already started to set it up. Some will still complain and not listen due to your age, but when they see your ideas, I think they may be willing to change."

Gareth gave a sly grin, "I know your parents are working on a human marriage for you two this summer. I am planning on having them here for it. There are going to be about eight to twelve packs represented. It is not going to be very big; mainly just those packs who are here or around the two we have taken down."

Adam and Brook looked a little pale but nodded.

Maria continued, "It is also so you two can formally sign onto the Inter-Pack Treaty."

"I was wondering about that." Adam smiled, "It will immediately be fully ratified, as I have already gotten agreement from the pack, and the rules are in the Pack Laws. We spent half the morning going over them and had almost consensus on accepting them. We then used the afternoon to go over other pack laws; I shamelessly took a copy of MacLaren's as a starting point. A couple laws were re-written, and a couple removed." He had looked over at the Inter-Pack Treaty and having the rules already in the laws showed clearly the pack accepted them, so signing off on the treaty would make them officially in effect and show the other packs they were willing to treat the other packs reasonably.

Gareth shook his head, "You have had a very busy day," he commented, as Robin brought them refills for their plates. "I want a copy of the changes; I haven't done a major review on the laws, ever. I don't think even Ralph did, after they were made when the pack settled here. We may follow your lead on the changes."

Adam smiled, "A copy is already in your mail slot. I noticed there was a pile of requests for pack transfer on my slot, too. I'll get you a list of them, and if I would accept them." Nodding in the direction of the packs, "If they find mates, I am willing to accept them." He could feel Brook's silent agreement as well.

Gareth smiled, "I think we're going to see if we can get some gear to clean snow from the work site, instead of waiting for it to melt. I want your pack house built before we get any more! This place is actually over the capacity it was designed for. The loft was actually a retrofit; it was originally designed as just storage." Remembering the request from the night before, "The elders have placed the urn with some of the ashes in your room; they actually liked your ideas. The rest have been scattered as per tradition. Before you ask, some was or will be scattered in all three territories by the patrols. Some from the two we lost was also placed in your urn, as they gave their lives to help bring about the changes."

Both Adam and Brook were deeply moved by the show of respect to their pack and were not able to voice words of thanks but shared with the other pair how deeply they felt over it.

As they had finished eating, "Well, time to mingle," Gareth commented.

*****

Mingling with the pack, they chatted with many wolves; Adam used it as a less formal way, to get to know some of his wolves and to congratulate the three pairs. He excused them from the hunt, if they wished, to find somewhere cozy instead. All three asked to join the new pack, and he nodded; the ones who had been already chosen were also changing their bonds over the next few days. It let Adam and Brook deal with having responsibility, but he could learn in more of a controlled environment.

Chris came up, "I take it you know Alpha Gareth told you I was approved to be turned?" he said without preamble.

Adam smiled, "Yes, and about your transfer. We're doing the ones approved after the formal bonds for the formerly Night Depths, so they are not sitting with just the tentative bonds any longer than they have to be. As for the turn, I want things to settle down a bit. You would need to have one of us in constant attendance, at least for the first week or two. Once it is over, you would be confined to the close pack territory, where there aren't humans, until you are confirmed as in control."

Chris nodded, "I understand. Couldn't there be anyone else who cares for me?"

Adam shook his head, "From what I have heard, only the alphas do that sort of turn, but I am trying to find out why or if it is just tradition. We are trying to clear our schedule to have the time for you."

Chris looked a little disappointed, "Understood. I'll have to think on it."

"Give us a week. This is just a very busy time, for everyone." Adam told him, gripping his shoulder, commiserating for the delay.

"I just didn't want to do it while they were doing the sensors."

Adam grinned, "Well, we can put off the installing till you are back on your feet, but you still would be here doing the remote work while the stuff is out there."

Chris smiled and nodded, heading off to talk to others.

The older woman, who he had learned was the senior-most Elder, or Eldest, asked, "Did I hear right, that you're turning him, even without a mate?"

Adam nodded, "Yes, Elder Elise. Alpha Gareth approved the turn, in consultation with the elders of his pack. He is a member of the pack, even though he is human—there is another human as well who doesn't have a mate—and is trusted. To me Chris feels like a wolf, as well. He is also moving to the Wild Valley Pack. Right now, he is in charge of IT security, and one of two managers of the passive automated defences."

"What sort of defences?" Was the sharp question.

Shaking his head, "Alpha Gareth's orders, which won't be discussed till the fully bonded, sorry. Already said too much. All the Elders will be briefed as soon as we are done."

She frowned, "Do you do everything Alpha Gareth orders?" Not liking the idea of *their* Alpha taking orders from another.

He knew where she was coming from, "While we are still living here, we decided he and his mate were the ultimate authority, and we would respect them till our own pack house is ready. So we are basically functioning as Seconds for the MacLaren, and mostly as Alpha for our own pack, with very few limitations. Doesn't mean I can't question it, which he supports, since we know we are very young, and we want to learn the skills from an experienced Alpha. In this decision, I totally agree with him and his reasoning."

He had expected her to frown some more and to be told off immediately, but she stayed silent until her face lit up, "I never thought about it that way. Having two sets of Alphas as equals usually causes interesting issues, especially over a longer period. The fact you two have worked them out before there was an issue shows you are both forward thinking, instead of reactionary. I think you'll do well."

Adam smiled back, "Thank you. I will respect the Elders as well. I will accept your advice, but I will not let you dictate my decisions."

Elise grinned even bigger, "That is how it is supposed to be. It will be a whole new world for the pack. There are stories of Elders who try to dictate the way of the pack who end up holding the pack back, but also of Alphas repeating history because they refuse to listen to the Elder's advice and experience to avoid the issues."

Adam nodded, "Yes, I am fairly sure on it being much different than it has been, and it will be a bit different even for those coming from MacLaren. I am trying to make it as long lasting as possible. Soon after the bonds are done, my mate and I will sit down with all you Elders and brief you on what plans we have, and what goals we have for the future."

She smiled, nodded, and after sharing a hug, headed off to chat with some others. Adam headed off to chat with others in the pack. He had a glow inside, as he seemed to have the approval of the elders—or at least the Eldest—of his pack.

Heading towards the fire pit, he started the slow migration and helped get the fire started. It would be a bit before it was going well, but with the additional wolves, the entire length of the long pit was going to be used. Getting it going took a fair amount of work, to ensure entire length was lit.

Once the fire was lit, he smiled as Brook handed him a mug of apple cider and curled up at his side. They had place of pride at the centre of one side, and Gareth and Maria would be on the other, when they arrived.

Some pulled out the sticks and started roasting marshmallows or meat on sticks. Adam declined when offered, while Brook accepted one of marshmallows. Adam shared one, but still didn't really like the processed sugar taste of it much; one tasted good but any more didn't.

Many enjoyed the time to chat and sing around the fire pit, and when someone pulled out a guitar, the singing started. Many of the newest were surprised but joined in. Eventually, they were having a good time as they relaxed into the new way of doing things.

Looking over the fire as it started to burn down, Maria caught Adam's eye and nodded; it was time to start gathering for the hunt, *Head east. We haven't hunted over that way in a while, and there have been reports of too many elk there* She passed on.

Adam's wolf was all for getting some nice fresh meat. Heading away from the fire, he followed Brook. When she started to shift, he followed her lead. Since he led the hunt last month, it was her turn. He joined in on her howled call to gather. They were quickly surrounded by wolves who were wagging their tails and licking their snouts in greeting.

Why is she leading the hunt? Came one wolf's dismissive complaint.

Both halves of Adam didn't like the slur on their mate, and growled, as he stalked stiff-legged to the offender as everyone between them scrambled out of their way, *I will never hear a slur on any female again. They are just as able to lead a hunt as any male. You will really not like what I will do if you voice a comment like that in the future.*

The wolf knew he was in big trouble and rolled on his back, **Yes, Alpha. I will keep my human in line,** Came the soft reply.

Adam gave the exposed neck a lick to show he accepted the submission. *You are to stay with Brook now, so you can see firsthand she is capable of leading a hunt!*

Yes, Alpha, Came the reply, from the human side this time, as he quickly moved to be near her, and crouched down, tail still tucked between his legs as she looked down her long nose with disapproval.

Brook gathered those for the hunt, as Adam gathered those for the ambush. As they had expected, some of MacLaren had joined them. Looking them over, they realised many were those who asked for transfer, but some just joined them to even out the numbers. All told, there was almost four hundred wolves staying at MacLaren, and even the hundred and fifty who were out hunting with them was a very large number. This was more to appease the wolf with a taste of fresh meat after a hunt and a time to bond than a time to fill the belly.

Heading out, they had some of the older pups learning tracking and how to tell what the scents were. They had a permit to take down five elk tonight.

Once they were in position, the pups were told to stay back, as they couldn't help with the takedown. Adam crouched and waited for Brook to chase them their way. When he saw one of the ones they had singled out head straight for him, he pounced and for the first time, he got the timing exactly right. Knocking the animal off their stride and since they had an injured leg, it collapsed, and they fell over. He quickly broke the animal's neck and while the meat was still warm, took a couple of tasty bits before backing off for more of the pack to enjoy. The pups whined but were pushed forward by the MacLaren wolves to get a piece of meat each, before others descended.

With the number of wolves, taking five animals down was not hard. They really needed to start using the farther areas, so they didn't overhunt. Luckily, they had several farms which shipped them meat, so they didn't have to subsist on hunting.

Brook and Adam took the fed wolves on a good run, although they paced it fairly slow for them, ending up in the field in front of the pack house. Sprawling out on the well paw-packed snow was fairly comfy, and they were soon piled upon by the others and curled up to sleep the night away.

Adam had trouble stopping the listing of things which needed to be done, till his wolf swamped his mind with sleep, and he relaxed against his mate. The work for the future and their pack could wait for when they were awake. Wolf-Adam knew they would be good leaders.

Epilogue

MacLaren's Next Alphas returned and were astonished by the changes which had happened during the time they were away but enjoyed them. Adam, Brook, and the two Next-Alphas passed their trials without issue, which surprised very few.

Eventually, Adam and Brook had their summer wedding, so they could show off to his human family their commitment to each other. The number of wolves who turned up was larger than the humans, with many of the leaders and elders of packs all around them showing up to show the support of the youngest Alphas around. For many, it was their first meeting of them and came to get a little bit of a feeling for them before the conference.

During the Alpha conference to formally have them accepted into the Inter-Pack Treaty, the support for the young pack came from many different places, including some unexpected ones with unexpected offers which would help put them on the map globally which would be great for the pack, long-term. They also had a couple of packs who clearly showed how some leaders were stuck in the past and they would be a thorn in the paw of the new pack in the future. Some contacts with others were also made, with a couple of packs in the US who also had representation at the conference.

The new pack flourished with the members able to tell the new Alphas would care for them as they needed, not just looking out for themselves. There were still some who don't think they are old enough to be Alphas, but both Adam and Brook know they couldn't please everyone, so they didn't even bother trying.